"Virginia Kantra delivers."

—*New York Times* bestselling author ~~Jay~~

"It's always a joy to read Virginia Kantra."

—*New York Times* bestselling author JoAnn Ross

"Hums with the rhythm of life . . . I loved it."

—Mariah Stewart, *New York Times* bestselling author of
At the River's Edge

"Intimate and inviting. . . . Contemporary romance at its most grati-
fying."
—*USA Today*

"If you have not yet visited Virginia Kantra's Dare Island, I enthusiasti-
cally encourage you to do so. . . . Learn why many readers, myself
included, have fallen in love with these wonderful characters and the
island they call home."
—The Romance Dish

"A wonderful love story."
—Fiction Vixen

"Her wonderful characters . . . engage and inspire me. . . . I love this
series, and if you're looking for solid romance with a generous helping
of steam, Dare Island is a great place to get lost in."

—The Bookish Babes

"A sizzling good time. Kantra's story building is excellent."

—*Publishers Weekly*

"Kantra is a sensitive writer with a warm sense of humor, a fine sense
of sexual tension, and an unerring sense of place." —*BookPage*

Berkley titles by Virginia Kantra

Home Before Midnight
Close Up
Meg & Jo

THE CHILDREN OF THE SEA NOVELS

Sea Witch
Sea Fever
Sea Lord
Immortal Sea
Forgotten Sea

THE DARE ISLAND NOVELS

Carolina Home
Carolina Girl
Carolina Man
Carolina Blues
Carolina Dreaming

NOVELLAS

Midsummer Night's Magic
Carolina Heart

To my mother, Phyllis S. Kantra,
with thanks for everything you taught me.
And in loving memory of Robert A. Kantra.
I miss you, Dad.

ACKNOWLEDGMENTS

First off, I owe an enormous debt to Louisa May Alcott, whose *Little Women* has inspired me in so many ways.

Huge thanks to my editor, Cindy Hwang. I'm so glad we got to do this together. It is a joy, always, to work with you. And thank you to Danielle Keir, Angela Kim, Jessica Plummer, Colleen Reinhart, and all the wonderful team at Berkley!

At Writers House, I'm so grateful to my agent, Robin Rue, who believed in this story from the beginning. Thank you and Beth Miller for reading it (over and over) and making it a better book.

To my sister, Pam Archbold. Because whatever happens, we have each other.

To my sisters-in-law, Mary Keefer and Ginny Grisez, for letting me be part of the Rockettes chorus line.

To my sisters of the heart, Carolyn Martin Buscarino, Kristen Dill, and Brenda Harlen, who persist in thinking I can do things.

Thanks to Mary-Theresa Hussey, for your insights and for sharing the story of your mother, Sheila Hussey, with me. To Kathy Hamilton and Lisa Jackson, for being at the bottom of the driveway when I had a question about soccer or needed a sympathetic ear. To Kristan Higgins, who told me to shut up and write the book (but much more nicely than that, because she is the nicest person) and Eileen Rendahl; to my Fiction From the Heart pals—Jamie Beck, Tracy Brogan, Sonali Dev, Kwana Jackson, Donna Kauffman, Sally Kilpatrick, Falguni Kothari,

Priscilla Oliveras, Barbara O'Neal, Hope Ramsay, and Liz Talley—for your fellowship; and to Suzanne Brockmann and Ed Gaffney, for taking me to Orchard House.

Thank you Jean, Andrew and Celia, and Mark and Katie, for the privilege of watching you become the people you were meant to be. And to Katerina Abigail, who I hope will one day take this book from the shelf and see her name.

To Michael. *Tell your story,* you said. You are my hero. There are no stories without you.

And finally, thanks to you, dear readers, for sharing your time with me. You are the best.

PROLOGUE

Christmas Eve, Then
Bunyan, North Carolina

"Christmas won't be Christmas without any presents," grumbled Jo, lying on the rug.

White Christmas was playing on the TV, but this year the scenes of soldiers far from home made her throat ache. It felt weird to be watching the movie without Dad. Everything felt wrong this year.

Meg sighed. "It wouldn't be so bad if we were home."

Jo propped her chin on her hands to look around the old frame farmhouse—the wide-plank floors imbued with the smell of woodsmoke and tobacco, the faded hydrangea wallpaper their grandmother had hung before they were born. "We are home," she said.

"You know what I mean," her older sister said.

Jo did. It wasn't fair to lose Dad and the house at the same time. Their father was in Iraq. *"Called,"* he'd said, to give up his congregation to serve as an army chaplain.

Jo understood that Daddy was doing good work, important work, serving their country far away. But that didn't change the fact that the new minister and *his* family were living in the girls' house now, and

Momma and Meg and the rest of them had been forced to move to the farm.

When the girls were all little, they'd loved to visit their grandparents' farm. There were woods to roam, if you weren't particular about ticks and poison ivy. A long slope down to the river, with a tire swing over the water and a splintery old dock where you could fish or swim or simply lie on your back and stare at the clouds.

But it was different actually living here. Like moving to another planet.

Jo ran cross-country, so she didn't mind walking the extra mile to the bus stop. But Amy whined that she missed her friends, and Meg complained because their parents couldn't afford to buy her a car like Sallie Gardiner's parents had done.

Of course, just about any boy in high school would be happy to give Meg a ride anywhere she wanted to go. But Momma was strict about things like that.

"At least we don't have to share a bedroom anymore," Jo pointed out.

She had begged to be allowed to move into the converted space in the attic, to have what Virginia Woolf called "a room of one's own" to write in. Their mother worried the attic would be too cold. But Daddy had intervened. *Let the girl have her privacy. It's not like she's entertaining boys up there,* he'd said. So eventually Momma relented and agreed.

The attic *was* cold. Especially in December. But Jo liked the funny peaked window with its view of fields and trees. She loved having her own space.

Ten-year-old Amy looked up from the coffee table, where she was making something out of the scraps she'd begged from Miss Hannah's quilting bag. "We still have to share a bathroom. That's worse. Your hair clogs the sink."

Beth spoke up from her corner of the shabby couch. "Whatever happens, we have each other," she said, quoting Momma. "At least we're all together."

"But we're not," Jo said. "Daddy's not here."

Silence fell over the living room, broken only by the muted dialogue from the television.

Crap. Jo bit her tongue. Keeping her mouth shut was not her specialty.

"But he will be," Meg said with a glance at the younger girls. "Soon."

His unit had been gone almost a year. He *must* be coming home soon. They'd all agreed to put off opening their presents until his return.

A month ago, the decision hadn't seemed so hard. But now . . .

Their gifts sat wrapped and waiting under the tree. Artificial, this year, to last until their father came home. Jo missed the sharp, resiny, real-tree smell of Christmases past.

She missed Dad.

"Anyway, Momma said we could each open one present tonight," Meg said.

The back door opened, releasing a draft over the threshold. Momma appeared, wearing a faded work shirt over her jeans, bringing with her the scent of frost and the barn.

Warmth prickled Jo's cheeks at the thought of their mother doing chores while they lolled inside, lazy and warm. Granny and Grand-daddy had worked the farm together until a lifetime of sweat and ciga-rettes had carried them off. But except for Miss Hannah, who helped in the cheese room, Momma did everything herself.

She smiled around at them. "Merry Christmas, girls. I have a sur-prise for you."

"Kittens?" asked Beth.

"Not until spring," Meg said.

"Better than kittens," Momma said.

Amy's face lit. "Daddy!"

Jo winced. It was the fault of all the local stations running those cheesy holiday homecoming videos on the evening news, fathers in uni-form coming up the driveway, striding into a classroom, showing up at their kids' ball games . . .

Momma nodded. "He's going to call this afternoon."

A phone call. Jo swallowed her disappointment. She didn't really expect Dad to pop out of a box like the fathers on TV. Anyway, even hearing his voice would make Christmas more, well, Christmassy. He usually called when they were in school. Because of the time difference, Momma said.

Talking it over one night after Beth and Amy were in bed, Jo and Meg had decided their parents were trying to protect them. As long as they didn't expect to hear from him every day, they wouldn't worry on the days his calls couldn't get through because of a sandstorm or an attack.

The phone rang.

"Jo, turn that volume down." Momma picked up the phone, tugging off her bandanna with her free hand. "Hi, honey." She ran her fingers through her hair as if Daddy could see her. "Merry Christmas!"

Jo couldn't hear his reply, but their mother laughed. "I will." He murmured something else. Her cheeks turned pink. "Yes. I'm putting you on speaker now."

Jo couldn't wait to hear his voice. But they had to take turns speaking, because if they all talked at once he got them mixed up. Of course, Meg, being the oldest, got the receiver first.

Jo jiggled from foot to foot as Meg told their father about organizing the canned-food drive at school. As if she hadn't spent the last student council meeting flirting with Ned Moffat.

Finally, it was Jo's turn. She reached for the phone, but Amy snatched it away.

"Hey!" Jo said.

"Ssh. It's all right," Momma said.

It wasn't all right. It wasn't fair. Jo needed to talk to Dad. And he wanted to talk to her—she knew he did. At the dinner table, while the others chattered about movies or friends, she and Dad always talked about what she was reading or thinking, tossing sentences back and forth the way another father and daughter might play catch.

But Amy got away with it because she was adorable. Not responsible like Meg or good at school like Jo or sweet like Beth, but small and super cute—their own little Disney princess with big blue eyes and smooth blond hair. Standing next to her, Jo felt like a giraffe, all long legs and knobby knees and spots.

Amy shot her a triumphant look and tucked the receiver out of reach beneath her chin. "I'm making you a present," she told Dad. "A wallet with all our pictures in it."

Which explained the mess on the coffee table.

"Thank you, Princess," Dad said.

"You won't have it in time for Christmas, though," Amy said.

"That's okay. I got the care package you sent," he said. "I appreciate the cookies. And the movies."

"Give me the phone," Jo said.

Amy angled her body away, still holding the receiver tight. "I put in *White Christmas*."

"I saw," Dad said. "It made me think of you."

"Are you watching it?"

"Not tonight," Dad said. "One of the other soldiers needed it tonight. He came into my tent to browse the DVDs and stayed awhile, talking. But I'm listening to your Christmas CD."

"That's from Beth," Amy said.

"Mouse? Is she there?"

Amy thrust the phone at Beth, who clasped her hands in front of her, twisting her fingers together. "Oh, but I . . . What about Jo?"

But Bethie needed to talk to Daddy even more than Jo did. Hardly a week went by without Beth reporting to the school nurse complaining of cramps, a headache, an upset stomach—whatever ailment would get her excused from class that day.

"She's adjusting," Momma had said.

To the move? Jo wondered. *Or to their father being gone?*

"It's okay." Jo forced the words out. "We have plenty of time."

Fifteen minutes. Eleven of them gone already, whizzing by like bullets. One for every month that Dad had been away.

"I say my prayers for you every night," Beth told Dad.

"That's my good girl," he said. He asked how she was feeling, if she was still practicing her guitar.

"Jo's turn," Momma said at last.

Jo took the phone eagerly. But when she tried to speak, all her emotions rushed in on her, congesting her chest, sticking in her throat. "Hi, Daddy." Her voice cracked.

"Hey, little woman."

"How . . . How's your Christmas?"

"Good," he said heartily. "They made us a real holiday dinner here on base. Turkey and stuffing."

"We're having turkey, too," she said, hungering for his attention. His approval.

Momma held up a finger. "One minute left."

"I love you," Dad said. "Take care of Momma and your sisters for me."

Jo swallowed hard. "I will."

"I'm proud of you," Dad said. "Proud of all my girls. I think of you every day and ask God to bless you and keep you safe and strong. Let me say good-bye to your mother now."

"Love you," Jo choked out.

She surrendered the phone, her heart burning. She hardly got to talk to him at all. She didn't get to tell him about the poem she published in the student newspaper or the English paper she wrote on the Brontës or . . .

"She's fine," their mother was saying. "We're all fine. We love you."

"We're getting cut off," Dad said. "Love you, too, honey. Merry Christmas. God bless you."

"Merry Christmas!" they all chorused.

The connection cut off. Silence fell, as cold as snow. Beth's eyes swam with unshed tears. Amy's face was blotchy.

God bless us, every one. Dickens, Jo thought, but Daddy wasn't here to appreciate the reference.

"Well." Momma took a deep breath. Released it. "Time for some Christmas music."

Jo stared. But then she saw how their mother gripped the phone like she couldn't bear to let go.

All those years their father was a minister, their mother never once complained about his hours or his charity cases. When he gave up his congregation in town to join the army, she talked about his sacrifices. But she sacrificed, too. It couldn't have been easy for her to move back down on the farm, to make the transition from pastor's wife to goat farmer.

"We could put on Bethie's Christmas CD," Meg said. "It'll be just like listening with Daddy."

Not really, Jo thought. But Beth's face glowed.

"What a wonderful idea," Momma said.

Beth jumped up to put the music on.

"And we can open presents," Amy said.

"Not until after dinner," Meg, the rule-follower, said.

"Actually, I think now is the perfect time," Momma said. "You girls deserve a treat."

"Me first," Amy said. "I'm the youngest."

Momma smiled at Jo. "I think Jo should choose first."

And that's when Jo knew what she had to do. Pretty, responsible Meg took after Momma—the model daughter. But Jo had always considered herself their father's child. She was determined to live up to his expectations.

"Take care of Momma and your sisters for me."

Jo surveyed the piles under the sad, stiff, artificial tree. That flat rectangle? A book, for sure. The bigger box . . . Well, she'd asked for a laptop this year, but it was probably only clothes—new pajamas, maybe, or a hoodie. Hey, plenty of kids didn't get that much. She ought to be grateful.

"This one," she said, and laid a squashy package in her mother's lap.

Momma looked down at the lopsided bow, a pucker between her brows. "But, honey, this has my name on it."

"I know." Jo stuck out her chin. "The rule is, we each pick one present. I want you to open this one."

Momma smoothed the crinkled paper without speaking as Bethie's carols played from the old speakers. *Silent night, holy night* . . .

"And this one," Meg said, sliding another present from under the tree.

Their mother frowned. "Oh, I don't think . . ."

"My turn!" Beth added her gift to the others.

"Girls . . ." Momma stopped, her hands stroking the bright packages in her lap. "This is so incredibly sweet. I am so proud of you. But you should open your own presents tonight. It's Christmas Eve."

"Christmas is about giving," Meg said. "That's what you always tell us." She looked meaningfully at Amy.

Their little sister sighed. "I got you something, too."

She dug under the tree, adding a bag covered in glitter to the pile on their mother's lap.

"Well." Momma smiled around at them all, her eyes shining. "I don't know what to say."

"Open them," Jo said.

"Yeah, open them!" said Amy.

Their mother peeled the tape from Jo's present. Later, Jo knew, she would fold the wrapping paper to reuse again next year.

"Slippers!" Momma said, holding them up.

Jo shuffled her feet. "I thought you could keep them by the back door. To change into when you come in from the barn."

"They're perfect," Momma said. "So warm."

Meg gave her work gloves. "To keep your hands nice," she explained.

Amy had made their mother a necklace, a sand dollar and some beads threaded on a silk cord. Beth's gift was a pair of ceramic salt and pepper shakers shaped like bluebirds.

"Beautiful," their mother said.

Beth blushed. "It's not much."

None of their presents were expensive or grand. But Momma acted as if they'd showered her with the contents of the jewelry counter at Belk department store. She touched and exclaimed over each gift, offering hugs and praise as the younger girls perched on the arms of her chair. Meg's face was wreathed in smiles. Jo's eyes were wet. The music wrapped them in ribbons of sound.

O holy night, the stars are brightly shining . . .

Jo sniffled happily. Finally, it felt like Christmas.

CHAPTER 1

Jo

Our mother taught us girls if you can't say something nice, don't say anything at all. But Momma wasn't trying to make it as a food blogger in New York City.

Negative reviews got a lot more clicks than positive ones. And I still had three hundred more words to write today.

A distant burst of car horns drifted up the fire escape to my apartment, the rush of traffic like the city breathing. I tightened my ponytail. Typed: The food at Earl's Eats in the East Village is not your momma's cooking. And not in a good way. Neither original nor authentic, the stereotypical menu clings to cliché without delivering either the heart or soul of true Southern home cooking.

My phone chirped on the table beside me. Did I have a blog comment?

Nope. A phone call.

"Hey, Jo. Whatcha doing?"

I smiled at the sound of my sister's voice. In the last few weeks, my circle had shattered. The friends I laughed and bickered and shared everything with had moved away. My roommate Ashmeeta had followed a job to Boston. My pal Rachel had followed a boyfriend to Portland. But I could always count on Meg.

"Working."

"I thought you were off today," Meg said.

A siren whooped in the distance. "From the restaurant, yeah. I'm writing."

"Oh, your blog." I could hear one of the twins—two-year-old Daisy, or maybe that was DJ—chanting in the background: *"Mommy. Ma. Mamamama."* "How's it going?"

I smiled. "Good."

Okay, not *Julie & Julia* or *Smitten Kitchen* good. Mine was not a success story. Or an interesting story of failure, like the gritty novels admired by my faculty advisor, where the small-town girl falls into a life of drugs and prostitution. Or even a Hallmark screenplay, where the heroine goes home to embrace her small-town roots and marry her high school sweetheart, finding love and purpose along the way. There was no big book advance, no movie deal, no guest appearance on the Food Network in my immediate future. Nope. The blog was more a fallback position than the fulfillment of my Life Plan. But I was slowly picking up readers. Instagram followers. E-mail subscribers. Even a few advertisers, which helped pay the rent since I'd been laid off from the newspaper. *"Last hired, first fired,"* my editor had explained regretfully when he let me go.

My dismissal had come as a shock. Yeah, yeah, I knew all about the dismal decline of print journalism. But I was supposed to be the smart one. The successful one. Certainly back when I wrote the school play and edited the school paper, graduating summa cum laude from the University of North Carolina and earning an MFA from NYU, I never imagined a future as an anonymous food blogger.

But I was determined to make this work. I earned a little money as a prep cook. The experience—and the insider's view of a top restaurant kitchen—were great. I hadn't given up my dream, I explained to my father on my last visit home. After all, I was still *writing*, getting comments (reader feedback!) on a daily basis. The book deal would come.

After, you know, I scraped together a book. I just had to survive until then.

"I tested a new recipe yesterday," I said. "For mac and cheese. Did you see it?"

"On your blog?"

"Yeah."

"No. I mean, not yet. Sorry," Meg said. "No, Daisy, that's DJ's cup. *This* is your cup."

"That's okay," I said.

"It's just I've been so busy with the twins . . ."

"I understand," I said.

And I did. Why should my sister read about my life when we talked almost every day? No one back home in Bunyan followed my blog. They went out for barbecue or home for Sunday dinner. They weren't interested in the restaurant scene in New York City. Or in the people who ate there. Or in the person I'd become. Fortunately for me, New Yorkers searched for "places to eat" almost as frequently as "the Mets" or "rent-controlled apartments."

"How are my adorable niece and nephew?" I asked.

"The kids are great," Meg said.

A crash, followed by a wail.

"Oopsie," Meg said. "I have to go. Daisy threw her milk."

"It's okay." I pushed back from my desk, almost bumping into the opposite wall. My Chelsea studio on the fringes of public housing was half the size of my attic room back home. No real stove, no storage, no homemade curtains framing a view of pasture and pine. Since Ashmeeta moved out, I struggled to pay the rent. But I was still living on my own in New York City, epicenter of the food scene and the publishing world. The capital of reinvention, where being a single woman over the age of twenty-seven was not an aberration. "I'll hold."

"Are you sure?" Meg asked.

"Me, Mommy, me." I smiled at the imperious tone on the other end of the line. Definitely Daisy this time. "I talk with Auntie Jo."

"Give her the phone," I said.

"You don't mind?" my sister asked.

I wandered the two steps into my two-burner kitchen. Reached for the bottle of wine I'd brought home from work the night before. Was it too early to start drinking? But no, it was almost . . . Well, not dinnertime, but definitely after lunch. "Are you kidding?" I asked. "Put her on."

I adored my niece and nephew, the warm, sticky clasp of their starfish hands, their cries of *"Auntie Jo! Auntie Jo!"* whenever I visited home. Not that I was ready for babies of my own. Meg was the maternal one. But I loved that while my sister cleaned the spilled milk on her kitchen floor, I could pour my wine and listen to her children on the phone. First Daisy ("I haz bangs," my niece announced with glee) and then DJ's earnest, heavy breathing, like an obscene phone caller or Dan, the homeless guy in front of the bodega where I bought my morning coffee.

"Sorry," Meg apologized breathlessly, coming back on the line.

"No problem. So . . ." I took a sip of wine. How a customer could leave a sixty-nine-dollar bottle of cabernet sitting half-full on their table, I'd never understand. "Daisy has a new haircut?"

"They're working on scissor skills in preschool," Meg said ruefully.

I snorted with laughter. "Let me guess. Daisy decided paper wasn't enough of a challenge."

"When I went to pick her up, all her beautiful baby curls were gone. I almost cried."

"Look on the bright side," I suggested. "She could have an amazing future as a surgeon. Or a seamstress."

"Or a hairstylist."

"At least hair grows," I offered.

"That's what John said."

"How is my favorite brother-in-law?"

My only brother-in-law, actually, but I liked my sister's solid husband. I really did. When they got married, I thought Meg was awfully young—only twenty-six—but by Bunyan standards she was practically an old maid.

"Oh, he's fine. Everything's fine," she said. Which is what she always said. Living the dream in Bunyan, North Carolina.

Her dream, anyway.

Meg had planned her life in careful steps, from a sensible major—business—to a practical career as a loan officer at the bank. Managing risk. She was good at that. She dated John for a year before they got engaged and produced two adorable children only a little ahead of schedule.

I waited for her to tell me again about her handsome husband, her fantastically satisfying life, her yard.

"Guess who's coming to Thanksgiving dinner?" she asked.

I blinked at the change of subject. "Um . . . Aunt Phee?"

Our great-aunt Josephine spent most holidays with our family. No one else would have the old bat.

"Who else," Meg said.

"Mr. Laurence." Our next-door neighbor.

"Both the Laurences," Meg said. "Trey's home."

My wine sloshed. I set the glass down hastily. "I thought he was in Italy. Driving Maseratis or something for his grandfather."

Theodore Laurence III—Trey—was old Mr. Laurence's grandson. We'd practically grown up together. I hadn't seen him since July, when he had a layover at JFK on his way to Florence. We'd fought—again—both of us too stubborn to change our minds and too proud to apologize.

"Ferraris. He got back last week," Meg said. "He was asking about you, John said."

Trey was John's boss at the Laurences' car dealership. I was vague on the details. "I hope John told him I was great."

"Well, of course." A pause, while I listened to a jackhammer across the street. "Trey didn't know you'd left the newspaper."

Sweet Meg. She made it sound as if my being let go was my decision.

"We kind of lost touch over the summer," I said.

He'd stopped following me on Instagram, Facebook, Twitter, Tumblr, Snapchat, and Pinterest. We were still friends, though. His face showed up occasionally in my various newsfeeds, usually tagged in a photo by some unknown Ashley or Jennifer. I told myself that was a good sign he was over me.

"So, do you think you two will ever get back together?" Meg asked.

"There is no together," I said. "We never were together."

Which wasn't, strictly speaking, true. Trey was my buddy, my oldest pal and coconspirator, one of the few friends I'd kept in touch with after high school.

But when I left for New York, Trey, instead of being happy for me, had sulked for months.

"You're not seeing anybody else," Meg said.

I took a deep breath. My sister only wanted me to be happy. In her world, as in Shakespeare's comedies, marriage was the restoration of the social order. I couldn't get her to see that my staying single was not a tragedy.

I went out a *lot*—to keep an eye on the competition, to gather grist for the blog mill, to indulge in the usual late-night, postshift rituals of kitchen workers everywhere. But I didn't date. Nobody outside the restaurant industry understood the insane, pressure cooker hours, the nights-and-weekends schedule. And dating someone on the inside . . . Well, aside from the drama, I didn't want to risk writing, even anonymously, about someone I'd had sex with.

"I don't have time for a relationship," I said.

"Or you haven't found anyone you can love like Trey," Meg said.

"Of course I love him. As a friend. But if we had to live together, we'd kill each other."

"You were best friends in high school."

"You're my best friend." We had always been close, paired together in age like Jane and Elizabeth Bennet. (In my imaginings, of course, Meg was Jane, and I was snarky, independent Lizzy.)

"Aw. Love you," Meg said. "I wish you could be here for Thanksgiving."

This year, I wouldn't be going home. Or taking New Jersey Transit from Penn Station to Summit, where Ashmeeta's parents lived. No Thursday turkey with a side of *palak paneer* and naan. No Friday night *Girls* marathon and martinis on the couch with Rachel.

This year, I was alone for the holidays.

"At least you'll see Beth," I said. Our sister Beth, after a couple of false starts, was back in college at Greensboro, studying music. But she went home every holiday. Most weekends, too.

"And Amy," Meg said.

"I thought she was going back to Paris. Doesn't she start that job this month?"

Amy, after sweet-talking Aunt Phee into giving her a trip to Europe as a graduation present, had schmoozed her way into an internship with Louis Vuitton.

"She put them off until after Thanksgiving," Meg said. "She feels bad enough about missing Christmas with the family."

I took another sip of wine. "How's Dad?" I asked.

"Dad's fine. He's going up to Walter Reed this week to visit some of his old battalion."

So that was good.

After 9/11, our father had left his congregation to join up as a military chaplain. After his first fifteen-month deployment, he'd re-upped again. And again. Even after he got out of the army, he had rejected assignment to another church, instead founding a nonprofit that worked with returning veterans, helping them reintegrate into civilian life, providing counseling for PTSD.

I was so proud of his service. Even when it took him away from us.

"Mommy, down," Daisy demanded in the background.

"Hang on, sweetie. Let Mommy wipe your hands first," Meg said.

"Done. Down now."

"DJ, don't you want more apple?" Meg asked.

"He's not hungry, Mommy."

"Okay," my sister said in a cheery voice. I was impressed by her patience. Not to mention her ability to conduct two conversations at once. "Let's get you both cleaned up and—"

"Done. Done. Down." An escalating wail.

"If you need to go . . ." I said.

"In a little while. DJ needs a clean shirt." A pause. "Possibly a bath. He's got peanut butter in his *ears*."

I laughed. "I think you're amazing," I told my sister honestly.

"Thanks, sweetie. Some days I don't feel so amazing. This morning when I left the house, I didn't even put on makeup."

I grinned. "Oh, the horror. Appearing in public without mascara? They're going to revoke your Southern Woman card for sure."

"So funny. I know you don't care about stuff like that. But I do."

"I remember." Back in high school, borrowing clothes from each other's closets, fixing each other's hair for prom. Okay, sometimes Meg loaned me her clothes. She declared she wouldn't be seen dead in mine. And after that time I singed her hair with the straightening wand, she refused to let me near her head.

"Maybe you should get John to take you out," I suggested idly. Not that there was anyplace to *go* in Bunyan. Not like New York. "Like a date night."

"Maybe. Usually we just collapse on the couch and watch *This Is Us*. Well, I watch. He sleeps. He works so hard."

"So do you," I pointed out.

"Anyway, I've never left the kids with a babysitter."

"Okay." I took another sip of wine. But it seemed a shame my pretty, sociable sister couldn't get dressed up and go out for one night. "I bet Momma would watch them if you asked her."

"I can't. She's still having that back pain. Especially at night. And now that her legs are bothering her—"

I set down my glass. "What back pain?"

"Didn't she tell you?"

"No, she never said a word." *And neither did you.* "How long has this been going on?"

"I guess . . . Three weeks?"

"Three *weeks*," I repeated, stunned. Stung. Yes, I had sworn never to return to Bunyan. But Meg always kept me in touch. "Has she been to see a doctor?"

"Dr. Bangs." Who had been our family doctor since before I was born. "He wants her to get an MRI."

Wait. *What?* "Is she going to be all right?"

"She says she's fine."

"Right. And if she chopped off her arm, she'd tell you she had a hangnail," I said. This past summer, when she'd gashed her shin almost to the bone on portable paddock fencing, she'd bandaged it up herself and gone back to herding goats.

"Don't worry," my sister said in her warm, reassuring Meg way. "I'm here."

I felt a wave of love along with the teensiest surge of guilt. She was the best sister. The model daughter. *"Never a minute's trouble,"* Aunt Phee liked to say. Usually with a glance at me. *Not like that one,* her look implied.

"Is there anything I can do?" I asked.

"You want to come home?"

"Ha-ha," I said.

Bunyan, North Carolina, could have been the setting for a Lifetime channel movie or a romance novel. Stuck in the middle of miles of farmland, past hand-lettered signs offering pine straw delivery and tarot readings, the small town clung to the bank of the Cape Fear River like a patch of daylilies, sturdy and bright. The lampposts all had flags, the front porches all had rockers and deep eaves. There was a bandstand on the river walk and a farmers' market on Saturdays. The main street boasted a library, a bank, a struggling art gallery, and three churches. A jumble of storefronts sold postcards and ice cream and secondhand clothes, bait and paint and appliances. It was the kind of place you wanted to raise a family in or move to in retirement. A good place to come from.

But not where I was going.

"I'll see you at Christmas," I promised. "Only six weeks away."

"We'll miss you at Thanksgiving."

"I'll miss you, too," I said.

But not enough to jeopardize my job, I thought as we ended the call. Not enough to disrupt my life.

They would all have to get along without me, Meg and John, Daisy and DJ, Momma and Daddy. Beth. Amy. Even Aunt Phee and old Mr. Laurence.

And Trey.

My heart tripped. My decision to stay away had nothing to do with Trey.

I scowled into my wineglass. Nothing at all.

I was fifteen the summer Trey Laurence came to live with his grandfather.

"*The boy next door,*" Amy called him, which I thought was ridiculous since he lived a mile away up the road.

Our big orange barn cat, Weasley, had gone missing the day before. Beth was making herself sick, worrying he had encountered a coyote. More likely a truck, I thought, but I'd promised her to keep an eye out when I went for my run.

So when I saw the orange shadow slink through the gap in the hedge by the Laurence place, I was relieved. Well, relieved and annoyed, because now I was going to have to break pace, and it was going to be really hard to get my body moving again. Also, I had no idea how I was going to get the cat home. But I pushed through the bushes anyway, scratching my arms, whistling the way Beth did when she was calling the cats to feed them.

Naturally, Weasley ignored me, streaking toward the antebellum-style house.

I jogged up a long gravel drive through an avenue of trees like a dirt-scratch farmer come to beg a favor at the Big House, growing hotter and sweatier and more exasperated by the minute. *Damn cat.* If I hadn't promised Bethie . . . I whistled again, following the flick of the cat's tail as it rounded a corner of the porch.

And there, sitting on the back steps, was a boy scratching our cat under the chin.

I stopped, eyeing him warily. He was about my age, with dark curly hair and faintly golden skin.

He looked up at me and smiled. "It's not a dog, you know. It won't come when you whistle."

I crossed my arms over my chest. "It's my cat."

"I've been feeding it."

I noticed the open can of tuna on the ground beside him. "Which explains why Weasley hasn't come home for two days."

"Weasley, huh?" The cat leaned into his fingers. "Ron, I presume."

A fellow Harry Potter fan. "Well, he's definitely not a Ginny. Eighty percent of orange cats are male."

He raised an eyebrow in acknowledgement.

I uncrossed my arms. "I'm Jo March. I live down the road."

He nodded. "I see you sometimes. You and your sisters. I'm Trey."

Trey. Theodore Laurence III.

I'd heard of him, of course. In the country, you might not see your neighbors every day, but you talk about them plenty. Even I knew about old Mr. Laurence's son, who ran off to Miami and married a club singer. He'd died a couple months ago, along with his Cuban-born wife—a boating accident, the gossips said.

"You're old Mr. Laurence's grandson," I said.

"That's right."

I didn't know what to say. I'd never known anybody before whose parents had died. Our dad was in Iraq. If something happened to him, it would be like the sun had gone out of our sky, but our lives would basically go on as usual, anchored in our routine orbits by our mother's steady gravity.

"Sorry about your folks," I said.

He nodded once, shortly, his black-lashed gaze sliding away.

"Well . . ." I shifted my weight from foot to foot. "It was nice, uh, meeting you. I gotta run." Like, literally.

He uncurled from his seat on the porch. He was taller than me, strong and lean. "What are you, in training or something?"

I stuck out my chin. "Yeah, actually. I'm on the cross-country team."

"What's your time?"

"Twenty-three minutes." *Give or take a minute.*

"Pretty good." His smile flashed, exposing nice white teeth. "For a girl."

I grinned back. "Whatever. I don't see you running."

His dark eyes met mine. "Maybe you will."

We stood a minute, awkwardly. Something about the way he was looking at me in my sports bra and running shorts made my face get even hotter.

"So." I refastened my ponytail. My hair was thick and curly like my father's, either my best or worst feature, depending on my mood and the humidity. "I guess I'll see you around."

"What about old Weasley here?"

I looked at the cat hunkered down at the tuna. "It's fine. I mean, it's not like I can carry him home with me. At least now I can tell Beth not to worry."

"Beth. Is that your sister?"

"My middle sister, yeah."

He nodded again.

With a little wave, I turned and loped away, aware of him watching behind me.

I finished my run—four miles in twenty-nine minutes with time out for the cat, not bad—thumped up our front steps and into the house. Meg was in the kitchen making a salad while Amy set the table.

I grabbed a pitcher of water from the fridge.

Amy wrinkled her nose. "Get away. You smell."

I ignored her. "Guess what? I just met our new neighbor."

"You mean Trey?" Meg asked. "Seriously, Jo, you should take a shower before dinner."

"Oh my God, he's so gorgeous." Amy sighed dramatically. "Like Edward Cullen."

"Language," Meg said. The Reverend Ashton March's girls did not take the name of the good Lord in vain. Leastways, not when anybody could hear.

I lowered the pitcher. "Wait, you saw him?"

Trey's hair was black, not bronze. But I could see how my *Twilight*-obsessed little sister could compare him to a sparkly vampire. There was that golden skin. That tall, lean build. Those almost black eyes, like he was hungry for something.

"He stopped by while you were gone," Meg said. "To drop off Beth's cat."

"Oh." I felt oddly deflated at having my big news scooped. "Well, good."

It wasn't like Trey was my exclusive property or anything.

But the following Monday at school I discovered that we were in the same grade. We took the same classes—Mrs. Ferguson for AP English, Mr. Clark for chemistry—even if Trey never exerted himself the way I did. "*Suck-up*," he'd tease when he came over to our house to study. "*Slacker*," I'd retort. We both went out for the school play, both ran cross-country in fall and track in spring. We were *friends*.

Which was why it was such a mistake to complicate our relationship with sex.

I saw that now. Why couldn't Trey?

CHAPTER 2

Meg

When we got married, I promised John—I promised myself, really—I wouldn't go running to Momma with every little thing. I didn't want John thinking I depended on my mother for advice. Anyway, we both agreed a married couple should solve their own problems.

Not that we were having problems. Every day I told myself how lucky I was to be living the life I'd always wanted. The life my parents had.

I buckled the twins into the big white Ford Explorer John insisted we needed. They looked adorable in their car seats, all dressed up in matching red-and-white outfits like little Prince George and Princess Charlotte.

"Juice," DJ said.

I kissed his smooth head. "Not now, honey." Even the lidded cups with straws I used in the car were no guarantee he wouldn't dribble all over his tiny jacket. "We're going to the fire station."

Daisy bounced in her car seat. "See Santa!"

"That's right." I adjusted the barrette holding down her hair, suppressing a sigh over the loss of her pretty baby curls. "Santa will be there."

Along with half the population of Bunyan. Every November, the volunteer fire department and rescue squad held a fund-raiser with free blood pressure checks and a Fire Safety House and Santa riding in on a shiny red fire truck. The early visit gave parents a jump on their children's wish lists and the local merchants a jump on the mall.

When we were first married, we'd gone together. John and me. Not to see Santa, of course. But on weekends when he didn't have a wrestling tournament—or a meet or a practice on Saturday morning—we wandered the stalls at the farmers' market, holding hands and sampling cider. Part of the community. Everybody knew and liked the Caswell Cougars' wrestling coach.

I'd always known I wanted a family, to share the kind of love my parents had. When I binge-watched *Pride and Prejudice* with my sisters growing up, we all accepted that book-loving Jo was destined for Darcy. But that was okay. One day, I knew, my Bingley would come. I waited patiently while my girlfriends from high school all paired off, while my sorority sisters went out to bars and created online dating profiles, fell in love, and got engaged. In the two years after college, I bought six bridesmaids' dresses with matching shoes, shopped for shower gifts and wedding presents, organized bridal luncheons and bachelorette weekends in Myrtle Beach and Charleston.

And then John walked into my life. Into the bank, actually, where I was working as a loan officer. One look at him—those warm, brown eyes in that comfortably handsome face, that too-short hair with the adorable cowlick—and everything else faded to gray while Shania Twain sang "From This Moment On" with all the violins. It was love at first sight.

"No such thing," Jo scoffed when I called to tell her. "It's a biological construct. Chemical attraction to promote pair bonding."

For an English major, she could be awfully dense sometimes. I knew better. This was the man I was going to marry.

After I got pregnant, he quit teaching and went to work for Mr. Laurence at his big car dealership. I missed our time together, the lazy

Sunday afternoons, the long Christmas break. The evenings when he used to come home without stress bunching his jaw and shoulders.

But we couldn't raise a family on his teacher's salary, John had explained earnestly. And one of us needed to be home full-time with the twins.

Well. I knew how his own mother had struggled to make ends meet. I remembered how our lives had changed after Daddy gave up his congregation. Like most parents, we made sacrifices.

Not that my staying home was a sacrifice.

In the car, I sang. *"Over the river and through the woods to Grand-mother's house we go . . ."* Daisy chirped along. DJ kicked his feet in time to the music. Love for them squeezed my chest so tight I could scarcely breathe.

Bunyan had grown in layers, like an onion. At the center was the historic district full of retired lawyers and B and Bs, within walking distance of the church, the library, and the waterfront. Then the gated communities, springing up like cattails along the river with their boat slips and golf course memberships, where my friend Sallie Moffat lived. Our neighborhood was beyond that, on the road out of town, a neat subdivision bulldozed in between the trailers and old tobacco barns quietly going to ruin under veils of kudzu.

The parking lot was full of shoppers in town for the farmers' market. But I found a spot two streets over, down by the waterfront. Slinging my giant mommy bag over my shoulder, I lifted Daisy out of her car seat ("I walk, Mommy!" she insisted), buckled DJ into the stroller, and handed him his blanket. Picking up and moving things—bags of groceries, stacks of mail, scattered toys, the kids . . . That was my day. Actually, that pretty much summed up my life since Daisy and DJ were born. Two and a half years ago, two minutes apart.

In the delivery room—before DJ was whisked away, before my tummy was stitched and stapled—the nurse held each baby close to my face so I could touch them with one hand, kissing their precious, pink, squishy cheeks while they cried. I'd cried, too, tears of relief and joy and exhaustion. Even John's beautiful brown eyes were wet. *This is it,* I'd thought then, overwhelmed with love. Marveling at their tiny fingernails, their adorable pursed lips, the delicate fringe of their eyelashes. *This is everything.* Finally, like my sisters, I had found my calling. Not a writer like Jo or an artist like Amy or a musician like Beth. I was born to be a mom. Like our mom.

We made our way along the river walk. Daisy skipped beside me in her sparkly shoes, mostly listening to my admonitions to stay out of puddles and off the grass. The sound of her giggles lifted my heart. Last night's rain had washed the sky to sparkling blue. The furled masts of sailboats stood out against the bright sky. The white steeples of Bunyan Baptist and First Methodist Church rose over the town. Where Daddy used to preach before he went to war. Before we moved to the farm, back when we had money.

I held Daisy's hand crossing the street; levered the stroller over a storm drain and onto the curb. The back wheels caught. I was stuck like a rock in a stream of holiday shoppers, couples strolling hand in hand, parents with their children in tow or riding on their fathers' shoulders.

Not a problem. I yanked. Nothing.

There was a time when I would have looked around for help. When guys leaped forward to open my door or motioned me to go ahead in the checkout line or at intersections. Now? Not so much. I was a mom now. It was like the stroller had some magic power that rendered me invisible to men.

I set my teeth and shoved.

A strong hand gripped the front of the stroller and lifted. The wheels cleared the curb. I looked up, smiling my thanks.

A man—a young man with a short, reddish beard—smiled back. "Heya, Meg. Meg March, right?"

I straightened, flustered. "I . . . Yes? I mean, no. It's Meg Brooke now."

"From the bank, right?"

I tugged at my sagging T-shirt. Smoothed my hair. He was very cute. And vaguely familiar, which in a town the size of Bunyan was no surprise. "Yes?"

He gave a short, satisfied nod. "I thought so. It's Carl," he said. "Carl Stewart."

"The sweet potato guy." I remembered now. His family owned a farm on the other side of town. "You applied for a loan."

Carl had graduated from NC State a few years ago, full of plans to convert the farm to an organic operation. He'd started implementing organic practices right away. But because of regulations, his produce couldn't be certified as organic for three full years. He'd needed a bridge loan to meet expenses until then.

"And got it, thanks to you."

I flushed a little with pleasure. "You got it because you qualified."

"After you went to bat for me."

"All part of the job." My favorite part, actually—guiding applicants through the loan process, making sure they had the best shot at getting the credit they needed to upgrade operations or expand their businesses. The loan business wasn't all about assessing risk. It was helping people realize their dreams. "So, how's the organic farm business going?"

"Good. Great, actually." A smile cracked his scruffy jaw. "Everybody wants sweet potatoes this time of year."

I laughed. Not flirting, just . . . Well, flirting a little. Totally innocent, perfectly safe. I was happily married. "I'm glad to hear it."

"Sales are up. Way up. We're in All Seasons now."

All Seasons Market, a small produce and grocery chain gradually spreading throughout the Carolinas. "I'm impressed," I said.

"Thanks. I was talking to Abby about expanding distribution. But I guess you know all about that."

"Not really." My mother and I didn't talk farm business. Our conversations focused on the twins or John. "How are your folks?" I asked.

"They're good. Ma and Pop are figuring they can finally buy that RV, drive cross-country the way they've always talked about."

"That's wonderful."

"Yeah." He scratched his beard with the back of one hand. "Although they're leaving me in a bit of a jam. I'm actually looking for somebody to take over the books now."

"Mommy, *Santa*," Daisy said.

"In a minute, honey."

Carl glanced down. "These yours?"

I'd always dated clean-cut, clean-shaven types, like John. The beard, though, was kind of hot. I blinked. What was the question again? "Yes. Daisy and DJ."

"Cute. I don't suppose you're interested?"

A flush swept my face. Had he caught me staring? "Excuse me?"

"In keeping the books," Carl said.

"Oh." I was relieved. And maybe just a little . . . disappointed? "Oh no. I'm not . . . That is, I don't . . ."

"Course, we couldn't pay what you're making now. It's not really a full-time job. Compared to the bank, a spread like ours is pretty small potatoes." He smiled at his little joke.

I couldn't help smiling back. "It's not that," I assured him. I'd always liked working with small businesses. But . . . "I'm not at the bank anymore. I'm home with the kids."

It's what I wanted. What John wanted, after having to raise himself and his brother while their mother worked two jobs to support them.

"Then this job is perfect. You could do it from home. In your spare time. Say, twenty hours a week? Less."

I laughed and shook my head. "I have twins. There is no spare time."

Certainly not twenty hours a week. Not even one. Every second of every day was taken up taking care of other people, doing all the things my mother seemed to manage so effortlessly. If my house was never as clean, my cooking never as good, my children never as well behaved, it wasn't for lack of *trying*.

"Gotcha," Carl said. "Well, if you ever change your mind, you should call me."

"Thanks."

Not that I ever would. But still, it was nice to feel wanted.

The line for Santa wended past the fire safety display and the cake walk table. A female firefighter with elf ears and a clipboard took our names. Another manned a camera set up by the fire truck. DJ kicked his feet in the stroller as Daisy danced forward in line.

"Look, DJ. It's Santa."

He smiled his slow, sweet smile.

Clipboard Elf beckoned. "Next."

But as I lifted DJ from the stroller to pass to Santa, seated on the textured metal step at the back of the fire truck, his little body stiffened. "No."

"It's Santa, honey," I said. Actually, I was pretty sure the guy behind the fake white beard was Randal Collins, the assistant fire chief, but to DJ, he was a strange man in a red fat suit. "Don't you want to see Santa?"

"No. NO!" he screamed, and twisted away.

"He doesn't *want* to, Mommy." Daisy, two minutes older than her brother, was fierce in his defense.

It took almost three minutes of coaxing and the promise of a cookie when we were through to settle my children onto Santa's lap. Even so, DJ fussed until I hauled myself onto the truck, conscious of all the mothers waiting in line with their perfectly behaved children. I squeezed into the frame, grabbing Santa's knee for balance.

"Ho ho ho," Randal said.

"Smile!" commanded the elf.

Years from now, I knew, we'd look back on the pictures of Daisy scowling and DJ bawling on Santa's lap, and think, *How cute. How precious. How hilarious.* But it wasn't funny as I climbed down, murmuring apologies to the other parents in line.

"Meg? Meg! Over here!"

I looked around, my face hot. There. By the new ambulance. Sallie Gardiner Moffat and her older sister, Belle. Sallie and I had been on pep committee and homecoming court together. She was a buyer now for Simply Southern, an upscale women's boutique in a restored Victorian between Connie's Cupcake Confections and Bunyan Hardware.

She waved. "Meg! How are you? It's so great to see you! I barely recognized you."

Sallie looked exactly the same, like the cheerleader she'd been in high school, like she could climb to the top of the pyramid and backflip off: ponytail hair, full face of makeup, coordinated outfit.

I finished buckling Daisy into the stroller and handed DJ his blanket. "Hi, Sallie. Hey, Belle. We were just visiting Santa."

"Bless your heart," Belle said.

Belle was a mommy, too, but she looked like she'd stepped out of a magazine or one of Sallie's display windows. Highlights, Botox, mascara, and manicure. I could almost hear Jo snort. *Here's your Southern Woman card.*

I tugged on my top and smiled at her. "Where are your kids today?"

"Oh, Harper has a soccer game. Have you seen five-year-olds play soccer?" Belle shuddered delicately. "Running up and down the field like a giant amoeba. No idea of position at all. Incredibly boring. So George took them."

"Oh. Well, that's . . . That's good."

She raised a slim shoulder in a shrug. "I suppose. Children need sports, right? Physical activity. Harper has soccer and ballet. And tae kwon do, of course. I signed up both children as soon as they turned three. Yours are almost old enough."

"I don't think . . . Our pediatrician says at this age they get most of their activity from play."

"They still need structure."

"They go to preschool," I said. "First Methodist, two mornings a week."

"Harper and Logan are at Sterling Academy." Belle smiled faintly. "It's not for everyone, of course."

That was for sure. My children were never going to learn Mandarin at their preschool.

Sallie nudged her sister. "We loved First Methodist. Remember the youth group?"

"Mommy, go!" Daisy demanded. "Cookie time!"

"In a second, honey." DJ's blankie was dragging on the ground. I stooped to retrieve it. "I promised them we'd get cookies. We all deserve a treat after Santa."

Belle raised perfectly waxed brows without wrinkling her forehead. "Do you think that's wise?"

I bristled. "Daisy's in the thirtieth percentile of weight gain for her age." Twentieth for height. Developing normally, the pediatrician said, a little ahead of her twin. She certainly wasn't *fat*.

"I meant for you," Belle said.

Sallie grabbed her sister's arm. "It's been great seeing you, Meg," she said, sounding sincere. "We really need to get together."

"I'd like that. Any special plans for the holidays?"

"Not really. Ned is taking me to Hawaii in January. So we'll probably just go to the beach house with the family." Sallie brightened. "You should come."

I blinked. "I'm afraid Hawaii is a little . . ." *Out of our budget.* "Far away."

"Not Hawaii, silly. The beach. There's plenty of room."

Oh. Longing swept me. John and I had spent our first night together at Carolina Beach. But the years when I could take off for the beach with nothing but a swimsuit and some sunscreen were gone. Nowadays, it was an effort to pack the twins to go to the grocery store.

"Aren't you sweet. Thank you. But we're going to Momma's for Thanksgiving this year." The way we did every year. John's family wasn't really into holidays. "Beth and Amy are coming home," I added, by way of explanation. "And Momma's invited Mr. Laurence and Trey."

"Clever Momma," Belle drawled. "Inviting the boss to dinner. Didn't you used to go out with him?"

I flushed. Aunt Phee always said it was as easy to love a rich man as a poor one. But Momma wasn't like that. Our parents had raised us to value love, not money.

Mischief seized me. I shook my head. "He's a little old for me," I said demurely.

"What are you talking about?" Belle asked.

"Mr. Laurence," I said. "He must be seventy, at least."

Sallie laughed.

"I meant Trey," Belle said.

"He's too young. It would be like dating my brother."

"Or your brother-in-law," Sallie said. "Remember? He and Jo had a thing for a while," she said to Belle.

"*Jo?* But she's so . . ." Belle took one look at my face and stopped. Too late.

"Smart?" I suggested sweetly. "Sure of herself?"

"How *is* Jo?" Sallie asked, making peace. "She's living in New York now, right? When is she coming home?"

"Soon." Not soon enough. "Christmas."

"Won't that be nice."

"Yes."

"Well." Sallie bit her lip. Glanced uncertainly at Belle.

Sallie and I had grown up together. Her birthdays had been a series of firsts for me: my first unicorn ride (a white pony with a glitter horn), my first spa visit, my first party with boys.

Three years ago, she had asked me to be in her wedding party. When I told her I was pregnant with twins, she'd been all concerned. How would I manage getting in and out of limos and being on my feet all day? What if the excitement sent me into early labor?

Belle was the one who told me a pregnant bridesmaid would just ruin the pictures of Sallie's big day.

So I'd said no. The thought still gave me a pang.

Water under the bridge, Momma would say.

I smiled. "You all have a great time at the beach. Maybe I'll see you when you get back."

"Absolutely." She hugged me tight. "Ned and I are having a Christmas party on the tenth. I'll call you."

And maybe she would, I thought, as I wheeled the stroller toward the market farm stands. Maybe John and I would have our night out after all. If Momma could watch the twins.

What would I wear?

I bought cookies for Daisy and DJ at the bakery booth. And one for me. Crunching away, I turned the stroller up the row toward Momma's stall. SISTERS' FARM, read the sign, after Momma and her sister Elizabeth, who had died when they both were just girls. But the tables were empty. Momma wasn't there.

My stomach clenched. Mom wouldn't miss the market the weekend before Thanksgiving. Unless her back was bothering her again.

I stopped by the farm on the way home, bouncing up the rutted gravel drive to the back door. A few goats rambled in and out of their shelter, pulling lazily on bales of hay. As the foliage died, my mother rotated the herd from the woodland perimeter to pastures by the barn.

I'd asked my mother once why she had decided to build a herd of dairy goats instead of finding a job in town.

"Goats are easier to keep than cows. I could do most of the work myself and be home for you girls." That was our mother, always practical. She looked out over the herd, her face softening. "Besides, goats have *personality*."

I'd nodded, but I didn't get it. I mean, Aunt Phee had personality, too, but I didn't want to spend all my time with her.

I parked, careful to avoid the puddles from last night's rain. Daisy held up her arms to be released first.

I set her on her feet. "Stay next to Mommy," I said, and ducked my head back in to unbuckle DJ.

Daisy took off toward the kids' paddock, thick with grass, squishy with mud. Empty now, thank the Lord, except for a battered preschool playset my mother had purchased at the church yard sale years ago. "Goats!"

"No, Daisy," I said. "No baby goats. Not until springtime."

Undeterred, she toddled faster. "Slide!"

Hitching DJ and his blanket on my hip and my giant bag over my shoulder, I ran after her, catching her by the back of her full skirt. She stopped. Dropped. Fell on her bottom, right into a puddle. Shocked, she looked for my reaction, her little mouth comically ajar, wavering between tears and outrage.

I opened my mouth in an exaggerated O of surprise. Widened my eyes. "Splash!" I said with a big grin.

The storm cleared. She smiled back tremulously.

"Come on, baby." I crouched beside her, still holding DJ, and helped her to her feet. Water drenched her little bottom, splotched her skirt and stockings. I lurched to my feet, balancing DJ and Blankie on one arm, taking her hand with the other. "Let's get you cleaned up."

Crisis averted, we picked our way through the puddles to the house. Daisy tugged against my hold. "Goats," she insisted. "See goats."

"We're going to see the kitty," I said. Weasley, my mother's ginger barn cat, was almost twenty now and mostly retired to the house.

"Key?" Daisy asked.

"That's right." I glanced toward the kitchen door, surprised our arrival hadn't summoned Momma. Her truck was in the drive. Where was she?

"Up the steps, sweetie. Here we go." I opened the back door. Unlocked, as always. "Mom?" And then, more tentatively, "Dad?"

Not that he would be any help. My father loved his grandchildren, of course. Whenever he noticed them, he smiled and patted them on the head. But his attention was always fixed elsewhere—on his all-important work, his men, his mission.

A plaintive yowl answered me. Weasley slunk into the kitchen.

"Key!" Daisy yanked free.

The cat, no fool, bolted. My daughter, deprived of the object of her affections, let out a wail of frustration. Poor baby. John and I had talked about getting the children a pet, but right now I wasn't ready to take on responsibility for one more living thing.

"Momma?" I called again.

No answer. Maybe she was in the barn. I let DJ slide from my hip to the floor. Rummaging in my bag, I handed a toy truck to DJ and dug out dry leggings for Daisy. Since the twins started toilet training, I never traveled without a change of clothes. Stripping Daisy of her sodden stockings, I helped her step into dry panties. "Here we go, sweetie."

DJ approached his crying sister to give her a kiss. My heart melted. My sweet, serious boy.

"No." Daisy pushed him away.

He hit her in the face with his little Ford truck.

Daisy shrieked.

"Demi John!" I swooped DJ into time-out on a chair (*"We do* not *hit.* No *hitting."*), grabbed a dish towel from a drawer and a bag of frozen peas from the freezer. I was at home in Momma's kitchen. Maybe more so than in my own.

"Cold!" Daisy sobbed, twisting away.

"I know, baby. But it will make your cheek feel better."

I sat with her on my lap, petting and soothing until her tears subsided. "There we go. All better," I said. She would have a bruise by morning.

I hung the dish towel to dry on the oven door. Glanced out the window. Still no Momma. I felt a sticky tickle of unease, like walking into a cobweb. Mom did most of the farmwork herself. But still, there wasn't that much to do this time of year.

"Come on, my babies." I hefted DJ on my hip, held out a hand for Daisy. "Let's go find Marmee."

The air in the barn was thick with the dusty summer smell of hay, the salty sweet scent of the goats. The milking does—already pregnant with next spring's kids—raised their heads as we passed their open

pen. The younger ones butted against the fence, seeking affection or feed. I held Daisy's little fingers tight, mindful of nibbling teeth.

"Mom?"

A low moan answered me. An animal in pain.

"Momma." Oh, dear God in heaven. My mother lay on her back on the feed-aisle floor, surrounded by scattered stubble. I dropped to my knees beside her. "What happened?"

"Fell." She arched her back as a spasm hit her, straining, gasping for breath.

"What can I do?"

Her gaze found DJ in my arms. "Take . . . the children . . . house."

"I'm not leaving you," I said fiercely.

Should I move her? I didn't dare.

Daisy tugged at me, upset. "What's wrong with Marmee?"

DJ, alarmed by his sister's tone, started to snuffle. "Marmee!"

My mother closed her eyes, turning her head away. I struggled to my feet, dragging Daisy by the hand into one of the birthing stalls. I sat her on a bale of hay. Plopped DJ beside her.

Daisy opened her mouth to wail.

I gripped her shoulders. "Stop it," I snapped.

Shocked, she met my eyes, her little face red.

"You stay here," I commanded. "Stay and watch DJ. You understand? You watch your brother."

Because she was the oldest. By two minutes. *Only two minutes,* my conscience cried.

But, miraculously, she understood. Her mouth closed. She nodded solemnly.

"That's my girl."

I patted her shoulders and hurried back to my mother.

T he last time I was at the hospital, John and I were bringing DJ home, a week after the twins were born. *"Breathing problems,"* the nurse had explained as they hustled my baby away. *"For his own good."* Nothing I could do.

Even though I accepted the rightness of their decision, even though I was grateful for their expert medical care and the comfort of Daisy's warm, swaddled weight against my breast, I felt the wrongness of his absence in my womb, in my bones. My body, after sheltering his for thirty-eight weeks, protesting his loss.

Sitting in the emergency department waiting room, holding my mother's purse, I felt the same. Bereft.

I'd called Dad from the car—he was in a meeting at Fort Bragg, almost an hour away—and again as soon as we reached the hospital. He was on his way, he told me. Until he got here, my mother was my responsibility.

I'd held her hand, sitting on the cold barn floor, waiting for the ambulance to arrive. In between spasms, when she could find breath, she kept telling me not to fuss, she was fine, everything was going to be all right. Trying to take care of me.

I blinked back tears.

"I'm sorry," she repeated over and over. As if her weakness were something she needed to apologize for.

"Ssh, it's okay. Don't move," I told her.

Stupid thing to say. She arched and writhed, trying to escape the pain.

I covered her with my sweater, moistened her face with a diaper wipe from my giant bag, but it didn't seem to help. Nothing helped. She lay where she fell until the paramedics showed up.

I couldn't ride with her in the ambulance. I loaded my babies into their car seats and followed the blinking lights, watching from the drop-off lane as the paramedics unloaded Mom's gurney. As they wheeled her away through the sliding doors of the hospital, she said something that made one of them laugh. The ache in my chest intensified.

When I returned from parking the car, the receptionist would not let me back to see her.

"She's in triage now. As soon as she's settled in a cubicle, someone will be out to bring you back." Her round, dark face was vaguely familiar. Her gaze dropped to the stroller. "Do you have someone to watch the children?"

"What?"

"Patients in the emergency department are only allowed two visitors at a time. And we discourage children under twelve."

"But they're with me."

"I'm sorry. Hospital policy. Of course, if your mother is admitted, I can take you up to her room." Her dark eyes were sympathetic.

I wondered if she knew my mother. If she recognized her. From church, maybe, or the farmers' market or the checkout line at the grocery store. Bunyan was a small town. Our mother ran errands for our neighbors when they were sick, took meals to mothers of new babies, volunteered in all our classrooms. *Do all the good you can, in all the places you can, to all the people you can,* our father liked to preach, quoting John Wesley. Everyone admired our father. Nobody praised our mother. Her goodness was the quieter sort. She just was *there*. Always.

"What's wrong with her?"

But nobody would discuss Mom's condition with me.

"I brought her in," I protested.

"Are you her designated care partner?" one of the nurses asked.

"I'm her daughter," I said.

"I know. I'm sorry. But HIPAA rules . . ."

I had already spoken to Dr. Bangs's office. Nothing to do now but wait. I retreated with the stroller to the row of scratchy chairs and sat, holding my mother's purse like a talisman in my lap. DJ rubbed the satiny edge of his blanket against his face, a sure sign he was tired. Daisy struggled against the stroller strap.

"Up, Mommy," she insisted. "Want up."

I lifted her from the stroller, reassured by her wriggly warmth, her solid weight in my lap. Which meant DJ wanted up, too. I wedged him beside me.

A mother and daughter sat in the chairs opposite mine, the little girl in shin guards and a ponytail, her wrist at an awkward angle. An elderly woman held her husband's spotted hand. There was a dog-eared copy of *Arthritis Today* on the table beside me, along with a stack of medical pamphlets and a five-month-old issue of *People*. Nothing to distract tired two-year-olds. I rummaged in my bag for board books. For juice boxes.

"Need potty, Mommy," Daisy said a few minutes later.

Of course.

When we got back from the public restroom (*"Mommy will hold you. Don't touch anything."*), the mother with the soccer player sent me an understanding smile. "How did it happen?"

"Excuse me?"

She nodded to the bruise rising on Daisy's face. "Did she fall?"

Her brother hit her in the face with a truck, I did not say. "She's fine. I'm here with my mother," I explained. "She came in earlier. In the ambulance?"

"Oh." The woman withdrew slightly, as if our tragedy was somehow catching. "I'm sorry."

I nodded, accepting her sympathy, and called John again at the dealership. This time he picked up.

"Where are the twins?" he asked after I'd explained where I was.

"With me." Where did he think they would be? It was a Saturday. We never hired a babysitter, never left the twins with anyone but my mother. His mother was remarried and living in Florida. "I just wanted you to know."

"Okay," John said. "I'm glad you called. Try not to worry."

Like not worrying was an option.

There was a child-size table and chairs in one corner of the room, with one of those wire maze contraptions with sliding beads. I wiped everything down with diaper wipes and Purell—this was no time to fret over the long-term effects of hand sanitizer—and for a while that kept the twins occupied. But they were reaching their limit, poor babies. So was I.

I checked in again with the receptionist and then called Jo.

"Jesus," my sister said, taking the name of the Lord in vain, and for once I didn't correct her. Prayer or swear seemed equally appropriate. "Is she going to be okay?"

Looking to me for answers, for reassurance, the way we'd always looked to our mother. I felt like I was five years old again, playing dress-up, teetering around in Momma's Sunday shoes. Off-balance.

"I think so," I said. *I don't know.* "Her blood pressure's high, but the paramedics said that could be because of the pain."

"What's wrong with her?"

I tightened my grip on our mother's purse. "That's what they're figuring out now. They're running a bunch of tests."

"What kind of tests?"

"Blood tests. An MRI." Dr. Bangs's nurse had told me that much, after I reminded her how long our family had been going to his practice.

"I wish I could be there. What can I do?" Jo asked.

"Nothing." Which was true. "I just wanted to give you a heads-up."

In case I was wrong. In case the doctors were wrong. In case Jo needed to be here suddenly.

"I'm glad you did," Jo said. I could hear traffic rumbling in the background, the gust of a bus like a beast breathing. She must be on her way to work. "How are you doing?"

"I'm fine." This wasn't about me. This was about Mom.

"*Fine* isn't *good*," my sister observed. "Have you told the girls?"

"Not yet. Not until I know what's going on."

"Smart," Jo said approvingly. "No point in scaring Beth into coming home."

"Or Amy."

"Oh, Amy," Jo said dismissively.

"Amy would come," I said. Amy, the baby of the family, did tend to slide away from anything unpleasant. But she was more sensitive than Jo gave her credit for. "She has to work."

"I thought she didn't leave for Paris until after Thanksgiving."

"She still has her job at the boutique," I said. Amy worked retail in Raleigh, at some high-end women's store near the NC State design school.

The sliding doors opened. A man strode into the waiting room. Not Dad. Tall and broad, with short blond hair that looked as if he'd dragged a hand through it recently. *John*.

A warm relief washed over me.

Daisy looked up from the wire maze. "Daddy!"

"I have to go," I gabbled into the phone. "John's here."

"'Kay. Love you. *Call* me," Jo said.

"I will," I promised.

John straightened, his arms full of twins, DJ's little head resting trustfully on his shoulder. He looked kind and calm and utterly trust-worthy. Coach John.

I swallowed. "Thanks for coming."

"Of course," John said matter-of-factly.

I wanted to hug him. I repacked the board books and DJ's blanket. John watched as I wiped the kids' hands again with Purell and buckled them into the stroller.

He seemed to be waiting for something.

"What?" I asked.

"Are you okay? Do you need anything?"

Darling John. He'd left work in the middle of the day to be here. How could I tell him how overwhelmed I felt? How scared?

I shook my head. "I'm still waiting for Dad. I'll be home as soon as I can."

"Don't worry about it. I'm staying home."

I stared at him in mute gratitude. "What about work?"

"The dealership can run without me for one afternoon. You should be here." He bent and kissed my forehead. "With your mom."

Tears flooded my eyes. I blinked and looked away before I started bawling like Daisy.

Somewhere beyond those steel doors was my mother, separated from me by cold hospital corridors and regulations. My entire life, our mother had been there for us girls, calm and sure, guiding and reassuring.

Now I had to be there for her.

CHAPTER 3

Jo

Thwack. I smacked the cleaver down. I was cleaning sardines for the appetizer special, bloody guts and pinbones all over my board.

The Gusto kitchens looked like a casting call for *Chopped*, seasoned pros rubbing elbows with misfit stoners sporting mohawks. I was one of Chef's charity cases, along with Frank-the-ex-felon and Constanza, single mother of four. Although they both pulled more weight in the kitchen than I did, my previous restaurant experience being limited to a couple years in campus food service. My occasional contributions to the What's Cooking? column for the *Empire City Weekly* apparently didn't count.

I tossed a fish head into a stock pan.

Technically, prepping the plats du jour was the sous chef's responsibility. But the sous—who ranked right below Chef at Gusto, which in the kitchen hierarchy put him two steps below God—had delegated the task to me after I'd requested Thanksgiving off.

Of course he'd said no. And then punished me anyway, for daring to ask.

I didn't mind doing the sous chef's dirty work. But there was no way I could accept his decision.

I thwacked the head off another sardine.

The back door burst open on a blast of cold air from the loading dock, and Chef blew in, his big voice booming, electrifying the air. He moved down the line, greeting everyone from the sous chef, Ray, to Julio, the morning dishwasher, clapping shoulders, shaking hands, shaping us into a team. "Ray, my man, ¿va bien? Hey, Constanza, how's your little girl? Julio, ¿que onda?"

The replies echoed back. "All good, Chef." "Much better, Chef." "¿Todo bien contigo? Gracias, jefe."

In the kitchen, his authority was absolute. He was always jefe, "Chef," never dude or dawg or bro. With his Michelin-star-studded résumé and James Beard Award, he could have been a consultant or celebrity chef anywhere. Paris. London. The Food Network. But here he still made food, cooking almost every day by choice. Gusto was his livelihood. His life. His mission.

Which made what I was about to do really stupid.

I wiped my hands on my apron, fingering the outline of my phone in my pocket. I hadn't had a text from Meg in over an hour. "Chef?"

He looked over from his discussion with the sous, one eyebrow lifting. A big, dark-skinned man closer to forty than thirty, totally in command of himself and his kitchen.

My heart hammered under my white coat. "Could I talk to you a minute?"

Ray, the sous, scowled.

But, "Sure," Chef said easily. "I've got the squab," he said to Ray. "Get Lucas on the tagliatelle while you do the pork belly, yeah?"

"Yes, Chef."

He approached, his keen gaze sweeping my bloody station. "What's this?" he asked, indicating the flat stainless pan filled with the heads and bones of decapitated fish.

"I'm prepping the sardines. With the carrot fennel slaw? I thought I'd make a fish stock later," I added, proud of my initiative.

Chef shook his head slowly, almost sadly. "Snapper and bass, March. Halibut, okay, or cod. But not sardines. Nothing dark or oily. Not for fumet."

His voice was kind, his rebuke audible throughout the kitchen.

My face burned. I should have known. I should have tossed the scraps to the skinny black cat that lurked around the Dumpster outside. Ray smirked.

Bite me, Ray, I thought.

"Yes, Chef," I said.

"Was there anything else?" he asked gently.

From across the kitchen, Lucas, one of the line cooks, shot me a sympathetic glance.

I should say no. I needed this job. Not so much for the pay. I could have made more as a dog walker in Manhattan or working front of house almost anywhere. Although, as an out-of-work writer, I didn't have the looks or the moves to command the kind of tips the auditioning dancers and aspiring actors could earn. But I didn't want to lose my front-row seat to the food show, my chance to learn from an award-winning chef who didn't throw tantrums or knives in the kitchen.

"Amy would come," my sister had said. *"She has to work."*

I stuck out my chin. "If we could . . . I only need a minute."

A long pause, measured in heartbeats.

"Sure," he said at last. "Let me see the reservation book," he said to Ray, and turned on his heel.

I trailed after Chef toward his office, resisting the urge to poke at my hair, bundled for work on top of my head.

The room was the size of a closet, cramped, cool, and dim. Chef tossed his leather jacket on top of the desk, which was already spilling over with invoices, menus, and samples.

"Talk to me," he ordered.

Unlike a lot of top male chefs, Chef didn't treat his staff as though having a dick entitled him to act like one. I took a breath. "I can't work Thanksgiving."

He grabbed the neck of his sweater, tugging it one-handed over his head. "Tell Ray."

"I did."

His face emerged from the pullover. His gaze met mine. "Ah."

I stood my ground. "I wouldn't ask if it wasn't important."

The sweater joined the jacket on his desk. Stripped, his shoulders and arms were broad and hard, his belly slightly soft. A chef's body, sculpted by years of commanding the pass, hefting and hauling, tasting and testing, marked by full-sleeve tattoos.

I averted my gaze, uncomfortable seeing him out of his professional whites. At the same time, my hands itched for a camera to capture those tattoos: kitchen knives, a flying pig, and a single word, *soigné*. I recognized the reference from Julia Child. It meant good cooking or elegance in preparation. Something like that. I was already framing shots, writing captions in my head. *Under the white coat*? No, too medical. *Chef, Exposed*. Ick. That sounded like a porn flick.

"Who died?" Chef asked.

What? Momma wasn't dead, she couldn't *die*, she was just . . . And then I realized he was being sardonic. "Nobody."

He maneuvered around me to the locker stuffed with white jackets and houndstooth pants. Years of working at top speed in tight kitchens had made him as agile as a boxer. But this proximity, off the line, felt different. Awkward. Intimate.

He shrugged. "Then . . ."

"It's my mother," I blurted before he could tell me no. "She went into the hospital today."

"Ah. I'm sorry. She will get better?"

"Yes. I think so."

Meg said so. My poor, capable sister, dealing with everything by herself.

"Good."

He pulled on his white coat. Unlike my anonymous polyblend, his chef's jacket was fresh-pressed, high-thread-count cotton, vented in the armpits, his name embroidered above the pocket.

"The thing is . . . After she gets out, she'll need help. I need to go home. Just for a few days."

He looked at me sideways. "How old are you, March?"

Why did he want to know?

"Twenty-eight." I tried not to sound defensive. At least I hadn't moved back home to live with my parents. Yet.

"College graduate?" he asked in the tone of somebody back home. Kind. Dismissive.

But I was in New York now, free to be whatever I made of myself.

"English major." I added, deadpan, "My faculty advisor told me it would be good preparation for any career." I didn't mention my MFA in creative writing, a two-year investment that had produced a handful of sentimental stories and put me more deeply in debt.

His eyes crinkled at the corners. Not a smile, but a sign that he found me amusing, at least. "And you chose . . . this."

I hesitated, wondering how much I should tell him. Nodded.

"You think when I was training that I went home to my mother every night?" he asked. "That I asked for weekends and holidays off?"

"No, Chef."

"I was sixteen when I dropped out of high school to work in my first kitchen," he said. "No Le Cordon Bleu for me, no culinary degree. I begged jobs from anyone who would teach me."

I knew all this already. I'd researched him online. Eric Bhaer, the son of an American serviceman and a German mother, had risen through the culinary ranks in Italy and France, working eighteen-hour days in two- and three-star kitchens in exchange for food and a cot. A hint of Old Europe still rolled around his voice like butter melting in a pan.

"I can learn," I said. "I want to learn."

I had always been a good student, having figured out early on that education was my ticket out of Bunyan. Always knowing there would be no money for college—not the kind of school I dreamed of attending—beyond what I earned or borrowed myself.

"Technique, sure." Chef slipped his feet into handmade clogs. "You have promise, March. You don't wait for everything to be handed to you. You show up on time, you pay attention to detail, your knife skills are improving. But the good cooks, the great chefs, they have passion, you understand? Dedication."

Another nod. Because I did understand. I watched the other members of the kitchen team stumble in day after day, shift after shift, underpaid, overworked, sleep-deprived, sick, or hungover. Cooks, driven to cook the way writers are driven to write.

"I like to cook," I said. Not to mention that there were way more job opportunities for inexperienced prep cooks than downsized journalists in New York.

Chef gave me a look, skewer bright and sharp, over his shoulder. "Why are we here, March?"

Not like, *here*, in his office. *Here* at Gusto. "To feed people?" I ventured.

"We feed them, yes. So simple. We take care of them, yeah? So basic. Service," Chef said, giving the word its French pronunciation. He reached for his knife kit, gearing himself for service like a knight preparing for a tourney. "Everything is for the guest. This is our calling. To be a chef, you must *love* to cook. You must live to cook, yeah?"

"Yes, Chef."

I couldn't match his dedication to service. The way he poured out himself in every dish, on every plate, night after night, for every diner who came to his table . . . That wasn't me. But I admired it—I admired him—so much. His integrity as a chef was one of the things that had drawn me to his kitchen, one of the reasons I liked talking about food, writing about food, sharing some of his enthusiasm, his passion.

Not that I could tell him that. My blog was an anonymous insider's view of the city's food scene. Confessing I was a food writer would put me on the other side of a professional divide. A critic, not a cook. No longer one of Us, but one of Them.

"Look, I know it's not the same," I said. "But my sister's in North Carolina dealing with everything herself, and she's got kids, twins, two and a half years old. And there are a ton of people invited for Thanksgiving dinner. I guess I thought . . ." That he would take my part against his sous, his second? I must have been out of my mind. "I thought if I went home, I could at least help cook."

He didn't say anything. He didn't have to.

"You gave Frank the weekend off when his sons came to visit," I said. "And Constanza . . . When her sitter quit, you let her bring Tina into work for almost a week."

"Where in North Carolina?"

"Um. Bunyan." Which nobody in New York had ever heard of. "It's on the Cape Fear River. Near Fort Bragg? My dad was stationed there."

"Yes, I know. I also have family there," Chef said.

"Your dad, right?" I felt a prickle of hope. We were both military brats. Would that make a difference? Would he let me go?

"My sons. Bryan and Alec."

"Oh." His bio hadn't mentioned children.

"They live with their mother. She's a support officer with the 82nd Airborne."

Or an ex-wife, either.

"It's not easy for families," I ventured. "Military life, I mean."

"Neither is restaurant life," Chef said.

Right. *"You must live to cook,"* he'd said. No wonder he was divorced.

A shadow appeared in the doorway. Ray, with the reservation book.

"Thanks." Chef took the book and flipped it open, scanning the day's entries.

I stood there, ignored. Dismissed?

"The *Times* is coming at nine," he said to Ray. "Move the ten-top to table twelve. VIPs in Jackie's station."

"Yes, Chef."

"And call Aaron, see if he wants to work Thanksgiving. March, here, is out."

"Out?" Ray repeated.

I held my breath. *Out?*

"On vacation," Chef clarified. "Aaron can cover her shifts."

Ray's lips pulled back from his teeth. "Yes, Chef."

"Thank you," I said after Ray left the office.

"You'll be back for Saturday service."

"Yes, Chef. I can be back by Friday, if you need me." If I had to be.

Chef regarded me, a rueful twist to his mouth. "Ray won't be easy on you when you get back."

"That's okay. It's worth it," I said.

"Scheduling the staff is his responsibility. I will not intervene again. There would be . . ."

Gossip. Resentment. Charges of favoritism.

"Consequences," he said.

Good word.

He was my boss. He was eight, maybe ten years older than me. The restaurant was a rude, crude, testosterone-fueled hierarchy. If Chef showed me any special treatment, everybody in the kitchen would talk. Hell, they were probably talking right now, wondering what I was doing in here with him.

But Chef had always seemed above the usual bed-hopping and partner-swapping that went on between the front and back of house. Despite the notorious sexism I'd blogged about in restaurant kitchens, he treated all the women who worked under him—the runners; the bakers; Constanza, our garde-manger—with the same exacting professionalism he showed the men.

"I understand. Thanks for giving me the time off." *Go, go,* my brain urged. My feet didn't move. "Why did you?"

He settled on the edge of his desk, arms crossed, legs spread. "If I had said no, you must stay, would you have quit?"

"I . . ." My heart beat faster. I should have left when I had the chance. What if I told the truth and he changed his mind? On the other hand, I'd done nothing but lie since he hired me. Maybe I owed him a little honesty. "Yes."

His eyes crinkled in another near-smile. "And that's why I'm letting you go. I don't want to lose a good prep cook."

I beamed back, relieved. "Yes, Chef. Thank you, Chef." He picked up one of the menus on his desk. Definitely my cue to leave. And yet, faced with the loss of his attention, I said, "How did you know it's the *Times*?"

He looked up, his brow wrinkling.

I tried again. "The nine o'clock reservation? I thought the *Times* reviewers were anonymous."

He grunted. "He's been in before."

"Oh. Well. Congratulations. I mean . . . The *New York Times*. That's a big deal."

"Fucking critics." Chef shook his head. "He'll order the fish. They always do."

I gaped at him.

"It's all right," he said, misunderstanding my reaction. "At least he's not an idiot hipster food blogger. Just make sure you prep those sardines for the appetizer properly."

Time to get while the getting was good. "What have you got against bloggers?" I asked.

"Parasites," he answered promptly. "They feed on the work of others."

"You don't write about something unless you love it."

He looked amused. Like he couldn't believe I was still standing there arguing with him. "They don't do it for love. They do it for profit."

"The restaurants benefit, too, you know. From the publicity."

"Fine. It's a transactional relationship."

"You mean, like prostitution?" I asked dryly.

The amusement spread. "It has its place. But it's not the real thing, yeah?"

I opened my mouth. This was the perfect opportunity for me to Tell All. To launch into an impassioned defense of the role of food bloggers in guiding the hungry, in creating the buzz that could make a deserving restaurant.

And yet . . .

He thought I had *promise*. He was letting me go home for Thanksgiving. Did I really want to see myself change in his eyes to an *idiot hipster food blogger*?

His brow rose at my continued silence.

Right. "I, um. I should get back to work," I said. "On the, um . . ."

"Sardines."

"Yeah. I mean, yes, Chef," I said, and escaped, my face burning.

CHAPTER 4

Meg

After thirty-six hours in the hospital being poked and prodded, x-rayed and imaged, our mother declared herself ready to go home, diagnosis or no diagnosis.

Momma came from country stock, with no time for doctors or what her mother called *fuss*. Granny could butcher a hog and handle a fishing pole or a shotgun as well as Granddaddy. Every now and then for Sunday dinner, our grandmother would kill one of the chickens pecking in the yard, making Beth cry and Amy threaten to turn vegetarian. Jo and I would watch, squeamish and impressed, as she prepped the chicken for the pot, fingers and feathers flying.

"Tough old bird," Jo would say, meaning Granny as much as the hen, and we'd sputter with laughter.

I'd never seen our own mother kill anything larger than a copperhead, whacking off its head with a shovel. But she had definitely inherited her mother's toughness.

She couldn't drive on pain meds. So Monday morning, after dropping off the twins at preschool, I went to the hospital to fetch her.

The discharge—against doctors' orders—took forever. I had to call John to pick up the twins.

"I'm fine," Momma said as I helped her up the steps into the house. "Go home to your family."

"Let me just pick up your prescriptions first," I said.

I did her grocery shopping while I was out—Thanksgiving was only three days away—and then milked the goats. I'd never been a farm girl like Beth or a tomboy like Jo. But I was our mother's daughter. All her life, Abby March had done for others, the perfect pastor's wife, the perfect officer's wife, the perfect example. The least I could do was keep things running until she was back on her feet.

When I got home, the twins rushed to greet me the way they usually ran to John, Daisy's bare feet thumping (where were her socks?), DJ dragging Blankie. *Mommy, Mommy! Momma's home!* I squeezed them tight, inhaling the salty sweet smell of their necks, absorbing the comfort of their warm, wriggly little bodies. John smiled at me over their heads. A rush of love swept over me for him, for them, for this life we'd made together.

"Thanks for watching the kids this afternoon."

"We had fun," John said, a trifle smugly. "I took them to the playground."

"I bet they loved that."

I could hear the television blaring from the family room. *Frozen.* I could sing that soundtrack in my sleep. I settled the twins in front of their movie, adjusting the volume down. Maybe they were getting too much screen time, but at least I wasn't damaging their ears.

"How's your mom?" John asked when I returned.

"She says she's fine. Better."

"Good."

I swallowed hard. "They're still not sure what's wrong with her. It could be anything." Infection. Inflammation. *Cancer.*

"They gave her something, though, right?"

I nodded. "Some antibiotic. And Vicodin, for the pain." I'd lined the bottles up on the windowsill, with a pencil and paper so she could keep track of her pill schedule, just like she used to do with our meds when we were little.

"The good stuff."

"I'm worried about her," I confessed. "I almost wish she'd stayed in the hospital. Who's going to take care of her at home?"

"Your father?"

I gave John a doubtful glance. My father visited wounded and incarcerated soldiers all the time. But Momma was the one who took our temperature and changed our sheets, who brought us ginger ale and soup on a special "sick day" tray. "That's not really his thing."

"So, Beth is coming tomorrow," John said. "And Jo gets in Wednesday. Let your sisters take some responsibility for once."

It wasn't that he didn't *care*, I reminded myself. But my sisters weren't the ones who found her writhing on the dirty straw. I was. "They don't know what to do."

"They're college-educated women. They'll figure it out. Your mother's laid up, not in a coma. She can tell them if she needs something."

Problem solved. Except I didn't need him to solve my problems. I wanted him to *sympathize*.

I caught myself. *Don't fuss. No fussing allowed.*

"You're right." I managed a smile. "You must be starving. I'll get started on dinner."

Back when John and I started dating, he'd fixed all his meals from a can. As if he were still nine years old, earnestly heating Dinty Moore stew and chicken noodle soup for himself and his little brother. I'd promised myself that once we got married, my husband would come home to a hot dinner every night. I would cook for him the way Momma cooked for us. The way his own mother, bless her heart, never had the time to do. For the past five years I'd kept that pledge as seriously as our wedding vows. Even when our babies were born (thirty-six hours of labor followed by a C-section, thank you very much), I'd prepared all

John's meals in advance, two whole weeks' worth of dinners with simple reheating instructions taped to each Tupperware lid. Cooking for John, caring for him in such a basic, intimate way, let him know how much I loved him.

"No rush," John said. "I fed the kids on the way home."

I took in my first full view of the kitchen. There were the twins' winter jackets, heaped by the door. Their muddy shoes, half under a chair. Their dirty school bags, smack on the center of the kitchen table, waiting for me to unpack. And there, on the counter, were . . .

I raised my eyebrows. "Happy Meals?"

"Chicken nuggets and apple slices. With milk." He shrugged, a little defensively. "They seemed okay with it."

Of course they were okay with it. It was *McDonald's*.

I could hear Elsa in the next room singing "Let It Go."

"Sounds like fun," I said lightly. "Let me get something for you, then."

I opened the freezer and found a steak. John's favorite. I popped it in the microwave to thaw.

He turned from the fridge, beer in hand. "You want anything?"

Pizza. A hug. A really large glass of wine. But I didn't know how to say so without sounding selfish. "I'm good, thanks, honey."

No time for baked potatoes. I went back to the freezer for Tater Tots. John tipped back his bottle, watching me, a warm look in his eyes.

I felt a little flutter of pleasure. Not that I could do anything about it now.

While the oven preheated, I unzipped the kids' book bags to retrieve their snack containers. The unmistakable whiff of poop wafted from a knotted grocery bag.

"Oh, that," John said. "DJ had an accident at school today."

"Thanks. I see that."

Gingerly, I untied the bag. There were the sweatpants DJ had worn this morning. His socks. His . . . everything. I took a deep breath—*big mistake*—and threw it all in the washing machine.

"Oh, and somebody's mom wants to know if you can send in three dozen reindeer treats."

The microwave beeped. Schools ran on the volunteer power of parents. Of mothers. Momma, with four daughters and a hundred goats to raise, was always baking or making or buying or selling something.

"Of course." I set the washer to presoak.

"I figured that's what you'd say." John sipped his beer. "So . . . Treats for reindeers. What is that, like, carrots?"

I smiled, my mind already leaping ahead. "Carrot cake, maybe." Carrot muffins? With powdered sugar instead of icing. Without nuts, obviously. Something kid-friendly that wouldn't trigger allergies. "Thanks for letting me know."

I washed my hands and opened the dishwasher, still loaded with clean dishes. Nothing to worry about now. First we had to get through Thanksgiving. I yanked open a drawer to put the flatware away.

John shifted out of my way. "The teacher said their class is doing some kind of skit."

I nodded. "Next month. They're singing 'Jingle Bells.'" We'd been practicing in the car all week. "With reindeer costumes." The costumes were done, thank goodness, antler headbands and white bibs sewn onto brown sweatshirts. The twins looked adorable.

John grinned. "I'd like to see that. I told her I'd try to take an early lunch that day, catch the performance."

I grabbed another handful from the dishwasher. "That's great, honey." The teachers *loved* it when fathers came to the preschool programs.

John came up behind me. "So it's a date."

"Sure." I sorted flatware. *Spoon, spoon, spoon, fork* . . . "I'll meet you there."

He rested a hand on my waist. Nuzzled my neck. His lips were cool from the beer. "You feel great." His standard opening line for fooling around.

I dropped a knife. "John," I said. Amused. Protesting.

Daisy ran into the kitchen. "Elsa, Mommy. Elsa."

I listened to the soundtrack from the family room. "The movie's over, sweetie. It's time to go upstairs now." I stooped for the knife and laid it on the counter. "I'll be back in a minute," I promised John.

He scooped up Daisy. She clung to his shoulders as he pretend-chomped her fingers, making her squeal with delight. DJ ran in, drawn by their noise, jealous of John's attention.

"Okay, everybody settle down," I said mildly. "It's bedtime."

John grabbed DJ, tucking him like a football under his other arm. Our son's head and feet dangled two feet above the floor. "I'll put the kids to bed. You can finish dinner."

I wavered, tempted. But taking care of the twins was my job. My only job, since our babies were born. John had left work twice in the past week to watch the twins while I dealt with Momma. It wasn't fair to ask him to tackle bedtime, too. "I can do it." I smiled to show him how much I appreciated his offer. "You'll just get them all wound up. They're used to things a certain way."

His mouth compressed. "No, Meg, you're used to things a certain way. Your way."

I stared at him, stricken. That wasn't it at all. Was it? Couldn't he see I was trying to be considerate?

"Sorry, honey." He rubbed the back of his neck. "It's been a full day."

Hurt dissolved into guilt. "Then you should relax," I said in my cheerful mommy voice. "Dinner's almost done. I'll be right back down."

"Whatever you want," he said.

He set the kids on their feet and kissed them good night. No kiss for me. But as I shepherded the twins toward the stairs, he asked, "Want me to open a bottle of wine?"

I smiled back, relieved. *Forgiven.* "That would be wonderful."

Two stories later, I closed the book and smoothed back Daisy's toothbrush bangs. "Sleepy time, my babies."

Now that they were toddlers, John had suggested we move the kids into separate bedrooms. I knew how important it was for him to provide our children with their own space. Cheryl, John's mom, told me that for the first year after her divorce, John and his brother had slept together on a pullout couch in their living room.

But I loved this room, our babies' room. I'd painted the walls myself a soft green (*"best color for a learning environment,"* I'd read) and made the white curtains with Momma's help. Amy, the artistic one, had added murals of the Hundred Acre Wood, sweet, old-fashioned line drawings of Piglet and Pooh based on the original illustrations. Along the opposite wall she'd painted a quote from Christopher Robin in flowing script: *"Promise me you'll always remember: You're braver than you believe, and stronger than you seem, and smarter than you think."*

I remembered how pleased I was, after years of sharing with Jo, to move into a room of my own. Filled with the dignity of my sixteen years, I'd picked out paint and grown-up curtains, pleased with my new status and closet space. But lying alone in bed at night, I'd listened to Beth and Amy in the other room, their whispers carrying through the wall at the head of my bed, and felt . . . Well. Wistful. Like I was missing out on something.

I wasn't ready for my babies to grow up and into separate rooms. Not yet. Maybe not for a long time. I'd read all those articles about twins' special bond. Anyway, we might need that third bedroom. If, say, I got pregnant again . . .

I clenched deep inside. I wasn't ready for that, either.

DJ was warm and damp against my side. Maybe too warm and damp? I checked. Yep.

I smooched the top of his little blond head. "Let's change that diaper, sweetie."

He lay quietly, rubbing the satiny edge of his blanket against his cheek as I took care of business. When I was done, he rewarded me with his slow, sweet smile. His big brown eyes were so much like John's. I smiled and planted a kiss on the bottom of his foot, eliciting a giggle.

"I pee, too, Mommy," Daisy said jealously.

I straightened. "Do you need to go potty again, sweetheart?"

"Need diaper," she insisted.

"Don't you want to wear your big-girl panties to bed?"

Her lower lip stuck out. "No."

My baby girl. So precious. So precocious. Ever since her first cry, two minutes ahead of her brother's, Daisy had taken the lead. Quicker to talk, to walk, to toilet train. The one who was expected to do everything first, to get everything right. Why *should* she have to put on her big-girl panties simply because she was the oldest? Let her sleep in a diaper for one night.

I changed her out of her pretty flowered panties and dimmed the lights. "Good night, my sweeties." I bent over their beds to kiss their foreheads. "Sleep tight."

When I got downstairs, John was in the family room watching *SportsCenter*. There was a beer in his hand, a bottle of wine and two empty glasses on the coffee table.

He looked up. "Kids down?"

"Yes." Should I apologize it took so long? "Dinner will be ready in a minute."

"No rush. Let me know if I can help."

Come keep me company, I almost said. But he'd already turned his attention back to the TV. Well. My father never helped my mother in the kitchen, either.

I cleared the fast-food boxes from the island, checking to make sure the toys weren't a choking hazard. I worried too much, John said. And obviously, the twins were fine. Everything was fine.

There was an extra Big Mac wrapper in DJ's box.

I balled it up and threw it away. John was a grown man, not a child. If he spoiled his appetite, that was his choice.

"Time to eat!" I called ten minutes later.

John strolled in, carrying his beer in one hand, the wine bottle in the other. I could still hear *SportsCenter*. I dashed into the family room to shut off the TV, came back to find he'd poured my glass of wine.

I sat and smiled at him. "Isn't this nice."

"Yeah." He sipped his beer.

We said grace. I stabbed at my salad. John sawed at his steak.

"I'm sorry it's overcooked," I said.

"It's fine. It's good. You didn't need to go to all this trouble for me."

"Maybe you're not hungry," I said.

He looked sheepish. "I picked up a burger earlier when I was out with the kids."

"I know. It's okay." I offered him a tiny smile. "I had a candy bar at the hospital."

I chewed and chewed, the steak like gristle in my mouth. "John." I swallowed. "Do you remember Carl Stewart?"

"No. Should I?"

"His family owns a farm on the other side of town. Organic produce?"

"There was a Dwayne Stewart came in last month looking for a new truck. To haul a camper, he said."

I nodded eagerly. "That would be Carl's father. His parents are retiring, and Carl is looking for someone to take over the books for the farm." I peeked across the table, searching for his reaction. "I was thinking maybe I could do it. Help them out."

John lowered his fork. "You want to go back to work?"

"Not full-time," I said. "Less than twenty hours a week, Carl said."

"I thought you were busy."

"I am. But this would be something different." *Something I was good at.* My heart pounded. "And the money would be nice, with Christmas coming."

His face froze, his jaw hardening in a way I knew well.

"Not that we need the money," I added hastily.

John frowned at his plate. "Who would watch the kids?"

"I'd work from home."

He looked up. His deep-brown eyes held mine. "Whatever you want," he said quietly.

Making it my decision. My responsibility. Part of me was grateful for his support. And another, smaller part wondered if this was a test.

"What do you want?" I asked.

John shook his head. "What I want doesn't matter."

I sucked in my breath. "That's a terrible thing to say." Even if it was true. Maybe especially if it was true.

He saw my face, and his own expression changed. "Christ, Meg, don't look like that. I just meant . . . I took this job so you would have a choice. I'm not going to tell you what to do."

My stomach clenched. He worked so hard. Especially in the beginning, when he still worked on the sales floor, on commission. I didn't regret those sleep-deprived days, when we were both bleary-eyed and exhausted, when John put in sixty-hour weeks to prove himself at the dealership, and I stumbled out of bed every hour to breastfeed the twins. But I wondered sometimes if he regretted leaving teaching, if he missed the autonomy of his classroom, his authority as a coach, the adulation of his team. It didn't help that his boss, Trey, was the owner's grandson and three years younger than John.

He'd taken the job at the dealership for us. For me. So that I could stay home full-time. So that we could give our babies the childhood he'd never had, with no financial worries and their mother's full-time attention.

The last thing I wanted was for him to think I didn't appreciate his sacrifice.

We finished dinner in silence.

Five years ago, I knew exactly what I wanted.

It was a Friday night, and everybody in town was at the high school to see the Caswell Cougars play the Cape Fear Falcons. I went with Sallie, which seemed like a healthier option than staying home watching *Say Yes to the Dress* and eating Ben & Jerry's Chocolate Chip Cookie Dough out of the carton.

Sallie, a former cheerleader, was critiquing this year's squad. "That girl in the back faked her handspring. And her nail polish is too dark. Ooh, is that the new coach?"

I looked and there he was, big-framed, good-looking, his fair hair gleaming under the Friday-night lights. It was like the marching band burst into the love theme from *Titanic*. "Wrestling coach. His name is John." My heart was pounding, my voice carefully casual. "John Brooke. I think he helps out in the weight room."

"You know him?"

"He comes into the bank sometimes."

Three times, to be exact. Each time, my heart gave a little bounce of happiness and excitement.

"He's cute. Dibs," Sallie called, even though she and Ned were already an item.

But I didn't care what Sallie thought. I saw him first. And after the game, he came over to talk to me, leaning in to listen, fixing me with those warm, brown eyes. We went out for ice cream—along with Sallie and the football team and half the year-round population of Bunyan.

"Can I take you home?" he asked me in the parking lot afterward.

I could have pointed out I had my own car, a practical Prius with side airbags and great gas mileage. I could have given him my address, a sensible one-bedroom in a recently built complex close to work.

I stood there, struck dumb with happiness.

"Or . . ." He watched me. "We can drive to the beach. Spend the night. Watch the sun come up."

I was the sensible sister. The responsible firstborn. *"Never any trouble,"* as Aunt Phee liked to say. Not the type of girl to hook up on the first date. To hop into the car of a near-stranger and drive an hour to the beach for tear-your-clothes-off sex.

Of course I said yes.

We checked into a room in Carolina Beach. We made love against the *wall*. And on the bathroom counter in front of the giant mirror. I couldn't look at my reflection for days afterward without blushing. Even now, the memory made me tingle.

I never told anybody. Not Sallie, who would have cheered me on, or Amy, who was way too young. Not even Jo. I had to set a good example.

I told Momma we met at the bank. Well, it was true.

"I can't believe I got lucky," John confessed to me later, after we'd been dating a few months.

But I knew I was the lucky one.

I moved in a year later; we married the following June, with Daddy officiating and my sisters as my bridesmaids. Momma rented a tent for the reception in the upper pasture, and Amy decorated the long tables with lace runners and mason jars of peonies and cornflowers.

"*Cheap,*" Aunt Phee had sniffed. Referring to the flower arrangements, I hoped, and not my future husband.

It was true John didn't make a lot of money, even with his coaching stipend. But he was steady and hardworking, patient and firm with his students, encouraging with his team. He would make an excellent father. Everybody liked him. Even my father, who rarely showed any interest in my life—Jo was his prize student and Amy his pet—expressed approval. Well, what he actually said was, *"He seems like a stand-up guy. Just tell me one thing that he stands* for."

"*Ashton, hush,*" Momma said.

For once I didn't care what my parents thought. John made me feel needed. Desired. Loved.

Even now, the smell of him, warm and familiar, sent pleasure signals to my brain. I stretched between the sheets, relishing the unfamiliar luxury of lying in bed beside John while the dawn edged the shutters with gray light. What day was it?

He nuzzled my ear, his early-morning stubble scraping my nerve endings to life. "You feel great."

The familiar line made me smile. I tilted my head to give him better access. Encouraged, he slid a hand to my breast.

"The kids will be up soon," I murmured.

John kissed the side of my neck. "I'm up now."

My smile spread, my eyes still closed. "I noticed." He felt so good wrapped around me, a blanket of muscle. "Don't you have to leave for work?"

"It's Thanksgiving."

Thanksgiving. The word bolted into my brain. I jerked away. "I should call Momma."

"It's too early." John's lips brushed my temple. "Let her sleep."

"Are you kidding? She's probably making stuffing right now." Cleaning stalls. Canning applesauce. Splitting firewood.

"Jo's home. Let Jo help her." He kissed my shoulder. "Relax."

He didn't understand. The only way to stop Momma from doing something was to get to it first.

But his hands, roaming under my nightshirt, were sneaky and persuasive. His body was warm and solid. Despite the drumbeat pulse of things to do, my breathing hitched. I shifted to my side to face him. He kissed me, soft, married kisses, coaxing. Tender.

I raised my head. "Do you hear the kids?"

"Nope. Don't worry." Another kiss. "I locked the door."

"John." I drew my head back on the pillow. "You have no idea what those children can do if you leave them alone for ten minutes."

He waggled his eyebrows. "I know what I can do."

A bubble of laughter rose in my chest, warm and expansive. "In ten minutes." I was skeptical but oh-so-willing to be cajoled.

He grinned. "If that's all I've got."

He was so dear. So close. It had been so long since we'd had sex. "Show me," I said.

He did, and it was good. Not Carolina Beach good, but warm and easy. He touched me, inciting, teasing, before he rolled me to my back.

We fit. We always had. I clung to his shoulders in gratitude, stroking his back as he finished.

Just in time.

A door creaked down the hall.

John raised his weight on his elbows, pressing warm lips to my forehead. "Get some rest."

"Can't." Little feet running in the hall. "That's Daisy." A thump. "And DJ."

"I'll get up with them."

John's idea of getting up with the twins was plopping them in front of the TV while he scrolled on his phone. Well. Watching cartoons had never stunted his brain development, he said.

"I'll do it." I tossed back the covers. "I won't go back to sleep anyway."

I stooped for my nightgown, self-conscious even after sex. My boobs were okay, even after all those months of breastfeeding. But there was a little pudge above my so-called bikini scar that guaranteed I'd never wear a bikini again. And my butt . . . I straightened hastily, pulling my nightgown over my head.

John lay naked in our bed, on full display. He'd developed a bit of a dad bod in the last three years—my cooking—but the extra weight looked good on him.

"You know, you don't have to do everything yourself," he said unexpectedly.

"I don't *have* to," I said. "I want to."

He worked so hard. He deserved a day off. He had told me how it was for him growing up, how their house was always dirty and the fridge empty sometimes. How, when his momma slept in after working the night shift, he used to go to the neighbors' to borrow eggs so he could fix his brother breakfast before they went to school.

"You want sausage or bacon this morning?" I asked.

"I thought you had to make pie."

"Just the fillings," I said. "I have plenty of time to cook you breakfast."

"Then . . . Bacon would be great." John smiled. "Thanks, honey."

Plenty of time, I told myself as I cleaned up after breakfast and mixed pie filling. Time to make icing, to wipe down the kitchen counter and the twins. Time to grab a shower while they napped. Time to take them potty and change their clothes.

The twins slept late. But we were still only a little behind schedule, I thought as I hunted for Daisy's shoes. "DJ? Daisy, where's your brother?"

I found him standing behind the sofa, grunting in concentration. Ah. The pediatrician said little boys trained later than girls. Nothing to worry about.

"Everybody poops!" Daisy sang as I led her brother back to the bathroom.

I stripped DJ of his stinky diaper, conscious of time, ticking. Of my mother, waiting. How had she managed with four of us?

John, after one look at my face, offered to get Daisy ready.

"That's okay," I said cheerfully, kneeling on the tile floor, trying to avoid smearing poop on my sweater. "We'll be done in a minute."

Ten minutes. Fifteen. We were definitely going to be late.

Daisy came running into the bathroom. "Look, Mommy! I haz shoes. Daddy put on my shoes!"

John had, indeed, put on her shoes. And mismatched socks, I saw, but his effort warmed my heart.

"Thank you, Daddy. Very pretty," I approved. "Where are your barrettes, baby?"

"I didn't see any barrettes," John said.

"They're sitting right on the dresser." Along with her socks.

Something tightened in his face. "I don't do hair."

"I know. It's fine." I was lucky he was trying to help. Not like some fathers. Not like my father. "Thanks, honey. I'll do it."

That was me—the mommy who could do it all, the sister who had everything. It wasn't John's fault if everything I ever wanted suddenly felt like more than I could handle.

CHAPTER 5

Jo

Our mother stood at the kitchen island, dicing celery and onions for her corn bread dressing with slow, precise cuts.

"Why don't you sit down, Momma?" Beth asked.

"Can't," our mother said.

Because she had too much to do? I wondered. Or because it hurt her back to sit?

Part of me wanted to grab her knife away and show her what I'd learned at Gusto. *This,* I imagined myself saying proudly, *is how you chop an onion.* Hearing Chef's voice, seeing the blur of his knife and hands.

But this was Momma, the *real* housewife of Harnett County. This was her kitchen. Her stuffing. Despite the pill bottles lining the windowsill, she was still competent. In charge. No matter how many professional techniques I learned in faraway kitchens, at home I was only her sous chef.

Honestly, I didn't have many memories of cooking with our mother. Meg was the one who helped in the kitchen while I holed up in my room, reading and scribbling. Or spent the time out in the barn. Or off with our father. Before he was deployed—and after, when he got back—he took me with him to serve Thanksgiving dinner for the homeless. *"My daughter,"* he would introduce me in the line, and I would glow with pride.

But Beth had already tackled the barn chores. And for the first time ever, Dad had gone to the veterans' center alone—the only acknowledgment from either of our parents that this holiday was not like other years.

"Your mother needs you," Daddy said as he left.

What about you? I wanted to ask. *Doesn't she need you?*

I bit my tongue. The truth was, my mother never seemed to need anybody. For years, she did the work of the farm alone, managed the house and the budget, drove us girls to the doctor's or to play practice, packed our lunches, cooked our dinner, poured our father's coffee. Daddy's job was taking care of others; Mom's was taking care of us.

I'd always considered myself my father's daughter.

But maybe in some weird way, he was counting on me, like he used to. "Take care of Momma and your sisters for me," he would say before he left for the base or Afghanistan. We all had been raised to respect our father's service. He poured out his life for others. Making a bed or a meal or a home seemed pretty unimportant in comparison.

But people had to eat. Feeding them . . . Wasn't that important, too?

I couldn't fix whatever was wrong with our mother. But at least I could be her hands in the kitchen.

She shifted her weight, leaning against the counter. "Do you have the onions?"

I scanned the glistening pile on her cutting board. "Do you need more?"

She shook her head. "The crispy ones. For the casserole."

Right. That would be the traditional casserole made with canned green beans, canned cream of mushroom soup, and canned crispy fried onions on top. Not exactly the locally sourced, seasonal ingredients I was used to at Gusto. I could just picture Chef's quizzical look as he surveyed my work space. *No cans, March,* I imagined him saying. *Not for green beans.*

I patted the red-and-white container. "Right here."

The front door opened. Our mother glanced toward the living room. "Is that Meg already?"

"It's Amy!" Beth cried, darting from the kitchen.

"She must have got an early start." Mom shuffled toward the living room, delivering a pat on my shoulder as she passed.

I wiped my hands on a dish towel and followed her.

"Jokies!" Amy disentangled herself and grabbed me, her smooth cheek pressing mine. That's what she called me, what she'd always called me since she was old enough to think the nickname was funny.

I patted her back awkwardly. "Hey, Ames." I didn't call her *Princess,* the way Daddy did. Even though she looked the part: deep-blue eyes, tiny waist, funny snub nose. Like the princess in Disney's *Tangled,* with a choppy blond haircut that would have looked at home in New York's Fashion District.

"Can I get your stuff from the car?" Beth offered.

"Not yet." Amy stretched luxuriously, her crop top sliding up to reveal her pale, flat stomach. "I want to enjoy being home for a while."

"Come into the kitchen, then," our mother said. "Plenty of work to go around."

Amy pouted. "But I just got here. Aren't we going to watch the parade?"

Momma smiled. "Turn on the TV. And then you can set the table."

Under our mother's direction, we executed her Day of Thanksgiving Plan, scrubbing, chopping, grating, and arranging to the muffled sound of the Macy's parade. Amy was in the dining room, setting the table the way our mother liked, with the good china that had belonged to her grandmother and the pinecone turkeys Amy made in second grade.

"The minute I walk into this house, I feel like I'm twelve," she observed.

I grinned. "You act like you're twelve."

She stuck out her tongue.

"Proving my point," I said, and she laughed.

Beth paused in her straightening of the living room to turn up the volume on the television. "Momma, come quick! The Rockettes are on!"

Amy dropped a handful of silverware. "Chorus line!"

I watched, bemused, as our mother left her work in the kitchen. My sisters positioned themselves on either side of her, lining up in front of the TV, giggling and grabbing each other for balance. Momma couldn't kick, but she laughed and lurched along with them.

They'd done this before, I realized. Watched the parade together, stepping along with the Rockettes, while I was off with Daddy feeding the homeless.

Amy stumbled. Laughed. "We need Meg."

I jumped in at the end of the line, wrapping my arm around Beth, matching my steps with my sisters', doing my best to support Mom in the middle. We giggled and kicked our way to the end of the song, hopping and breathless.

"Ooph!" Amy collapsed into a chair. "That's it. I'm done."

"That was so fun," Beth said.

Our mother eased herself onto the couch, smiling. "I always wanted to visit Radio City Music Hall. See the Rockettes in person."

Which was news to me. She'd never said anything. Never taken a day off in her life. "Maybe you should come for a visit," I suggested.

But she wasn't listening to me. "Have you heard anything yet from Branson?" she asked Beth.

Beth shook her head.

"Who?" I asked.

"Nothing," Beth said.

"Branson, Missouri." Our mother's voice warmed with pride. "Your sister tried out for one of the Christmas shows there."

"My voice teacher thought the audition would be good practice."

"Mouse! Good for you! That's awesome."

Beth smiled wistfully. "Remember when you used to write those plays for us?"

I nodded. "On the parsonage porch. Meg charged all the neighborhood kids a quarter to watch."

"You and Meg always got to be the heroes," Amy said.

"Or the villains," I said. "Because we were tallest."

"And I was the golden-haired princess."

"Because you were too young to remember your lines."

"Only a year younger than Beth."

"I was the prince once," Beth said.

Our Bethie had never sought the family spotlight. I smiled at her affectionately. "You played a selection of kindly retainers."

"And the prince's horse," said Amy.

"And now you're going to be a star!" I hugged Beth. She was so talented, a voice major at UNC Greensboro. She deserved a chance to shine. "Why didn't you tell me?"

Beth's cheeks turned pink. "I didn't think I'd get a part."

"But you did. She's an angel," Mom said to me. "In the chorus."

"Typecasting," Amy said.

"It's not a real part," Beth said. "I'm only an alternate. They're not going to call me unless somebody drops out of the cast."

"It's all good experience," our mother said. "Colt Henderson is one of the headliners."

Country music was one of those things I swore I'd left behind when I fled home, like sweet tea and church homecomings. But even in New York I'd heard Colt Henderson's music, heartland rock with a country core.

"I'm impressed." I was, too. And a little hurt I was the last to know. In spite of the four-year gap between us, Beth and I had always been close. She was my baby, the way Amy was Meg's. "I thought Branson just did big family acts. The Trapp Family Singers. The Osmonds."

"He has a new Christmas album," Beth said.

"Nice," Amy said.

"Your sister got to rehearse with the cast in September," Mom said.

"Very cool." I frowned. "How far away is Branson?"

"Fifteen hours," Beth said.

"You have to follow your heart," Mom said. "No matter where it leads."

I managed not to roll my eyes. "Right."

Our father was the one who had pushed me in school, who had encouraged my writing, who told me there was a whole wider world out there for me. He had taught me, by example and sometimes with praise, to follow in his footsteps. To pursue my own vocation, while my mother stayed in the background. *"You could always come home,"* Momma said. *"To save money,"* after I graduated. *"To figure out your next step,"* when I got laid off from the paper.

She wasn't wrong, just practical. But her constant offers of support made me feel like she was waiting for me to fail.

She raised her eyebrows at my tone. "Excuse me?"

"You never went anywhere," I said.

"Because this is my home," she said a little stiffly.

I felt guilty. I wasn't trying to upset her. We'd had to leave the parsonage when Daddy enlisted. Aunt Phee had never offered to take us in at Oak Hill, the big white house that had belonged to my father's grandparents.

And anyway, our mother wouldn't take charity. She moved us to the farm because we had no place else to go.

"Sorry, Mom. I know you didn't really have a choice."

"This farm is my choice," she said. "My heritage. I always figured that was worth preserving."

"Okay."

"You girls may not care about it now, but this land is your heritage, too. Sisters' Farm."

I gaped at her. I'd always figured the "sisters" were my mother and my unknown aunt Elizabeth, the one who died when they both were young. The one Bethie was named after.

"I care," I protested. Our grandparents were homesteaders, small-scale farmers living off the land. Rednecks, to my friends in New York. After they died and we moved to the farm, our mother slowly built up the goat herd and started making and selling cheese. There was something cool about growing up on a farm that had been in our family for generations, that our mother owned and operated herself. I just didn't want to actually live there.

My mother smiled wryly. "Of course you do." She pushed to her feet, clutching the sofa arm for balance.

Anxiety spurted inside me. "Are you all right?"

"Just tired. Don't fuss, Jo," she said, channeling Granny.

"I'm tired, too," Amy said. "I was up all night, packing."

"Why? You don't need a lot of clothes. You're only here for a couple of days."

"Not for here." Amy smiled, a little smugly. "I leave for Paris on Monday."

Right.

"You should take a nap," our mother said.

"I will if you will," Amy said.

That was Amy, bargaining for what she wanted. Which in this case . . . I looked at her with sudden appreciation. She was trying, in her own way, to get Momma to lie down.

Our mother hesitated.

"You go," I said. "Everything's under control."

After executing a full evening service at the restaurant, I figured I could handle one Thanksgiving dinner. Mom took Amy's arm to go up the stairs.

And now that I had the kitchen to myself . . . I glanced at the wall clock. This morning I'd posted a recipe for sweet potato soufflé on my blog. Not the standard Southern casserole with marshmallows and pecans, either, but a real French soufflé with Gruyère cheese and whipped egg whites. I'd barely checked in with my followers all day. But it would be nice to share some photos with them. Maybe I wasn't going to Paris. Or even Branson. But I had my own dreams to chase, my own work to do.

Opening the pantry door, I pulled out three large jewel yams.

Beth stood in the middle of the kitchen floor, watching me. "What can I do?"

"Want to peel potatoes?"

Beth smiled. "Sure."

"So . . ." I hauled out a saucepan, nudging Beth aside with my hip to fill the pot at the tap. "Tell me about this Branson thing. It's a big deal, right? Good exposure."

"Not that anybody's going to see me. The show opened three weeks ago." She smiled shyly. "I did get to meet Colt in rehearsal."

Colt Henderson was one of the new bad boys of country music, a former studio guitarist who'd been on tour with Taylor Swift. "And now you're on a first-name basis," I teased.

"He told me to. He's very friendly."

"Define *friendly*," I said. Looking out for her, the way I used to.

She turned pink. "Not like that. He was nice. He asked me to play a song for him."

"One of your songs? Beth, that's so cool. Which one?"

"'Leave a Candle in Your Window.'"

"I haven't heard that one. Will you play it for me?"

"Maybe later. He said I showed promise."

"So much promise."

She ducked her head over the sink. "Not enough to land the job," she said. Turning to me for confidence, the way she always did.

"Maybe not this time." I rummaged in the junk drawer for a second peeler. "But you wait. There will be other auditions. Other songs. You just focus on school and the rest will come."

Beth concentrated on the potato in her hand. Peelings flew.

Uh-oh. "Bethie?"

"I was thinking . . ."

"Always a mistake."

"Ha-ha. The thing is, Mom could really use some help right now. Around the farm, you know? And I'm good with the goats. I was thinking maybe I'd stay home after Thanksgiving. Go back next semester."

"Beth." Impossible to keep the dismay from my voice. "You've missed so much school already. What about your classes? What about finals?"

"I already talked with my teachers. I could take incompletes." A flush climbed her cheeks. "It would just be for a little while. Just until Momma's feeling better."

Her thoughtfulness put me to shame. "What does Mom say?"

"I haven't told her yet."

I pointed my peeler at her. "Because you know she'll hate the idea."

Beth's chin came up. "I'm twenty-three. Old enough to make my own decisions."

"I just hate to see you wasting your talents in Bunyan."

"You know, not everybody thinks living here is some kind of prison sentence," Beth said quietly.

My mouth opened. "I don't think living here is a prison sentence." *Did I?*

T he soufflé was in the oven when the front door opened again.
"Dad?" I called.

But it was Meg with John and the twins. "Sorry we're late," my sister said breathlessly. "Oh, I'm so glad to see you!"

I hugged her. "Hi, munchkins. Hi, John. Happy Thanksgiving."

My brother-in-law smiled his slow, attractive smile. "Same to you."

DJ regarded me suspiciously as I swooped in for a kiss.

Meg handed over my niece, a warm, lovely weight in my arms. "He's still tired. They just got up from their nap."

Amy emerged from her room. "Hey, me, too." She kissed our sister, John, the twins. "Cute socks," she said to Daisy. "Very fashion forward."

Mom came downstairs, holding tightly to the banister. The rest had done her good. There was color in her cheeks that hadn't been there before. Or maybe that was makeup. "Meg, are these your pies? They look gorgeous."

We swept to the kitchen on a flood of hugs and greetings, carrying the twins and dessert along with us. The rise and fall of our voices filled the air along with the scent of roasting turkey.

"I love your sweater."

"Here, taste. Do I need more salt?"

"Where should I put this?"

"Don't touch, DJ. Hot."

I leaned against the counter, immersed in family, feeling the tug and strong flow of love. All of my sisters together at last. "Get you a beer?" I asked John.

Smiling, he shook his head, a rock in the chattering stream. "I'm good, thanks. I think I'll turn on the game."

It *was* a little noisy in the kitchen, I admitted, watching his retreat to the living room. Where was Dad? Shouldn't he be home by now?

The doorbell chimed. Aunt Phee with her little dog, Polly, and her sidekick, Wanda Crocker.

"The Croaker," Amy murmured in my ear.

I suppressed a snort. "Because one old lady criticizing your hair and life choices is never enough."

"Puppy!" Daisy cried, toddling forward.

Polly promptly squatted and peed on the rug.

"She's not used to children," Aunt Phee announced.

Meg grabbed Daisy protectively.

"I'll get some paper towels," Beth said, escaping to the kitchen.

Smart move.

"Why are you standing around half-naked?" Aunt Phee asked Amy. "Go put on a sweater before you catch your death."

"This is a sweater, Aunt Phee," Amy said.

"Half a sweater, maybe. I'm getting cold just looking at you." She turned her attention to me. "Don't stand there like a beanpole, girl. Give me some sugar."

Obediently, I stooped to kiss her moisturized cheek.

"Well?" she demanded. "Did you bring your boyfriend home to meet me?"

My eyeball twitched. "I don't have a boyfriend, Aunt Phee."

She sniffed. "What's the matter with those men in New York City? You're not bad-looking. Or you wouldn't be, if you fixed your hair."

I had my father's hair, thick and curly. Momma cut it once when I was eight or nine, creating a giant brush, an uncontrollable explosion of hair. Ever since middle school, I'd worn it long, bundled out of the way.

"I heard the men in New York are all gay," Miss Wanda said.

"The men are fine." Jeez. "New York is fine. I'm just not looking for a relationship right now."

Beth kneeled out of the line of fire, blotting the rug.

"By the time your mother was your age, she had the three of you and another one on the way," Phee said.

"If you mean Amy," I said, "I'm pretty sure she was a mistake."

Aunt Phee's mouth quirked before she pressed her lips into a thin coral line.

Amy narrowed her eyes at me, silently promising retribution. I grinned.

Meg, flushed and pretty with Daisy in her arms, came between us. "Hello, Aunt Phee."

Aunt Phee presented her other cheek for my sister's kiss. "Don't think you're off the hook, either, missy. This one needs a little sister to play with."

"She has a brother," Meg said.

"Go, Meg," I said. "No gender typing here."

"Meg and John have plenty of time to think about expanding their family," Mom said. "DJ is still in diapers."

Daisy wriggled down to toddle after the cat.

"How old is he now, three?" Miss Wanda said.

"Two and a half," Meg said.

"Old enough to be toilet trained," Aunt Phee said.

I rolled my eyes. John turned up the volume on the television. The front door opened, admitting a blast of cold air and our tall, lean, aristocratic-looking father. *Finally.*

"Girls. Abby," he greeted us. He stooped to kiss my mother. "I brought some guests home from the center. You remember Captain David Lewis."

Who?

"Of course. I'm so glad you could join us for dinner, Captain," Mom said, sounding like an officer's wife.

"Dave, ma'am. Appreciate you having us."

They started coming through the door behind him, four men I'd never seen before, young ones with beards, old ones with service caps, all of them wearing some kind of camo. Vets? Homeless? Homeless vets?

Polly yapped. I scooped her up before someone stepped on her, and she sank her little needle teeth into my wrist.

"Ouch. Your dog bit me," I said, handing her to Aunt Phee.

"She's not used to so many people," Aunt Phee said.

"Neither is Jo," Amy said. "But you don't see her biting anybody."

"Give me time," I said.

"Welcome," Mom said. "You're all very welcome."

The thanks and introductions went on. The house filled. Cars and trucks littered the driveway. Aunt Phee retreated to a corner with Wanda Crocker, feeding her dog from the platter of shrimp. Daisy had pinned Weasley in a corner and was sticking her chubby fingers into the cat's ears.

"Gentle," Meg warned. To which of them, I wasn't sure.

"John, please bring some more chairs from upstairs," Mom said, raising her voice over the noise of the football game. "Meg, there are extra cups in the pantry. Can you make sure our guests all have something to drink?"

Forget drinks, I thought, counting heads. What were they all going to *eat*?

"Do we have enough food?" Meg whispered to me.

Seven, eight, nine . . . There was a sixteen-pound bird in the oven. Enough for guests and leftovers, I'd thought. Figure fifteen adults at a pound and a bit per person . . .

"I'll go check," I whispered back, and escaped into the kitchen to take inventory.

In the back of my head, I heard Chef's voice: "*We feed them, yes. So simple. We take care of them, yeah? So basic. Service. Everything is for the guest.*"

So, okay. Counting the soufflé, we had plenty of sides. If I added more noodles to the mac and cheese . . .

I filled a pot in the sink.

"They're here!" Beth's voice sang out.

More guests.

I glanced out the kitchen window. Sure enough, there was old Mr. Laurence's long black Lincoln turning into my parents' driveway. And there . . . Yep. That was Trey at the wheel, bringing them both to Thanksgiving dinner.

Setting the pot on the stove to boil, I resecured my hair and crowded into the hallway with the rest of the family to greet them.

Trey had brought flowers and beer, and Mr. Laurence, wine. Our parents were not big drinkers, but John took a beer and passed the rest around. Captain Lewis opened the wine, pouring pinot noir into red plastic cups. At least all the activity covered the awkwardness of seeing Trey again.

Mom and Meg both exclaimed over the big bouquet of sunflowers and roses.

"I'll just get these in water," Meg said as Trey enveloped me in a hug.

Well, everybody was hugging everybody.

I turned my head, aware we had an audience. Amy looked away as his kiss landed somewhere above my ear. He smelled the same, like bergamot and starch, the only twentysomething guy I knew who sent his shirts to the dry cleaner's. Or could afford to.

"Hey, Trey," I mumbled against his shoulder.

"Jo." He backed to arm's length, still holding both my hands. "You look amazing."

He did, too. His hair had grown, dark curls tumbling around his face. Very Lord Byron. *"Bedhead,"* I used to tease, back in the days before we'd been to bed together.

Now I said nothing.

He ran his finger along the strap of my borrowed apron. "This is a new look for you."

I jerked back a step. "I'm giving Mom a hand in the kitchen."

"Jo made almost the entire dinner this year," Momma said. "She's a chef now."

Trey gave me a speculative look. "Really."

"Prep cook," I said.

I'd been let go from the paper less than a month after our last fight. *"I don't need this,"* I remembered yelling at him.

He'd glared at me, sulky and gorgeous. *"You mean, you don't need me."*

I didn't *want* to need him. I could not be his instant family, his next step to achieving manhood.

So I'd turned him down, turned him away. Again.

I tightened my ponytail. "Speaking of cooking, I left a pot of water on the stove."

"I'll take care of it," Mom said.

My parents had always welcomed strays, on the farm and around the table. I admired their easy hospitality, my father's determination that no soldier should go hungry on our national holiday of Thanksgiving.

But honestly, what was he thinking, springing guests on her an hour before dinner? Not that I would have noticed a year ago.

"I got it, Mom," I said.

Daisy wriggled down from the stranger's lap. "I help, Auntie Jo," she announced.

DJ lurched for me, holding out his little arms.

"Oh, I don't think . . ." Meg began.

"Absolutely." I hefted my nephew onto my hip. Smiled at my niece. "You can . . ." What? Toddlers had terrible knife skills. "Put out some more napkins and forks, okay?"

While Daisy and DJ trotted importantly back and forth from the dining room, I grabbed butter and cheese to make a roux.

"There's no more room at the table," Meg said, bustling in. "I told John to set up TV trays."

Beth slipped in from the dining room. "I can eat in the kitchen."

"Ha." Amy came in for another bottle of wine. "You just don't want to sit next to Aunt Phee."

Beth half smiled. I wondered how my shy, performance-averse sister would manage if she ever actually got a singing part in a show. But she didn't have a bad idea. No making conversation with bearded strangers, no Great-Aunt Josephine, no Trey . . .

"Why don't the four of us eat in here?" I suggested. "It would be like old times."

"We're a little old to sit at the kiddie table," Meg pointed out.

"Although it does sound nice," Beth said.

"As long as we have alcohol." Amy carried the open bottle out to the living room.

I opened the pantry.

"What can I do?" Beth asked.

"I'm fine," I said.

Meg returned carrying a stack of dirty cups. "You know, it wouldn't kill you to ask for help every once in a while."

I snorted. "Look who's talking."

"She's right," Beth said.

"Fine. Grate me some cheese."

"Aunt Phee wants to know what time we're eating," Meg said.

I threw a look at the kitchen timer. "Ten minutes?"

"Great." Meg stooped to retrieve DJ from under the kitchen table. "And we need more chips."

"I'll get them," Beth said.

She collided with Trey in the doorway. He steadied her, rescuing the chips from spilling. Beth blushed and thanked him, ducking under his arm to carry the bowl to the living room. It struck me—not for the first time—how good he was with her.

And then—definitely for the first time—how good she would be for him. How good they could be for each other. He would take care of her. She would admire him.

Maybe Trey had fallen for the wrong sister.

Huh.

"Get out," I said. "I have work to do."

He held up his hands in an I-come-in-peace gesture. "Come on, Jo, don't be like that." He flashed his boyish, ingratiating smile. "I've missed you."

The words, the familiar smile, went straight to my heart. I grabbed the pasta off the stove and drained it in the sink, raising a cloud of steam. My cheeks flushed from the heat. Or maybe that was annoyance.

"I missed you, too," I admitted.

He propped his lean hips against the counter, hanging around the way he always did. Teasing. Distracting. In my way.

I hefted the pot. "Move your ass, Laurence."

He shifted a few inches to avoid getting burned. "So you're a cook now."

"Among other things." I banged the pot onto an empty burner. Adjusted the heat under the roux. "I write a food blog."

He nodded. *"Hungry."*

I was pleased. Surprised. *Hungry: Taking a Bite Out of the Big Apple* was the name of my blog. "You read it?"

"Your sister said something about it." He plucked a shred of cheese from the bowl. "Mm. Good. What happened to the newspaper gig?"

I slapped his hand away. "The paper downsized. I was let go."

"You didn't tell me."

I shrugged. "You were ignoring my texts. Anyway, I figured it was better if you didn't know."

"Better for what? Your pride?"

He had never understood my determination to stand on my own two feet. Never accepted my decision to move to New York in the first place.

I looked up from the cheese sauce to meet his gaze. "Our friendship."

Our eyes locked. He smiled a little crookedly. "Fair enough."

I took a quick survey of the kitchen: turkey resting, green beans and gravy keeping warm, butter melting on mashed potatoes. Glanced again at the clock. "Tell me about you," I said. "How was Italy?"

"It was all right."

"That doesn't sound very enthusiastic. I thought you were looking forward to seeing Europe."

"I was looking forward to seeing Europe with you."

I sighed. "Trey, we've been through all this. I have to work. I have a job."

"Not anymore. Not a real job."

Ouch. My teeth gritted. "Thanks, pal. I appreciate your support."

He pushed away from the counter, catching my hands again. His were warm and firm. "Come on, Jo, I didn't mean it that way. I *want* to support you, I swear I do. Let me prove it. Let's do it. It's not too late. Let's take that trip we always talked about in college."

I tugged on my hands and snatched up a set of pot holders. "Trey, I can't do this now."

"Then after the holidays," he said, following me. "Think about it. You've always wanted to visit Paris. Rome. Barcelona. We can go anywhere you want. Dine our way through Europe, eat at every Michelin-starred restaurant, any weird hole-in-the-wall you say. You could write about them for your blog. I can give you that. Let me give you the break you deserve."

"I mean, I'm *busy*."

I had a sudden image of Chef expediting dishes at the pass, legs planted like tree trunks as the storm of dinner service swirled around him, sending everything out to the table at just the right moment. How did he do it?

That soufflé had to come out of the oven. Now. I grabbed the green bean casserole and shoved it, pot holders and all, into Trey's hands. "Take this out to the table. Dinner's ready."

Without waiting for his reply, I whirled to the stove. Eased open the oven door. The soufflé was puffed and golden. I released a breath of relief. Whipping out my phone, I snapped some quick pictures for the blog before I slid the soufflé from the rack. Holding the dish chest high like a trophy, I turned. And . . .

The top crust listed. Steam escaped before the whole creation collapsed gently on itself.

Crap.

Squaring my shoulders, I marched into the dining room, carrying the deflated soufflé.

"What's that? Where's the turkey?" Aunt Phee demanded.

"In the kitchen." Meg stood hastily. "I'll get it."

When she returned with the turkey platter, Daddy led us in grace, holding hands around the table, two TV trays placed awkwardly at one end to accommodate our last-minute guests. I watched as my father's lean, elegant fingers enclosed my mother's smaller, callused ones. They were high school sweethearts, a small-town love story, the boy from the big white house on the hill and the farmers' daughter. No wonder everybody in Bunyan thought I'd end up with Trey. History repeating itself.

But my parents truly loved each other. My mother always said how much she admired my father, his sense of purpose, his rigorous intellect, his deep devotion to God and country. And he loved her because she was devoted to . . . him, I guess.

I flushed. That wasn't fair to either of them.

Bowing my head, I let the familiar words wash over me. *"Bless, O Lord, this food to our use and us to thy service . . ."*

Aunt Phee poked her soufflé with a fork. "I don't see any marshmallows."

Daisy bounced in her high chair. "Marthmellowth!"

"No marshmallows. Sorry, Daisy." I smiled at my niece. "Sorry, Aunt."

I'd wanted to bring something of myself to the table. To show my family what I'd learned. How I'd grown. Big mistake.

"Have some cranberry sauce," Meg said, passing the cut glass bowl.

Aunt Phee peered at it suspiciously. "What's this?"

"Real cranberries, Aunt. Try it. You'll like it."

"Real cranberry sauce has ridges," Miss Wanda said.

Right. From the can.

"I love the soufflé," Amy said unexpectedly.

I looked at her in surprised gratitude. "Thanks, Ames."

At least my father's guests weren't picky. They loaded their plates as if this were their first decent meal in days, or their last. For some of them, maybe it was. Our mother, on the other hand, struggled to eat anything at all. I wondered if pain or the pills she was taking had killed her appetite. More likely, she was trying to save some turkey for her guests.

Dad was quietly talking with Captain Lewis—Dave—about an upcoming workshop.

". . . critical to keep the focus on our veterans who have experienced actual trauma," my father was saying.

"I agree. But we can't ignore that listening to stories of the same events, horrible stories, day after day, makes caregivers vulnerable to the same symptoms," the captain said.

My father's face folded into hard, cool lines like a marble statue in St. Patrick's Cathedral. "You're talking about secondary traumatic stress."

The captain shrugged. "Or compassion fatigue, if you feel that term is less stigmatizing."

"My feelings are not under discussion," my father said.

"But that's the point, isn't it? Military culture, medical culture, ministers—we're all trained to tough it out so we can take care of others. We cope by ignoring our own emotions. But eventually, those feelings can't be ignored. And that creates a problem."

"It's not just military culture," our mother said. "It happens in families, too."

Meg shot our mother a quick, troubled look from down the table.

But our father ignored the interruption. "It's not a problem for me. It doesn't stop me from doing my job."

"Yes, sir," the captain said. "I just thought you could drop in and give your perspective. Since you're going anyway."

Wait. What?

"Going where?" I asked.

"The military caregivers' conference in D.C. next month," the captain said.

"Perhaps if you weren't so busy in the kitchen you would be able to follow the dinner table conversation," my father said.

I scowled. I could follow the conversation just fine. He was leaving. For D.C.? Five and a half hours away.

"You can't go," I said. "Not now."

All those faces swiveled toward me. Like I'd yelled out *shit* in church or something. I couldn't believe I had to explain. I looked at

Beth, but she was staring at her plate. If she wouldn't say anything . . .
And Mom wouldn't say anything . . .

"Mom needs you here," I said. "She's sick."

My father looked more like a saint than ever. A martyred mission-
ary, maybe, forced to reason with rebellious natives. "It would be
unthinkable for me to withdraw. I am one of the organizers."

Right. Mission first.

My chest burned. "But—"

"Don't fuss, Jo," Mom said. "I'm sure I'll be fine by then. The conference is weeks and weeks away."

An awkward silence fell.

I wanted desperately to believe her. But before we even served dessert, she needed to go upstairs. She shuffled toward the stairs, leaning
heavily on Beth.

"Let me help you, ma'am."

A rough, bearded soldier came forward to take her arm. Beth
flushed and moved away.

"Thank you," my mother said.

I glanced at our father—was he really okay letting some strange
man walk Mom to their bedroom?—but he was still deep in conversation with the captain.

"Well, at least we have enough dessert," I said glumly to Meg as we
cut and plated pie. "These look great, by the way."

"Thanks. Dinner was delicious," she added kindly.

"The soufflé fell." It sat on the counter, looking like a deflated
football at the bottom of the dish. *I should take a picture of* that *for
the blog.*

"The twins loved your mac and cheese."

I snorted. "They're two-year-olds. They would have loved Kraft
from the box."

"They love mac and cheese in the box. Which makes it even more
impressive that they liked yours. John, too. And Dad."

That was my sister, always making everybody feel better. Her words salved some of the sting I felt, that sense I got whenever I was in Bunyan of being judged and found wanting. Visiting home as a starving grad student or a rising journalist in the Big City hadn't been so bad. I'd had a purpose, a direction, then. *"Writers change the world,"* my father used to say. Food bloggers? Not so much.

I hated disappointing him. Maybe I wasn't writing the Great Southern Novel. My advisor told me kindly that the stories I'd written for my master's project were "sentimental" (not a compliment). But at least I hadn't quit.

I cut another wedge of pie. "I can't believe he'd go off like that and leave Mom."

Meg dolloped whipped cream onto plates. "Who, Dad? He goes away all the time."

"Not to D.C."

"That's not until after Christmas," Meg reminded me. "You'll be back home by then."

"Only for a couple days." Assuming I could even get that much time off after skipping out on Thanksgiving.

Meg didn't say anything.

"And you're here," I said, reassuring myself.

"I'm always here."

"You say that like it's a bad thing."

"I did not. It's not." She loaded dessert plates onto the special tray our mother used to bring us meals when we were sick in bed. "I'm taking these in. You coming?"

I shook my head. "I'm not leaving the kitchen until Aunt Phee is gone."

"Coward," Meg said, picking up the tray. "Slacker."

"Hey, I'm doing the dishes." But I felt a wriggle of guilt anyway. Not about Aunt Phee. But Meg definitely did more than I did to help out our parents. On the other hand, it was her decision to live so close to home. I *had* to go back to New York.

"Great pie," Trey said from the doorway.

"Meg made it." My sister's dessert choices, like everything else in her life, were sweet, traditional, and family approved. There was a lesson there somewhere.

"John's a lucky guy," Trey said.

"Thank you." Meg dimpled. "Tell him he should bring you home for dinner sometime."

"I'll do that." He stood aside to let her through to the dining room.

I turned on the water in the sink.

"So, you got any more?" Trey asked.

I glanced at him over my shoulder. "I can't believe you're still hungry."

Trey assumed an injured look. "It's for Granddad."

I sighed. "Fine. Pumpkin or pecan?"

"Both, please," he said meekly. "To go. I've got to get the old boy home."

I wiped my hands. Grabbed a knife.

He held up both palms. "Don't stab me."

"Don't tempt me." I cut two large wedges and covered them with foil. "Here."

"Thanks." He accepted the plate from me. Paused. "Jo—"

"Am I interrupting something?" Amy asked from the doorway.

"No."

"Yes," Trey said at the same time.

I scowled at him. "What do you need?" I asked Amy.

"Oh." She took a step forward, looking uncharacteristically uncertain. "I just wanted . . . I came in for . . ."

"More pie?" I asked.

"Whipped cream."

"In the fridge."

Trey shifted out of her way. She grabbed the bowl and left.

"Why don't I swing back later?" Trey said. "Take you out for a drink."

I raised an eyebrow. "There are actually bars open in Bunyan on Thanksgiving Day?"

"There's Alleygators."

A dive bar on the river near the trailer park. "Ha. No, thanks."

His mouth curved. "I'll keep you safe."

"Please. I live in New York. I can take care of myself. Which means I'm not hanging out with the drunk and desperate on a holiday weekend."

"We can go to my house, drink up Granddad's whiskey."

I crossed my arms against temptation. "I really should stay home tonight."

"Tomorrow."

He was too used to getting his own way. And too old for me to let him get away with it anymore. "I go home tomorrow. Back to New York," I added, in case it wasn't clear to both of us that's where I belonged.

"So soon?"

Not soon enough. "I have to work."

"I'll see you at Christmas, then." Trey moved in. *Mr. Smooth.* This time I didn't turn my head fast enough. His kiss landed squarely on my mouth. His warm lips lingered. Whispered. "It's no good you trying to avoid me, Jo. I've got my eye on you."

I laughed and pushed him away. "You are so full of it. I am not avoiding you. I have things to do, that's all."

He continued to smile, his dark eyes somber. "That's what you always say."

Boy, did that bring back memories.

J unior year. Trey sprawled on my narrow dorm bed, six feet of lean, frustrated male.

"Come on," he wheedled. "They're showing *The Half-Blood Prince* at the auditorium tonight."

I hunched over my laptop. "I have to finish this paper."

He unfolded from the bed to read over my shoulder. "'*Love and gluttony in Shakespeare's* Twelfth Night.' Aren't you acing that class anyway?"

"So?"

"So you can afford to slack off. It's one paper out of thousands."

Right. Easy for him to say. Trey had charm, he had his grandfather's money, he had a job waiting for him when he got out.

I, on the other hand, was trying to figure out how to swing grad school without asking my parents for help. My only hope was to earn a fellowship.

"No, I can't. This is due tomorrow. Why don't you ask . . ." I tried to remember the name of his current flavor of the month. "Brittany to go with you?"

"We broke up."

"Which explains why you're here. And in such an excellent mood, too."

"Wow. You could show a little sympathy."

I grinned. "Maybe if you weren't such a man whore, I would. Trey, I really do need to work now."

"All work and no play . . ."

"Means I might actually get a stipend next year." The Creative Writing Program at NYU awarded all incoming students departmental fellowships. The prospect of doing nothing for two whole years but concentrate on my writing seemed like heaven to me. The MFA program even had a writers' residency workshop in Paris. Not that I could afford that. But to get in, I needed more than an offer of half-tuition remission. I needed a full ride.

I resecured my ponytail. Trey's pacing was getting on my nerves. "You know, it wouldn't do you any harm to study now and then."

His face clouded. "You sound like my grandfather."

"I like your grandfather."

"Because he respects *you*. He doesn't tell *you* that you're worthless and irresponsible."

My own grandfather—my mother's dad—died when I was little,

leaving behind a faint, comforting impression of tobacco and whiskers and strong, callused hands. I never knew my father's father at all. But in his pictures, he looked a lot like old Mr. Laurence—same ramrod posture, same pride and privilege, same clean, white, ironed shirt.

Trey might have a job waiting for him upon graduation. But . . . Well, he'd be working for his grandfather, right? Mr. Laurence was proud of his grandson, no doubt about it. But he must be over seventy now, a generation older than my parents. A tough old bastard. It wasn't always easy for Trey, growing up as the sole focus of his grandfather's attention and ambition.

"What happened? Are you two fighting again?"

Trey gave me a smoldering look. "He said no to my study abroad next semester."

"Oh, Trey." I closed my laptop. Paper or no paper, we were friends. And friends sympathized with each other's disappointments. I knew how much he'd been looking forward to spending a semester in Italy. "I'm sorry."

"He threatened to cut off my tuition."

I winced. *Ouch.* "He's afraid of losing you." *Like he lost your father,* I thought.

"I should just drop out." Trey flung himself on the bed. "Go anyway."

I sighed. "Don't be stupid." I sat beside him on the bed. "At least wait until after graduation."

"Is that what you would do?"

"You know I want to go to New York." As much as I wanted to travel, my student loans wouldn't wait while I backpacked across Europe. Over the summer, Aunt Phee had hinted she might come through with a nice graduation check. But I'd already earmarked that money for grad school. "Anyway, we're not talking about me." I took his hand. "It's only another year or so. You just have to make the best of things until then."

Trey's hand tightened on mine. "I wouldn't mind so much if . . ."

I squeezed encouragingly. "If?"

He turned his head to look at me. "If I had a reason to stay."

Oh.

Our eyes met. My throat went dry. Trey was my friend. The best friend I had, next to Meg. I needed to keep him that way. Because if I didn't . . . And then we broke up . . . Well, I'd seen how rapidly he discarded his old girlfriends.

He kissed me.

Surprise, curiosity, compassion held me still. My thoughts churned. My stomach fluttered. It was not, after all, like kissing my brother. If I had a brother. Which, much to our father's disappointment, I didn't. Oh, I did my best to fill the role—the family tomboy, the son he never had. We didn't watch football together or shop for power tools or anything. But he'd taught me to stand up for myself and encouraged me to read. When some parents petitioned to have *The Handmaid's Tale* removed from the AP English curriculum, Daddy was the one who went with me to the school board meeting to defend my reading choices.

I remembered how scared I'd been. Not of the grown-ups seated behind the long table, but of letting him down. And then my father caught my eye from the front row of folding chairs, smiling faintly the way he did when he was pleased. He looked so handsome in his uniform, the cross of his chaplaincy on his lapel, and my whole body flooded with courage.

Hm. Apparently my brain wanted to think about anything but this kiss.

The truth was, sex wasn't really my thing. Not that I'd taken a vow of celibacy or anything. But unlike Meg, who dreamed of love and romance, or Amy, who thrived on drama, I wasn't looking for love. Sex made things messy.

I tried to focus as Trey kissed me again, with more confidence and tongue. Giving him a chance. Giving *us* a chance. It was . . . nice. Not that I had a lot to compare it to, but it was better than in high school.

He drew back. His gaze met mine, his eyes dark and expectant.

I cleared my throat. "Pretty good."

"Thanks." He leaned in again.

I leaned back. "Must be all the practice."

"Don't hold it against me."

My cheeks started a slow burn. "I don't. The thing is . . . I don't think you should practice with me."

"Not with you. For you." His eyes held mine with dark, disconcerting sincerity. "Everything I've ever done . . . It's all for you, Jo."

My heart lurched. "Trey, stop."

"Why?"

"I've told you before. We're too young."

"We *were* too young. We're twenty now."

"Exactly. We have the rest of our lives ahead of us. Places to go. Things to do."

"That's what you always say."

The memories followed me to bed that night, clustering like shadows in the corners of my attic room. Eventually, I sat up, my back against the wall, and scrolled through the day's blog comments. Thirty-four little notes, pictures from cell phones and cries for help, including some guy in New Jersey who had failed to defrost his turkey in time and wanted to know if he could quick-thaw the bird in the dishwasher. *Um, no.* Honestly, hadn't these people ever heard of the Butterball Turkey hotline?

I responded to every comment, congratulating, commiserating, offering thanks and advice, grateful for the distraction, for every post reminding me that I had readers, friends, and followers outside Bunyan, North Carolina. I had an identity: Jo March, the *Hungry* blogger, biting into everything life had to offer.

I typed "Gusto" into my browser, immediately noting the *Times* review near the top of the search results. I clicked and read eagerly. The restaurant was an unpretentious oasis, the monkfish seasonal, stylish, and straightforward, the quail with fig puree uninhibited and presented with flair. Yay! Not that one review would change Chef's opinion of food critics, but . . .

On impulse, I sent a message to chef@gusto.com:

Something to be thankful for.

With the link.

And waited.

No answer.

I closed my hand on disappointment. Well, what did I expect? It was barely midnight. The last orders would be trickling into the kitchen at Gusto, the cooks already packing up their mise en place, scrubbing down their stations, snapping towels and cracking jokes and counting the minutes until they could all go out drinking. Plenty of bars open in New York at the end of the night, even on Thanksgiving. Chef would stay behind, calculating portions and proteins and the night's receipts. He wouldn't be wasting his time checking the restaurant's e-mail accounts.

I tossed back the quilt and padded half a flight down to the bathroom, feeling my way in the familiar dark, my feet wincing from the cold plank floor. Trying to soothe myself with rituals like a child, one more drink of water, one more trip to the potty, before I returned to bed.

A message lit my phone screen. I snatched it up.

He ordered the fish, Chef had typed.

I grinned foolishly. In the hustle of service, I'd missed the orders going out to the VIP table. They always do, I typed back.

I climbed into bed, staring at the little screen, my heart beating unaccountably fast as three dots appeared, followed by, How was your dinner?

Not a terribly personal question.

Good, I replied. Thanks for the time off. I hesitated. I'd read the restaurant menu: turkey two ways and planked salmon, grilled lobster and roasted root vegetables, brussels sprouts with lardons.

I made green bean casserole, I confessed.

A pause.

With the little fried onions on top?

Yep.

A longer pause. I pictured him sitting alone in his office as the clamor of the kitchen faded, surrounded by paperwork, the task lists and shopping lists for the morning.

My ex makes that. The boys love it.

Aw. *The boys.* His sons, Bryan and . . . Who was the other one? Alex? Alec. They must spend the holidays with their mother. I wondered if he missed celebrating with his family or if he was glad to be in New York, cooking dinner for paying guests with discriminating palates. But then why bring up his sons at all?

Chefs at the holidays. It would make a great blog post.

Not that I could ever ask him.

Maybe you should put it on the menu, I typed.

Nothing.

I swallowed. Right. What was I doing, feeling sorry for Chef? Imagining we'd forged an intimate connection over green bean casserole. I was an idiot. The man was God. I flopped back on my pillow. Turned out the light.

My phone screen glowed softly, like a message from heaven. We could have used you tonight, March. I hope your mother is well. Happy Thanksgiving.

Simple words. They filled me, satisfied me like bread. I had purpose. I was appreciated. Valued.

Smiling, I typed, Happy Thanksgiving, Chef. I fell asleep holding the phone like a talisman that would take me back to my real life.

The next day, I had to put my phone on airplane mode for the flight to New York. So I missed the call from Meg.

It wasn't until I was on the ground in LaGuardia that I saw her text: Mom back in hospital. Call me.

CHAPTER 6

Meg

I could take care of this. I took a deep breath of cold air and knocked on Hannah Mullett's door.

I was good at taking care of things. Helping people with their problems. That used to be my job, helping people who needed money, making the numbers work so they could get a loan, buy a car, start a business, everything in black and white. Now . . . Well. I didn't see the solutions so clearly now. I shivered in the yellow porch light.

The moon shone over the skeletons of trees. Through the bare branches, against the twilight sky, I could see the pitched shadow of the old mule barn—our barn. The Mulletts' trailer sat on Laurence land, near the edge of our property. Our mother did most of the farmwork herself. But even before Miss Hannah's retirement—she had been the science teacher at Caswell Middle School—she crossed the fields to help our mother make and pack the cheese. After all, you couldn't raise a family on a teacher's pay, John always said. Not in North Carolina.

The door cracked and then swung wide.

"Meg." Miss Hannah smiled in welcome. Beneath her cap of charcoal hair, her face was smooth and ageless. "It's good to see you, honey. How's your momma?"

I opened my mouth. My throat closed. To my horror, I couldn't speak.

"Come in out of the cold." She took my arm, drawing me across the threshold. "I'll get us some coffee."

I smelled like the barn. There was goat slobber on my jeans and the Lord only knew what on my sneakers. "I'm all dirty," I said. "I can't . . . I'm fine. I don't need anything. Thanks."

She gave me a look, like I was still in her seventh-grade science class. "You just set," she said, and sat me down at her scrubbed wooden table while she bustled around the narrow galley kitchen.

And, oh, it felt so very good to be mothered. To sit as she laid out mugs and spoons, sugar and cream. Real cream, in a ceramic pitcher shaped like a cow. A hand-pieced quilt hung on one wall along with pictures of her kids: James, all serious in his naval uniform, and Daphne in her cap and gown, beaming at her Howard graduation. I remembered when they used to play in the barn with Amy.

Miss Hannah set a plate of cookies—homemade, chocolate chip— on the table. I eyed the plate. I'd always done my best to follow my mother's rule, *No snacks before mealtime*. But some days required chocolate. *Or vodka,* my sister Jo's voice said in my head.

I got up to wash my hands. Took a cookie. "Thank you."

"So what did the doctors say today?" Miss Hannah asked.

The crumbs caught in my throat. "Mom's biopsy results are back. She has a bone infection." *"Osteomyelitis,"* the orthopedist said. I'd made him spell the word twice so I could look it up later. For the first few minutes all I'd really heard were the words he didn't say, *Not cancer, not cancer, not cancer,* beating over and over in my brain.

"An infection," Miss Hannah repeated.

I nodded. "From when she cut herself moving the paddock this summer? Apparently the bacteria traveled through her bloodstream and got into her spine."

"So what are they going to do?" Miss Hannah said.

"Well." I swallowed. "They put a port in her arm. For her antibiotics? But it takes, like, four hours for her to get all her medication through the IV, and she's still in a lot of pain. The doctor says that at some point she might be able to get the drugs as an outpatient. But until she can manage basic daily activities on her own, they want her to go to rehab." Four to six weeks, the orthopedist said. Through Christmas. The lump in my throat developed spikes like a seedpod from a sweet gum tree.

"Well, that's a blessing."

"Excuse me?"

"Abby needs somebody to take care of her. Lord knows your father can't do it." Miss Hannah stirred her coffee vigorously. "Bless his heart."

I blinked. To the patriotic folks of Bunyan, our father was a hero. A saint. All the church ladies had a crush on him, so handsome, tall, and lean, his thick chestnut hair going to gray, his high-bridged nose, his rather thin mouth. Jo looked like him, though nobody ever called her beautiful. I took after our mother.

What would Momma say?

"He's never had to," I said. Defending him, the way she would have.

"Well, that's the truth. That man can't find the coffeepot without your mother."

A spurt of laughter escaped me. Granted, Hannah had never been a member of Daddy's congregation. She taught Sunday school at Greater Zion Baptist Church on the other side of town.

"He's been eating at the hospital most nights," I said.

"Cafeteria food." Hannah sniffed. "I'll make him my Brunswick stew."

In birth, death, sickness, and natural disasters, any Southern woman worth her salt showed up at her neighbors' with a sympathy dish. With Daddy being a former minister and all, the poultry offerings were piling up: chicken and rice, chicken chili, chicken breasts with broccoli and cream of celery soup.

"I'm sure he'd love that," I said.

"Anything I can do, honey. You know that."

"Thanks." I cleared my throat. "Actually, I came to ask your advice. I've been helping out at the farm since Momma's in the hospital. But . . . Well. Daddy's so busy now, and I've got the twins. I can't do it all myself."

"You have enough shit in your life already," Jo had said on the phone. *"I mean, come on. Poopy diapers and dirty straw?"* I had laughed, because she wanted me to. But it was true.

I crumbled my cookie. "And now we know that Mom will be in rehab . . . Even after she gets out, she won't be able to work like she used to. Maybe not for months. We really need to hire somebody to handle the farm chores."

Hannah's eyes were dark and kind. Troubled. "Meg . . . Did you talk to your parents about this?"

I shook my head. Between the pain—and the pain meds—my mother was in no condition to make decisions about the farm. My father had never really asked for my help, or volunteered any. He spent his days counseling veterans in a rented storefront in a run-down part of town, an old insurance office that held a desk, some chairs, a computer, and a coffeepot. At night, he ran a twelve-step program in the church basement, down the stairs from the twins' classroom, or visited the hospital, sitting with Momma, dropping in on the wounded warriors in rehab.

It was as if he expected life to simply go on revolving around him. Which, of course, it did.

"Honey . . ." Hannah studied her mug, which was a cheerful yellow with *Think like a proton . . . Stay positive!* printed on one side. Science teacher humor, I guess. "Your folks are good people. Abby and I have been friends a long time. But you're talking about, what, three months?"

I nodded. "I can't help you. I won't be here. I'm visiting James over the holidays." Her son in California.

"I'm not asking you to do it," I assured her. It was one thing to work in the cheese room, cutting curd and draining whey. But Hannah was past retirement age, too old to be hauling hay and mucking out stalls. "I figured you might know someone who could use the work, that's all. It won't pay a lot, but . . ."

"Meg." Hannah met my gaze, her eyes regretful. "Your mother doesn't have the money to pay anybody right now."

My jaw unhinged. But . . . Okay. Granted, I hadn't worked at the bank in a while. But I understood the problems farmers faced with cash flow. Market prices and milk production went up and down. Feed costs and vet bills were constant. Any large, unexpected expense could plunge you into the red.

For some reason, my heart was racing. "Are you saying . . . Miss Hannah, does Momma owe you money?"

"I told Abby not to worry about it. You're getting into the lean season now. Pretty soon those goats dry up. So do customers. Abby always counted on her holiday sales at the farmers' market to see her through till spring."

But my mother hadn't been at the farmers' market, I remembered. She'd been in the hospital.

"But what about you?" I asked. "Are you all right? For money, I mean."

"Don't you worry about me." Hannah patted my arm. "I still have my retirement. And my quilt sales. Why, I got another commission last week." She kept talking, snatches filtering through the noise in my head. Something about her trip at Christmastime. Another grandchild.

She'd made us a wedding quilt. Me and John. A traditional double-ring design for the queen-size bed in our first apartment. I'd loved that quilt. But it didn't match the style of our new house. Now we had everything matching, coordinated drapes and duvet cover and lots of fussy pillow shams that John threw on the floor.

Not that it mattered. I guess my brain didn't want to face up to what she was really saying: I couldn't hire anybody to help on the farm. There wasn't any money.

Hannah paused, looking at me expectantly. The blood rushed in my ears. Had she asked me a question?

"Excuse me?"

"When are your sisters coming home?" she repeated.

"Christmas." Almost three weeks away. "Well, Jo is coming. Amy is in Paris." She'd cried, leaving. "And Beth got a part in a show."

Our mother wouldn't hear of them changing their plans simply because she needed, in her words, *a few medical tests.* That was her way. Keep going, keep moving, keep working, through deployments, disappointments, dry wells, and broken hearts.

"I heard Beth auditioned for something," Hannah was saying. "In Branson, right?"

I nodded, pulling myself together. "She got the call last week." Before we knew Momma would spend Christmas in rehab. "Colt Henderson wants to use one of her songs in his show, so they added Beth to the chorus. She's playing an angel, I think. Oh, and an elf."

"That's wonderful news. Good for her."

"It *is* wonderful. She's so talented."

"Gonna be hard, though."

"Yes." My sisters and I had never been apart for the holidays. Ever. "They'll be all alone on Christmas."

"I meant for you. All that work."

"Oh. Yes."

"You want to lay off milking now anyway," Hannah said. "Those goats will start having babies in a couple months. Give you all a little break before then."

I nodded. "Do you know . . . Is there enough inventory that I could sell at the farmers' market on Saturday?"

"Should be. The chèvre's still good for a couple weeks. And that marinated feta, that keeps awhile. Check the walk-in."

"I will. Thanks."

Miss Hannah watched me, a frown creasing her dark face. "You never did like working with a lab partner. It's a big step for you, coming here to ask for help. I'm just sorry I—"

"No, I'm sorry. It's not your problem." It was mine. "I'll talk to Dad,"

I said. I wondered what kind of salary he drew from his nonprofit. Enough to pay Hannah the money Momma owed her?

"Honey, your daddy doesn't do a damn lick around the farm. I'm talking about John. Your husband."

"John's so busy," I said. Making excuses for him. Although just this afternoon, he'd picked up the kids from preschool so I could be at the hospital. "I can't ask him to do any more."

"Well, you know what's best," Hannah said, in that doubtful tone teachers sometimes used. Like I was twelve years old and about to set the lab on fire. (Which I never did, by the way. That was Jo.) "If there's an emergency or you need a break, you call me. I'll be in town for another two weeks."

A rush of guilt and gratitude choked me. "Thanks." I hesitated. "I wonder . . . That is, Sallie Moffat is having a Christmas party on Saturday. I figured we'd stay home. I mean, I've never left the twins with anyone but Momma. But . . ."

"You want me to watch them for you?"

"Yes. Please. If it's not too much trouble."

"No trouble at all." Hannah smiled. "Kept an eye on you and your sisters often enough. And it will be good practice for when I visit James."

"Oh, thank you, Miss Hannah!" I hugged her awkwardly, leaving bits of hay on her purple fleece sweater. Flushing, I brushed at her shoulders. "Sorry."

"It's all good, honey. Take some cookies with you."

"Oh, I shouldn't . . ."

"For John and those babies."

So I left with cookies and Hannah's promise to come over Saturday at seven.

I checked my messages in the car. Nothing from my mother. There was a string of texts from John, starting with, Hey, hon. We're home. and ending Where r u? I stopped at the Piggly Wiggly to pick up a rotisserie chicken, my mind already calculating ahead. I wondered how much

Carl would pay me to do the books for his farm. Enough to hire a sitter? Enough to hire help with the farm?

Maybe I should talk to John after the twins were in bed tonight.

But when I pulled into our neat little subdivision, there was another car sitting in our driveway. A red new-model Ferrari with dealer's plates. What was Trey doing here?

"Hello?" Dropping the grocery bag on the island, I walked through the empty kitchen to the family room.

Beer bottles and sippy cups covered the coffee table. Trey lay on the carpet, DJ bouncing on his chest. Daisy crawled on all fours, eating fish crackers out of a bowl on the floor. Without her hands.

John looked up from his phone, relieved. "There you are."

"Mommy!" DJ tumbled off Trey and ran to me.

"Hey. Hi, baby." I hefted DJ, bent to smooch the top of Daisy's head.

"I a key cat, Mommy!"

"Such a nice kitty cat." I tugged on my shirt, embarrassed. I looked a mess. My house was a mess.

Trey rolled gracefully to his feet and kissed my cheek. "John invited me for dinner. But if this is a bad time . . ."

Tell him he should bring you home for dinner sometime, I'd said at Thanksgiving. "No, of course not." I smiled. "This is great. It's great to see you."

"I called you," John said. "I left a message."

Not his fault. "This is great," I repeated.

"We can order a pizza or something," John said.

DJ removed his thumb from his mouth. "Pizza."

"Pizza, pizza, Mommy!" Daisy chanted.

Trey held up his phone with a smile. "I've got Domino's on my favorites list."

Maybe I wasn't a chef like Jo. But if I'd learned anything from our mother, it was how to stretch a meal to feed an extra mouth. I could manage one home-cooked meal for Trey, the boy I'd known since high school. John's boss.

"Don't be silly. By the time they deliver, I can have dinner on the table," I said.

The answering machine in the kitchen was blinking. John, telling me Trey was coming to dinner.

I poured canned stock and cream of chicken soup into a pot. Mixed together flour, salt, baking powder, butter, adding just enough milk to make a sticky dough. I rolled it out, cut it into strips, and dropped the dumplings into the broth to simmer while I attacked the chicken.

"Something smells good," John said while I set the table.

"Chicken and dumplings."

Trey grinned. "You're amazing."

I blushed with pleasure.

"Can I help?" John asked.

I smiled and shook my head. "All under control." Well. Almost under control. DJ had stripped to his diaper and was squatting on his heels while Daisy fed him crackers one by one. "Come on, kitties," I coaxed. "Time for dinner."

"DJ no key," Daisy said. "He a puppy."

"Ruff, ruff," DJ said.

"Okay, big dog." John lifted him by the waist, making him shriek with delight. "Let's wash those paws."

"Careful," I said automatically.

"I a puppy!" Daisy said as John carried a kicking, giggling DJ off to the bathroom under one arm. "Daddy, I a puppy, too!"

"Let me open some wine," Trey said.

It was a relief to sit down to supper. Of course, the twins had no appetite. All those crackers. But eventually they ate enough that I could wipe their hands and set them up with coloring books in the kitchen.

"You should get those kids a dog," Trey said when I returned.

"We've talked about it," John said.

"We will. When they're a little older," I said.

"Be good for teaching them responsibility," Trey said.

I smiled at him affectionately. "Which is why you never had one."

"I always wanted a dog," John said.

But who would end up feeding it? Walking it? Cleaning the yard? Me, that's who. I swallowed some wine, searching for another subject. "I saw Miss Hannah today. She's coming over to watch the twins on Saturday. So we can go to Sallie's party."

"Great." John dug into his bowl. "Did you talk to her about hiring somebody to help out at the farm?"

"Sort of."

John put down his fork. "Meg, we agreed you can't do it all yourself."

"I know. But money's a little tight for my parents right now."

John nodded. "Medical bills."

Oh God. "No." I didn't know. My parents were both self-employed, but surely Dad had veteran's benefits or something. "I haven't asked."

"You know, if your folks need anything . . . Anything at all," Trey said.

"Oh no, they're fine," I said. Although I wasn't really sure. "It's just Mom always sees her biggest sales around the holidays, and since she can't go to the farmers' market . . ." I took another sip of wine, for courage. "I thought I could do it. Just for one weekend."

"You? Why not your father?"

Because he doesn't do a damn lick around the farm. But I couldn't say that. I was his daughter. Growing up in a minister's family, in a military family, you learned not to air your dirty laundry. "He sees clients on Saturday." I forced a smile. "Anyway, do you really see my dad selling cheese at a stall?"

"Not really," John admitted. "But it's not your job."

"Somebody has to do it." And there was only me. Doing it all. I swallowed again. "I'm the only one here."

John sighed. "Honey, I appreciate you wanting to help your parents. But your dad's not the only one who has commitments on Saturday."

"Oh." I bit my lip. "Of course."

"You've been busting your ass," Trey said easily. "Take the day off.

The dealership can manage without you one more day. Assuming you don't have to be somewhere else."

I blinked, confused. Where else would John be?

John's jaw set. "I guess that's all settled, then."

I knew he didn't want special treatment from the boss. I admired his independence. But Trey was like my brother. "I'll get dessert," I said hastily. "Miss Hannah made cookies." Cookies made everything better.

And I should check on the twins anyway. Ten minutes ago, I'd left them coloring happily at the table. Now they were . . .

Not at the table.

The flour canister I'd used to make dumplings was on the floor, along with the empty sugar bowl. Daisy stooped and then straightened, flinging fistfuls of flour into the air above her head. Flour and sugar were everywhere, a gritty mix dusting the cabinets and counters, caking the floor.

"Daisy! DJ?"

My little boy turned his white face to me. White hair, white clothes, white eyelashes, all of him, white.

A bubble rose from my chest to my brain, making me light-headed with laughter. Or hysterics.

"He a snowman, Mommy," Daisy chirped. "I make it snow for Kiss-mas."

Trey, behind me, started to laugh. John chuckled.

"Who wants to make snow angels?" Trey asked.

The bubble swelled. Burst in a laugh. "Don't encourage them."

"Honey, relax."

Like I was at fault. "John, look at this mess!"

"So? We can clean it up," he said reasonably.

Irrational tears stung my eyes. "I'll do it."

His gaze fixed on my face. "Right," he said slowly. "Bath time, kids. Up to bed."

"No!" Daisy said. "Want snow!"

John scooped her up, flour and all. "We'll make bubbles," he promised. "Snow bubbles in the tub."

"Bubbows," DJ said happily.

"Snow! Snow! Snow!" Daisy said, patting her father's shoulders, leaving little white handprints against the blue cotton.

"Make sure you stay with them," I warned. "Don't let DJ play with the faucet."

"Meg, I know," John said.

The impatience in his tone tightened my throat. I was only trying to help. How did that make me the bad guy?

I opened the hall closet to get the vacuum. I'd be finding flour in the cracks and corners for weeks. Ants, too, probably, with all that sugar.

"Let me give you a hand," Trey said.

I blinked hard. "I've got it."

"At least let me clear the table."

"Trey, I'm fine."

"No, you're not. Your mom is in the hospital and you're wound tighter than a clock."

"Sorry," I said.

"Hey, it's okay." He caught me in a one-armed hug, his body lean and comforting. He gave my shoulders a little shake. "You know, it's okay to accept help sometimes."

"Unless your last name is March," I mumbled into his chest.

I closed my eyes, leaning my head against Trey's shoulder. He smelled like starch and beer, with a whiff of some expensive cologne. The sound of the children's laughter floated light as soap bubbles down the stairs. I sighed. "I don't want to be selfish."

"You'd rather be overwhelmed?"

"Don't be silly."

"Miserable?"

I gave a watery chuckle. "Maybe."

"How about bitchy?"

I opened my eyes. Glared. "I am not . . ." *Oh.*

Trey grinned. "Gotcha."

I smiled back reluctantly. "Fine. Just for that, you can load the dishwasher."

"That's my girl," Trey said.

It was nice having his company in the kitchen. And maybe he had a point.

For the next three days, I tried extra hard to be patient and cheerful. To be my mother, baking cupcakes at eleven o'clock at night, rehearsing songs with the twins in the car, collecting pinecones at the farm to make Christmas tree ornaments.

On Thursday, when John came to the twins' program at school, he sat beside me, his right hand holding my left, making the diamond twinkle in the light. Part of a row of parents and grandparents, side by side.

The kids filed in from the hallway holding hands as the teachers half led, half herded them into a ragged line facing the chairs. Miss Julie turned on the music. Miss Nancy passed out jingle bells. Three-year-old Kaylee Upton's thumb crept into her mouth as Chris Murphy's dad squatted in the aisle, holding up his cell phone to record.

My mother would have loved this, I thought with a pang. She would have admired the children's costumes, complimented my nut-free, gluten-free carrot cupcakes.

In the front row, DJ stood stock-still beside Kaylee, hands thrust into his little pockets. Daisy spotted us and waved. Behind her antler headband, her bangs stuck up in every direction.

"Pretty damn cute," John murmured.

I squeezed his hand.

"Jingle bells, jingle bells . . ."

I leaned forward with the other mothers, nodding encouragement, mouthing along.

"Jingle all the waaaay . . ."

My phone rang, garnering dirty looks from everyone around us. I flushed and dug in my bag, glancing at the caller ID. *Mom.*

Anxious anticipation tightened my chest. I hit MUTE. "I have to take this," I whispered to John.

"Can't it wait?" he murmured.

Little Kaylee, overwhelmed by attention, broke down and had to be led to one side. Chris Murphy sat down and began taking off his shoes. ". . . *one-horse open sleigh-aaay!*"

I shook my head. "It's my mother."

"Honey, she's fine."

Miss Nancy coaxed Chris Murphy back into line.

"You don't know that," I said.

John gave me a patient look. "If something was wrong—something important—the rehab center would call you."

Doubt made me pause. At the front of the room, Daisy jumped up and down, vigorously shaking her jingle bells.

But as soon as I met John's eyes, I knew—he knew—what I was going to do.

"I'll be right back," I whispered.

And left my husband and children and went into the hall.

I can't believe the case manager didn't call me," I said to John.

Parents and children eddied in the hall around us, spilling out of the classroom toward the parking lot.

"Honey, your mother fell. She's fine," John said with heavy patience. "Maybe next time she wants to go to the bathroom, she'll remember to use her walker. Or wait for help."

"I did bells, Mommy," Daisy said.

"I heard, sweetie. Wonderful bells. So loud!" I smoothed her bangs under her reindeer headband. Turned back to John. "They still should have notified me."

John plucked Daisy from the current, hoisting her in his arms. "What do you think you could have done?"

I didn't know. Something. She'd *cried* on the phone. My mother, who never cried about anything in her life. High, weak, gasping sounds that tore my heart. "I'm her daughter."

"Right. Not her doctor. Or her husband."

"Daddy didn't even answer his phone," I said. My father had been counseling a client in his storefront office when my mother fell. "Careful, DJ."

I plucked him back from bumping into three-year-old Matthew Mackay. "Sorry," I mouthed to Matthew's mother. That's how we identified ourselves in Bunyan. As somebody's mother, as somebody's wife.

She smiled. "They're fine. Merry Christmas. Oh, your husband's here. Aren't you lucky."

I took a breath. Released it. "Yes. Merry Christmas."

John waded into the stream heading for the exit. "To be fair, your dad didn't know anything was wrong."

I grabbed DJ's hand. "That's no excuse."

John looked back at me over his shoulder, Daisy in his arms. I flushed.

"Give the staff some credit for handling the problem, Meg," my husband said quietly. "They're trying to take care of her."

"Then they should do a better job," I said, frustrated by my own helplessness. I was supposed to be the good daughter. What good was I if I couldn't protect my own mother? "What if the fall damaged her spine?"

"Then we'll deal with it," John said.

I was irrationally encouraged by that "we." "*We'll deal with it.*" Like we were a team. Like the early days.

I looked at him, seeing the tired lines in his face, the oxlike set of his shoulders. He'd been bringing work home this week, staying up late in his office, making up for the time he'd taken off so I could be with my mother.

How could I ask him to do any more?

"Thank you, honey."

CHAPTER 7

Jo

When I moved to New York, I started running again. I memorized landmarks, learning my way around my new neighborhood: the brown spire of the Episcopal church, the plywood construction barriers, the Greek produce stall, the Korean dry cleaner on the corner. I ran in the early morning, before or after the sun came up, when the air was cool and full of promise, after the garbage trucks came through. Alone, except for Dan the Homeless Guy on his cardboard patch in front of the bodega, and a few people walking to the subway or waiting for the bus. The thump of my running shoes measured my progress, claiming my territory.

In those early days, I was in love with the city, like Joan Didion, drunk with adulthood and freedom. Five years later, my affair with New York was what I imagined marriage might be—inconvenient, sometimes disappointing or exhausting. But I was committed now. I kept running after I lost my job at the paper, staying a few steps ahead of panic.

It was cheaper than paying for a gym membership. Or a shrink.

After I was hired at Gusto, it got harder to force myself to stumble out of bed in the mornings. But on Friday, I laced up my shoes and ran through the Meatpacking District to the High Line, the old elevated freight rail turned public park beside the Hudson River. The path was clear of tourists and of snow. The cold quiet was an antidote to the noise and smoke of the kitchen, the stress of orders rattling in, the bodies bumping in tight space. The grease that coated everything like the miasma of failure. The fear that I wasn't measuring up. That I was letting people down. That I wasn't, in my father's words, *"fulfilling my God-given potential."*

Between the blocks of buildings, the pale sun sparkled on the distant water. The pressure to succeed, to perform, built in my chest, knifing my lungs like cold. I ran, chasing . . . something. A dream.

As far back as I could remember, I'd wanted to write. Stories scribbled on notebook paper, stitched with yarn or stapled along the edges to resemble the real books I borrowed from the library. Plays on the parsonage porch performed with my sisters.

The first Christmas our father was in Iraq, I'd written him a letter. More of a journal, really, day-to-day stories about our family and the farm, complete with pictures. Like a blog, only there were barely any blogs back then. I worked on it for ages, adding and polishing, taking pages to Mrs. Ferguson, my AP English teacher, for feedback.

And then . . . Nothing. All my effort, wasted. All my work, gone.

All my fault.

I t was one of those warm North Carolina days that happen sometimes in winter. The trees stood like sentinels along the bank. Our footsteps rustled as Trey and I picked our way to the dock, the slope to the water littered with decaying leaves and fallen pines. The brown river reflected the blue sky, like a child's landscape decorated with puffy white clouds.

Our family had two boats, an old johnboat we used for fishing and swimming on summer days, and my father's canoe that he'd made himself at summer camp in Maine. Very Hiawatha.

Trey rowed the flat-bottomed johnboat out to the middle, away from the weeds and mud and encroaching trees. Away from everything. A blue heron hunted motionless in the shallows. The wind wrinkled the glassy water. I tilted my face to the sun, breathing deep, trailing a hand over the bow. Beneath the sunny surface, the water was winter cold.

"Jo! Jo!" Amy cried from the dock. I turned my head away. "Jo, I'm sorry!"

Trey lifted the oars, raising an eyebrow in question. "Go back?"

I glared, annoyed he'd even suggest it. My grievance burned inside me. I was so *mad* at Amy.

How *dare* she delete my letter to Dad?

Meg said I could write another. Mom said I needed to forgive. Even Beth—my baby, my ally—suggested wistfully we should make up after Amy had apologized.

They didn't understand. I'd worked on that letter forever, one day, one page at a time, making it the best I could, polishing it like a college application. And Amy deleted it all out of spite because Trey and I wouldn't take her with us to a stupid party at the Gardiners that she was too young for anyway. Before I sent it. Before I printed it. Before I backed it up.

I couldn't forgive myself for being so *stupid*.

Or her, either.

"No." It was easier to be mad at Amy than to blame myself.

"She's got the canoe."

I looked indignantly toward the dock, where our NO TRESPASSING sign was stapled to a tree. "She can't take that. It's Dad's. Anyway, she can't get it into the water by herself."

We both watched as Amy half lifted, half pushed the upside-down canoe from its rack and dragged it to the splintery dock. Squatting, she gripped the gunwale on both sides. I felt a moment's unease. Amy was not an experienced canoer. Or a strong swimmer.

"She'll give up when she figures out she can't paddle solo," I said. To Trey? To myself?

But Amy, undeterred, shifted her weight over the boat's centerline and put one foot, then the other, into the canoe. Without a life jacket.

I cupped my hands and yelled, "Don't! It's not safe."

"So come back!"

"Go away!"

She pushed off from the dock. "I want to talk to you!"

The canoe wobbled into the current. Amy paddled ineffectively, digging too deep. She was sitting, not kneeling, which made her center of gravity too high. The canoe turned sideways, scraping close to a gnarled log jutting out of the water.

"Be careful!" Trey shouted.

"Go back!"

She grabbed for an overhanging branch. The abrupt shift in weight tipped the canoe. It flipped, dumping her into the freezing water.

Amy shrieked. Trey swore.

"Amy!" I cried. She thrashed. Splashed. The cold water sank into her clothes, darkening them. Amy sank, too. "Grab the canoe!"

She reached for the hull. The upturned boat spun, bumping her. Her head went under. Resurfaced. Trey was rowing, pulling powerfully toward Amy, who was gasping and struggling in the water.

I fumbled with the buckles on my life jacket. "Don't hit her."

"Take an oar. Quick, quick!"

I scrambled to hold the boat steady with one oar while he stretched over the side, trying to reach Amy with the other. Her hands kept sliding off the paddle. She was clumsy with cold. Her lips were blue, her eyes wild.

I sobbed. Pulling off my life jacket, I threw it at her. She struggled to raise her arm.

Trey jumped into the water beside her. She gripped him like a monkey as he hauled her to the rowboat. I grabbed her under the arms. Together, we pushed and lifted her over the side; she was sputtering, freezing, crying.

My heart constricted with fear and shame. It was all the fault of my shitty temper. My fault my sister almost died.

I should have gone back.

My chest burned. My breath made little clouds in the air as I ran along the High Line. *Ha ha ha. Hee hee hee.*

I pushed harder, my heart pounding, my soles pounding the path. Two miles and turn. A combination of cold and sweat stung my face like tears. Three miles. Four. My emotions tangled, my brain on some stupid treadmill, covering the same ground over and over again, spinning and spinning and going nowhere.

I huffed. Jesus, I was pathetic. I pulled out my phone. No text from Meg yet today. That was good, right? At least, it wasn't bad. I started taking pictures at random, finding spots of color in the winter-brown landscape. A spray of red berries against the wall. A clump of seed heads—coneflowers—that reminded me of home. Nothing I could use. I wasn't writing a nature blog.

A big man in a green knit cap and navy Windbreaker was practicing tai chi in the wide space created from an old train platform. Not a class. Just this one guy, moving with fluid strength against a backdrop of sky and water. I stopped to catch my breath, watching him.

He looked so . . . centered. Calm. His powerful body flowed from one pose to the next, relaxed and graceful. Grounded. On impulse, I lifted my phone to capture his picture. He turned, revealing his face.

Oh. It was Chef. I sucked in my breath.

His gaze met mine. *Oh*.

For a second, he looked . . . I don't know how he looked in that moment before his expression shuttered, became benign, impersonal and familiar.

He nodded. "March."

My face went as hot as if I'd been dipped in boiling water. I was dizzied, disoriented with embarrassment and heat. Well, I'd been running. I could blame it on that.

"Chef." I lowered my phone. "I didn't recognize you."

One corner of his mouth curled up slightly. "You take pictures of strangers."

Was that a question?

"Sometimes," I admitted. "Well, people. Places. Food."

Because I was *an idiot hipster food blogger.* I winced.

It felt weird to see him away from the kitchen, out of context and his white chef's jacket. Like the time I'd seen Mr. Clark, my tenth-grade chemistry teacher, at the beach without his shirt. Not that Chef was shirtless. Nope. Arms, covered. Tattoos, covered. But the soft layers clung to his broad shoulders, stuck to his heavy chest. A line of sweat darkened the T-shirt at his neck.

I realized I was staring, and flushed. "We had a late night last night. I was just, um, going for a run."

"Clearing your head?" His deep voice sounded amused. Almost sympathetic.

"Yeah." *No.* He didn't go out drinking after service with the rest of us. I didn't want him to think I was hungover. "I just needed the . . ." *The escape.* "The exercise."

He nodded. "You make yourself strong."

It was nice that he saw it like that. Not running away. Not a coping strategy, a sign of weakness, but a kind of strength. It was nice that he said it, as if we were friends.

My throat felt thick. I swallowed. "I didn't mean to interrupt you."

He moved his big hand—a chef's hand, burned, scarred, and tattooed—in a dismissive gesture. "*Passt schon.* How is your mother?"

His interest wasn't personal, I reminded myself. He asked after all the staff, inquired about Constanza's daughter and Frank's parole meetings and Julio's sciatica all the time. It was one of the ways he made everybody feel better about showing up for work. The way he made us want to do our best.

But somehow his attention felt different, special, outside the kitchen, away from other ears.

"She's okay. Thanks," I added.

"Out of the hospital, then."

"Yeah. Well, she's in rehab."

"You have talked to her."

My eyes prickled. Shit. Oh shit. I was not going to cry. "Not today," I admitted.

He didn't say anything.

Which was all the encouragement I needed to start babbling. "She fell," I said. "Apparently she needed to use the bathroom, and when the staff didn't come right away, she tried to go by herself." Our mother had always liked to do for herself. The image of her waiting for assistance, alone and helpless, anxious not to soil her hospital bed, tore at my heart.

"I tried calling yesterday," I said. "But Meg says not to bother her at breakfast, because she needs to eat and the food is terrible even when it's hot, and she doesn't have any appetite as it is. And then the doctor does rounds, and after that they try to get her out of bed, and at that point she's usually too exhausted to talk to anybody. In the afternoon, I'm at work. I call her on break, but if she's sleeping, they don't put the call through. Or she's not sleeping, which means she's in this awful pain, so I want her to sleep. Only I can't . . . I don't . . ." I swiped at my face with the heels of my hands. Well, crap. Evidently I was crying after all. "Sorry."

Chef pulled a black chef's bandanna from his pocket and held it out.

I looked from the folded square to his face.

"Take it." His eyes did that attractive crinkle thing at the corners. "It's clean."

"Thanks." I blotted my eyes. "We didn't even talk that much before," I said, my voice muffled by the comforting folds of cloth. Dad was the one I talked to, whose interest and approval I craved. I'm sure Mom would have loved to chat with me about raising children and sewing curtains the way she did with Meg. Except I didn't have children. I barely had a window. "It's just . . . She's always been there, you know?"

In the background. Safe and sound and boring enough that I could live my life without ever having to think about home.

"How long will she be in rehab?" Chef asked.

"A month. Maybe two?" I blew my nose. "Sorry. I don't know why I'm bothering you with this."

"Because you have no one else to talk to."

"That's not . . ." I stopped. Okay, maybe, since Ashmeeta moved out, it was a little true. Rachel had followed her boyfriend to Portland. My college friends had gone on with their lives, finishing law school or internships at Ernst & Young, buying furniture at Ikea. My colleagues from the paper no longer called.

We have totally different schedules now, I told Meg when she asked.

But that was an excuse. Newspapers everywhere were closing, merging, downsizing. Being with me reminded them that their own jobs were at risk. And the truth was, I flinched from seeing myself through their eyes. *Poor, expendable Jo.*

"I talk to my sister," I said. "Every day."

But Meg had her hands full dealing with things back home. It wasn't fair to dump my feelings on her, even if she had time to listen.

"Your sister with the twins," Chef said. "In North Carolina."

He remembered.

I nodded. "Everybody's in North Carolina." Including his ex-wife. Oops. I bumbled on. "I mean, Meg and her family, obviously. My parents. Aunt Phee. Oh, and Trey."

Who hadn't called since I got back to New York. Probably a good thing. The truth was, I was lonely and at loose ends. Trey's familiar comfort was a temptation to be avoided.

He'd been so glad to see me at Thanksgiving. Why *hadn't* he called?

"Trey is your brother?"

For some reason, my face got hot. I shook my head. "A friend."

Chef looked at me, his hazel eyes unreadable. "Ah."

"My sister Beth goes to school in Greensboro. Well, not now. She's in Branson now. Missouri? She got a part in a Christmas show there." Like he cared. *Stop talking.* "And Amy—she's the baby—is in Paris." Dear God, I sounded like a travelogue. "Not that it makes any difference. It's always been me and Meg, really. We're the oldest."

"You protect them."

"Yeah. Kind of. Beth feels guilty enough already. And any conversation with Amy always revolves around Amy."

You're too hard on her, Meg said in my head.

"Amy is the pretty one," I said. "Very talented. She's doing an internship with Louis Vuitton."

Not that I was jealous. I could have gone to Europe. I'd come to New York to become a writer instead.

But Amy had never had to make that choice. It seemed my baby sister had it all, the glamorous travel and the fabulous career.

Fine. Maybe I was a *little* jealous.

"Your sister is the pretty one," Chef said in an odd voice.

"Well, yeah."

The eyebrows rose. "And what are you?"

My brain froze. Was he implying . . . Did he think I was *pretty*? I reached up and tightened my ponytail. "I'm the . . ." *Smart one,* I almost said, out of habit. Except, look at me. I wasn't anywhere close to the five-year plan I'd made my senior year of college. My time was running out, and all I had to show for it was a half-baked collection of random reviews, recipes, and rejection letters. My graduate school project—*"consisting of a substantial piece of writing,"* a collection of coming-of-age stories set in Bunyan—had been judged adequate to receive my degree but ultimately too *"immature"* to merit special praise or attention. I'd been let go from my newspaper job. Did New York need another food blog? No. Everything was happening on Instagram now anyway. Pictures, rather than words. But writing was all I knew how to do. Writing and cooking. And I wasn't that great a cook.

"I'm the one who talks too much," I said.

He put back his head and laughed. He had a great laugh. Against the darkness of his heavy stubble, his teeth looked very white. His throat was smooth and strong.

Yep. I was definitely feeling some feelings. Me. For my at-least-a-decade-older-than-me divorced boss. *Not smart at all*.

He held my gaze, that little smile tugging his mouth. My heart beat faster. Maybe . . . Was it possible that he felt something, too? Maybe with a little encouragement, he would ask me . . . What? To breakfast. For a drink after work. For sex.

His lips were moving, forming actual words, but my blood was pounding so hard I didn't hear them.

"What?" I asked.

"Why did you move to New York?" he repeated patiently.

I got a fellowship at NYU, I almost blurted. *And then I was a lifestyle reporter.* It wasn't exactly a secret. I'd listed my former employment on my job application. But Chef had probably never called my editor for a reference, maybe never even read my résumé. In the kitchen hierarchy, I wasn't that important. I shrugged. "You know what they say. If you can make it here, you can make it anywhere."

"There are other places for a chef to get training."

There were other places to be a writer, too. But after I was down-sized, moving away felt like giving up. Felt like failure.

"You're here," I pointed out.

"For now."

Something inside me sank. "Does that mean you would move? Sell the restaurant?" *But what about the people who worked there? What about me?*

"If I found a better opportunity, sure." He shrugged his broad shoulders. "Anyway, I wouldn't have to sell to start somewhere else. Ray is itching to take over the kitchen."

I fought an unexpected sense of loss. Of panic, almost. "But Gusto is *yours*. What about your dedication? Your, um . . ."

"Passion?"

I regarded him uncertainly, that curl still teasing the corner of his mouth, his eyes serious. Were we still talking about the restaurant?

Just for a moment I wished I had Amy's ease with men, her ability to make the perfect, light, flirty comeback. "That's what you said. Before," I reminded him. "You live to cook, you told me."

"I love to cook," he said promptly. "But this business isn't static. You are always on your way up or your way down."

Right. No question where he thought I was headed.

"Thank you for those words of encouragement," I grumbled.

His smile spread. "You should be encouraged. You think I hire every English major who walks through my door?"

As if I were special. As if he wanted me training under him. As if—maybe—he'd read my job application after all.

"Why did you hire me?" I asked.

He started to say something. Gave a quick shake of his head instead. "You are smart," he answered finally. "You work hard. You learn quickly. But I think maybe I made a mistake with you."

My lips felt numb. Was he . . . Oh God, was he letting me go? "If you don't want me . . ." I said stiffly.

"March." Another shake of his head, as if he'd caught me using the wrong knife. "Every kitchen you go to, you get what you want and move on. Move up. Get out. You serve me well. But I do not serve you. I do not think you find what you want at Gusto."

"But I do," I said desperately. "Maybe I don't belong in the kitchen for the rest of my life, but I don't want to leave you."

He gave me an intense look. "To leave Gusto."

Weren't they the same thing? I was using him. For inspiration, for a paycheck, for material for my blog. And I didn't have the guts to tell him so. "Right."

He regarded me for a long moment. "What *do* you want, then?"

I thought I knew, once. I wanted to be a writer. I'd followed my dream to New York City, to experience a bigger life on a larger stage than Bunyan. In the city, I was free to shine. Not with the reflected glow of a father, husband, children, but with the light of my own success.

Only now . . . I'd lost my job and my roommates. I worked in a restaurant like every other scrambling dreamer in New York, the actors, the dancers, the musicians, the writers. And for what? There was no book deal. There wasn't even a book. Meanwhile, Amy was in Paris, Beth was in a show, Meg was hardly home anymore, and Momma was in rehab. Maybe I needed to reexamine my priorities.

"I don't want to let everybody down."

Another serious look. "That is about them. Not about you."

"I guess . . ." I thought. "I don't want to let myself down. I want to do the right thing."

He nodded, once. "Then you will."

I snorted. "You can't know that."

"I know. For three months, I have watched you. Once you decide on something, you don't let anything stand in your way."

Wow. A compliment.

"Thank you," I said. A pause. "That's a good thing, right?"

Laughter leaped in his eyes. "I have always found perseverance a very attractive quality," he assured me.

Warmth flooded my chest. I grinned back. "Well, that's a relief."

More than a relief. It was reassurance, validation on a level I hadn't known I sought or needed.

Our eyes held. My smile faded. I shivered a little, all over.

"You are cold," he said, concerned.

My cheeks ignited. I was burning up. I wound my hair around my hand, resecuring my ponytail. "I'm fine."

"You should keep moving."

"Yeah." Before I did something else, said something more, to make a bigger fool of myself. "I guess I'll see you around, then."

I started to go, aware of his eyes on my back.

"March."

I turned hopefully. "Yes, Chef?"

"You are on the schedule tonight, yeah?"

I swallowed my disappointment. Of course he didn't keep track of my hours. My comings and goings were of no interest to him. Unless . . . *"For three months, I have watched you."*

"Yes, Chef."

"Good. You can do family meal."

The meal before service, when the restaurant was closed. Responsibility for the staff meal rotated. It was an opportunity for Chef to try new recipes, for Ray to use up leftovers from the night before, for Constanza to make her killer *asado de bodas* and tortillas. Being asked to cook was an honor, an accolade, an assurance I had a place in the kitchen.

I belonged.

Here.

My smile started deep inside and grew and bloomed. "Yes, Chef."

CHAPTER 8

Meg

The sky was still dark outside our kitchen windows as I made my way downstairs. John was already up, making breakfast with the twins.

"Pancakes, Mommy!" Daisy announced with glee. "I help."

"Frozen toaster waffles," John said, before I could speak. "I figured they had enough fun with flour when Trey was here."

I smiled. "It smells wonderful, whatever it is."

Like butter and syrup, like the Saturday mornings of my childhood. DJ was coloring at the table, a purple crayon gripped in his stubby fingers, singing softly to himself. *"Wish you a merry Kissmas . . ."* My heart melted.

"Coffee." John handed me a mug. "I figured you'd need it to face the farmers' market."

"Thanks." I took a sip, hot liquid and guilt scalding my throat. He was being so nice.

"How long will you be gone?" he asked.

I swallowed. "The market's open until two." After that, I needed to drive to the farm, feed the goats, make the bank deposit . . . No, that had to wait until Monday. "I'll be back before dinner. In time to get ready for Sallie's party."

He nodded.

"We haven't had a night out in a long time." I tried another smile, hoping for a response. "It will be like a date."

"Don't go, Mommy," Daisy said. "Eat pancakes wiv us."

I kissed her forehead. She smelled delicious. "I wish I could, sweetie. But Daddy will take good care of you. There are apple slices in the fridge," I told John.

"I was going to feed them Tater Tots and ketchup," John said. "That's two food groups, right?"

A joke. I smiled, relieved. "At least. Thanks for watching the kids."

"They're my kids, too."

"Sorry, honey. You're a wonderful father." He was. But being their mom was my job. This house was my surrogate work world. It was surprisingly hard to let it go. I offered him a weak smile. "I guess I'm just used to being in charge."

John's jaw tightened, the way DJ's did when he was frustrated. "So tell me what you want me to do."

I hesitated. John's mom, Cheryl, had worked like a dog to provide for her boys: second jobs, third shifts, whatever she had to do. No one to pick up the slack, ever. Except John. He was only nine when Cheryl started to leave him alone to watch his brother. Too much responsibility, I'd always thought, for such a little boy.

But he was willing to help. If I was willing to accept it.

"Maybe," I suggested, "if you see something that needs doing, you could just . . . do it? Like the other night, when you took the kids up for their bath without asking. That was really thoughtful."

John stared at me a moment. He nodded once, confident now that he had a mission. A plan. "I could help with the Christmas shopping. Buy presents for the kids."

I blinked. Christmas shopping? But why not? Did I really think it would stunt our children's development if John bought them a toy?

"That would be great," I said. "Thanks."

"Great," John repeated. He gave me a coffee-flavored peck. "We'll see you later."

"Bye, my babies! Have fun."

It was good for the twins to get away from me sometimes, I told myself as I pulled out of the driveway. To have special bonding time with their daddy. It was good for John.

Maybe it would be good for me, too.

At the farmers' market, the pumpkins and tomatoes had been replaced by apples, pecans, and first-frost collards, sweet from the cold. Jars of local honey and pickled okra gleamed on makeshift shelves. The tree farmers and Boy Scouts were doing brisk business in Fraser firs and wreaths, loading trees into pickups, securing car trunks with cord. The fresh pine scent swept over me, sharp as memory.

Two weeks until Christmas. I still needed to buy our tree. Or maybe two trees, one for our house and one for the farm.

Maybe Jo would help decorate when she got home, I thought hopefully, setting up my stall. Part of me wanted to have everything ready for my sisters' homecoming, to make Christmas for them the way our mother always had, to hang the star on the barn and the wreath on the door. Put candles in the windows and strings of lights everywhere, looping over the crepe myrtle and azalea bushes, twining the banister and railings of the porch until the house glowed inside and out.

The Saturday morning shoppers streamed past my stall, oblivious to the whiteboard sign with prices lettered in my mother's handwriting. Ignoring me, except to ask sometimes, kindly, how my mother was doing.

"Better, thank you," I lied.

Except she wasn't. Not really. Since the fall, her pain seemed worse, and she complained about the way the meds made her feel, lethargic and then irritable. The doctor had ordered a narcotic patch "to even things out." But it was too soon to tell if it was working.

I rearranged the display by the cashbox, jars of chèvre marinating in golden olive oil. They looked nice, peppercorns studding the white cheese like little jewels. When Amy was younger—twelve or thirteen— she used to decorate the jars for the farmers' market. I remembered her at the dining room table, earnestly tying quilting scraps with bits of ribbon around the lids. But Amy was in Paris.

Somebody called my name. Carl Stewart, the sweet potato farmer, a feed cap pulled over his reddish hair.

"Hey, Carl. What are you doing here?" I asked. "I thought you only sold in organic grocery stores now."

He flashed a smile. "I'm a single farmer. Where else am I going to meet hot women?"

I laughed.

"Anyway, local and organic is what it's all about. You don't get more local and organic than the farmers' market." He ran an assessing eye over my stall, as practiced and inoffensive as the look he'd given me. "How's business?"

"A little slow," I admitted. "Maybe I should hand out lollipops. Like at the bank."

"Not lollipops, samples."

"I was hoping to sell cheese, not give it away."

"Just a taste." Carl winked. "Show them what they're missing. Got any crackers?"

"Crackers? No. But . . ." I watched across the way as Connie of Cupcake Confections handed a cookie to a toddler in a stroller. *Samples.* What a good idea. "Maybe I have something better."

That's two baguettes and a loaf of walnut bread," Connie said a few minutes later. "You want me to throw in a couple of these little plastic knives?"

"That would be wonderful, thanks! What do I owe you?"

"Please." Connie waved my money away. "If you hadn't talked me through my loan application, I'd still be baking cupcakes in my kitchen. Tell your momma I said hi. And if anybody asks, you got your bread from Connie's."

Not everybody who took a sample bought cheese. But gradually a sort of line formed. The pile of bills in the cashbox grew.

"Meg, my dear, what are you doing here?"

Aunt Phee, wearing coral lipstick and a sweater set from Talbots. Her little dog stuck its head out of her bag, a matching bow in its topknot.

I tugged on the hem of my hoodie. Tucked my hair behind my ears. "Hey, Aunt Phee. Miss Wanda. I'm filling in for Momma today."

"Selling cheese," Aunt Phee said, in the tone somebody else might have used for *Pushing drugs*.

"Yes, ma'am."

She sniffed and fed a sample to Polly. "I'd think you'd have better things to do on a pretty Saturday morning."

Aunt Phee wanted her grandnieces in Junior League, not toiling on the farm. "I'm helping out while Momma's in rehab," I said. "It might be another month, the doctor said."

"Bless her heart," Miss Wanda said.

"Your poor father," Aunt Phee said.

I raised my eyebrows. "Don't you mean, *poor mother*?"

Aunt Phee's mouth puckered like the end of a coral balloon. "Abby has plenty of people making sure she rests. Bringing her little meals on trays. Who's looking after Ashton?"

I could have argued that my father was a grown man, perfectly capable of looking after himself.

But of course he never had. A son of privilege, he'd grown up cared for by devoted domestics at Oak Hill, the big white house that belonged now to Aunt Phee. Yes, he had turned his back on his family's wealth to go into the ministry. He'd given up a comfortable living to serve in Iraq. But his basic needs had always been provided for by his congregation. By the army. By his wife.

By me.

"I'm doing my best," I said.

"And how is *your* dear husband?" Miss Wanda asked.

"He's home today. Taking care of the twins."

"They grow up so fast," Miss Wanda said. "When are you having more?"

I felt a twitch of sympathy for Jo. *"That's all anybody ever asks,"* my sister had complained on one of her visits home. *"'When are you getting married? When are you having kids?' Like my only purpose in life is to procreate."*

I summoned a smile. "We're not in any rush. When it happens, it happens."

The Yorkie whined, eyes fixed on the plate of cheese. "You don't want to wait too long," Aunt Phee said, feeding another sample to her dog. "You're not getting any younger."

"No kidding. I feel like I'm dying standing here."

Aunt Phee emitted a snort of laughter, surprising us both.

"Did you want to buy any cheese today?" I asked, changing the subject.

"If the good Lord wanted us to eat cheese from goats, He would never have created cows."

"Polly seems to like it," I said.

Aunt Phee humphed. "I guess we could take some of that chèvre. You tell your father to come for dinner," she said as I wrapped it up.

"Yes, ma'am."

"Need another baguette?" Carl asked.

I looked over my dwindling pile of samples. "I can't leave my stall."

"I'll get it for you."

While I was counting money, Belle, Sallie's sister, surfaced from the crowd, her young children in tow. "Meg! I didn't realize you worked here."

"Just helping out Momma. Is this Logan? And Harper!" I smiled warmly at the kids. The little girl scuffed the toe of her pink UGGs on the ground. "You guys have gotten so big! Would you like to taste the cheese?"

Brightening, the child reached for a sample.

"No, no, Harper. She's not allowed to have cheese. Too much F-A-T," Belle explained, spelling the word out like something obscene. "Logan can have a piece, though."

The girl's face turned red. I smiled pleasantly at Belle, aware of Carl, hovering with the bread. "If you want a healthy snack for your children, you can't do better than goat cheese. Goat's milk is lower in fat than cow's milk. High in protein. And of course natural cheese doesn't have all those nasty emulsifiers and extenders and hydrogenated oils you find in other cheese products."

"How do you know all that?" Belle asked.

I'd looked it up on Google. "You forget, I grew up on a farm."

"We-ell . . . I suppose a little taste wouldn't hurt."

I handed the kids samples and was rewarded with shy smiles.

"I'll see you at Sallie's tonight?" Belle asked.

I nodded. "Looking forward to it. I thought I'd bring some of the marinated feta."

"Oh, I think she's got the food covered." Belle laughed. "Although, why not? We big girls need our healthy snacks, too."

"I always had fantasies about dating a farmer's daughter," Carl said when she'd gone.

I laughed. "Oh, please."

"It's true." He shifted out of my way so I could slice more bread. "I had a terrible crush on you in high school."

"You didn't even know me in high school."

"You didn't know me. I was only a freshman. Everybody knew you—the pretty senior on the homecoming court."

I turned my head, surprised and suddenly uncertain.

He winked. "Not that I would have done anything about it then."

I blushed. Not that I would do anything about it now. But it was nice to be, well, remembered. Noticed.

"So how about it?" Carl asked.

I stared at him blankly.

"The job," he said. "Doing our books. It's yours if you want it."

Temptation tugged. I'd always liked adding things up. Numbers in columns. Problems with solutions. I shook my head. "I've never kept books for a business before. You must know somebody more qualified."

"Nope," he said cheerfully. "There's just me now, and I can't run the farm and do all the paperwork."

"I'm sorry," I said regretfully. "Between the twins . . . and Momma . . . I really don't have the time."

"Could you at least maybe take a look? Ma's got her own special system, half on the computer and half paper files, and I can't make heads or tails out of any of it."

I smiled. "Sure, I could do that. Help you get organized."

"Great." He beamed. "That's just great. When can you start?"

"After the holidays?" I suggested.

"Whatever suits you. Unless you want to start now, earn a little Christmas money."

"Oh, you don't need to pay me."

"Sure I do. You're doing me a big favor."

I opened my mouth to protest. Held out my hand instead. "It's a deal."

He took my hand, tugged me forward, and kissed my cheek.

"Mommy, Mommy!" DJ and Daisy came darting through the legs of shoppers, holding up their adorable little arms. Where were their jackets?

"Hello, my babies." I stepped away from Carl. "Where did you come from?"

"Daddy brung us."

"We're Christmas tree shopping," John said.

I came around the table to give hugs. Raised my face for a brief, marital kiss. "What a nice surprise!" A memory stole over me like winter sunlight, John and me, shopping together for our first tree. Making love on the rug on Christmas morning, surrounded by tissue paper and the scent of pine. "Thanks for buying the tree. That's one more thing off my list!"

John offered a hand to Carl, sizing him up. "I don't think we've met. John Brooke."

"Carl Stewart."

They gripped hands a little too long, like arm wrestlers testing the competition.

"Carl has a farm stand, too. Over there." I stood, waving vaguely in the direction of the river. "He's been helping me."

"So I see." John gave me a level look. "I didn't mean to interrupt."

"You're not interrupting," I said.

"I'm just being nice so she'll come work for me," Carl said.

"Can I try that stuff in the jar?" a man asked.

"Marinated feta. Absolutely." I twisted open a lid. "It's a great appetizer. Or on salads."

He bought two jars of feta. I tucked his money into the cashbox. Almost out of singles, I noticed. I should have brought more.

"Come with us, Mommy," Daisy said.

"I wish I could, sweetie." Without her barrettes, her butchered bangs made her look like a little hedgehog. I smoothed back her hair, smooching her forehead.

"Mommy's busy," John said. "We'll get out of your way."

"You're not in the way."

A woman layered in scarves and sweaters, her feet in sandals—very earthy, very arty—picked up a log of chèvre. "Excuse me, is this cheese organic?"

I looked to Carl for guidance.

"Probably not certified organic," he said. "But humanely farmed and pasture grazed, am I right?"

I smiled at him gratefully. "Yes. And it's local."

"Cheese is cheese," her husband said.

He was talking about my mother's cheese. "Actually, cheese is an expression of the place where it's made. Like wine. So a cheese made from local goats has a flavor you can't get anywhere else."

"I'll take two," the woman said.

I wrapped the cheese, tucked their money into the cashbox.

A familiar wail jerked my head up. "Mommy, Mommy!"

"Mommy's busy." John had hefted Daisy in his arms and was holding DJ firmly by the hand. "Let's go."

"I'm never too busy for my babies," I protested. "I have to work, that's all."

"Right." His gaze flicked to Carl. "Say good-bye, kids."

"Bye, Mommy!"

"Bye!"

"Bye, my sweeties!" I gave them big, smacking kisses. "Ooh, your arms are cold. Where are your coats?"

DJ wriggled. "No coat."

"It's not that cold out," John said.

"You're right." I started to unzip my hoodie. "Here, why don't you—"

"Meg, they're fine. Keep your sweatshirt. We'll only be out a little while. You're here all day."

"Not all day," I protested. "I'll be home this afternoon. We're going to Sallie's tonight."

He looked at me a long moment. Leaning forward, he kissed me, a quick, skimpy kiss like the punctuation at the end of a sentence. A period, not an exclamation point. "See you at home."

I watched them go, three blond heads disappearing into the crowd.

CHAPTER 9

Jo

I wriggled my toes in Wonder Woman socks under my alcove table. It was Saturday morning, and I was putting the finishing touches on my blog. The topic—family meal—was sure to appeal to my New York hipster foodie audience. I'd posted the recipes I'd made last night next to surreptitious photos of hotel pans heaped with food.

I'd wanted my dishes to wow Chef, to prove to him I was worthy of his trust. But for most of the staff, family meal was the main—sometimes the only—meal they got all day.

"Why are we here?" Chef had asked me.

"To feed people."

I'd noticed that when the other chefs cooked, they prepared something hearty and filling, a pasta or a stew. So, resisting the urge to impress Chef with my technique (*Ha. Like that was ever going to happen*), I'd made comfort food from my childhood: smothered chicken, corn bread, and greens.

"This is fucking great, babe," Lucas had said, digging in.

Ray, the sous, had been less enthusiastic. "I would have blanched the collards," he said. But I noticed he took two helpings.

Too bad I didn't get a picture of *that*. No photos of the crew gathered like a big, happy, dysfunctional family around the table, dishwashers and back runners, cooks and servers, checking their phones, joking and talking in a mix of English and Spanish. I couldn't post anything that would identify them. Or me.

Unless someone recognized the food. But I hadn't photographed all the dishes, I reassured myself. No one was going to identify Gusto based on a chicken recipe that wasn't even on the menu.

I added a call to action at the bottom of my blog—What do YOU cook for a crowd?—before reading it over. Strategic content? Check. Long-tail keywords optimized for search? Check. Links to advertisers and related posts? Check and check. I'd learned a lot since those long-ago stories scribbled in my attic room. Or even since my first blog posts, written when I was still giddy with freedom, drunk on New York, swept off my feet by the experience of working in my first real restaurant kitchen under a Michelin-starred chef. *Hungry: Taking a Bite Out of the Big Apple* was my love letter to the food scene in the city, written with all the sizzle of service and the freshness of infatuation.

But lately I'd had this nagging sense of . . . I don't know. Something missing. As if I'd read everything before, on my own or someone else's blog. The thought filled me with mild panic.

I'd always known I was going to be a writer. I did not want—I couldn't afford—to fail. Again.

When we were growing up, our house was full of art projects Amy had started and abandoned, lopsided pots and half-pieced quilts and tangles of jewelry beads. *"An artist in search of a medium,"* our father called her wryly.

I never wanted him to say that about me. I was his dinner table audience, the straight-A student, the daughter who loved reading, the son he never had. When *Harry Potter and the Deathly Hallows* came out, he took me to the midnight release party at the bookstore. Not Beth, who was sick. Not Amy, though she begged and pouted to be allowed out past her bedtime. I'd grown up with Harry. I was wild to get my hands on the book. But the time with my father—just the two of us, alone—felt nearly as magical.

I shoved my hair into a ponytail and dragged a Windbreaker over my faded NYU sweatshirt. Hey, it wasn't like I was getting ready for a date. My idea of dressing up was basically throwing on a clean T-shirt and a pair of skinny jeans anyway.

I laced up my running shoes. Dressed and done.

At the bodega, I bought two cups of coffee, one for me and one for Dan the Homeless Guy. I walked down the street, sipping the hot liquid, warming my hands on the cup. The city that never sleeps was stretching and stirring, the rattle of early-morning construction like the twitter of birds back home. My feet took me back to yesterday's route, my body putting into motion a plan my mind hadn't quite acknowledged yet.

Ten minutes to the High Line. Pitching my empty cup into the trash, I headed up the stairs, my heart pounding as if I'd already run a mile.

A wind whipped off the river. The tall grass bowed and swayed. As I ran, my gaze bounced from the bright horizon to the graffiti-splashed buildings rising along the track.

And . . . He was there. Chef. In almost the same spot as yesterday.

Warmth flooded my midsection, more potent than the coffee. My cheeks were hot with happiness. *Stupid.*

He leaned against the wall of the shelter, watching the water. Waiting? For me?

I gave him a little wave, like a dope. "I'm not stalking you."

Laughter leaped into his eyes. "I am crushed," he said politely. "It is my dream that you follow me everywhere."

Ha. He'd made a joke. I thrust my hands into my pockets. "You're up early this morning."

Yesterday, I had almost finished my run and was on my way back before I saw him.

"Indeed. I have not been to bed."

"Late night?" I asked sympathetically.

It happened. When you were jazzed after a successful service—or,

God forbid, an unsuccessful one—after the kitchen was restored to gleaming order and the prep lists written up for the next day, it hardly seemed worthwhile to lie down for the few hours before you reported to work again. Chef didn't go out with the rest of the kitchen crew at the end of the night, doing the rounds of late-night bars and hookups. But maybe he'd stayed behind, working in the office. Maybe he had a whole other social life I didn't know anything about. Friends. A girlfriend.

The thought was vaguely depressing.

He shook his head. "I was home. I couldn't sleep."

"Gosh, I'm sorry. I hope it wasn't something you ate."

His eyes crinkled. "No. Your food last night was very good."

I flushed, ridiculously pleased. "Pretty simple stuff. I didn't season with anything but salt and pepper. Well, and a ham hock for the greens."

"Simple is best," Chef said. "That's how you honor your ingredients."

I grinned. "Right. By flattening the chicken in a cast-iron skillet and cooking the shit out of everything."

He laughed.

I grinned back, something inside me relaxing. My instructors at NYU had made it clear I would never be a Great Southern Writer. But I was a good Southern cook. Chef made me feel like it was okay to be myself. Like I was good enough without trying so hard.

Of course, he made everybody feel that way. The kitchen was full of misfits whose lives outside the restaurant were a mess. He taught them, trained them, inspired them to pull together as a team, to strive for perfection every night. Even me. The *idiot hipster food blogger*.

"They're my mother's recipes," I confessed. "We always had greens on the table."

"Ah yes, the collards." His mouth tugged in that small, ridiculously appealing smile. "Ray had seconds."

He'd noticed.

I glowed. "My mother always boiled them like that. For hours. To make pot likker."

"Vegetable stock."

I nodded. "With ham grease. It's a Southern thing. Sometimes she serves it in a cup with corn bread on the side."

That was what was missing from the blog, I realized suddenly. I'd listed the ingredients. I hadn't told the story.

"Then your food honors her, yeah?" His voice was kind. "The best cooking is from the heart."

My throat closed. I nodded, speechless.

"How is your mother?" Chef asked. As if he really wanted to know.

I swallowed hard. I was *not* going to weep all over him again. "They wheeled her to the dining room for dinner yesterday. And she walked down the hallway and back." A good day, according to Meg.

He nodded. His silence pulled at me like the end of the dock back home. *Jump on in. The water's fine.*

"The thing is . . ." I hesitated, then took the plunge. "My mother's always been so active. She runs that farm. Meg says she can hire someone to help when Mom gets out of rehab, but she's never had to depend on anyone before."

"I am sorry." His voice was kind, his eyes soft hazel.

I shrugged. "Whaddaya gonna do?" I asked, mimicking the New Yorker I'd tried so hard to become.

The real question was, What was I going to do?

But he took me literally. "I thought today I would run with you."

Wait. What? I looked at his feet. Yep, those were running shoes. Wide toe box, thick sole, well-cushioned and salt-grimed. Like mine.

He cocked an eyebrow. "Unless you prefer to run alone."

He made it sound like a choice. My choice. No pressure.

I smiled, suddenly light. Free. "Let's see if you can keep up."

I took off.

I heard the air escape his lungs—a gust of surprise or laughter—and then his shoes striking the path. For a big man, he was quick. The frantic pace of the kitchen, the constant cries of *Hot!* and *Behind!*, must have honed his reflexes. He caught up to me easily.

For a while we ran in tandem. Maybe I slowed down a little. Or maybe he adjusted his stride, matching his steps to mine. I snuck a look at his profile. He wasn't even breathing hard. I wasn't at race pace, but . . .

"How's your family? Your mother?" I heard myself ask.

His eyes did that crinkle thing, as if he found me amusing, but he answered politely. "She is fine, thank you. She and my father are spending the holidays with my sister in Frankfurt."

Ooh, a personal detail.

"You think when I was training that I went home to my mother every night?" he had asked me. *"That I asked for weekends and holidays off?"*

"I guess you won't be joining them," I said.

"Not this year. I will miss seeing them, of course. But Germany is not home for me. We were military." A quick glance. "You understand."

"Kind of. I mean, I get the whole military-culture thing. You must have felt it even more in a foreign country. But our family never had to move, except to the farm. We always had ties to the community."

To the land.

"Roots," Chef said, as if he could read my mind.

"Yeah."

Our feet pounded, side by side. Our breath puffed, intermingling in the cold air. I hadn't had a running partner since my cross-country days. I'd always liked running alone, with no one to measure against but myself. But running created an instant intimacy. Shared sweat or something.

"My mother says the farm is our heritage," I said. "But I couldn't wait to leave Bunyan. I always felt . . ." *Too bookish, too stubborn, too ambitious, too competitive.* "Like I didn't belong."

"Ah. In Germany, I was a *mischlingskinder*. Mixed race," he explained. "It is a term from the Second World War, when American GIs had brown babies with German women. The prejudice is not so bad as it was a generation ago, but . . ." He shrugged his big shoulders.

Not protesting the unfairness of it all. Just . . . sharing his feelings with me. As if I were somehow worthy of his confidence.

"There's prejudice here, too." Like he needed me to point that out. My hot face got hotter.

"Yes," he said simply. "But my roots are here, too. My boys are here."

His sons, I remembered, living with their mother near Fort Bragg.

I wondered how he'd met his ex-wife. How long had they been together? When did they get divorced? I wanted to know him better, beyond the bare facts of a Google search or the speculation in the kitchen. What was he looking for? But we didn't have the kind of relationship that I could ask.

We ran to the rail yards and back, a mile, a mile and a half, occasionally dropping into single file to pass a mother with a stroller, a tourist with a camera, an old couple holding hands. Always drawing level again, our shoulders rubbing, bumping companionably, the rasp of our breathing like a conversation without words. The sun painted a broad, broken swath of light across the river, splashing the tops of the towers with gold. Half a mile to go. Almost home.

I picked up my pace, pushing myself. Challenging him. Our rhythm changed. Our running transformed to something raw and alive, our breathing hard and ragged, our muscles hot and loose. My world expanded and contracted to the rush of my blood and the thud of our footsteps. It was exhilarating, like flying or swimming or sex.

When we reached the access stairs to the street, I pulled up, panting, perspiring, high on endorphins. Chef stopped beside me, radiating heat, his chest laboring in and out. I was laughing. He was not. Sweat trickled in the crease of his ear, under the curve of his jaw. I'd never minded sweat as a general thing. The body's coolant and all that. But now I wanted to lick his neck.

So this is lust, my mind said brightly. *Good to know. Pay attention to how it feels so you can write about it someday.*

Our eyes met.

I was drenched, my heart pounding. "Do you want to come to my place?"

That green gaze sharpened, bright as a broken bottle, all his fierce concentration focused now on me. "For breakfast," he said. Asking a question? Or setting a boundary?

My lungs burned. I could barely breathe. I'd never invested much energy in emotional entanglements. Relationships were messy. Demanding. Distracting. I tugged on my ponytail. "If that's what you want."

"What do you want?" he asked evenly.

Obviously he wasn't seized by a desire to drag me back to my place and rip off my clothes. Maybe he was afraid I'd accuse him of sexual harassment. Or maybe he had more self-control, more consideration, than any boy I'd ever been with.

My heart jerked.

He waited. Leaving the choice to me. Making my decision that much harder. That much easier.

"You have to follow your heart," my mother had said at Thanksgiving. *"No matter where it leads."* She'd been referring to Beth's audition, obviously, not my sex life. But she could have been talking about my move to New York. About taking a risk, about making a choice, about going for what you wanted with everything you had, even if you failed.

Chef Eric Bhaer was a risk. A bite of life I wanted desperately to take.

"I want you to come home with me," I said.

His smile—warm, approving, intimate as a kiss—started in his eyes. "I am hungry." His smile deepened mischievously. "Not for breakfast."

I led the way quickly back to my apartment, afraid to look at him in case he disappeared. Like Orpheus and Eurydice, and why I was even thinking about that now, I did not know. But he kept up with me, the way he had on the High Line. When we stopped to cross the street at the light, he took my hand. Startled, I glanced at him. Sex was one thing. Holding hands—in public, too—was something else, another level of intimacy, more Meg's thing than mine.

But his big, rough chef's hand felt so good holding mine. I held on, at least until we reached my building.

Climbing the steps to my apartment, I was aware of him behind me.

Not too close, just . . . There, muscled and sure, moving lightly, confidently up the stairs. I could feel his eyes on my butt. Or maybe that was my imagination.

I unlocked the door, squeezing to one side to let him enter.

Ashmeeta and I had chosen to sacrifice space for location, the way you do in New York. Even so, our studio apartment had always been big enough for the two of us. She'd had a bed by the window; I slept on a mattress on the platform above. Now that she was gone, I'd turned the alcove where her bed used to be into a space for my desk.

My desk. I threw a panicked glance at my laptop. Closed, thank you, Jesus.

Chef turned slowly in the center of my . . . Well, not a living room, exactly. One chair, two lamps, shelves crammed with books, cooking supplies, and photos from home. He was so much larger than Ashmeeta. Like a fire burning in the middle of the room, sucking up all the available oxygen.

What was I thinking, inviting him here? Into my space.

What was I supposed to say? *Want to climb a ladder and have sex?*

"I stink," he said. "Use your shower?"

Another question? Or a suggestion? I must stink, too.

"Uh, sure. Through there." I waved a hand in the direction of the tiny bathroom. Which I'd cleaned . . . Not recently. Damn it.

"Thanks." His eyes crinkled, and then he was gone, leaving me in possession of the empty room.

I drew a deep breath, wondering if I'd left hair clogging the drain. On the other side of the door, a faucet creaked on. I listened to the rush of water, imagined him tugging off layers of shirts.

His deep voice echoed in my head. *"What do you want?"*

Everybody I cared about was busy getting on with their lives, Ashmeeta with her job and Rachel with her boyfriend. Beth had her show, and Amy had Paris. Meg had John and the twins. I had . . . a blog. Readers. Advertisers, even. But I missed feeling connected to somebody by something more than words on a screen.

Before I lost my nerve, I stripped off my clothes and followed him into the bathroom.

Behind the steam-clouded glass, his shape moved, big and dark against the white tile. I opened the glass door.

He turned in a cloud of steam, soap lather sliding over his skin like foam on a wave. My heart was beating so hard I could almost hear it.

"March. You are . . ." He stopped.

"Naked?" I suggested.

Laughter leaped in his eyes. "I was going to say *beautiful*."

I grinned back, relieved. "For most guys, it's the same thing."

He shook his head. "Although naked . . . It's a good look on you."

"You, too," I said honestly.

His gaze met mine. His chest expanded. "Jo."

Just my name. Like he saw me. Like he wanted me, red face, wild hair, and all. My stomach relaxed and steadied.

"I thought you might need help scrubbing your back," I said, and stepped into the shower with him.

It was a tight fit. He had to put his arms around me so I could get under the warm spray. His body was warm, too, solid and slippery against mine.

His hand curved around my jaw. His thumb stroked my cheekbone, and then he was kissing me—slow, soft, unhurried kisses in delicious contrast to the hard demand of his body. He kissed like this was the main course instead of merely an appetizer, like he could go on kissing me for hours. Which was great, but I was hungry. Greedily, I ran my hands up his arms and around his neck, sinking against him, into him, trying to absorb as many textures as I could. He felt so good. I wanted to climb him like a tree.

He turned me, my back against the tile, protecting my face from the spray. "Jo." His voice was husky. "I didn't plan on . . . I don't have anything with me."

I was so drunk with what he *did* have—hot muscled smoothness—it took a moment for me to understand. "That's okay," I assured him. "I do."

Scrambling out of the shower, I lunged for the shelves, digging past the towels and toilet paper, grabbing and discarding boxes by feel. *Tissues, tampons* . . . There. At the back. *Condoms.* I'd bought them when I moved to New York, a single woman in the big city.

I turned, flushed with triumph at my foresight, brandishing the half-empty box like a prize.

He stood motionless under the shower, studying me as if I were a plate he was about to send through the pass. Serious. Focused. No smile at all.

"I don't do this a lot," I said. "Invite guys back to my apartment."

The corner of his mouth kicked up in that knee-weakening smile. "Then I better make it worth your while," he said, and pulled me with him under the spray.

In the cramped shower, he took up everything, all the space, all the air. He took *me* over, his hands following the flow of the water, gliding over my muscles and angles, the texture of his calluses grazing my skin. Broad hands, scarred, nicked, and tattooed. Strong hands, capable of breaking down a pig carcass or applying microgreens to a plate with delicate precision. Deliberate hands.

It was hot and wet, carnal and wonderful. I was drenched, drowning in sensation. In him. When the hot water finally ran out, when I was fed, filled, satisfied to bursting, he rolled me in towels and we staggered up to my loft so he could do it all again.

I didn't have my phone. For once, I didn't care. Chef sprawled on his back beside me, legs spread, one massive arm thrust under the pillow, the other anchoring the covers. The pale winter light illuminated the broad curve of his forehead, the shape of his lips, his curly lashes, dark against his cheek.

I snuggled into my pillow, relaxed, replete, simply existing in the moment. Fully present in my skin. I didn't need to check for comments on my blog. I wasn't worrying about texts from home.

But I did have to pee.

Cautiously, I sat, scooting toward the end of the mattress, holding my breath as I navigated over his feet.

My clothes still lay in a heap on the floor. I jammed them into my laundry bag and glanced at my phone on the dresser. Two messages from Meg—that's right, she was at the farmers' market this morning—and . . . Oh God, look at the time. I was going to be late for work. Surreptitiously, I scraped open a drawer.

If I took the phone with me into the bathroom, I could call Meg. I grinned a little. For once, I had something to tell her. I, prickly, unromantic, bad-tempered Jo, had just had wild crazy sexy times with my boss in the shower. And the loft. And it was awesome.

A sound, the merest vibration on the air, made me turn. "Chef."

The amused look was back. "Eric."

"Right." I knew his name from his bio. Not that I'd ever used it. I flushed, clutching my underwear to my chest. Like he hadn't spent the past few hours exploring everything I had to offer. "I didn't mean to wake you. I was just . . ."

"Getting dressed."

"Yeah." I watched as he turned and descended the ladder. Well, who wouldn't? He had a butt like a football player. Years of working in restaurant kitchens had made him agile in tight, confined spaces. As he'd already demonstrated this morning. Twice.

He stood before me, a large, naked man, at ease in his body.

"Do you want to, um, borrow a clean T-shirt?" I asked.

His expression climbed from a four to a six on the amusement scale. "I do not think your clothes will fit me."

"Very funny." I rummaged in the drawer again. "Here."

He looked at it for a long moment. Looked at me. Like maybe he didn't want to wear another man's shirt. And then, with a shrug, he pulled it over his head.

"I have a lot of them," I said.

"I see."

"I buy them big. To sleep in."

He glanced down at his chest. "NYU," he read, upside down. "This is where you went to school?"

"Graduate school. Yeah." Exchanging small talk, the way you did with strangers before you had sex. Something had been lost when I climbed out of bed. I swallowed. "Sorry. I'm not very good at this."

"On the contrary," he said politely.

"That's sex. I like sex." At least, I'd liked sex with him. Something to think about later. "I'm not very good at . . ." Relationships? We didn't have a relationship. He was my *boss*. "The part that comes after."

"This part."

"Yes."

He regarded me thoughtfully. "Sex is like food, yeah? Something the body needs. Maybe a dish is not prepared to your liking, but if you are hungry, you eat. Maybe next time you make it a little differently. Or you choose something else."

I nodded. What was he trying to say?

"But sometimes . . ." His hand curved around my neck, drawing me close. Closer. "You try something so much to your taste, you would not change a thing. So good," he whispered against my lips, "you don't want anything else." His thumb stroked the side of my throat, making my skin prickle to attention. "I have such a taste for you, Jo."

Everything inside me melted: my brain, my knees, my spine. He kissed me, warm, openmouthed kisses, coaxing my response, making me hungry for him all over again.

"I'm going to be late for work," I warned several minutes later.

He glanced over my head at the clock. "It's only noon."

Right. Because he came in later, after the rest of the staff, when the bulk of the prep work was done.

"I have to be there by one," I reminded him.

Reluctantly, it seemed, he released me. "Then I will take you."

"Um. I don't think we should go in together. I don't want everybody thinking I'm one of your . . ."

He raised an eyebrow. "One of my . . ." Definitely a question this time.

Well, shoot. In all fairness, he didn't have a reputation for shagging the staff—no more than I made a habit of inviting men up to my apartment. But I didn't want him to think I was angling to turn our hookup into, well, anything else.

"I don't want to put you in an awkward position," I mumbled, my gaze anchored to his chest.

"Jo." His voice was patient. "People will see what they want to see. Whether we walk in together or not."

"But they'll talk."

"Let them. If I walk down the sidewalk wearing a hoodie, to some eyes I look like a thug. But that's on them. I don't have to be limited by their vision. Who I am, what I choose to wear or do . . . That's on me, yeah? I am myself, whatever they choose to see."

"Easy for you to say."

"You think so," he said without inflection.

Oh God. Had I actually just told him that it was *easy* for him to be himself when other people—strangers, customers, cops—judged him by his appearance?

My face flamed. "I only meant . . . You're *Chef.*"

"Eric. And you . . . You are yourself." I looked up. He met my gaze. The curve of his mouth almost undid me. "Jo."

I smiled back uneasily. Because I hadn't been myself with him. Not completely.

It was okay to hide the whole blogger thing when he was simply my boss, I rationalized. I mean, I didn't know everything there was to know about him, either. But now . . . How much of the truth did I owe him now?

What did I owe myself?

CHAPTER 10

Meg

Even though I was gone from the twins all day, I showered and blow-dried my hair when I got home. Shaved my legs. Shaved everywhere, my heart quickening in anticipation. As if I had all the time in the world. As if I were single and childless again, getting ready for a big date instead of going to a Christmas party at Sallie's.

I'd always liked dressing up, doing my hair and nails and makeup. Unlike Jo, who considered most feminine rituals with scowling suspicion. When we were younger, I practically had to drag her to prom.

The whole concept of prom is an outdated fantasy," Jo had declared as we got ready in my room. Beth and Amy curled against the pillows, watching me primp, taking pictures, while Jo sprawled across the foot of the bed, her nose in a book, as usual. I glanced at the cover. *The Second Sex* by Simone Somebody. "Part of an archaic culture that perpetuates normative gender roles," Jo continued loftily.

I plugged in my flat iron, determined that tonight my hair would achieve the glossy smoothness of a model in *Elle* magazine. "If you're expecting me to make a snappy comeback, you're going to have to speak English."

Jo flopped onto her stomach, wrinkling her dress. "I mean, it's stupid. All that fuss, waiting for some boy to ask you out. I don't need a date to a dance to validate my feelings of self-worth."

"You only say that because Trey asked you weeks ago," Amy said.

"Because we're friends," Jo said. "At least Trey isn't going to get all weird on me."

"Prom isn't about your date. Not really," I said. "It's a rite of passage."

I was going with Ned Moffat. A sort of pity date, because Sallie got tired of waiting for him to ask and accepted Charlie Campbell's promposal instead. Trey was picking us all up in his grandfather's town car (Mr. Laurence had hired a driver and everything), and we were all meeting up at the Gardiners'—before prom, to get our pictures taken with all our friends, and for the after-party.

"It's about being with your friends," Beth said.

"Shopping for a dress," Amy said.

I nodded. "Buying shoes."

Jo regarded my pretty silver sandals doubtfully. "You'll probably break an ankle in those things."

Amy sighed with just a touch of envy. "I think you look beautiful."

"You both do," Beth said.

Jo clambered off the bed to stand beside me in front of the mirror. "I guess we don't look so bad, do we?"

I smoothed the skirt of my silver gown. I'd bought it off the sales rack at the old-ladies' shop in town, but Momma and Amy had transformed it, taking off the sleeves, altering the bodice to fit just right. Jo dug her dress out of the church donation pile, but if you didn't notice the stain on the skirt, she looked really nice.

I smiled. "Not bad at all." I tested the temperature of the flat iron. "All right, it's ready."

"Right." Jo brandished the hot straightening wand. "Let's do your hair."

~

My phone lit up, interrupting the flow of memories.

I smiled. It was like Jo was psychic or something.

But it wasn't Jo, it was Amy, WhatsApp-ing from Paris, four thousand miles and six hours away. "Hey, sweetie," I said warmly. "How's life in the fashion world?"

I propped the phone against the mirror so I could see her face as we talked. Or rather, as she talked and I listened, making occasional encouraging noises.

Our Amy would never admit it, but she sounded homesick. Well, it had been hard for her, leaving Mom. She'd had only a week to settle into her new job, her new digs. I reckoned she must be feeling lonely.

I listened as she hinted at some workroom drama, told a story about a club she went to the night before, a British boy band she followed on YouTube. "You went by yourself?" I asked. "What about your roommate? Chloe?"

A hesitation, so short I could blame it on the phone app. "She had other plans."

I dotted concealer under my eyes. "You could have asked somebody else."

"Meg, this is Paris," Amy said. "People here stick to themselves. Unless your French is, like, perfect. Anyway, it was a good thing I was alone, because I went around back afterward. To meet them, you know? And Fred Vaughn was trying to talk to his fans, and I got to translate for him, and . . ." She paused dramatically. "He asked me to hang out with them backstage!"

Of course he did. Because things happened for Amy. She made them happen. "That's amazing."

"Right? So then I followed him on Instagram, and Meg—this is the best part—he just followed me back!"

Carefully, I applied eye shadow. "Why is that the best part?"

"Because he's got over a hundred thousand followers. Even more on

Twitter. So if he follows me, and his followers follow me, it builds brand recognition for my line."

I smiled at her enthusiasm. "You have a line now?"

"I will," Amy said. "Anyway, Vaughn invited me to New York to see them play at some club on New Year's Eve. It's not Times Square, but still . . . New York! I've always wanted to visit the Garment District. Go to Mood!"

I lowered my lash brush. "I thought you had to stay in Paris this Christmas."

"I do. Not that there's anything really happening here over the holidays. The studio is clearing out already." Amy sighed. "But I can't afford to come home."

"If you need us to help . . ." I offered. A last-minute ticket over Christmas would cost the moon. But it would be worth it, to have my sister home.

"No, no," Amy said. "I'm fine. You know me, I'll find something to do. How are you all? How's Mama?" She pronounced the word the French way, *MaMA*.

"Momma's fine." Should I tell Amy about the fall? But she'd been so upset, leaving when our mother was in the hospital. I didn't want to worry her more. "Sweetie, I have to go. John and I are going to a party tonight at Sallie Moffatt's."

"Oh." Amy's pretty face fell. "I should let you get dressed."

"I am dressed."

"Not for a party at Sallie Moffatt's."

I glanced down at my black slacks and sweater. "What's wrong with what I have on?"

"Nothing, if you want to look like Mom. Do you still have that red dress? The wrap one?"

"It doesn't fit."

"How do you know?"

"Amy, that dress is older than the twins. I bought it before I got pregnant."

"It looked great on you. You should try it on. With shapewear, obviously."

Five minutes later, I eyed my reflection in the mirror, my face almost as red as my dress.

"Hot," Amy said.

"Very hot. I'm sweating from getting into this thing. And my stomach sticks out."

"Nobody's going to look at your stomach. They'll be staring at your boobs."

I laughed, slightly out of breath. The shapewear squished and reshaped my post-baby bod, squeezing my mommy tummy to cleavage. "Is that supposed to make me feel better?"

"It should. The girls look great," Amy said.

"Well." I twisted and turned in front of the mirror. The dress swirled and settled around my knees, pretty and feminine. "You don't think it's too much?"

"Nope," Amy said firmly. *"Très élégant."*

I checked my reflection one final time. Bank Meg smiled back at me.

"Don't you look pretty," Miss Hannah said as I came downstairs.

"Thank you! Thanks for coming tonight."

"It's my pleasure. You all have a good time."

I turned hopefully to John. He looked me up and down, smiling in the old way, his brown eyes warm. "Nice," he said. "New dress?"

I twirled. "This old thing?"

"Pretty, Mommy!" Daisy said. DJ watched mistrustfully over his thumb.

"Thank you, sugarplum." I stooped to kiss their smooth blond heads. Despite the shapewear, I could still bend. I breathed in their good, fresh-from-the-bath baby smell. "Be good for Miss Hannah now. Say night night to Daddy."

They bounced into his arms. "Night night, Daddy."

"Daddy, night."

He hugged and kissed them. "Good night, cookie monsters. I love you."

They hugged him back, all smiles. But when I got my coat, DJ clung and Daisy wailed.

"You go on," Miss Hannah said. "We'll be fine."

I handed DJ over to her capable arms, feeling guilty.

"I've never left them with anyone but Momma," I said to John in the car.

"They'll settle down as soon as you leave."

I snuck a look at his profile, lit by the glow of the dashboard. "They're probably upset I was gone all day."

"They'll get over it."

I clasped my hands in my lap. "I thought maybe you were upset, too."

"I don't like to see you work so hard all the time, that's all." He glanced my way. His slow smile warmed me from the inside out. "It's good for you to get out sometimes."

An electric pulse flickered inside me, like the tick of the turn signal. "It's good for us to get out."

He didn't say anything. Communication wasn't our strong suit. But he reached across the console and took my hand, holding it on his thigh all the way to Sallie's. His hand was warm and firm on mine. The flicker became a current. I felt happy, breathless, and not just because the shapewear was cutting off my air. The white lines on the road beyond our windshield flashed by like we were finally getting somewhere.

Sallie and Ned had bought a house on a golf course in the same gated community as her parents. We drove past lit tennis courts and landscaped ponds, up a long, circular driveway to a parking area filled with Lexuses and Land Rovers, Teslas and Maseratis.

"There's Trey's car," I said.

A valet opened my door. I stepped out, off-balance in my party heels.

John handed the valet the keys and came around, steadying me with a hand on my elbow. He shot a wry glance up the curving double staircase to the front door. "You didn't tell me your friends lived at Tara."

"We've been here before," I said.

"You were here," he said. "For a shower or something."

A baby shower for Belle, back when John and I were first married. Before I got pregnant. I squeezed John's arm as we went up the steps. "It does feel a little like a movie set." Or a magazine spread, the December issue of *Architectural Digest*, maybe, or *Southern Living*, white lights everywhere, twining on the crepe myrtles in the yard, glowing in the windows, twinkling along the path to the boat dock. Full-size Christmas trees, decked in more lights and red ribbon, framed the open door and the people milling around inside.

"Thanks for buying the tree today," I said to John.

He shrugged, handsome and uncomfortable in a navy blazer and tie. "One tree. Big deal."

"If I don't have to do it, it is a big deal." He slanted a look down at me. I stumbled. "I mean . . ."

"I know what you meant," he said quietly.

"Meg, you came. How nice." Belle, materializing out of the glittering crowd in the foyer, wore wide-legged silk pants and a very sheer top. Obviously she didn't need shapewear. Or a bra, apparently. "And you must be Jim."

"John."

"Of course. Welcome."

My dress was all wrong, I thought as we exchanged air kisses. I resisted the urge to tug at the nylon creeping into my butt crack.

"Hey, Hot Mama." Sallie's husband, Ned, appeared, drink in hand, and moved in for a hug. "You're on fire tonight."

I smiled and hugged him back, flattered and reassured. For a very, very short time our junior year, Ned and I had been a couple. "Thanks. John, you remember Ned."

They shook. "Let me get you a drink. What's your handicap now?

Sallie's around somewhere," Ned said to me, waving toward the guests circulating downstairs. "You should let her know you're here."

"Where should I put this?" I raised my decorated bag of marinated feta.

"Oh, you brought a gift. This way." Belle navigated the crowd, confident as the queen bee she'd always been. I followed her, part of her court.

The guests ranged from our age to our parents', the women all shiny, the men in khakis and button-down shirts. Except for the waiters, John was the only man in a tie. A server offered me champagne on a tray. Other servers passed plates of giant shrimp, tiny sandwiches, little bites on skewers. Like at a wedding reception. I looked over my shoulder for John.

"Meg! Oh, I'm so glad to see you!" Sallie embraced me, careful not to spill my wine. "Is this for me? You are so sweet. Everybody, you know Meg."

I did know them, most of them, Sallie's posse, high school pals. Susie Perkins, May Chester, Rose Campbell and her adopted sister, Phebe. Members of Sallie's wedding party, friends from her neighborhood, all with white, white smiles and expert manicures.

"How was the beach?" I asked Sallie.

She shrugged, flipping her perfect highlights over one shoulder. "Oh, you know. Sterling got stung by a jellyfish, and the boys were off playing golf all day, and Mother got mad because Belle complained about missing all the Black Friday sales when everybody knows she does all her shopping online. She won't set foot in the mall. So Daddy . . ."

I sipped champagne as the conversation shifted to ski trips to Park City and Banff, cruises and Caribbean vacations. Sallie and Ned were going to Hawaii in January. Belle was talking about Mexico. I liked listening to them, the gurgle and flow of feminine voices as familiar and comfortable as waves rippling on shore. I helped myself to a slider filled with some kind of spicy meat—Jo would know—washed down with more champagne.

"I haven't done Cancún since spring break days," Susie said.

"We go to Sanara in Tulum," Belle said. "The yoga studio is right on the beach."

Across the room, John stood, hands in pockets, head to one side, part and yet apart from the group discussing golf or whatever it was men talked about at parties. Cars? He had probably sold, serviced, or financed most of those fancy vehicles outside. The sight of him—blond and broad-shouldered—kicked my memory.

John, his fair hair shining under the stadium lights, making his way purposefully toward me on the sidelines. "Hello, Meg."

"You remembered my name."

He looked adorably, momentarily confused. "Why wouldn't I remember your name?"

"Because we're not at the bank. I'm not wearing my name tag."

He smiled. "You don't need a name tag. I know you."

"Are you and John going anywhere after the holidays?" Rose asked politely.

"Oh. No." I took another sip from my champagne flute. "We can't leave the kids. Or my mother. She's still in the hospital."

Belle and Sallie exchanged a quick, significant glance.

"I heard. I'm so sorry," Rose's sister, Phebe, said.

"How is your mother?" Sallie asked kindly.

My head was pleasantly fizzy. Maybe I couldn't afford a trip to Hawaii. But at least for tonight I wanted to escape my everyday self. My everyday life. My to-do lists.

Ned swam up by my shoulder, red-faced and hospitable. "Your glass is empty. Let me get you a refill." He signaled to a waiter.

"Oh, I don't . . . I shouldn't . . ." I looked around for John. He'd left the guys and was talking to one of the servers with that caring attention that was so attractive.

"Haven't you had enough?" asked Sallie. I set down my flute in confusion. "Not you, Meg. Ned, you know what the doctor said about motility."

"Christ, Sallie, for one night, can we not talk about my sperm?" Ned picked up my glass and his own. "Come on, Meg. Let's get away from Debbie Downer here."

I looked at Sallie.

"Ned's right. It's a party." She waggled her fingers, her diamonds catching the light. "Go have fun."

It's a party, I repeated to myself as I tagged after Ned. Maybe John would follow? Ned grabbed drinks from a passing tray. We circulated, making our way toward the back of the house, pausing to chat, saying hi to people I'd known since high school.

"Like old times," Ned said as we found a quieter spot overlooking the water.

"Boys on one side of the room, girls on the other?"

"Sneaking wine coolers on the back deck."

I laughed. "My choice in drinks has improved." So had my choice in dates. I glanced over my shoulder at John. He was still in the corner listening to the waiter, a youngish man, not much older than the boys John used to teach. His students had loved him. He could focus on you like he was genuinely interested in what you had to say, like you were the most fascinating, important person in the world.

He'd looked at me that way. *"Can I take you home?" he'd asked, watching me with those warm, brown eyes. "Or we can drive to the beach. Spend the night. Watch the sun come up."*

I smiled harder at Ned, compensating for my husband's inattention. Ned slid closer, whiskey on his breath. I pretended not to notice.

"I thought I saw you out here." Trey swooped in and kissed my cheek. "Hey, Ned. Great party."

Ned eased away. "Thanks, man."

"Picked up some cigars for you when I was out of the country. Cohibas."

Ned's eyes got big, like a child's on Christmas morning. "Cuban?"

"Box says Dominican." Trey winked. "Left them under the tree. Merry Christmas."

"Wow. Thanks." Ned glanced from me to Trey. "Guess I'll go blow a cloud. Excuse me."

"Impressing a client?" I asked when he was gone.

"Impressing the old boyfriend?" Trey returned dryly.

I flushed. "I'm just having fun."

"Are you?" Trey asked quietly.

No. "Of course." Flirting with Ned . . . It was silly, harmless high school behavior.

"Where's John?"

"Talking to a waiter."

Trey quirked an eyebrow. "I didn't expect someone from your family to be a snob."

"I am not a snob. I'm . . ." *Let down. Lonely,* I admitted to myself. The one person I really wanted to spend time with was John. For one electric moment in the car, feeling the flex of his thigh under our joined hands, I'd felt that old chemistry. That familiar connection. And now the evening had gone as flat as the bubbles in my champagne. "I don't know why John can't relax and mingle with everybody else." I winced at the whiny sound of my voice. Took another sip of wine.

"Give him a break, Meg. He's the new kid here. You all have known each other since kindergarten."

"You didn't have any trouble fitting in when you moved here."

"You and your sisters made sure of that. Besides . . ." Trey stopped.

His hesitation, the turn of his head, jolted me out of my self-absorption, reminded me of the lonely boy we had befriended almost fifteen years ago. "Besides . . . ?"

He met my gaze. "Money buys a lot of friends."

"Oh, Trey." I felt an almost maternal tug. "People don't like you because you have money. You're a good guy. You're kind and smart and fun to be with. And you're not exactly ugly."

"I wish your sister thought so."

I knew, of course, which sister he referred to. "My sisters love you," I said. "We all love you."

"Sure." His smile flickered. "Thanks."

"Come on." I tucked my arm in his. "Let's go back to the party."

We mixed and mingled. So many people wanted to talk to Trey. A lot asked after my mother or my father. I thanked them, smiled, and moved on, looking in vain for John. I felt like a Cinderella who had stayed too late at the ball. My feet hurt. My shapewear chafed.

"You okay?" Trey asked as I squirmed.

"Yes, I just . . ." I was not confessing to Trey that my underwear was rubbing a blister in the crease of my butt. I set down my empty glass. "I don't feel so good. Excuse me a minute?"

The powder room was already occupied. I backed away from the door. Glanced up the stairs. Surely Sallie wouldn't mind . . . ?

Her bedroom door was open, coats piled on the bed. I nipped in, out of sight of anyone passing in the hall, and hiked my skirt to my waist. I stretched and jiggled, trying to shift my shapewear. A toilet flushed. I froze as a door on the other side of the room opened, and Ned walked out, his pants gaping. *Ack! Ick!*

"Shit!" he yelled.

"Sorry!"

Ned fumbled for his zipper. "What are you—"

Trey stuck his head in the door. "Are you all . . . Oh. Hey."

Heat swarmed my face. My entire body burned. His black, observant gaze skipped from my exposed underwear to Ned's unbuckled belt. I dropped my skirt hastily. "I just came up to fix my . . ."

"I had to use the bathroom," Ned blurted.

"Meg?" It was John. Of course he'd come looking for me *now*. "You ready to go?"

I smoothed my dress over my thighs with fingers that trembled only slightly. "Yes."

John's brows flicked together. "Everything okay?"

I nodded, wordless with embarrassment.

Trey looked like he was trying not to laugh. "She wasn't feeling well. I brought her upstairs to get your coats."

It wasn't a bad lie. But . . .

"She didn't have a coat," John said.

Trey shrugged. "I didn't know."

John looked at me. "You didn't tell him?"

"No coat. Sorry," I said to Trey. Or John. I wasn't sure.

John frowned.

"Well. Time to go. Thank you for a lovely party," I said to Ned.

And escaped.

D id you have a nice time?" I asked John on the way home. "It was fine."

"I was looking for you. I missed you," I said.

"It looked to me like you were having a pretty good time without me."

"With drunk Ned?"

"I don't pick your friends."

I shifted on the soft leather seat, trying to dislodge my wedgie. "They're your friends, too."

John grunted. "They're customers, Meg. I'm just the car guy."

"So, what did you all talk about all night?" I asked. "Cars?"

"Boats." John slid a glance at me, a hint of humor softening his set expression. "Apparently size matters."

I smiled. "I can see why you decided to hang out with the waiter."

"The waiter? Oh, Hunter. He's home from college, making a little money over the holidays. He was in my American history class. On the wrestling team, too."

"He seemed very interested in what you were saying."

"He's a junior now. Starting to think about careers." John glanced at me. "He wants to be a teacher."

"You were a great teacher. Not that you're not wonderful at your job now," I added quickly. Being supportive.

He didn't say anything.

I tried again. "And of course you make more money at the dealership than you could in teaching. Teachers don't get paid anything close to what they deserve."

"That's what I told him. But it's a great job, teaching. If you don't have a family to support." John switched on the radio. We listened to music the rest of the way home, James Taylor singing "Have Yourself a Merry Little Christmas" in a mournful key.

I'll be right up," I promised John after Hannah had gone.

He did not look at me. "Take your time. I've got some work to do."

Again? But how could I complain? It was my fault he had to work so late.

I drifted through the downstairs. Miss Hannah had left our house as tidy as her own, all the toys picked up, the counters wiped free of crumbs. I transferred a load of laundry from the washing machine to the dryer. Added soap to the dishwasher. Adjusted the thermostat.

My phone buzzed with a message from Jo. Call me!!! ☺☺😳♥, the giddy string of emojis more like Amy than Jo.

I smiled wistfully. Something had made my sister happy—something besides her usual fabulous life in New York. I wanted to hear all about it. But not tonight. Hard enough to pretend to myself that everything was all right. I'd never fool my sister.

I texted her a brief update on Momma and then—feeling guilty for dodging Jo's call—sent her a picture of me in my dress.

I couldn't wait to take it off.

I went upstairs to check on the twins. They looked so sweet in the dim glow of the night-light, like cherubs, like sugarplums. "God bless, my babies," I whispered. "Sleep tight."

John's light was on at the end of the hall, but I didn't go to his office.

I peeled out of my clothes, the hated shapewear like a cicada chrysalis, pale brown and shiny, the corpse of my pre-baby body. I stuffed it into the hamper and got into bed, lying with my eyes closed as John came in and turned on the shower. He always showered at night. I loved the way he slipped into bed, smelling like soap and clean, male skin.

He kissed my cheek.

"John?"

"Mm?" He moved down to my neck.

"Is everything all right?"

"Mm."

"I just wondered . . ." I squirmed. His mouth was hot and gentle on my breast. "You seemed kind of upset earlier."

"Honey, I'm fine."

Of course he was *fine*. When you're the oldest child, you're always *fine*, because there's always somebody younger than you who's *not* fine and needs attention.

"It's just . . . We never talk anymore."

"We talk," he said a bit defensively.

"About our schedules. Or the kids. Not about us. Not about our feelings."

"Honey, I'm a guy. We don't sit around discussing our feelings."

"We used to," I reminded him. "We used to talk for hours." About everything and nothing at all. About our hopes and fears, our plans and our dreams, about where to go out for dinner or what was on TV. Or we could sit in silence and be perfectly in tune.

He sighed and rolled away, punching his pillow to stuff it under his head. "Fine. What do you want to talk about?"

I didn't know how to ask for what I wanted. I didn't want to sound as if I was complaining. "Tell me something important," I said.

"Like what?"

"Tell me what you want out of life."

"Besides sex?"

I sputtered with laughter. "John!"

He turned on his side to face me, his warm, brown eyes on mine. His thumb traced the shape of my smile. "There it is," he said quietly. "I want you to be happy, Meg."

My heart melted. "Oh, John." That was so lovely. How could I be anything but grateful? "That's it?"

"That's not enough for you?"

I grabbed his hand. "Of course it's enough. It would be enough for anybody. But what about you? What do *you* want, John?"

"I want to take care of you. You and the kids."

"You do. You work so hard. I love you, John."

His face was sober. "Love you, too, honey."

"But I want you to be happy, too."

"I told you, I'm fine." I searched his face, unconvinced. "Let it go, Meg," he said in his Coach voice.

I could push. But I didn't want to fight. And maybe there was a chance we could get this night back on track. I squeezed his hand again.

John raised on one elbow to kiss my forehead. "Good night, honey."

"Are you tired?"

"Kids will be up before you know it," he said. "You should get some sleep."

"You're right." I kissed him back softly. "Good night, John."

But it was a long, long time before I fell asleep.

CHAPTER 11

Jo

"Hot, hot!"
    "Knife."
"Behind!"

All around me, manic cooks stirred, seared, and sautéed, clanking pans and scraping spoons like the rhythm section of a dysfunctional orchestra. Fat sizzled. Pots bubbled. Intake hoods roared. Two hours into service, the bar was buzzing and the dining room packed. The printers spat orders nonstop into the kitchen.

Eric commanded the center of the storm at the pass, feet planted shoulder-width apart, a black bandanna knotted around his head like a pirate's. My fingertips tingled, itching to push beneath the texture of his hair, to find the strong shape of his skull.

I expelled my breath. *Hoo, boy.*

"Rib eye up," Lucas yelled from the meat side, his voice fraying.

I jerked forward, pot in hand. My elbow knocked a half-full hotel pan from the flat-top, spilling buttery browned circles of potato fondant all over the floor.

Crap. Crappity crap.

Ray, on fish, swore. "Get it together, March. What's got into you today?"

Your boss, I thought inappropriately. My boss. Eric.

All through service, I'd been acutely conscious of him, touching, tasting, plating, his strong hands coaxing and sure, teasing exactly the response he wanted from every gleaming entrée, every delicately placed garnish. The soft, secreted nerve endings inside me twitched to insistent life.

"Sorry," I mumbled.

I willed myself not to glance toward Eric. It wasn't his job to rescue me.

But of course he heard. He heard everything that went on in his kitchen.

"Veg on the fly," he said. "How long?"

Handling me—his clumsy prep cook, his onetime hookup—like one more spinning plate in his juggling act at the pass.

My face burned as I calculated my time. The goal was to get all the ingredients to the pass at the same time so that Eric could plate. A second pan of potatoes, already seared and seasoned, waited for the kiss of butter and thyme that would bring them back to life. "Three minutes, Chef." Impossible in this environment even to imagine calling him anything else.

"Push back the rib eye," he instructed Lucas. "Three minutes, yeah?"

"Yes, Chef."

Eric plucked a ticket from the rattling printer. "Ordering," he called, focusing all eyes back on him. "Table twelve, two charcuterie. Followed by one pappardelle, two sea bass, one rib eye, medium rare."

A chorus of assent echoed back. *Yes, Chef. Oui, Chef.*

I threw down pans for vegetables and heated up sauce. Beneath my cheap chef's jacket, I was sweltering. Sweating. I'd be playing catch-up all night now. Did I have enough? Should I have prepped more potatoes? Two minutes and fifty seconds later, I grabbed my pots and headed for the pass.

Eric accepted my offerings without a word. Deftly, he composed the dish, scattering gold coins of potatoes around the plate, dotting orbs of flavor in a seemingly random arrangement. Instagram stuff. #foodporn.

He paused. Considered.

I held my breath. Not that I needed his approval. He wasn't my father.

But he was my boss. He'd taken a chance on me tonight, putting me on entremets when Frank called out sick. Cooking was a job for me, not a career. But I wanted to impress him, wanted to believe my best was good enough. So, yeah, okay, a *little* approval would be nice.

He glanced up. His eyes crinkled, just barely, before he touched my shoulder. The fleeting gesture seared through my chef's jacket all the way down to my toes. Amazingly, I did not dissolve into a puddle of lust and relief on the floor.

"Service!" he called, and turned back to the board.

Good. Fine. No special treatment, no favoritism, no gossip.

I retreated to my station, my cheeks still burning with residual heat.

Five hours later, the last tickets—desserts and salads, late-night stuff—had been cleared from the rack. Eric called the last order and disappeared into his office, leaving Ray in charge of the pass. The crowd out front had dwindled to a couple of college girls on barstools flirting with the manager and a four-top of campers who wouldn't leave until we turned out the lights. I hauled my pans to the dishwashing station. Isaam and Tomas were moving mountains of pots and plates, the spray from their hoses raising clouds of steam. My back ached. My feet hurt as if I'd just completed a marathon. I was dehydrated, depleted, my blood buzzing with a potent cocktail of adrenaline and endorphins like a runner's high.

Ray shut off the heat lamps. "Right. Start breaking down."

My station looked like a battlefield, debris everywhere, shriveled corpses of potatoes scattered on the rubber mat by my feet. I attacked the mess, labeling and stowing the mise en place away. Scrubbed the tabletop, polishing the stainless until it shone. Knotted my trash chute bag and carried it out back.

Lucas was smoking by the loading dock, shoulders hunched against the December wind sneaking down the alley. He jumped as the door opened.

"It's only me," I said.

The cooks all copped their cigarette breaks when Chef wasn't likely to see them. Eric did not smoke. Bad for the palate, he said.

I looked around for the alley cat but it was off hunting. Or invisible in the dark.

Lucas took another drag. "Nice job tonight."

A little glow, like the spark from his cigarette, warmed my insides. "Thanks."

"Chef really threw you into the fire, putting you on the line like that."

I shrugged. "You know what they say. If you can't stand the heat . . ."

"Get out of the kitchen?"

I hefted the trash bag into the Dumpster. "Don't piss off the dragon," I said.

Lucas laughed, short and sharp. Together, we trudged back inside. I shook out the black carpet runner under my station. Swept the floor.

Kevin, the back waiter, almost unrecognizable in his street clothes, appeared. "We're headed to The Spot. You in?"

I hesitated. The bar would be packed with restaurant folk fresh out of service, flush with tips and gossip. Good blog material.

"Go. You've done enough here," Ray said.

"Gee, thanks. Was that supposed to be a compliment?" I asked.

The sous looked down his nose at me. "If you choose to take it that way." He pursed his lips. Added grudgingly, "You did all right tonight."

"Um. Thank you."

"Come on," Kevin urged. "I'll buy you a beer. You earned it, baby."

I needed a drink. I could almost taste the beer, crisp and cold, sliding over my parched palate, down my dry throat. I glanced toward the office. "You go ahead," I said. "Maybe I'll see you there."

Eric sat at his desk, an open bottle of water and a clipboard of things to do in front of him. I stopped in the doorway, unaccountably shy. Reluctant to interrupt.

Stupid. My clothes were in there. My coat. What was I going to do, ride the subway dressed like a giant marshmallow?

I marched to the closet and yanked it open.

"Good service tonight," Eric said behind me.

"I dropped the potatoes," I blurted.

"We all make mistakes the first time, yeah? That's how we learn."

I turned. He had leaned back in his chair, watching me. The top button of his chef's coat was undone, exposing the dark hollow of his throat. He looked tired. Well, I was exhausted, and he worked harder than I did.

I raised an eyebrow. "Are you speaking from experience, or is this some Teutonic aphorism you learned at your mother's knee?"

His face lit with laughter, and something turned over inside me. My heart.

Ray stuck his head in the doorway. Like he'd been hanging around outside, waiting for the perfect moment to interrupt. "Starting the menu meeting, Chef."

"Yes." Eric collected his legs under him. Looked at me. "You are not staying?"

I shook my head. I had my prep list for the regular Sunday brunch menu. Deciding the specials—what needed to be used up or added to the standing delivery orders or fetched fresh from the market—was the chefs' job. "I'll be in in the morning. Six o'clock."

Meaning, if I skipped the bar and went straight home, I could get, what? Four hours of sleep? My bones shuddered.

But life was full of trade-offs, right? Maybe I didn't have the career I'd always dreamed of, but I was still living the life I'd chosen in the city I loved. At least for now.

"I'll say good night, then," Eric said politely.

I looked at him, uncertain. *Will I see you later?* But I couldn't ask. Not with Ray standing there listening.

"Here." Eric reached into the minifridge beside his desk, where the expensive stuff was stashed, white truffles and osetra caviar, and tossed me a bottle.

I caught it. Pedialyte. Yuck. "Are you kidding? My sister gives this stuff to her two-year-olds."

His eyes narrowed in amusement. "You need electrolytes."

The glow spread. He was taking care of me. Of course, he looked out for everybody on his team. But his attention to me felt different. Sweet. Special.

"Oh. Well . . ." I raised the bottle in salute. "Cheers."

Maybe he'd call after he left the restaurant, I thought hopefully. Or text.

And maybe he wouldn't.

Sure, he'd texted me before. Or rather, I'd messaged him through his restaurant account. He could get my number from my file. But we weren't exactly a couple. He could have a girlfriend I didn't know about. A chef groupie. A regular booty call.

Sex was like food, after all. A basic need. That's what I'd always believed, no matter what Meg or Trey or all those poets I'd studied in college said.

"I have such a taste for you, Jo."

His whisper sparkled along my nerves, burst in my chest like a fistful of glitter. And my breath went all over again.

I walked through the kitchen on autopilot. Isaam gave me a friendly wave from the dishwashing bay as I passed.

"Good night," I called.

"Nos vemos mañana," Tomas said. *See you in the morning.*

It was almost one now. Outside, the glow of the streetlights obliterated the stars. The sidewalks glittered with frost. Going underground, the air was dank and cold. Huddled on the subway, rocking to the rhythm of the train, I unscrewed the Pedialyte and took a swig. Shuddered. Recapping the bottle, I pulled out my phone. Hoping.

A message from Meg lit up the screen. An update on Mom, still recovering from her fall. A mirror selfie of Meg in a red dress, head angled like a pro. Getting ready to go out! my sister had typed. It's not the same without you.

Unexpected tears stung my eyes. Darling Meg. I wasn't the same without her, either. She had dragged me to parties and dressed me for prom, her popularity smoothing my way through high school. She was my oldest ally, my other half. My better half, according to Aunt Phee. All our lives, people had compared me with my pretty, kind, sensible older sister. Without her I was less defined, less myself. Lizzy without Jane, a brain without a heart.

I didn't run to my big sister with every imagined romantic drama, the way that Amy did. But we'd shared a room until I turned fifteen, whispering secrets across the darkness between our beds. For every major event in my life, my sister was there. When I moved away to school, when I broke up with Trey for the final time, Meg called me every day to see how I was doing.

I couldn't wait to tell her about Eric.

Unless I never heard from him again.

I texted her back—Glad to see you and the boobs going out! Hope you had fun!—before scanning the rest of my messages.

Nothing from Eric.

What did I expect?

The subway car jolted to a stop. A night-shift worker in scrubs got off. A trio of student types with backpacks and earbuds got on. The train chugged away from the platform, escalating into the dark tunnel. I checked my blog. Scrolled through my notifications, liking, replying, and retweeting. I shared a picture of potatoes fondant to Instagram, promising to post the recipe tomorrow. And . . . Oh my God, there was Beth, in my newsfeed, tagged in an onstage photo of Colt Henderson. My sister never posted anything. Too shy. But that was definitely her.

The angle almost made it look like they were singing together, Bethie in her angel costume with her eyes half-closed, the show's star smiling behind his guitar. I typed a caption—A star is born?—added a smiley face and forwarded her the photo. Not that she'd see it tonight. It was after midnight in Branson, way past my sister's bedtime.

The train rattled and jerked to my station. I climbed the stairs to the street. Down the block, the bodega's windows glowed. A far-off siren wailed against the dark. Walking home alone at this hour used to scare me. Now it was routine. I lengthened my stride, watching the shadows, listening for footsteps, holding my keys ready in my pocket. My building didn't have a doorman.

I had locked and bolted the door behind me when the phone buzzed in my hand. Stupid with fatigue, I stared at the unfamiliar number, the single word message. Hungry? E

Hungry was my blog. But *E* . . . That *E* . . .

My heart tripped. It was Eric. He knew. I was busted as a food critic. An *idiot hipster food blogger.*

Except . . . I pressed my fingers to my eyes, forcing my sleep-deprived brain to think. He was texting me. At one in the morning. I knew what that meant. Booty call.

Hungry?

I smiled, sagging against the door, weak with relief and happiness. Starving, I typed.

The doorbell for the front entrance buzzed, making me jump and clutch the phone. Let me up?

I mashed the button to admit him to the building. Unlocked my door and threw it open. "How did you get here so fast?" I asked as he came up the stairs.

"Uber." He held up a white takeout bag. "I brought food."

My smile spread. "Of course you did." He lived to feed people. To take care of them. *Service.*

He gestured toward the tiny countertop. "Here?"

"Sure." I stood back as he unloaded the bag, his big hands quick and confident. The smells of ginger, garlic, and sesame oil filled my apartment.

That was it? We were just going to eat?

I cleared my throat. "That's an awful lot of little white boxes," I observed.

"I wanted to give you a choice." He met my gaze, his eyes steady on mine. "I didn't know what you wanted."

There was that glow, warming me from the inside out. Making me feel daring. Happy. "You," I said, and jumped him.

G od, that was good," I said much later.

Eric kissed my temple. "Yes."

We were naked in my loft, surrounded by half-empty cartons of Chinese takeout. I flopped back on my pillow. "I've never been so stuffed in my life."

His eyes crinkled.

"With *food*," I clarified, punching his bare shoulder.

"I'm glad you enjoyed it," he said politely.

"I did." I sat up again, kissing the place where I'd smacked him, warm, solid muscle and smooth skin. "All of it."

He turned his head, kissing my mouth. A rich, savory kiss, flavored with soy and sex. Umami, the elusive fifth taste. I leaned into him, craving more, chasing his taste with my tongue, and . . . *Crap*. I jerked back, yanking my hand from a puddle of kung pao chicken.

Smiling, Eric righted the carton. Holding my wrist, he ate from my hand. And then, when I was feeling all melty and squirmy, he gathered the remaining cartons and stacked them. To get them out of the way? In the kitchen, his section was always immaculate, his setups pristine, everything soigné.

He caught me watching him and raised an eyebrow. "More?"

Food? Or sex? My face heated. "Maybe later."

"As you wish."

Like the farm boy Westley declaring his love for the Princess Bride. My heart jerked. It was one of my favorite movies. Had he seen it? But when I tried to ask, my tongue tangled. This wasn't a fairy tale. And I was nobody's Buttercup. I could live my own adventure, thank you very much.

"I've got this," I said, grabbing a box. "I have to get up now anyway."

"You should rest."

"Can't. I have to be at the restaurant in . . ." I glanced at my phone. *Oh God.* "An hour."

Sleeping with the boss—or in this case, not sleeping—didn't mean I could call in late to work.

Eric nodded. "I should get going, too."

Right. He didn't come into the restaurant on Sundays, but obviously he couldn't stay in my apartment. He wasn't my boyfriend. I wasn't sure what he was, besides my boss, but I wasn't about to slap a label on our relationship and then sulk because it didn't live up to my assumptions. When he failed to conform to my expectations. I wasn't going to make the same mistakes with Eric that Trey had made with me.

Even if I felt things with him that I'd never felt for Trey.

I swallowed. *Don't overthink this.* "I'm gonna shower."

I slithered down the ladder to grab my clothes and whisked myself into the bathroom. Running away. When I got out, Eric was already dressed.

He slipped his phone into his pocket. "All set?"

"You bet," I said, as perky as I could be on no sleep. No coffee.

We went downstairs together. He didn't reach for my hand this time. I was annoyed with myself for noticing.

The sun wasn't up yet. Eric's Uber ride idled in front of my building, puffing clouds of exhaust into the air. He exchanged male-nods with the driver and opened the door.

"Well." I stood awkwardly on the curb. Did we kiss? Wave? "See you."

"Yes." He enveloped me briefly in a warm, hard hug and then stepped back, holding the door.

I looked at him in confusion.

"Get in," he said.

I obeyed out of habit, used to following his direction in the kitchen. When he didn't slide in behind me, I peered up at his silhouette, dark against the streetlight. "Are you . . . Aren't you coming? To the restaurant?"

He shook his head. "I don't want to cramp Ray's style."

"But . . ."

"See you," he said, like an echo, like a promise, and closed the door. The car pulled away from the curb.

Leaning forward, I addressed the driver. "What do I owe you?"

He met my gaze in the rearview mirror. *Why,* his expression asked, *do I always get the dumb ones?* "Forget about it," he said.

Right. Because Eric had already charged the fare to his card.

I sank back into the unfamiliar luxury of being driven to work. An hour before sunrise, the streets were stirring with cabs and delivery trucks, dog walkers and runners. Another morning, I might have been one of them. This morning was different. I felt different.

I couldn't wait to talk to Meg.

Not that I could call her now. Unless the twins woke her, she would still be in bed at this hour.

A n hour before service I snuck off to the loading dock like a smoker grabbing a cigarette break and checked my phone. There was a wordless reply from Beth—😊😊😊—and one new comment on my blog. I needed a fresh post. I texted Beth—WTG! ttys?—and called Meg.

Meg was getting the twins ready for church, which meant she had only minutes to talk. Instead of savoring my news, drop by delicious drop, I had to spill it all in a rush.

"What's up? Are you all right?" my sister asked.

"I'm fine. I'm great." I shivered a little with happiness and hormones. My chef's coat, designed to shield me from burns and spills in the kitchen, was lousy protection against the winter wind. "I'm seeing someone."

"You what?" said Meg, sounding distracted. "Sweetie, where is your bow? We need to do your hair."

"I brushed it," I said.

"Very funny," Meg said. "Wait. What? You met someone?"

"Not exactly. Not recently. Someone from work."

"You're dating a waiter?"

My huff of laughter hung like a cloud in the air. "No. God, no. You sound like Aunt Phee." I moved away from the kitchen door, so I wouldn't be overheard. "It's Eric."

Crickets.

I held the phone tighter. "Eric Bhaer?" I talked about him. All the time. Although maybe not by name. "Chef."

"Your boss?" Meg asked.

"Um. Technically. Yeah."

Another pause. I heard Daisy piping, "DJ has a stinky bottom."

"DJ, honey, did you poop?"

"He poop, Mommy."

"That's okay. Let's get you cleaned up, sweetie," Meg said. She was such a good mom. If I ever had children of my own, I hoped I had her patience.

Not that I was looking to have kids anytime soon. But the thought of some future baby, my baby, with hazel eyes and dark curly hair, momentarily stole my breath away.

A rumble in the background.

"No, it's all right. It's my sister," Meg said. "John says hi."

I smiled. "Hi, John."

The thing about having babies was, you needed a father. Or at least a baby daddy. Trey and I used to joke that if I were still single and childless at forty-two, he would make the perfect sperm donor.

"Can you . . . ? Thanks." A door closed. Meg took a deep breath. "All right. So, when did this start? The dating."

Eric and I weren't exactly dating. We were . . . We didn't need labels, I reminded myself. "Not long. I met him when I was out running on Friday, and then he asked me to cook the family meal, and . . ."

"Is it serious?"

Serious? I caught myself grinning at the Dumpster. "He hasn't given me his letter jacket yet. But it's pretty wonderful. He's pretty wonderful."

"It sounds . . . wonderful."

That was it? "I thought you'd be happy. You're always telling me I should be more open to finding . . ." *Love*. I cleared my throat. "Somebody."

"If you're happy, I'm happy," Meg said staunchly.

She didn't sound happy.

"Is everything all right?" I asked.

"Everything's fine. Did you hear about Beth?"

"I got a text. Good show last night?"

"She sang a duet. With Colt Henderson. That song she wrote, candle something."

So the photo of the two of them together hadn't been the trick of some camera angle. "That's . . . amazing. She called you?"

"Amy messaged me. It was on Twitter. So, that's one thing going right," Meg said.

I frowned. "How was the farmers' market yesterday?"

"Well, I sold a lot of cheese. I'm making a deposit at the bank tomorrow."

"Great. So everything will be back to normal."

"Not everything," Meg said.

I kicked myself. "I just meant you'll be able to hire some help at the farm."

"Yes." Something banged. "Look, I've got to go."

"Okay," I said, smothering my disappointment. "I love you."

"Love you, too," Meg said. "Take care."

Deflated, I ended the call. My sister was already dealing with Mom and the farm, I reminded myself. Not to mention getting my adorable, wiggly niece and nephew ready for church. I couldn't expect her to drop everything to share in my feelings. Especially when I wasn't prepared to give those feelings a name.

If Ashmeeta were here . . . No. My former roomie routinely rejected her loving parents' attempts to fix her up with well-educated, professional Indian men. *"Forget love,"* she would say. *"Work will give you everything a man can. And it doesn't expect you to cook dinner."* I could call Rachel. But along with enthusiasm, Rachel would bubble over with recommendations for lube and butt plugs.

Meg knew me better than anyone. If anyone could help me make sense of these new, big, confusing emotions, it would be Meg.

Or Beth. I called, but it went straight to voice mail.

"Yo, Jo. Break's over."

On Sundays, Gusto opened for brunch from ten until three o'clock. The dining room was full of churchgoers and Christmas shoppers, families coming early, friends lingering over drinks, tourists in town to see the ice-skaters at Rockefeller Center or the Rockettes at Radio City Music Hall. We squeezed two and a half turns into five hours, every table demanding refills on pastries and coffee. Under Ray's critical eye, I broke and beat hundreds of eggs; peeled and chopped garlic, potatoes, and apples; segmented oranges and grapefruit until my fingers stung. I was dead on my feet, making it through on adrenaline and coffee, determined not to fail. Too tired to focus on more than one task at a time. Too busy to think about Eric at all.

Liar, liar, pants on fire.

Finally, the brutal pace slowed. I scrubbed my station, staggered out with the trash, swept and mopped the floor. Untied my apron. "I'm out of here," I announced.

Lucas winked. "Have fun."

Ray gave me a funny look. "See you Tuesday."

Right. Tomorrow was my day off. Good thing. I wanted to fall in bed and sleep for the next twenty-four hours. Catch up on my blog.

Check up on my mom. Enjoy a long, cozy phone call with Beth. Read the new Kristan Higgins novel I'd downloaded on my Kindle.

Except . . .

Eric was there. In the office, at his desk, surrounded by menus.

My heart bounded and wriggled like a happy puppy. My brain scrambled, struggling to make sense of his presence. "You said you were leaving Ray alone today."

"I am. I'm in here, yeah? Not out there, looking over his shoulder." He smiled at me ruefully. "I seem to have more trouble staying away from you."

I gaped.

"I thought we could get something to eat," he said.

"Now?"

One eyebrow raised. "Unless you are busy."

"I have to go home," I blurted.

His face blanked. "I see."

"No. I mean . . . I can't go out like this." I was desperately tired. And dirty. I needed a *shower*. "Maybe later. I could meet you somewhere."

"Of course," he said politely.

Damn. I was missing something. Getting this wrong, getting him wrong somehow. If only I weren't so tired.

"Or . . . Or you could come home with me."

"Whatever you want."

I folded my arms. "Why do you always do that?"

"Do what?"

"Say that. *As you wish*," I mimicked. "*Whatever you want*. Like whatever happens next is up to me."

"Jo. Whatever happens *is* up to you. You work for me."

"So?"

"I am your boss. I do not want to . . ." He stopped. For a man so confident, so decisive, he seemed oddly at a loss for words.

"Harass me?" I suggested, grinning.

He did not smile. "Take advantage."

"You could try," I said. "I'm not powerless, you know. I can always say no."

He gave me a searching look. "Would you?"

Oh God. A memory surfaced of Trey's white face during our last, horrible fight, the hard glitter of tears in his eyes. *"Don't say it,"* he'd begged me in a choked voice. *"Say you'll think about it. Say you need time. Just don't say no."*

I'd hurt him so much. I'd broken his heart. That's what he said. *Heartless,* he'd called me. Because I wouldn't give in to friendship and our families' expectations. Because I didn't give him what he wanted. Because I couldn't be who he needed.

I'd always been selfish, Amy said. Willful, according to Aunt Phee.

"Yeah," I said slowly. "It's kind of my thing. Saying no."

Eric nodded. "Good."

Like I could tell him *no,* like I could be myself, and it would be okay.

"Er. So. Are you coming home with me or not?"

"Yes."

"I should warn you, I'll probably fall straight into bed."

"Fine." He smiled his full, knee-weakening smile. "I'll catch you."

CHAPTER 12

Meg

The Explorer had that mom-car smell, a compound of smooshed Cheerios, apple juice, and diapers. John had offered to take my vehicle to the dealership to be detailed. That's what marriage was all about. Doing things for each other because you could. Because you wanted to make the other person happy.

But I couldn't give up my car, even for one day. I reckoned I had just enough time to run my errands and drive an hour to the rehab center before I needed to turn around and pick up the twins from preschool.

I drove to the center of town, where Christmas lights shaped like holly and snowflakes hung from all the lampposts. Parked in the lot for the Cape Fear Bank and Trust, a few blocks from the waterfront.

"Meg!" Anita Jackson, behind the counter, waved me forward. "You coming back to work today?"

A joke. She asked the same question every time I came in.

"Not today," I said, smiling the way I always did.

"Too bad. We miss you around here," Anita said. "How's that handsome coach of yours?"

Three years since John left Caswell High, and he was still "Coach" in town. The time would come when folks wouldn't see him that way anymore. I would miss it, I realized.

So would he.

"He's fine." I swallowed. "We're all fine."

"So, what can I do for you today?"

I plopped my mom bag down on the divider. "I need to make a deposit to my mother's account. For the farm. Can you look up the number for me?"

"Sure thing. How's Abby doing?"

"Oh, you know. She has her good days and bad days." Yesterday she didn't want to get out of bed. Or even sit up in bed. Too much pain, the nurses said. Because of the fall? Or something else? "I'm going to go see her today."

Anita nodded. "It's a process. When my mother had her hip replacement . . ."

I half listened, making vague, sympathetic noises while I checked my phone. Nothing from Jo.

She'd sounded so *happy* when she called yesterday. I should have been more understanding. I should have asked more questions. At least I could have called her back.

Well. Something else to put on the list.

Anita peered at me over the top of her glasses, waiting for a reply.

I flushed. "Excuse me?"

"Did you want this to go to the equity line of credit?" Anita asked.

"No." What line of credit? "Regular checking. The farm account." I couldn't pay Hannah in cash, as if she were babysitting.

"I'm only asking because the payment on the equity loan was due three weeks ago," Anita said. "This would just about cover it."

"Sorry, what?"

"Your mother's loan payment. It's overdue."

I stared at her.

"We sent a notice," Anita said.

I thought of the mail, piling up at the house. "She's been sick."

"Honey, I know," Anita said. "There's a grace period, of course. Fifteen days. But she's a week past that now."

My mind stumbled. There must be some mistake. I had set up lines of credit for a lot of farmers to buy equipment or see them through unexpected expenses, a lean season or a bad year. But if my mother had ever applied for a bank loan, I would know.

Unless . . . Unease wriggled inside me, like the fuzzy worm at the core of an apple. Unless she'd done it since I left the bank.

Three years ago.

I took a calming breath. Obviously, my parents had to make adjustments when my father left active duty. Whatever salary he drew from his nonprofit could not equal his military pay. Three years ago, he had moved his ministry out of the church basement and into its current storefront location. The rent couldn't be that much. But . . .

"The deposit will cover the loan payment, you said?" I asked.

Anita nodded. "For November, that's right. The December payment is due on the twentieth."

Next Tuesday. Eight days away. My thoughts blurred. "Fine. Let's do that. Thanks."

I left the bank, my heart thumping.

Our father came from old money. Our mother came from none at all. My parents never talked much about finances. We girls were supposed to fix our thoughts on higher things. But I'd never once questioned if they had enough to live on.

My stomach cramped.

We were going to have to talk about it now.

A t the rehab center, I signed in, dropping off a tin of sprinkle-covered cookies with the ladies at the front desk.

"Bribing the staff?" an aide asked with a twinkle in her eye.

"I noticed some of the patients don't get a lot of visitors. I thought maybe . . ." I flushed. They'd want overdecorated Christmas cookies from my twins' sticky fingers?

"Aren't you sweet," she said. "I'll put these in the common room."

"Thanks." I scanned the schedule for my mother's name. "I'm looking for Abby March."

She glanced down at the visitors' log. "You're Meg Brooke?"

"Her daughter. Yes." Only identified "patient caregivers" were allowed to visit the rehab center during the day. No children under twelve. No ordinary visitors.

"She's in her room. She didn't go to therapy this morning."

"Is she all right?"

A brief, sympathetic smile. "I'm sure she'll fill you in."

The hallway was decorated like the twins' classroom with cutout snowflakes. Maybe the result of some school's adopt-a-veteran project. Or scissors therapy for the residents.

The rehab center treated veterans with spinal cord and brain injuries, seniors with joint replacements, stroke survivors, and amputees. I wished an old woman pushing a walker a Merry Christmas. Smiled at a young man in a wheelchair, who nodded and looked away.

My mother at least would get better. Not every patient, not every family, was so lucky.

As I approached her door, I heard a man's voice coming from inside the room. I tapped and poked my head in. "Dad!" He was sitting beside Mom's bed, his handsome head bowed over their joined hands, clasped in prayer. "I didn't know you were here."

He looked at me in mild reproof. Obviously, I'd interrupted. "We had a meeting with your mother's case manager this morning."

"What did she say?"

"Hello, sweetheart," my mother said before my father could answer. "This is a surprise."

"A nice one, I hope." I bent to kiss her, dodging the bright blooming poinsettia on her bedside table. She looked better, I thought. There were spots of color in her thin cheeks, and she'd raised her bed so she was almost sitting. She must have made an effort for the caseworker's visit. Or Dad's.

"Last week of preschool," I said. "We made you cookies. Well, I made cookies. DJ mostly ate dough."

Momma smiled. "And Daisy?"

"Daisy liked the sprinkles." I opened the tin to show her. "Lots and lots of sprinkles. On the cookies, on the counter, on the floor . . ."

That won a chuckle. "They do look very . . ."

"Colorful?" I suggested.

"Christmassy," she declared, offering the tin to my father.

He took one absently as I set her laundry on the narrow dresser. Five loose T-shirts, three bras, seven panties, five pairs of sweatpants.

"You didn't have to wash my things," she protested.

"You needed clean clothes." I smiled. "Anyway, it's not like I had to beat them on rocks and spread them on bushes to dry."

"No point in using the dryer when the sun works just as well," my mother said.

She'd always sun-dried our sheets, bringing them in stiff and fresh-smelling off the line.

"Mm." I started putting the clothes away. "I went to the bank this morning. To make the deposit from the farmers' market?"

"Sales should be good this close to Christmas," my mother said.

"Yes, ma'am. The thing is . . ." I cleared my throat. "I talked to Anita. At the bank? There was a little problem with the account. She thought the deposit should go into your equity line of credit."

My mother's brow creased. "That's not right. We pay all our bills out of the checking account."

"That's what I figured." I took a deep breath. There was no reason for me to feel apologetic. Money was my thing. Numbers. You could always make numbers add up. All you needed to solve any problem was the right variables. "There wasn't enough money in the account to cover the loan payment."

"That's all right. It's not due until next week." My mother shifted, her face twitching in pain. "I'd have to look to be sure."

Her back hurt. I should leave her alone. Let it go.

"The December payment is due next week," I said. "Anita was concerned because they hadn't gotten payment for November."

My mother looked at Dad. "Ash?"

He brushed crumbs from his fingers. Patted her hand. "Don't upset yourself, Abby." He glanced at me. "Don't you upset her, either."

His words stung. "I'm only trying to help."

"By meddling in our personal financial affairs?"

I inhaled. "There's not enough money in the account," I said carefully. "I thought Mom should know."

You should know. Why didn't you say something? I wanted to ask. *Why didn't you* do *something?*

But I didn't. We girls didn't question our father. Our mother taught us that. *"Don't worry your father,"* she'd said when he was deployed. *"Don't bother your father,"* she'd said when he holed himself up in his office for hours at a time while we watched TV with the volume turned down low. *"Your father is working,"* she'd explained every time he missed a concert or a track meet or a play performance.

We accepted that the Reverend Ashton March answered only to a Higher Power.

But now she was struggling to sit up. She looked at my father. "How much did you withdraw?"

"Abby . . ." He pulled back his hand, folding his long fingers together. "This is hardly the time or place for this discussion."

"Then, when? If I weren't sick, you'd never talk to me at all." She sounded like Granny.

My mouth jarred open. I'd never heard my mother use that tone with my father before. Never heard her breathe a word of criticism.

"I had expenses," my father said.

"Household expenses," my mother said. "*Farm* expenses."

He drew himself up. "Critical commitments. There are others in need, especially at this time of year, men and women who have sacrificed everything for their country. My obligation to them doesn't go away simply because you have a temporary setback."

"We can't keep funding the ministry if it means losing the farm," my mother said. "Our *home*."

"What setback?" I asked.

"Your family's home," my father said to my mother. "Your parents never made me feel particularly welcome there. I never understood your decision to go back."

"After you went into the army, after you gave up your living and the parsonage without consulting me, where were we supposed to live?"

"You could have moved to Oak Hill."

"I'm not taking charity from your aunt."

"On base, then. The Lord always provides a way for those who do His work. But you had to do things your way."

This was awful. "What setback?" I repeated.

My father spared me a glance. "Your mother can't do her rehab." He made it sound like that was her fault. "Without some improvement, they'll have to move her to a nursing home. So the doctors have decided—and we concur—that she needs surgery."

"Oh, Momma, *no*. What kind of surgery?"

"I'll be fine," my mother said. As if I had to be protected from too much information, like Daisy or DJ. Or Dad. "A couple of my vertebrae are compressed a little, that's all. So Dr. Chatworth is going to go in and stabilize things."

"Deteriorated from the infection," my father said. As if he were punishing me for coming into my mother's room, worrying her about money. That was okay. He couldn't blame me more than I blamed myself. "They have to remove the infected bone and put some kind of a cage in her spine."

"Oh my God," I said. A prayer, not a curse. "When?"

My mother made a face, twisting position in bed. I couldn't tell if she were struggling to get comfortable or avoiding my question.

"As soon as they can schedule the surgery with the hospital," my father said.

I swallowed. "I'll call the girls."

My mother's head moved back and forth against her pillow. *No.*

"Momma . . . They might want to be here."

"No," she said. "No fuss. They have their own lives. I don't want them coming home for me."

I looked at my father, hoping for reinforcements.

"That's up to your mother," he said. Leaving the decision, the responsibility, to her, the way he left everything else.

"They still should know," I argued.

"After the surgery," my mother declared. "You can tell them then. When you can say I'm better."

Unless she wasn't. What would I say then?

"Amy put off her trip already," Momma said. "And Beth . . . This show is her big chance."

"Dad?"

"You heard your mother," my father said. "Dealing with all you girls is too much. She needs to concentrate on getting better. Then everything will be fine."

Was he kidding? But he genuinely believed that, because that's what our mother had always let him believe. As long as he wasn't inconvenienced, everything *was* fine. He saw her inability to take care of him as her weakness, not his.

"It's in the doctors' hands now. And the Lord's. What could your sisters do?"

They could be here, I thought. *We could be here for one another.*

I swallowed hard and bent to kiss my mother. "Whatever you want, Momma."

Because what else could I say?

All my life I'd watched her care for my father. Care for us all, providing, managing, keeping everything running smoothly. *"The woman makes the marriage,"* my mother told me on my wedding day. But she couldn't do it alone. It was easy to blame my father for not doing more to help.

Maybe she'd never asked.

Well.

I got in my car and closed my eyes for a second. The smells of apple juice, pee, and Things Under Seats wrapped around me. Maybe I'd let John take the car to get cleaned, after all.

John. If I were in the hospital, my husband wouldn't be patting my hand, telling me how the Lord would provide, that was for sure. He'd get to work, making sure we were taken care of.

Exhaling, I opened my eyes and called Carl Stewart to ask about that job.

CHAPTER 13

Jo

I'm starving," I declared on Monday morning.

Eric's eyes crinkled.

"What?" I said. "We must have burned up, like, a million calories."

His lips curved. "Indeed."

I punched his arm. "From the run."

After a warm-up jog along the High Line, we'd descended the stairs at 18th Street. Energized by the cold and the city's pulse, we ran, past graffiti-decorated Dumpsters and storefronts, through the crowd of office workers and artists bundled in scarves and boots, around parents pushing strollers. Four miles, five, our feet hitting the cobblestones, our breath making puffs of fog in the air. I was glowing inside and out.

In my kitchen, I stretched, trying not to hit Eric with my elbow, sensitive to the twinge of underused muscles. "I'm not used to all this activity."

Eric lowered his water bottle. "I pushed you too fast."

Yes. No. I pulled out my hair elastic and put it back in again. Was he talking about the run?

He hadn't pushed me. I was the one who got physical, right? Determined to move on with my life, confident of my ability to set the pace. *Go, me.* But now . . .

"I've never had a guy spend the night in my apartment before," I blurted. "Not all night." Except for Trey. Another twinge. "I don't know what to do with you."

A hint of a smile. "I am not that complicated."

"But you're here." In my space. Even when I'd lived with Ashmeeta, our different schedules meant I had plenty of alone time.

The amusement faded from his eyes. "You want me to go."

I had always been comfortable alone. Curled up with a book, holed up in my attic room. I flushed. "No."

"Ah." He regarded me for a moment before he took me in his arms. He held me for a long time, until my muscles slowly relaxed, until our breaths matched, in and out, the way they did when we ran. He was so *big*. Maybe I was a little worried he would take over, the way Trey tried to do. That he would fill my thoughts, my space, until there wasn't any room for me anymore. "Jo." The sound of my name rumbled through me. "Maybe you stop overthinking things, yeah?"

Stop looking for something to go wrong. Stop looking for a way out. "I don't know how," I mumbled into his chest.

"Be in the moment." He stroked my back, my hair. "Be."

My body softened, molding to his. He was already half-aroused. I was, too. "I'll try."

His large hands cupped my head as he tipped my face back. Smiled into my eyes. "I will cook for you."

"What?" I blurted as he released me.

"I will cook. Breakfast." He maneuvered around me to open my fridge. "You don't have food."

I couldn't afford to buy a bunch of groceries. Which is why I always ate the family meal. "There's leftover Chinese." I spied a carton, lurking on a shelf. "And eggs."

"Eggs will work." He took them out. Taking charge, the way he did at the restaurant.

I folded my arms, watching as he cracked the eggs into a bowl. All the eggs, enough to feed us both.

"What are you making? An omelet?" The standard test for every beginning cook.

He shook his head, reaching for a pan, already at home in my kitchen. "You have no cheese. No herbs."

"I think there's a jar of parsley flakes around somewhere," I said.

He shot me an appalled look before he realized I was joking. "Funny girl."

I grinned. He moved with such deliberation, in full possession of himself, in command of his surroundings. I snuck a glance at his big hands, his calm face as he whipped the eggs to a creamy yellow froth. He swirled a knob of butter in the pan, calling attention to his thick wrists, the play of muscle under his pushed-up sleeves. He scrambled eggs like he was plating an entrée for dinner service, like he made love, with intense focus and attention to detail. Very hot.

Too bad I couldn't record him. A video tutorial of Chef Eric Bhaer demonstrating scrambled eggs would get a ton of hits. #sexycookingman

I pushed away from the counter. "I'll make toast."

He nodded absently, adjusting the heat of my crappy electric burner. "*Bitte.*"

It was like in the restaurant, me working around him, playing prep cook. Only . . . different. I nudged him with my hip to get to the toaster. He patted my bottom, shifting out of my way. I was embarrassed by how much I liked it, that light, affectionate slap.

"No snotty comments about the bread?" I asked.

Eric's lips quirked. "When Alec was five, he wanted peanut butter and jelly on plain white bread every damn day for lunch. With the crusts cut off. You cannot scare me with your bread."

Aw. "That's adorable." I was pretty sure my father couldn't name any of my favorite childhood foods. "You packed your son's lunch?"

"Certainly not," Eric said, squashing that little fantasy. "He was five. Old enough to pack his own lunch."

I cocked my head. "But you trimmed the crusts."

"No."

"No?"

He expelled his breath. "I bought cookie cutters," he admitted. "So he could do it himself. Stegosaurus, brontosaurus . . . He liked dinosaurs."

A piece of my heart melted. Having seen how he dealt with the misfits in his kitchen—his tolerance and support for his makeshift family—it was easy to imagine him teaching a curly-haired five-year-old to cut sandwiches into dinosaur shapes.

"You must miss them," I said. "Your sons."

"Yes." One word.

"Do they ever visit?" I said.

"Not often. It is difficult to find time."

"Right." I knew what it was like to have a father whose work took precedence over everything else.

"You must live to cook," Eric had said.

He slid me a look. "You and your father . . . You are close?"

"Yes. I mean, he wasn't around a lot. Because he was deployed." I watched Eric fold eggs gently from thé cooked edges to the center of the pan. "But this one time, in high school, I had this cross-country meet? And he was waiting for me at the finish line." I flushed, embarrassed by the wave of remembered emotion. I'd cried. "Total surprise. I wasn't expecting him until the next day. It was a moment. Like something on YouTube."

"Bryan is on the football team. Soccer," Eric corrected himself. "He has a tournament over the holidays, yeah? And Alec has play practice. The boys cannot come to me. So . . ." Eric shrugged his big shoulders. "I go to North Carolina."

I was oddly breathless. "When?"

"Christmas." He concentrated on the eggs. "Denise invited me to spend the holiday with them."

Denise? His ex-wife. Oh.

Oh. Whatever stupid fantasies I might have entertained about seeing Eric at Christmas, introducing him to my family, died a swift, embarrassing death. Not that I was jealous or anything, but . . . Fine. I was totally jealous.

"That's very . . . civilized."

"We are parents, yeah? It is best for the boys if we get along."

I nodded. That didn't sound like he was still hung up on his ex. But what did I know?

He slid the eggs from the pan, yellow as sunshine, soft as a cloud. The kitchen smelled like toast, like coming downstairs to breakfast on the first day of school with a new book bag full of sharpened pencils and the air rich with coffee and promise.

I slipped my phone from my pocket.

"What are you doing?" Eric asked.

I tapped the screen. *Perfect*. "Taking a picture."

He gave me a look of controlled patience.

"What?"

"Jo. Every night we work to get dishes to the tables on time. Everything on the plate à point, the right texture, the proper temperature. And then some idiot pulls out his phone to take a picture and the food gets cold while they frame their fucking shot to impress their friends."

I grinned. "You sound like my mother." Except my mother never dropped the f-bomb in her life.

He raised an eyebrow.

"Eat, before your eggs get cold," I explained.

His smile broke. When he smiled like that, with his whole face, I felt warm all over.

Encouraged, I continued. "Anyway, isn't that why you became a chef? To impress people with your cooking?"

"To impress you. I cooked for *you*. The point of making food is to feed people, yeah? The ones you care about."

My cheeks got hot. Meaning . . . He cared about me? Well, me, and everybody who ever ate in his restaurant. *Let's not get carried away here.*

We sat down to eat at my alcove desk table. I stuck a fork into the eggs. They melted on my tongue, the promise of butter, a whisper of salt, the taste of home.

"Oh," I said, a soft note of discovery.

Another smile. He looked pleased. Like my opinion mattered. "Wait until I cook you dinner."

"You cook dinner all the time." It was the highlight of the day, when he cooked for the staff. Most of us couldn't afford to eat his food otherwise. I ran bread over my plate, wiping up the last smear of silky goodness. *Wait.* "You mean, like, here? Tonight?"

"I thought we would go to my place." He watched me carefully. "Unless you would rather go out."

As if spending the day together, the night together, was a foregone conclusion. I swallowed. With Trey, I'd learned to always be on my guard, holding tight to my definition of who I was and what I wanted, constantly braced against the moment he would lunge ahead, dragging me with him.

But Eric . . .

"You're doing it again," I said. Giving me choices. Options. "I don't always need to be in control, you know. What you want matters, too."

"I know what I want." His gaze met mine, making my insides shimmy. "I don't know how you feel."

"I *jumped* you at the *door.* I'm pretty sure that was a clue."

A glint of a smile. "And I'm grateful."

"Amy—my sister Amy?—says men don't like aggressive women."

"You are passionate."

I flushed. "Blunt."

"Honest."

I squirmed, trying not to glance in the direction of my laptop. I hadn't been all *that* honest. "You only say that because you don't have to live with my big mouth."

"You speak your mind. That's a good thing. Otherwise nobody pays attention until everything goes to shit."

"Speaking from experience?" Momma taught us girls not to ask personal questions. But I wasn't simply curious. I . . . cared.

He shrugged. "I was a bastard husband. Typical chef, working all the time."

So his hours sucked. Like my father's. But despite Eric's devotion to his work, his ambition, his passion, I didn't see him as uncaring. Or self-absorbed.

"It's not like you were cheating on her," I said. "Unless . . . Oh. Um. Sorry."

Eric gave me that look, the one that said I amused him.

I bumbled on. "It's just that Trey—my friend—says given the chance, the majority of men would sleep with the majority of women. Of course, he's . . ." A *horndog.* "He's hardly a relationship expert. He doesn't know you at all. Obviously you wouldn't cheat on your wife."

Eric smiled wryly. "Only with the restaurant."

"You were a chef when she married you, though, right? You didn't change."

"Maybe I should have. She deserved better from me. I should have paid more attention. I should have been there for her." His eyes met mine. "I won't make that mistake again."

I lost my breath. There was definitely not enough air in my apartment. Not with him in it. Did he mean . . . ?

"You mean, when you see her again? At Christmas."

"Jo." His voice was deep, a vibration along my nerves. "I am there for Christmas with the boys. Nothing more. I am with you now."

The words wrapped around me like a blanket.

"With me," I repeated, testing the idea. I waited for the familiar stifling panic to envelop me but . . . Nope. Nothing. Only that odd, lovely warmth.

I grinned. "Then I guess we're going to your place."

"Good." He smiled.

For a minute, we just sat there, looking and smiling at each other over the breakfast dishes, and it was . . . pretty great, actually.

Eric swore. "*Scheisse.*"

"What?"

"I have to meet the liquor distributor today."

"Okay."

"And"—he shot me a guilty look—"I need to go in and talk to Ray about the specials."

Like he had to apologize for being . . . Chef. I widened my eyes in mock horror. "On your day off? I'm shocked."

"There are no days off when you own a restaurant," he said a little grumpily. "Ray can handle the service, no problem. But it isn't his name on the menu."

My name was on my blog. Well, my pseudonym, actually, but the principle was the same. I couldn't take the day off, either. "It's fine. I'm used to having my own space."

His brow wrinkled.

"Really," I assured him. "Actually, this will be great."

Maybe me being myself gave him the freedom to be himself, too. Or was it the other way around?

He raised an eyebrow. "Trying to get rid of me?"

"No. Kind of. I just . . . I have work to do, too. You can do your thing and I'll do mine."

"Your thing?"

I opened my mouth. Shut it again. He thought I was honest. "*You speak your mind,*" he'd said. But I wasn't prepared to tell him about *Hungry* yet. Everything between us felt too new. I didn't want to spoil the moment, the day, his good opinion, by confessing I was an idiot hipster food blogger.

He was waiting for an answer, watching me with interest. Paying attention, damn it. I had to say something.

"I'm a writer. *Was* a writer. Before I was let go."

He nodded. "From the newspaper. I know."

I looked at him, surprised.

"I read your job application," he said. "You were a reporter."

"Lifestyle journalist. Weddings, science fairs, parades." I forced myself to meet his gaze. "Restaurant openings."

His eyes lit with amusement. "So, maybe you are glad to get fired, yeah? What are you writing now?"

For some reason, for no reason at all, I thought of my abandoned master's project, all those finished files going nowhere. My writing was *"quite competent,"* my adviser had said kindly, sticking a knife in my dreams. If only I could overcome my insistence on sentiment, my dependence on plot.

I cleared my throat. "I want to write a book. Eventually. When I have enough material."

"I would like to read it."

A chasm yawned at my feet. "You don't want to do that."

"Why not?"

"Because. Even my own mother doesn't read my . . ." *Blog. Don't say* blog. "It's not the sort of thing you'd be interested in."

Fucking critics.

"Jo." My name, in his deep, slightly accented voice. "I am interested in you. You wrote it, put your heart on the page, the way I put my heart on a plate every night. I want to know your heart."

My breath went. It was so unfair. Who talked like that? Besides poets and heroes in romance novels. I could feel myself teetering closer to the edge. So close. So far to fall. My heart pounded in panic. How was I supposed to answer him?

"It's not, er, ready." *I'm not ready.* "Anyway, don't you have to go buy booze? See Ray about a menu?"

Something flickered in his eyes. "Unfortunately, yes."

He stood, carrying his plate. I followed him into the kitchen and trailed after him to the door. He turned.

I folded my arms, hugging myself tight. "So, I'll see you tonight."

"Yes," he said again.

He kissed me, hard, hot, and deep, and I kissed him back, rising on tiptoe to meet him, clutching him for balance. Giving him everything I had. When it ended, my lips were tingling and my brain was numb.

His breath was warm against my mouth. "Enjoy your space."

My head wobbled up and down. *Yes.*

"Come early. Five o'clock. I'll text you the address."

"Sure. Five." I turned, staggered, and walked into the wall. *Oops.*

Eric grabbed my elbow, keeping me upright. "Careful," he said mildly. "Don't fall."

Too late, I thought as I locked up behind him.

I'd fallen already, fathoms deep. I wasn't sure if I'd ever climb back out again. Or if I even wanted to.

That night, Eric pulled back from our hello kiss to look down at the pie dish in my arms. His eyebrow raised in the way I was coming to love. "What is this?"

"I brought dessert." I thrust it at him.

He took the plastic-wrapped plate. "You made this?"

"Hey, I can cook."

"I know you can cook. But . . ." He regarded the plate in his hands, seemingly at a loss.

"What?" I asked. "You don't like apple pie?"

"No." He shook his head. "Jo. I love that you made pie. Baking is different, yeah? Special. I just . . . Nobody ever cooks for me."

Of course not. He was Chef. Nominated for best 30 Under 30 chef the year he came to America, winner of a James Beard Award. The best cook, the best butcher, the best baker at Gusto.

"Because you intimidate everybody," I said.

His gaze met mine. "But not you."

His look warmed me to the soles of my feet. My toes tingled. "Oh, I'm intimidated," I said airily. "But I figured you might like a home-cooked dessert for a change."

"You are good to me."

I snorted. Bethie was good, and Meg was nurturing, and Amy knew how to get along with everyone but me. I was stubborn and bad-tempered. *Selfish,* according to Aunt Phee. *Heartless,* Trey had said.

I wasn't like Momma, that was for sure, needing to take care of everybody all the time. But this afternoon, after I'd finished writing my blog (*Low and Slow: How to Make the Best Scrambled Eggs Ever!*), I'd wanted to do something for Eric. He made me feel bigger somehow. More generous. Like I could give a little of myself and still have something left over.

"You haven't tasted it yet," I pointed out.

"I can't wait."

He hung my coat on a hook in the hall. His gaze warmed as he looked at me. "You look beautiful, Jo."

I managed not to squirm. Because, yeah, I had gone to extra effort tonight. Fixed my face, left my hair out of its ponytail, dug a soft blue cashmere sweater—a castoff from Amy, actually—from the back of my closet. "You clean up pretty good yourself."

Very adult, right? Date-like. Date-ish.

He guided me forward, one hand at the small of my back.

"Wow," I said. "You have a fireplace."

A working fireplace with burning gas logs.

His building was a few blocks and a world away from mine, a reno-vated co-op with a doorman and an elevator and a view. Through the windows, I could see bare tree branches and the Christmas lights in the apartment across the street. Not a lot of furniture, but what there was looked sturdy and comfortable—an oversize leather couch, a big new TV. High-end guy stuff. A granite bar top separated the living area from the kitchen. He seated me at the counter, gave me a glass of wine, and went back to stirring something on the stove. A Viking range. Six burners. And a dishwasher.

I sniffed appreciatively. Butter, sage . . . "What are you making?"

"Duck breast with tart cherry confit." He lifted the lid off a pot of boiling water. "And my mother's pierogi."

I watched his muscled forearms as he fished out dumplings with a slotted spoon, fighting the itch to take notes. Or pictures. Pictures would be good. I cleared my throat. "I haven't seen those on the menu at Gusto. Pierogi, I mean."

"Not yet. I am playing with the filling. Sweet potatoes instead of white, a little red cabbage." He swirled the pierogi in the pan of browned butter, plated one, and slid it across the bar in one smooth move. "What do you think?"

Like my opinion mattered. I picked up the fork that appeared with the plate. The tender dough gave easily, the insides spilling like a sunset, red and orange and caramelized gold. The first forkful melted in my mouth with a kiss of butter and a bite of something savory.

"Yum," I said. "I thought it would be sweet, but it's not. Onion?"

He nodded, looking as pleased as if I'd left him a five-star review. My stomach hollowed. I really needed to tell him about my blog. Later. Tonight. Maybe.

I swallowed. "What does Ray think?"

"Ray." A huff of amusement or acceptance. "He wants to elevate everything. Until you can't taste the heart anymore."

"He does have kind of a stick up his butt," I said around another mouthful of pierogi.

"Ray's a good guy. A good cook," Eric said. Defending his sous. That was the kind of boss he was, seeing the best, encouraging the best, in everybody.

"So why hasn't he left to become executive chef somewhere?"

"He has the résumé. He is ready for the responsibility. But he is afraid to take the risk, yeah? He holds back from putting himself on the plate. He wants too much to impress, I think."

I thought of the pie. The sweater. The extra fifteen minutes I'd spent flat-ironing my hair, trying to get it smooth and straight. *Right there with you, Ray.*

I took another sip of wine. "I guess I get his point. I mean, that's why people go out. Because they want something they can't find at home."

Were we still talking about food?

"Sure," Eric agreed easily. "But not every dish has to amaze. Sometimes you simply want to eat. To be fed." He looked up, that little smile tugging at the corner of his mouth. "To be satisfied."

A great wave of lust and longing shook me to my knees. Good thing I was sitting. He could satisfy me, I thought. He could hoist me up on the counter. I could wrap my arms around his neck, my legs around his waist. We could . . .

He cracked the oven door to check the duck. "Almost ready," he promised with another smile.

Definitely talking about the food this time.

I swallowed my disappointment along with another gulp of wine and slid off my stool. "Right. I just need to . . ." *Don't say* pee, Aunt Phee instructed in my head. Southern ladies did not have bodily functions. "Wash my hands."

"Second door on the right," Eric said.

"Thanks."

I used the bathroom (which was pretty amazing. No tub—this was New York, after all—but lots of granite and a bunch of high-tech water jets in the shower) and then, unable to resist, peeked in his open bedroom door. His bed was as big as the rest of his furniture, his nightstand and dresser top as neat and organized as the kitchen before service. Next door, another room with a dormitory-size twin and a futon. The price of a two-bedroom in Chelsea must be over the moon. I guessed Gusto was doing well.

There were pictures on the wall. I stepped closer to see them. A younger, beardless Eric holding a scrunch-faced newborn in a stocking cap. A standard beach shot, two little boys playing at the edge of the water. A more recent photo of Eric and both boys, squinting into the sunlight against the background of an unfamiliar city. In Germany, maybe? I didn't know. I'd never been to Europe. Something about the last pose tugged at my heart, the easy way Eric hooked his arm around his older son's shoulders, the way the younger one leaned into his side. My father the minister had rarely touched his adolescent daughters.

"*Do they ever visit?*" I'd asked.

"*Not often. It is difficult to find time,*" Eric had replied.

But here was their room, kept in readiness, just in case.

And here . . . Another photo. Their mother, Eric's ex-wife, smiling into the camera, the boys—maybe seven and ten?—beside her. She was dark eyed, dark skinned, and very beautiful. I felt oddly . . . jealous. Depressed. Which was stupid. I knew he'd been married before.

I whisked myself out of the room, my heart pounding. Served me right for snooping.

Eric was plating in the kitchen.

"Can I do anything?" I asked.

He shook his head, smiling. "It's all done."

He'd pulled a small, square table in front of the fire. There were place mats. Candles. Everything soigné. Very romantic. I stared down at my plate arranged like an artist's palette, pink slices of crispy skinned duck with maroon cherries, golden pierogi, haricots verts, and wondered what the hell I was doing here.

Eric raised an eyebrow. "Everything all right?"

"Great. Thanks." I pulled myself together and dug in. "So. This is your idea of home cooking, huh?"

His eyes crinkled. "My heart on a plate. For you."

I almost choked. Swallowed hard. He ought to be careful about saying stuff like that. If I were somebody else—somebody pretty and sweet, somebody like Meg—I might take him seriously. "The napkins are a nice touch."

He laughed. "It is all just stuff, yeah? That's what my father would say."

"Mine, too."

"Military families. Every time my father was transferred, my mother would have a yard sale."

I chewed, relaxing. "We didn't move so much. My dad didn't join the army until after 9/11. But he's a minister. You know, '*Set your minds on things above, not on earthly things*'?"

"And your mother?" Eric asked.

"She's not exactly a material girl, either. But . . ." I swallowed, thinking of the farmhouse. Of Great-grandmother's quilts and Granny's china and Amy's craft projects, all lovingly preserved. "She likes to hold on to stuff."

"It falls to her to make the home," Eric said. "It is important for the children to have their things around them."

I remembered the photos in his sons' room, and my heart melted a little more.

We ate. The wine went to my head, or maybe it was Eric's attention. I found myself talking about everything and nothing: about my sisters and the goats; about running in the city; about my AP English teacher, Mrs. Ferguson. He was a good listener. His eyes never once glazed over the way a guy's do when they wish you'd shut up and have sex. Like I was interesting enough simply being myself. Well. Mostly myself. I didn't tell him about my blog. I asked about his family. His father had retired from the military. His parents still lived in Germany, near his mother's family. His older sister was a vice president for international relationship management at some bank.

"My sister works in a bank, too. *Worked* in a bank," I corrected myself. "Before the twins came along. She's an awesome mother. And daughter. And sister. And wife. I don't know how she does it all, honestly."

"She is happy, your sister?"

I hesitated. "*If you're happy, I'm happy*," Meg had said. Living for others, that was Meg. Except . . . She didn't seem so happy lately. I'd texted her on my way over, asking if I could call, and she messaged me back. Sorry. Really busy. Maybe later?

Meaning, *Later, maybe*. She *was* really busy. Or maybe she didn't want to talk to me. Which was totally unfair. *I* wasn't the one questioning *her* choices.

"She's a better person than I am," I said, dodging the question.

"You seem like a good daughter to me," Eric said. "A good sister."

"I mean, I couldn't give up my career to have a family."

"You could have both."

My heart stumbled. "That's not what you said before. Cooking is your passion, you said."

"I love to cook," he said promptly. "When I was starting out, I worked twelve, fifteen hours a day, seven days a week. But I don't have to make every plate anymore. I don't need to be on fire, in the heat, on the line, all the time." He reached out, his hand covering mine, clutching the fork. "Maybe I can learn to love more than one thing now, yeah?"

Warmth flooded my cheeks from his touch or the wine or the fire. I jabbed randomly at my plate, ridiculously happy.

After dinner, we did the dishes together. While he made coffee, I studied the shelves above the wine rack, where his cookbooks stood side by side like old friends. Alice Waters, *The Art of Simple Food*. Ferran Adrià's *El Bulli*. Dornenburg and Page's *The Flavor Bible*.

Eric came up behind me and dropped a kiss on the back of my neck, sending a pleasant shiver down my spine. "See any of your favorites?"

"Hm. No Charlotte Brontë. No Jane Austen." I grinned at him over my shoulder. "And where's your Harry Potter collection?"

"In the boys' room," he said.

That did it. Or it would have, if I hadn't fallen for him already.

My fingers skimmed the spines. "Oh, look, Bill Neal's *Southern Cooking*. I used to eat at his restaurant all the time when I was in college! Well, when I could afford it. Crook's, in Chapel Hill." Unable to resist the feel of a book in my hands, I took down *The French Laundry Cookbook* and flipped to the title page. Signed by the author. "Thomas Keller," I said reverently. "You met him?"

"I worked for him at Per Se." Keller's New York restaurant. He said it so casually, as if he rubbed elbows with legends all the time. "I learned a lot from him."

"Until you left the nest," I said.

"He kicked me out." Eric's voice was easy. Amused. "Time to fly on my own, yeah? Cook my own food. Find my own voice."

I turned my head. "You should write a cookbook."

I knew he hadn't. I would have bought it.

"What I have to say, I say with food."

"I get that. But not everybody has the chance to eat at your restaurant. You could share your recipes, your food, your story with more people," I said with building enthusiasm for the idea. "People who might never come to New York."

He shook his head. "I am a cook, not a storyteller."

"A cook with a James Beard Award," I pointed out.

"Awards do not make me a writer." He met my gaze and smiled. "Maybe you should write my cookbook."

"I . . . You're not serious."

"You are a writer, yeah? Lifestyle journalist," he corrected. "You wrote about restaurant openings, you said."

Oh God. He remembered.

"I didn't set out to be a food writer," I said. "I just . . . I needed a job. A writing job. I wanted to stay in New York. And I love to eat. Writing for the *Empire City Weekly* . . . It was a way to explore the city. To try new foods. Knishes. Noodles. Everything sort of snowballed from there."

He turned me in his arms. Boy, he smelled good. Like cherries and wine, like laundry soap and woodsmoke. "Jo, you don't need to apologize for doing what you love. Not to me."

But I did. I was already using him for inspiration. Without his knowledge. For him to suggest that I draw on his experience, his recipes, his passion in the kitchen, to write a book—his cookbook, with his name in big letters on the front . . .

"I don't want to take advantage of you," I said.

"Maybe I am taking advantage of you."

"I don't think so." I had to tell him about the blog.

"No? Not when I do this?" His lips brushed my jaw. "Or this?" I felt the scrape of his beard as he kissed my neck. His body was hot and solid against mine. *Oh, glory.*

"You're just after my pie," I managed.

His smile curved against my throat. "I am after all of you."

I put my hands on either side of his face, raising his head so I could look into his eyes. Clear, warm eyes that saw and promised so much.

"I'm not just using you for your recipes, you know," I said.

"No?"

"Nope." Rising on tiptoe, I whispered close to his ear, "I'm also attracted to your great . . . big . . . *bed!*"

Laughing, I whirled and ran. I heard his low laugh as he followed, chasing me down the hall.

We ate the pie in bed.

CHAPTER 14

Meg

"Once I get all your customers set up, this program can generate invoices directly," I told Carl on Thursday. "Plus, I can integrate the accounting system with your farming software so you can see all your orders, which will make it much easier to track your inventory."

Carl winced slightly. "So, every time I make a sale, I have to enter it in the computer?"

"You can do everything from your phone." I clicked a few keys. "Or you can leave the receipts in a basket to deal with later, the way you did when your mother was keeping the books."

"This is incredible. Thanks for getting me organized."

"You should see my Tupperware drawer." Smiling, I pushed back from the desk in his farm office. "The initial setup will take a while, but eventually this system is going to save you a ton of time."

He propped a hip against a corner of the battered desk. "You trying to talk yourself out of a job?"

My smile grew. "Not at all. But you probably won't need me for more than five hours a week. Then once a month, I'll balance your bank account, and you'll be set."

"Seriously, you're amazing."

He was such a nice guy. Why was he still running around avail-able? Maybe I should fix him up with Beth. "You remember my sister, don't you?"

"Jo? Sure."

"Beth."

Carl rubbed his beard with the back of his hand. "The blonde."

"That's Amy." Everybody remembered Amy. "Beth is the older one. She was a year behind you in school."

"I don't . . ." He shrugged. "Maybe."

Well. It was just an idea. I shouldered my giant mommy bag, pre-paring to go. I'd dressed for this meeting in cute boots and a new sweater, applied mascara, flat-ironed my hair, even shaved my legs. To-tally wasted on Carl, of course, but the small rituals made me feel more confident. More like my old bank self.

"So I'll see you Saturday," Carl said. "At the farmers' market."

"Oh. Yes."

I felt bad about asking John to take off work again so I could sell cheese. But it was only for one more week, I told myself as I left. And maybe I could find a way to make it up to him. The twins were in ex-tended care today. Maybe I should stop by the dealership on my way to the preschool and tell him how the meeting went with Carl. We could celebrate. Go out to lunch.

Barbecue, I thought as I drove. I could pick up something on the way. We could eat in his office. Like a picnic. With the blinds closed, for privacy. No one to see, no babies to interrupt, just two consenting adults sharing lunch over a large, horizontal surface.

I'd told John I wanted him to be happy. Barbecue and sex should do the job.

I pictured myself walking into his office. *Hello, you,* I'd say. *I have plans for you.*

I'd lock the door to his office, and he'd smile at me, that slow, it's-going-to-be-good-honey smile, and I'd grab his tie, tugging him closer, pulling him to stand between my shaved legs. He'd sweep the papers

to the floor with one arm and lay me down and we'd do it on his desk,
in his office, surrounded by windows. My blood surged.

Ssh, he'd whisper, while he touched me, his hands making me hot
from the inside, and it would feel so right, so good I'd scream . . .

No screaming. Not at the dealership. Trey's office was right down
the hall. The receptionist, Kelly, would hear. John would be horrified.

Or maybe not. Maybe . . . My heart beat faster, thinking about it. I
could hardly wait.

The holiday sales event was in full swing at the dealership. A big red
bow decorated the shiny Ford truck at the showroom entrance.
Clusters of red and green Mylar balloons floated over the receptionist's
kiosk.

"Merry Christmas, Kelly!" I called cheerfully. "Is John with a client?"

Kelly looked up from her monitor. "Hey, Meg. No, he's—"

"Good. Don't buzz him." I smiled. "I want to surprise him."

"He's not here."

"But I brought lunch," I said stupidly. Like that made a difference.
"When is he coming back?"

"Not until two. Sorry." Her sympathy sounded genuine. "I'll be sure
to tell him you stopped by."

"Meg!" Trey emerged from the glass-fronted offices behind her,
looking like an Italian car ad in a slim, dark suit with a slim, dark shirt
open at the neck. No tie. If you were the owner's grandson, you didn't
need to follow the dress code. "What a nice surprise. Getting the car
detailed today?"

"I came to see John."

"He's not here."

"I told her," Kelly said.

Trey's gaze fell to the white barbecue bag in my grasp. "Is that from
Hooper's?"

His hopeful expression reminded me of the hungry boy who used to hang around Momma's kitchen, looking for cookies and invitations to dinner. "It is." I pulled myself together. "Want a pulled-pork sandwich, extra slaw?"

"That would be great. I'm starving. Come back to my office and we'll eat."

"Well. If you're sure I won't be interrupting . . ." I still had an hour before I had to pick up the twins.

"I always have time for your family, you know that. Kelly, can you grab us some sodas?"

So I had my picnic after all. In Trey's office. With the blinds open.

I swallowed. "Sorry about Saturday."

"What are you talking about?"

"When I flashed you in Sallie's bedroom. With Ned standing right there."

"Oh, that," Trey said easily. "I thought that was my Christmas present."

I smiled, grateful despite my hot face.

"I always wanted a threesome with old Ned," Trey added outrageously.

I threw my crumpled napkin at him. "Pervert."

He caught it and tossed it back. "Tease."

We grinned at each other.

His face sobered. "How's Abby doing?"

I filled him in as we ate, telling him all about Momma's lack of progress in therapy and the upcoming surgery on her spine. Not about the outstanding loan on the farm, though. Or the unsettling crack I'd glimpsed in my parents' seemingly perfect marriage. Trey was like a brother to me. But some things you didn't share.

Except with John. I could tell John.

Assuming we ever found time to talk.

I collected our lunch trash and stood to go. "Thanks for keeping me company."

"Thanks for the barbecue. John will be sorry he missed you."

"I should have called first."

"How would you know? He usually goes later, after school. But they had an early practice today. Teacher workday or something."

"I . . ." *What?*

"He felt bad about missing their tournament on Saturday," Trey said. "But he's making it up to the guys this week."

There was a faint buzzing in my ears. *"Their tournament." "The guys."* The wrestling team? Through the static, I remembered John's comment the night Trey came to dinner. *"Your dad's not the only one who has commitments on Saturday."*

"How did they do?" I heard myself ask.

Trey grinned. "They won. John didn't tell you? He was pretty pumped. At least he's not giving up all those lunch hours for nothing."

"All those lunch hours . . ." And Saturdays, too. I felt numb. "There's been a lot going on," I said. "It must have slipped his mind."

But I knew my husband hadn't forgotten. He deliberately hadn't told me he was volunteering to coach the wrestling team. All those Saturday mornings I thought he was at work, he was at the high school.

I felt so stupid. So blind. How had I failed to see what everybody knew?

When we girls were growing up, we always decorated the tree together, Beth humming carols while Amy flitted like a butterfly, arranging crocheted snowflakes to perfection, and Jo hung the funniest, ugliest ornaments at the top of the tree.

I wanted my babies to have what we had.

John had wrestled the tree into the stand and kept the twins occupied while I strung the lights. Now Daisy lay on her back under the Christmas tree, staring at the decorations twinkling overhead. DJ toddled around her, loading all the red balls onto a single branch in the center of the tree.

I reached into the last box of ornaments, sifting through memories.

A pottery heart—*Our First Christmas*—from John. A pair of baby rattles, pink and blue, Amy had made to mark the twins' birth. The Popsicle stick reindeer they'd glued together in preschool. Older ornaments, too, from my childhood, one for every Christmas growing up, hidden away in the toe of my stocking. Momma had saved them all to give to me the year I got married.

I glanced at John, methodically stacking empty cartons to go back into the attic. He didn't have a box from his mother. No ornaments, no traditions carefully preserved and passed on. He didn't have the example of two parents sticking together for better or worse, in sickness and in health, through chores and children and deployment. The only father he'd ever known walked out on his family when John was a little boy, leaving him without a male role model.

Carefully, I hung an angel on the tree. "I stopped by the dealership today."

"Yeah, Trey told me." Was it my imagination or did John sound wary? "Sorry I missed you. How'd your meeting go with Carl?"

"Well. The new accounting system will save him a lot of time. And I think I'll be able to do some of the work from home."

The overloaded branch finally gave up its burden, sending red balls bouncing and rolling all over the living room rug. Daisy shrieked—in outrage? delight?—as DJ stooped to grab a ball and threw it again at the tree.

"Good arm," John said.

"He must get his athletic ability from you." I dropped to my knees, digging under the couch for a rolling ornament. "Daisy, honey, it's all right."

John hooked a finger in the back of DJ's overalls, hauling him away from the tree. "That's good. As long as you're happy. You have enough on your plate right now dealing with your parents."

"Actually, I wanted to talk to you about that." I sat back on my heels. "Do you think you could stay home with the twins again this Saturday? It's the last farmers' market before Christmas."

John picked up Daisy. "I can do that."

"You can make more selling cars than I can selling cheese."

He shot me a glance. "It's not about the money, Meg."

"No, it's not." I took a deep breath. "If there's something else you have to do that day . . ."

His eyes flickered. "It doesn't matter. You heard Trey. The dealership can manage without me for one more day."

"And the wrestling team?" I asked in a steady voice. "Can they manage without you, too?"

John set our daughter carefully on her feet. "So you heard about that."

"Trey said something. I sort of guessed the rest. How long has this been going on?" I asked. Like I'd caught him having an affair.

He looked away, at the tree. "At first it was just . . . I dropped in every once in a while. To see how the team was getting on. But this summer, the coach quit to take a teaching job in Virginia, and Ben—you know Ben Hardy in the math department—took over the program. He means well, but he doesn't have any coaching experience. I'm just helping out until he learns the ropes."

DJ hung another red ball on the tree.

"I wish you'd said something."

He shrugged. "I didn't want to worry you."

"Not talking to me . . . That's what worries me. It's like my dad, keeping secrets from my mom. Or my mom, not telling my sisters about her surgery. You should have told me."

"Honey, it wouldn't have made any difference. It's not like I'm going to quit my job."

"Well, that's a relief," I joked.

He didn't say anything.

"John?"

Daisy picked a red ball from the floor and hung it on the tree.

"Mine!" DJ grabbed the ornament. Daisy smacked him.

I leaped to separate them. "No, no. Are you okay?" I asked DJ.

He clutched the red ball to his chest. "Mine."

"Sweetie, I know you like the red ones. But you have to share. And Daisy, no hitting. We don't hit. We have to use our words, okay? Tell DJ you're sorry."

"I not sorry. DJ bad."

"Nobody's bad," I said.

Daisy scowled. DJ's little face was flushed, his lower lip jutting dangerously.

"All right, kids, hug it out. Come on," John ordered when they dragged their feet. "Bring it in. Group hug."

He swept them into his lap, hugging them, loving them, tickling them. *Wrestling* with them until they giggled and squirmed.

"John." I hesitated. *Use your words.* "Do you have a tournament this weekend?"

His jaw set. "Doesn't matter. You're going to the farmers' market."

"Could we at least please talk about it?"

He kissed the top of Daisy's head. Set DJ on his feet. "Nothing to talk about."

"I could take the twins with me," I said.

"To the farmers' market."

I smiled. "Better than to a wrestling match."

He didn't laugh. "Why don't you ask Hannah to watch them?"

"She's in California, visiting James. Anyway, I can do it."

Shouldn't he be relieved? Why couldn't he just say *thank you*? I was trying to be supportive here.

Oh. *Oh.* I covered my mouth with my hand. All those times he'd offered to help and I'd turned him down . . . I'd never realized how it felt from this side. His side. Not good. "Please, John," I said. "Let me do this for you."

He rubbed the back of his neck. "If that's what you really want."

"I want us to be . . ." *Together. Connected. The way we used to be.* "Partners," I said.

"Then . . . Thanks." He met my eyes. "Partner."

CHAPTER 15

Jo

Y ou know, if you feed it," Frank said on Friday morning, "you'll never get rid of it. You're only encouraging it to stay."

You and me both, cat.

I straightened from my crouch in the alley, scaring the skinny black cat into retreat under the shadow of the Dumpster. The midday sun barely penetrated between the buildings. A crust of salt caked the curb, and icy slush filled the potholes, but everything inside me was sunshine and rainbows. "Who says I want to get rid of it? Cats keep down the mice."

"You're such a hick," Frank said.

"Please. Every bodega in the city has a cat. They chase the rats out of the snack aisles."

Truth. But I would have fed the cat anyway. Spreading the joy, right? Sharing the love.

My face flushed despite the cold. Not that this was love. Exactly. Yet.

I hugged my arms around my waist. If it were love, wouldn't I know? The way Meg had, the first time she met John. *"Love at first sight,"* she had claimed, and I'd rolled my eyes. My feelings for Eric had come on more gradually, respect and infatuation mixed with a healthy dose of lust. And trust. All I knew was I'd never felt this way before, never been able to feel for Trey the things he claimed to feel for me. Not that I didn't love Trey, in my own way. I certainly never wanted to hurt him. But I'd never been able to hear him say those three words without feeling panicky. Or suffocated. Or sorry. I sure as hell had never felt tempted to say them back.

"Whatever." Frank exhaled a stream of smoke. "Boss wants to see you when you clock in."

"Ray?"

"Chef."

My heart bumped pleasantly. "He's here?"

Frank pitched away his cigarette. "Just said so, didn't I?"

I was surprised. Eric had left my place around dawn. More convenient for me, since I needed to be at work before he did. I'd been busting my ass all week, determined to pull my weight in the kitchen. With Frank back on the line and the weekend looming, I had a ton of prep to do.

Maybe, I thought, he wanted to talk about the cookbook.

He hadn't mentioned it again. But the idea had stuck with me, like the smell of the kitchen that clung to my hair, sinking into my skin, gradually becoming part of me. I walked around with it for days. It rode with me on the subway and followed me to work. *You are a writer. Maybe you should write my cookbook.*

I tugged on the back door, releasing a gust of fat and garlic into the alley.

We needed to talk. This weekend, away from the restaurant. I didn't even question anymore that we would spend Eric's day off together.

Stupid me.

I ducked inside. The cooks were stocking their stations, slicing, chopping, joking, yelling, but as I entered the narrow work aisle, the kitchen fell suspiciously silent. A trio of back waiters nudged one another, one of them slipping his phone into his pocket in an elaborately casual gesture. I looked at Constanza for guidance, but our motherly garde-manger was deep in conversation with the dishwashing crew. Tomas caught my eye and winked.

"*Chula!*" Constanza bustled over. "How *are* you?"

"Fine. Why is everybody acting so weird?"

But I thought I knew. Gossip traveled like cockroaches through the kitchen. No matter how professionally Eric behaved, no matter how hard I worked, sooner or later word would get out I was sleeping with the boss.

"Not weird. No weird," Constanza said. "*Jefe*, he wants to see you."

"Thanks. I heard."

I wanted to see him, too. Anyway, I needed to change into my chef's coat.

I headed for the office, ignoring Lucas's sympathetic look as I passed. Ray was just leaving Eric's office. Ray handled routine staff matters—requests for overtime, advances, and days off. He was probably in there reminding Eric that women were trouble in the kitchen and I was a lawsuit waiting to happen.

He nodded stiffly. "March."

I gave him a dead-eye stare. "Chef."

Eric was standing at his desk, his back to the door.

"Hey." I smiled. "You wanted to see me?"

He turned. No answering smile. "Close the door, please."

I complied. He didn't move to kiss me. Didn't quite meet my eyes. Didn't acknowledge in any way that we'd been together last night. Which was fine, I told myself. Even with the door closed, the restaurant was no place for Public Displays of Affection. I'd never been touchy-feely anyway.

I angled my head. "What's up?"

He shifted, giving me a clear view of his desk, and nudged the computer so the monitor was facing me. "You tell me."

My heart moved into my throat. I looked at the screen. Oh. Oh *crap*.

There was my banner, *Hungry*, with its familiar apple-missing-a-bite graphic. (So far, Snow White and the computer people hadn't written a cease-and-desist letter demanding their logo back.) The headline was from two days ago: *Dumpling Love, A Taste of Home Wherever You Are*.

I'd written about mothers and comfort food, about the combinations of protein and noodles that spelled and smelled like home—Asian dumplings, Italian ravioli, Momma's chicken and dumplings, and . . . Yeah. There it was. A recipe for sweet potato pierogi. My own recipe, okay? No red cabbage. But still . . . Pierogi.

My stomach sank. When I checked this morning, I had thirty-two comments and almost a dozen shares on social media. Not my best-performing post, but close. Now there were eighty-one comments.

No, eighty-two. I blinked. Eighty-three.

Crap. "How did you . . ." Of course. "Ray."

"He follows this . . . *Hungry* on Instagram. Naturally, he didn't know it was you." Eric looked at me briefly. *Neither did I*, his eyes accused.

"Yeah." I swallowed. "Look, Eric, I . . ."

"I didn't believe him," my lover continued evenly. He reached for the keyboard, careful not to touch me, and scrolled down. "Until he showed me this."

Monday's post filled the screen. *Low and Slow: How to Make the Best Scrambled Eggs Ever!* I'd done my best to follow Eric's technique, beating and folding the eggs myself, staging a photo to go with each step of the instructions. The final shot, though, I'd taken earlier in the day. Those were Eric's eggs, fluffy yellow and perfectly smooth. That was his arm, holding the plate. And . . . those were his very recognizable tattoos.

I felt sick. I'd cropped that photo. I knew I had, to hide his identity. But maybe, in my hurry to get the blog done before our date, I'd uploaded the uncropped photo by accident.

"*There are no accidents,*" Momma used to say. Or maybe that was Freud.

"You wrote about me," Eric said. "About us."

"I wrote about dumplings." I glanced at the screen. Ninety comments. Ninety-four. Shit. I was going viral.

Something flickered in his eyes. Pride? Hurt. "I made you my mother's pierogi."

"They were delicious." Unable to help myself, I started reading the comments.

The first one was innocent enough. Great eggs, thanks!

I'm lactose intolerant, read the second. Can you use olive oil instead of butter?

Very "soigné." ☺, Sousbaby wrote. Who's your kitchen helper?

"I was honest with you," Eric was saying. "I opened myself to you, yeah? And you never said a word about this . . . this . . ."

I tore my eyes away. "It's a food blog, Eric. I'm a food blogger. It's not a big deal."

"Then why not tell me?"

"Because I knew you'd react like this!"

His face changed without moving, flesh into stone.

My throat thickened. I looked away again, toward the screen.

I usually add milk to my scrambled eggs. Can't wait to try this.

Hey, isn't that Eric Bhaer? asked Foodie10012. The chef at Gusto?

How can you tell? You can't see his face.

The flying pig. That's totally his tat.

I bit my lip. "At least they like the eggs."

Eric's eyes went flat. "This is a joke to you."

"No."

He folded his tattooed arms across his massive chest. "Did you see everybody out there? Do you know what they're talking about? You've made me look like a fool to my staff."

"I never mentioned you by name."

He started to reply. His cell phone buzzed. He looked at it and put it away, his lips tightening.

Not just the Gusto staff, I thought. Not if he was getting texts from outside the restaurant. Normally, I was happy when a post took on a life of its own. But this was awful.

"I trusted you," Eric said. "Like a fool. Like a lovesick teenager. And you lied to me."

"I didn't lie." Exactly. "I just . . ." *Didn't tell you.*

"Took something that was personal, private, and put it on your fucking blog without telling me."

"You knew I was a writer."

"A writer, yes. Not a blogger."

"Don't dis bloggers. I make money from that blog."

"Because you write about me. About my restaurant. You used me." My eye twitched. "I'm sorry."

"Sorry does not fix this."

"I made a mistake."

He folded his arms across his chest. "So did I."

My temper—my terrible temper—sparked and ignited. "By trusting me, you mean? Or by sleeping with me?"

"Shout a little louder," he said in a hard voice. "I don't think they can hear you in the kitchen."

The twitch became a throb. "You know, it's not like I deliberately set out to hurt you."

"How would I know? I do not know you. You tell me nothing."

I threw my arms wide. "What do you want me to say, Eric? What can I do?"

"Take it down."

"I can't. It's too late. It's already out there."

I'd linked my blog to all my social media accounts, Instagram, Facebook, Twitter, and Pinterest. Once a post got picked up by other bloggers, once it was tweeted and retweeted, liked and shared . . . Yeah. The food scene in New York fed on itself like a rat snake. The online community depended on networking. I couldn't have other sites, other bloggers, other influencers, clicking on a broken link.

I tried to explain. "It's not just one post. I can't delete the whole blog. I have a commitment."

"*You* have a commitment."

The scorn in his voice lashed heat to my face. My temper flared. "Yes. To my readers. To my advertisers."

"What about your commitment to me?"

A moment of electric stillness, charged with emotion, swirling with the bitter echoes of every argument I'd ever had with Trey. I would *not* give myself up to be with him.

"What commitment? We hooked up. We had sex. I'm your booty call."

He went very still. "You work for me."

He didn't contradict me, I noticed. *"We had sex. I'm your booty call."* Not, *We made love.* Not, *I love you.* Never that.

Not that I wanted that. My pulse throbbed in my head. "Maybe I should quit."

"Fine." His voice was a near-growl. "Walk off. Walk away four hours before service."

"I wouldn't do that." It was the cardinal sin of the kitchen, to call out without a substitute. "I'll give you two weeks' notice."

He said something in guttural German. "I don't want your fucking two weeks' notice."

"Don't you swear at me," I said.

"*Swear* at you? I'd like to . . ." He broke off, glaring. "Go. Just go. You're right. This situation—you working for me—I knew it would be a problem."

My vision blurred. My headache was blinding me. "Yes, *Chef.*"

I fumbled for the locker, my jacket, my knives. Pulling myself together to face the fire outside. To get back on the line.

E at," Constanza said, handing me a generous slice of flan. "You'll feel better."

If I ate anything, I'd throw up. "I'm good, thanks."

"I saw your review of Earl's," Lucas said. "Man, that was brutal. What does a guy have to do to get a good review from you?"

Frank snickered. "Ask Chef."

At least they weren't mad at me. They clustered around, curious and sympathetic. Suffocating.

Ray's face folded like a wet towel. "All right, back to work. All of you." His gaze flicked to me. "You good to go?"

"Go. Just go."

Out of his face? Or out of his kitchen? I couldn't leave. I couldn't walk off the line, leaving the kitchen short-staffed a few hours before service. *"What about your commitment to me?"*

"I'm fine." I was furious. Shattered.

"I want you on batch work today," Ray said.

I nodded. The assignment—making the vinaigrettes and aiolis the whole kitchen would use over the next two days—was a mark of his confidence in my ability to follow a recipe. Or maybe he just wanted to keep me out of Eric's way.

Smart move.

I blew my nose and washed my hands. Focusing on the ingredients, chopping and measuring, helped keep my mind off the fight in Eric's office. And if occasionally my eyes watered, hey, I blamed it on the onions. Anyway, I made it through the afternoon somehow without cutting myself or stabbing anybody with a kitchen knife.

An hour before service, Malik, the headwaiter, bustled into the kitchen with the reservations book. "Heads up. The phone's been ringing off the hook. We added twenty covers to the second seating."

Lucas swore. "I need to prep more sunchokes."

"You knew we'd be slammed. It's the holidays," Ray said.

"It's that blog. *Hungry*," Malik said. "Nothing brings out the foodies like thinking they know something nobody else don't know."

"We should sell tickets," Frank said.

"Give sex tours," Kevin suggested.

Lucas laughed. Constanza hit him with a spoon.

"What? Oh." He cleared his throat. "Sorry, Jo."

"It's fine," I said.

Not fine. I didn't want them to censor themselves on my account. I wanted the comfort of being one of the guys, part of the team.

When Eric called us together to demonstrate the day's specials, I hung back, not pressing with the others around the table. I watched over Constanza's shoulder as Eric layered colors and flavors on the plate, his hands beautiful and sure. I snuck a glance at his face once or twice. Okay, maybe three or four times. But he would not look at me.

When the staff gathered afterward for family meal, I fled to the storeroom, seeking out the deepest, darkest aisle behind the wire shelves. I was not going to snivel. I was not the type. I pulled out my phone, like a teenage boy surreptitiously surfing for porn.

The torrent of comments had slowed. One hundred fifty-eight. But interspersed with the usual comments (Yummy. Hate dry scrambled eggs. And Do you know where I can buy fresh farm eggs in Millington, New Jersey?) was speculation on Eric's identity. On mine. On our relationship. (I love it when my boyfriend cooks for me. And So does Bhaer wear the chef pants in the kitchen?)

You took something that was personal, private, and put it on your fucking blog without telling me.

Meg had messaged me a picture of a Christmas tree, a cluster of red balls weighing down one branch, a snapshot of her small, bright, perfect life. Decorating with Daisy and DJ!

A swell of longing for my sister swept over me. I tapped my phone once. Twice. *Don't go to voice mail, please don't go to voice mail . . .*

"Jo?"

I swallowed hard. "Hey, Meg. Whatcha doing?"

"Just throwing dinner together." Something clattered on the stove. "What's up?"

I couldn't speak.

"Jo?" The concern in her voice nearly made me cry. "Can you hear me?"

I cleared my throat. "I'm here."

"What's the matter?"

I slept with my boss. But I posted his mother's recipe for pierogi on my blog, and I lied to him, and now he's acting like I released a sex tape.

"I just wanted to say hey."

"Hey back at you. No crackers, Daisy. Mommy's making dinner."

"I hungry now, Mommy."

"Sorry. You're busy," I said. Meg was always busy. She had twins. Not to mention she was visiting our mother in rehab and shoveling out the goat barn on a regular basis.

"A little," Meg admitted. ("*I starving to deaf,*" Daisy said in the background.) "I'm doing the books for Carl Stewart now. And I've got to work the farmers' market again tomorrow."

"Who's Carl Stewart?"

"He was a couple years behind you in school? He took over his parents' farm."

"Oh. That sounds like fun," I offered.

"So much fun," my sister said dryly.

I held the phone, reluctant to let her go. "How's Momma?"

"*No, Daisy.*"

"Meg?"

"Sorry," my sister said. "You know Momma. God forbid we make a fuss."

"A fuss about what?" Silence. "Meg?"

"She doesn't want you to worry."

A sickening feeling settled in my stomach. "Meg! You can't say something like that and then *not* tell me. I'll only worry more."

Meg sighed. "Okay. But you can't let on I told you. She has to have an operation on her back. On the twenty-third."

"Oh God. Is she going to be all right?"

"I think so. The doctor says so. Apparently she has a pinched nerve in her spine. The surgery is supposed to relieve the compression. But you can't tell Beth and Amy."

"Of course not." Bethie felt horrible enough already about missing Christmas with the family. Any more stress, any more pressure, any excuse to come home, and she'd crack like an egg. And Amy couldn't afford the airfare. I frowned. "You said the twenty-third?"

"That's the only time the OR was available. I guess they have a lot of surgeries scheduled before the end of the year."

"That's right before Christmas."

"I know." My sister sighed. "Listen, sweetie, I have to go."

"Meg . . ."

"I'll call you later."

She disconnected, leaving me alone in the dark. The door to the storeroom opened. I looked up, a quick flutter of hope in my chest.

"March?"

It was only Ray. Damn it. Probably worried I was going to leave him shorthanded.

I wiped my nose on my sleeve. Tightened my ponytail. "I'll be out in a minute."

"Aaron is here. You've got time." The sous appeared around a corner of the shelving, his white coat dimmed by the shadows. "I brought you stew."

That was a surprise.

"I'm not hungry," I said. My stomach felt filled with cement.

"Eat." He held out a bowl and a fork. "We can't have you fainting on the line."

He watched, a little frown between his brows, as I poked at the bowl's contents, chicken thighs in a stock of parsley, mint, and onions over rice.

"*He wants too much to impress,*" Eric had said. But for the first time, I could see the sous chef's fussy manner as part of a genuine desire to please.

"Thanks." The warm broth soothed my aching throat.

"What are you going to do now?" Ray asked.

After tonight, he meant. The realization roused a near-panic in my chest. I had an education I wasn't using and a studio I could barely afford. My mother was facing surgery, my sister was distracted, and my boss/boyfriend didn't want to look at me.

"*Go. Just go.*"

"I don't know." I swallowed. "I need to think."

CHAPTER 16

Meg

At five minutes after nine, the sun was shining. The market was filled with people pushing strollers, sampling apples and cookies, carrying bulging bags of carrots and cabbage, collards and kale. The air smelled like Christmas, pine with a hint of cold, as if the tree sellers at the end of the lot had brought the mountain air with them.

I lowered the Explorer's rear seats, making a play space in the back of the SUV, spreading out blankets and pillows, unpacking board books and blocks, arranging the twins' car seats like chairs around a plastic play table behind the cargo net.

"This is your fort," I said. Making it a game.

DJ smiled and crawled under the table.

"Is a tent, Mommy," Daisy said.

I smiled at her in gratitude. "That's right. It's your tent to play in while Mommy's working."

"Nice setup," Carl Stewart said behind me.

"We camping," Daisy informed him with pride.

"Good for you." Carl glanced at me. "No fair, using your cute kids to sell cheese."

I unzipped their jackets, unpacked snack cups and juice boxes for each of them. "You could rent them. For the right price. Sell more sweet potatoes."

He grinned. "You should bring them to the buyer's meeting."

I turned. "What meeting?"

"I mentioned your operation to my buyer at All Seasons. Talked up the family farm angle, said how you were taking over from your ma. He said you should call, set up a meeting. If he likes you, he'll kick your product profile over to the specialty buyer—their cheese guy. You interested?"

"Carl, that's amazing. But . . ." *All Seasons?* I shook my head to clear the dollar signs dancing in my brain. "We're not big enough."

"They don't want big. They're looking for local. Anyway, Abby was talking about expanding. Before she got sick, I mean."

"But wouldn't she need . . ." *Inventory. Employees.* "A business plan?"

He smiled. "I reckoned you'd be helping her with that."

My mind spun. "I could." I *could*. The prospect made me dizzy. "I'd have to talk it over with her first."

"Sure. You decide you want to go for it, I'd be happy to walk you through the process."

"That . . . That's incredibly generous of you."

He winked. "Hey, you're helping me. I'm just returning the favor."

My mother needed money. Getting into All Seasons was like an answer to a prayer. A solution to all her problems. If I could do it.

Daisy was feeding Cheerios one by one to DJ.

"Excuse me, are you open?" a woman asked.

"Yes, ma'am. What would you like to try?"

"You're Coach Brooke's wife, aren't you?" she asked as I rang up her purchase.

"I'm just the car guy," John had said the night of Sallie's party.

I smiled. "Meg Brooke. Yes. Hi."

She nodded in satisfaction. "I thought I recognized you from

Patrick's season. I'm Lisa Roberts," she added. "Patrick's mom. His brother Jason is a freshman on the team now."

"Nice to see you again. Good luck in the tournament today."

"Oh, I don't go to the matches anymore." She leaned forward confidingly. "I can't stand to watch Jason compete. He's so small compared to the other boys."

"You do know they wrestle by weight class," I said.

"That's what Coach says. But Jason is my baby. Thank God your husband's there."

"Yes. I mean, thank you. That'll be fourteen dollars."

"So, I'll see you at the athletic banquet?" she said as I handed her her change. "After States?"

"I'm not sure. That's in . . ."

"February," she said.

Months away. I couldn't look beyond Christmas, couldn't see past every day's list of Things To Do.

"I'll have to talk to John," I said.

At the next break in the line, Connie dashed from her bakery stall with fresh baguettes and cookies for the kids.

"You have to let me pay you," I said.

"No, no. You sent a ton of business my way last week."

"Cookie," DJ said, crawling out from under the play table.

"Not now, sweetie. You have Cheerios," I said.

"No!"

"Do you want apple slices?"

"*No!*"

"He wants a cookie, Mommy," Daisy said.

"And these are for you," Connie said. She handed me a short stack of her bakery's business cards. "If you don't mind putting them out with the samples, maybe?"

"Not at all. I can put them in the bags, too. They're pretty." I fingered the thick card stock, admiring the whimsical font. Made on her home printer, I was sure, but . . . My mind went to the buyer for All

Seasons. Wouldn't I need business cards if I went to meet him? "I was thinking we should get some made up for Mom. As a Christmas present, maybe."

Amy had a degree in art. She could design something. Maybe an updated logo. Labels. Branding was important.

"Abby would love that," Connie said. "How's she doing?"

"She needs spinal surgery," I heard myself say.

Connie's smile dissolved in sympathy. "I'm so sorry. When?"

"The twenty-third."

"Right before Christmas?"

I nodded.

"Mama. Cookie," DJ insisted.

"You haz to eat your Cheerios," Daisy said.

"No!" DJ said, giving his sister a push.

I intervened. "DJ, do you want some juice?"

"No! Cookie!" DJ shouted, flinging himself at the cargo net. "Cookie, cookie!"

I grabbed him before he flipped over onto the asphalt.

"I should go," Connie said, backing away. "You have customers."

I did. All of them looking at me like I was the worst mother in the world. I gave DJ a cookie.

"Me, too, Mommy," Daisy said. "I want a cookie, too."

So I gave them both cookies because, you know what? They deserved cookies. "Who wants to watch *Frozen* on Mommy's iPad?" I asked.

"*Frozen!*"

Daisy beamed. "Peez, Mommy."

For the next hour and forty-nine minutes, they were little angels. With one eye on the back of the Explorer, I offered samples and sold cheese, made change and conversation.

"Mommy."

"Yes, baby?"

"I haz to pee," Daisy said.

Too many juice boxes. My bad.

I did a quick calculation. The library restroom was too far away. The park was closer, but that would involve a detour to the playground. I looked at my daughter's anxious face, at DJ, idly rubbing the satin edge of his blanket against his cheek. It would have to be the playground.

"What a big girl you are. Thank you for telling Mommy."

"Meg! I was just fixing to call you."

Sallie.

I snapped the cashbox closed. "Hey, Sallie. I should have called you. To thank you for the party."

"You left early. I barely saw you."

Ned saw me. Clear to the waist. I stooped to zip DJ's jacket, hiding my hot face. "Well, you know . . . The kids . . ."

"I haz to pee *bad*," Daisy said, right on cue.

"In a minute, honey. I'm taking them to the park," I said to Sallie. "There's a restroom there."

"Oh." Sallie's face fell and then brightened. "I could go with you. Like old times."

The times when we did everything together, including go to the bathroom. Sneaking off to reapply lip gloss, to check our teeth in the mirror and readjust our thongs. Dragging each other off to compare notes on our dates, for pep talks or a good cry. Always a pair, Sallie and Meg.

A thirtysomething wearing a knit toboggan hat stepped up, recalling me to the present. "You got any of that cheese from last week? In the jar?"

I cleared my throat. "The marinated feta? We sure do."

Daisy danced from foot to foot. *"Mommy."*

"Sorry," I said. To the guy in the knit hipster hat? To Sallie? "I'll be right back."

"Let me take her," Sallie said.

"I don't . . . DJ should go, too."

"I can take both of them."

I hesitated. Hipster Hat was waiting.

Sallie smiled winningly. "Please?"

"Peez!" Daisy repeated.

"They can be a handful. Do you want the stroller?"

"Do you guys want the stroller?" Sallie asked my children. "No? Let's go, then. Maybe after we go potty—"

"And wash our hands," I added automatically.

"Go potty *and* wash our hands," Sallie said without missing a beat. "Your mommy will let us go to the playground."

DJ clapped.

"I Daisy. Who you?"

"I'm Mommy's friend Sallie."

I watched her skip off hand in hand with the twins, my stomach squiggling with the usual stupid worries. Did she know to take both children into the stall with her? To make sure DJ aimed up, not down? To wait for Daisy at the bottom of the slide?

More than an hour later, Sallie brought the twins back. The market crowd had thinned. I was out of singles, out of bread, almost out of fresh chèvre.

"Sorry we took so long," Sallie said breezily. "We stopped for cookies. I hope that's okay."

I looked at my babies. Daisy held on to Sallie with one hand, the other rubbing her eyes. DJ's head rested in the crook of Sallie's neck, his thumb creeping toward his crumb-streaked mouth. They looked tired. Grubby. Happy.

"It's great," I said sincerely. "Thank you so much, Sallie."

"They're kind of zonked." She nodded toward the back of the Explorer. "You want me to put Deej in there?"

I held out my arms. "I'll do it."

His warm weight settled on my shoulder. I inhaled as I buckled him into his car seat, tucking Blankie around him. He smelled delicious, like sugar cookies and little boy.

"No," Daisy protested as I lifted her into her car seat.

I let her lie on the comforter, smoothing back her bangs, kissing her forehead.

"Thanks for taking care of my kids," I said to Sallie.

"Anytime. They're adorable."

I wanted to kiss her in gratitude. I swallowed instead. "Sallie . . . About last Saturday . . ."

"This is about Ned, isn't it?"

"I . . . Well . . ."

"I knew he had too much to drink. Was he a total asshole?"

"*No.*" Oh God, no. "It's just . . . We were flirting a little, and I didn't want you to think . . ."

"That my husband was so insecure about his lousy sperm count that he'd hit on my best friend?"

I blinked. "Oh, Sallie. Oh, honey. Nothing like that. We were just talking."

"He won't talk to me," Sallie burst out. "He says all I care about anymore is my fertility cycle. Like I'm the only one who wants kids. He doesn't even want to have sex anymore. That's why we're going to Hawaii. I thought if we went away . . . Like he's going to get it up after six mai tais."

I didn't know what to say. I hugged her. "I'm so sorry."

She sniffled against my shoulder. "That's okay. You didn't know."

No, you didn't. Momma said the only people who knew what went on in a marriage were the two people in it.

And sometimes not even them. (An image of my parents arguing in my mother's hospital room rose like a ghost in the back of my mind. "*If I weren't sick, you'd never talk to me at all.*")

I pulled a tissue from the pack I always carried and handed it to her. "Ned loves you. I'm sure he does. You guys will figure it out."

"Thanks." Sallie blew her nose. "Mother says if I'd just relax and stop stressing, I'd get pregnant right away."

"Your mother is an idiot."

Sallie gave a watery chuckle. "Thanks." She dabbed at her eyes. "I feel better now that I've talked to somebody."

"Have you guys tried counseling?"

"Ned won't go. He says he's sick of doctors asking about his junk."

"He's a guy," I said, thinking of John. "It's hard for men to talk about their feelings."

"You're so lucky being married to John. You two have the perfect relationship."

"Even John doesn't tell me everything."

"At least your husband's not off getting drunk at parties."

"No, he just spent all evening with the waiter."

"What?"

Flushing, I shook my head. "It doesn't matter." Except it did.

After Sallie left—with many hugs and promises to keep in touch—I packed up and loaded the SUV with the twins, the car seats, the cashbox, the coolers.

John was still at the tournament. Maybe when he got back we could talk. Although part of me worried about digging too deeply beneath the surface of our happy life. Because we were happy. Mostly. Right?

I drove down the bumpy gravel road past empty fields toward the farm. The goats crowded the fence of their hay enclosure as they recognized the rumble of my car.

An unfamiliar car was parked in the driveway. The back of my neck prickled, and my fingertips. Which was ridiculous. This was Bunyan. My mother still left her doors unlocked. On the other hand . . . Who knew who might have followed or tracked my father home? It would be dark in an hour. I had my babies in the car.

The back door opened. My sister Jo bolted down the porch steps, letting the screen door crash behind her. "Meg!"

"Jo!" I fumbled out of my seat belt, tumbled from the car, and she ran into my arms.

CHAPTER 17

Jo

Meg insisted on staying with me at the farmhouse until Dad got home.

"What about John?" I asked. "Isn't he expecting you?"

"I texted him. He said it was fine." Meg unzipped DJ's jacket. "He's busy today anyway."

"Working?" I asked sympathetically.

"Wrestling tournament. He's been volunteering with the team."

Fine by me. Selfishly, I wanted my sister to myself for a while. My sister and the twins. Their welcoming cries of *Auntie Jo!*, the warm clasp of their little arms, were balm to my bruised heart. Two-year-olds do not judge. I hugged them close, breathing in the scent of their necks, grateful for their earnest self-absorption, their distracting wriggliness.

While I scrounged in the kitchen for dinner, Meg plucked Daisy away from Weasley's food dish, prying kibble from my niece's mouth with one finger. "No, sweetie. We don't eat cat food."

Daisy set her hands on her hips. "But I hungry, Mommy. I a hungry kitty."

"Does the hungry kitty want some noodles?" I asked.

"Yessss! Noodles! Noodles, Auntie Jo."

"Noodles," DJ said.

"Coming up in two shakes of a kitty's tail," I promised. I opened a Tupperware container and sniffed. Tomatoes, peppers . . . Chili? Spaghetti sauce, I decided.

"I can't believe he fired you," Meg said.

He. Eric.

"He didn't fire me," I said, determined to be fair. *He broke my heart. Or I broke his.* I dumped the frozen block into a pot and poked it with a spoon. "I quit."

"I cook, too, Auntie Jo," Daisy said, rattling spoons in a pot.

"I see that. Great job," I said.

"I feel guilty, sitting here while you do all the cooking," Meg said.

"I'm not cooking. I'm heating stuff up."

"Well, thank you for heating stuff."

"Don't thank me. Thank Dad's church ladies." I stirred the pot and held the spoon to her lips. "Wine?"

"It tastes fine to me," Meg said.

"I meant for us."

Meg laughed. "There's wine in the pantry. Left over from Thanksgiving."

Pinot noir. Trey could say what he liked about his grandfather, but the old boy knew how to buy wine. I opened a bottle and poured some vino into glasses. Splashed some into the sauce.

"I meant to go shopping before you came," Meg said.

"I'm a week early."

"Christmas shopping," Meg said. "I was going to buy a tree."

Oh. I looked around at the faded hydrangea wallpaper, the salt and pepper shakers shaped like birds, the windup kitchen clock. Everything the same, dear and familiar. The air even smelled the same, of old wood and books and, faintly, of the barn. But now that Meg had pointed it out, I could see neglect lying over the house like the patina of woodsmoke. A pile of mail instead of the Christmas village on the lowboy. A film of dust on the piano where the Nativity scene should be. No wreath, no tree, no candles shining welcome from the windows.

A longing for our mother pierced me. And for our father, although making the house ready for Christmas had never been his thing. Or mine, either.

"I could do it. Decorate, I mean," I said. "Now that I'm home."

Meg smiled. "We'll do it together. Like we used to."

"I'm so glad you're here," I said.

"I'm glad you're here, too."

"Whatever happens, you have each other," Momma used to say. I'd never been more grateful for my sister's presence.

We ate dinner together in the kitchen. Anyway, Meg and I ate. The twins dropped noodles on the floor and smeared red sauce on the table.

"They had cookies for lunch," Meg explained, mopping a milk spill. She turned her gaze on me. "What will you do now?"

I swallowed, my appetite gone. "I figured I'd stay here."

"For Christmas," Meg said.

"For Mom's surgery and Christmas." I shoved pasta around my plate. "Maybe longer. Until Mom's out of rehab."

Meg's eyes were full of doubt. "That could be weeks. What about your apartment?"

"I can't afford the rent as it is. I was going to have to let it go anyway. Move to the Bronx. Find another roommate." I shrugged. "Maybe I'll sublet."

"Won't that make it harder to go back?"

"What happened to, *'I'm glad you're here'*?"

"I am glad. It wouldn't feel like Christmas without you. Especially with the girls gone this year."

"The house is awfully quiet." I grinned. "No Amy drama."

"No Bethie singing."

"I can't believe our little Mouse is a YouTube sensation."

"Jealous?" Meg asked.

"No." *Maybe.* I drank more wine. "I'm proud of her. It's time she spread her wings."

"You don't think this Colt Henderson is taking advantage of her?"

"I don't want to take advantage of you," I'd told Eric.

"Maybe I am taking advantage of you," he'd said, kissing my neck.

The memory made me squirm. "He's using Beth's song in his show," I pointed out. "I'd say the advantage is on her side."

"I know. I only meant she's not very experienced," Meg said.

"Which is why this is such a great opportunity. She needs someone who can bring her out of her shell. Coax her into the spotlight."

"Professionally, sure. But she sounded a little starstruck on the phone."

Uneasiness slithered through me. "That's not necessarily a bad thing. Look at me and Eric."

"Because that turned out so well."

I flushed. "My point is, he didn't take advantage of me. Anyway, Beth would have told me if there was anything like that going on."

"I'm just worried. She's never even had a boyfriend."

True. Long after Amy had moved on to magazines and makeup, Beth was still taking care of our discarded Barbies, styling their chopped-off hair, bandaging their missing limbs.

I shook my doubts away. "If she's going to have any kind of career, she needs to get the hell out of Bunyan."

Meg gave me her Mom Look. "What about you?"

I swallowed. "What about me?"

"You couldn't wait to leave Bunyan and go to New York." Meg stooped to retrieve DJ's spoon from the floor. "I'm surprised you're giving up on it, that's all."

I stared at her, stung. I wasn't giving up. Eric wanted me gone, I was gone. Back home, where I was needed, where I was loved. "Hey. You're supposed to be on my side."

"I am totally on your side," Meg said. "You should sue his ass for sexual harassment."

Her unaccustomed fierceness made me grin. But some deep-rooted instinct, pride or fairness, made me say, "It wasn't harassment. Sleeping together was my idea. My choice." I gulped my wine. "My mistake."

Meg nodded. "So you ran away."

I lowered my glass. "What are you talking about?"

"Well." Meg took a sip of her own wine. "That's what you do. You ran away from Bunyan. You ran away from Trey. Anytime you get too close emotionally, you bolt."

Guilty. Damn it. "Not this time," I argued. "He rejected me. He said he didn't *know* me. After we'd been . . . You know. Intimate."

"After you'd had sex."

I scowled. "No. Yes. Meg, he slept at my *apartment.* We went running together. We cooked together. And then he dumped me."

"Asshole," Meg said.

I turned my fingers over to lace them with hers. I couldn't stay mad at my sister. It was easier—safer—to be mad at Eric. "I love you."

Meg squeezed my hand. "Love you, too."

"Ath-thole," DJ repeated.

Meg covered her mouth with her hand, her gaze darting to meet mine.

I fought a grin. "Sorry."

"I not a ath-thole," Daisy said. "I a kitty."

"Athole! Athole!" DJ said gleefully, banging his spoon.

Meg's laugh spurted. "And . . . It's bedtime."

I didn't want her to go. "So, shoo. I've got this." I stood to stack our plates.

"I'm not leaving," Meg said. "I'll put the kids down in Beth and Amy's room until Dad gets home."

Gratitude swamped me. If Mom were here . . . But she wasn't. And as close as I felt to our father, I could never talk to him the way I talked to Meg. Unless he was counseling one of his vets, heart-to-hearts weren't really his style. A daughter's breakup barely registered on his trauma scale.

Alone with the dishes, I listened to the twins' footsteps as they ran down the hall, the squeak of the old box springs, the rise and fall of Meg's voice as she read them a story. If I ever had kids—which was probably never going to happen, given how my life was going—I hoped I'd be as good a mom as Meg.

A snatch of lullaby drifted down the stairs. *"Silent night . . ."* A fat, hot tear slid down my nose and plopped into the sink. Crap.

"No use crying over spilled milk," Momma would say.

I dried my hands and reached for my phone. As if a handful of new blog comments would make me less alone. I checked my text messages. Nothing.

I mopped my eyes with the dish towel and went outside.

I teetered on the railing of the front porch, stretching for the hook I was sure our mother had screwed into the eaves.

"What on earth are you doing?" Meg asked.

I glanced at my sister, silhouetted in the doorway. "Putting up the Christmas lights."

"But it's dark," said my sister rationally.

"That's why we need them."

She tipped her head to one side, considering the open cartons and tangles of wires spread over the shadowed porch.

I held my breath, hoping she would understand my need to do something. Waiting for the *Jo, be reasonable* look she'd given me our entire lives.

"I'll get the ladder," my sister said.

An hour later, Meg was pink-cheeked with cold and exertion. I had scratches on both arms and a splinter throbbing in my thumb. Overhead, the stars shone, pure and clear as angel voices. I could not see the river, but I could smell water, like snow or promise in the air. Weasley, safe from Daisy, twitched his tail on the porch rail, lit by the glow of fat, multicolored lights. Candles shone from every window. More lights bloomed on the front of the house, festooning the bushes and twining up the crepe myrtle.

I was pretty sure our mother would have approved.

"It looks great," Meg said.

"Yeah." *Like home.* I shot her a sideways glance. "Want to do the tree now?"

She huffed with amusement. "We have to buy one first."

"There should still be an old one around somewhere. From when Daddy was deployed?" Our mother had always insisted we celebrate Christmas together as a family. One year that tree stood, covered in ornaments and dust, until February, when Dad came home from Iraq.

"The fake one? Great. Maybe we can get DJ to throw balls at it," Meg said.

I leaned my head against her shoulder, a little buzzed with wine and lack of sleep. "Thanks for being here."

She hugged me, enveloping me in her warm Meg smell, babies and Pantene shampoo. "What are sisters for?"

I felt a twinge of guilt. I hadn't exactly been there for her lately. "How are you doing?"

"Fine."

I snorted. "You sound like Mom."

"Yeah." Meg looked away.

"We should tell the girls about her surgery on Friday."

"I know. But what good would it do? It's not like they can come home."

"They still have a right to know."

"It's not our place to tell them."

"Have you talked to Dad?"

"To Mom *and* Dad. She doesn't want to worry them. And he doesn't want to upset Mom."

"I could e-mail them," I offered.

"Because that's reassuring," Meg said dryly.

I shrugged.

"Fine. I'll tell them," Meg said, taking Mom's role as she always did. Taking responsibility. *Thank God.* "I'll tell them everything's fine and they don't need to come."

"Thanks."

Her smile flickered. "It's what I do."

"Make everybody feel better?"

"Pretty much." Her tone was light.

I peered at her, trying to read her expression in the dark. Trying to imagine how it would be to have everyone depending on me all the time, to be responsible for everybody's feelings. "So, what's this about you going to work for Carl Stewart?"

"Oh, that. It's just part-time. A couple hours a week, helping out with the books since his parents retired. I can do most of it from home."

"Following your passion," I said, half joking.

"I don't have a passion. I'm an accountant."

"But you like numbers."

Meg nodded. "I like the clarity. The responsibility. And I'm not going to lie—I like getting paid."

"What does John think about you going back to work?"

"John says it's my decision. Whatever I want, he said."

"Well, that sucks."

She laughed. "A little. Like it's all on me. But, really, he just wants me to be happy. He gave up teaching so I could stay home with the kids. He doesn't want to take that choice away from me. I think maybe because his mom didn't have a choice, you know? She had to work."

"Whatever you want," Eric had said. Because he didn't want to take advantage of an employee. Because he trusted me to say no. Like I could be myself, and it would be okay. Me telling him what I wanted freed him to say what he wanted.

Until he wanted me to go.

Headlights swung up the drive. I raised my head, squinting against the glare. "Dad's home."

But he wasn't.

A white Mercedes pulled up to the barn, and a well-upholstered woman in a purple car coat climbed out, a plastic cake saver in one hand, her little dog cradled in the other.

"Aunt Phee," Meg said. "What a surprise."

"I could say the same." Our aunt's gaze swept the glowing lights and the bottle of wine before narrowing on me. "What are you doing here?"

"It's Christmas," I said.

"Not for another week. But I suppose there's nothing to keep you in New York now that you've lost your job." My job at the paper, she meant. But her words stabbed anyway. She was right. I was twenty-eight years old, underemployed, unattached, and back where I started. "Unless you're finally dating someone," she added, twisting the knife.

"Nope. Just having meaningless sex with my boss."

Aunt Phee snorted with laughter, surprising us both. "Well, you're honest, at least."

"*I was honest with you*," Eric said. "*I opened myself to you, yeah? And you never said a word about this . . . this . . .*"

"Jo came home to help Mom," Meg said.

"I hope your mother appreciates it. This whole hospital nonsense has been very difficult for your father." The Yorkie yapped as Phee climbed the stairs. Weasley jumped down with a disgruntled thump and slunk under the porch swing. Too bad there wasn't room under there for both of us. "Where is Ashton? He should be home by now."

"He's having dinner with Momma," Meg said. "At the rehab center."

Aunt Phee's coral lips pursed. "But I brought dessert."

I rolled my eyes. Who put on lipstick and drove across town at nine o'clock at night to deliver dessert to a grown-ass nephew?

Oh.

Somebody lonely, that's who. Aunt Phee had been widowed as long as I could remember. No living parents. No kids. All she had was a bad-tempered little dog. And our father.

"Is that your hummingbird cake?" I asked. "It looks awesome." Not that I could see much through the plastic shield.

Aunt Phee clutched the cake saver tighter. "It's for your father."

Right. Another offering on the altar of the Reverend Ashton March.

"Do you want to come in?" Meg asked politely. "I can make coffee."

"It's too late. Drinking coffee after three o'clock in the afternoon interferes with your sleep." She gave a pointed look at the bottle of wine. "So does drinking alcohol."

Meg and I exchanged glances.

"It *is* late," Meg agreed. I scratched the Yorkie behind the ears. "Jo's had a long day. Maybe we should all say good night."

"You certainly should," Aunt Phee said. "Before that husband of yours gets tired of waiting for you."

"John understands I had to work today," Meg said, sticking up for herself in her quiet way.

"Well, of course he'd *say* that. Bless his heart. His mother never stayed home with him, did she?"

Polly nipped the fleshy part of my thumb. I pulled back my hand, sticking the bite in my mouth. "Jeez. Somebody's feeling cranky."

"Polly is sensitive," Aunt Phee snapped. "And you're a fine one to talk, missy. I don't see anybody waiting at home for you."

Meg sputtered. I choked.

Aunt Phee nodded once in apparent satisfaction. She thrust the cake saver at me. "You tell your father to come see me," she said, and marched back to her car.

Gravel rattled beneath her wheels as she pulled out of the driveway. Meg bit her lip.

I caught her eye. "It's like being related to Almira Gulch."

Meg smiled. "Riding away on her broomstick?"

"Bicycle."

"Whatever."

I cackled. "I'll get you, my pretty. And your little dog, too."

"You made your bed," Meg said in her best Wicked Witch voice. "You ought to go lie in it." She wagged a finger at me. "Preferably with your husband."

I snickered. "At least you *have* a husband."

Somehow we were giggling, laughing, holding on to our sides and each other until Meg was wheezing and I was out of breath.

"Poor old Aunt Phee," Meg said.

"She's a bitch," I said.

"She's lonely," Meg said.

"I know." I squatted to hold out my hand, coaxing the cat from under the swing. "That'll be me in forty years. I don't have anybody, either."

"You have us," Meg said.

The cat sniffed my fingers. I rubbed his head. "And Weasley. Maybe I'll be a cat lady like Bethie."

"Or you could get a little dog," Meg said.

"Ha. Not in a million years."

"You're right. Dogs are too much work. Besides, you like being on your own," Meg said.

"True." We sat on the swing, side by side. I felt so close to her in the quiet dark. Like when we were little, whispering secrets across the space between our beds. "Sometimes I'm jealous of you," I confessed.

"Of me?"

"Of you and John," I clarified. "You have somebody you can count on. Someone who's *there*."

Meg's face looked funny in the blue glow of the Christmas lights. "If all you wanted was somebody there all the time, you could have married Trey."

Huh.

"Did you tell him you're back?" my sister asked.

I shook my head. "I didn't come home to repeat my mistakes."

"Are you so sure it would be a mistake? Trey loves you. He's always loved you."

"Trey loves his idea of me—the girl next door, his buddy, his pal. As long as he can imagine he's in love with me, he doesn't have to grow up. But I don't fit into his life. And he definitely doesn't fit into mine."

"You mean, your life in New York."

"I mean, we don't want the same things. We're not like you and John."

"Sometimes I don't know what John wants anymore."

I felt a little flare of alarm, like a moth flying into a bug zapper. "Meg?"

She looked down at her lap in the blue light, where her engagement ring shone like a star. "Did I ever tell you about our first date?"

"You went to a football game, you said. He took you out afterward for ice cream."

"Not only for ice cream."

"You mean . . ."

Her lips curved. "He drove me to Carolina Beach. We checked into a hotel."

"Shut up. You did not."

Her smile turned smug. "We didn't get home until Sunday."

"You told Mom and Dad you met at the bank. You dated for a year before you moved in together."

"Because I wanted them to like him. I didn't want them to think we were rushing into things."

"You were awfully young when you got married," I observed.

"I was not."

"Beth's age."

She gave a surprised laugh. "I guess you're right." A few late tree frogs peeped from beyond the porch. "I always thought John and I would have more time before we started a family," she confessed. "Nobody tells you how hard it's going to be."

I didn't know what to say. I squeezed her hand instead.

"He didn't tell me he was coaching at the high school," she said. "I found out from Trey."

A little silence, filled with the wind in the pines.

"Makes me wonder what else he isn't telling me," she said in a small voice.

Oh hell. "You think he's cheating on you?"

"No. No. John's not a cheater. But he's not . . . happy. I love our babies. I love our house. I love our life, most of the time. What if he doesn't feel the same way?"

"Ask him."

"Maybe I don't want to know."

"Meg." I bumped her shoulder. "Just talk to him."

"The way you're talking to Eric?"

"That's different. John loves you."

"And Eric doesn't love you." Her voice made it half a question.

I swallowed. "I thought he did." I'd thought he could. The trees whispered in the darkness. *"I have such a taste for you, Jo."* "When I was with him, I felt . . . accepted, I guess. Like he really saw me, liked me, warts and all. But he didn't want me. That blog . . . It was his cooking, but that's my writing. That's me. He rejected me."

We sat awhile longer. Clouds scudded across the moon, blurring its face. Meg handed me a tissue from her pocket, like a good mom.

"I'm not going to cry. I hate crying," I said, and burst into tears. She sat beside me, petting my hair, the way our mother used to. "I'm sorry."

"Have another tissue," Meg said.

I loved her so much. I sniffled. "How about more wine?"

"Definitely wine. And cake," Meg said, holding up Aunt Phee's cake saver.

"Definitely cake." I stood. "Let's go eat our feelings."

Meg smiled. "Spoken like a true March."

We went inside. Maybe I wasn't sure where I belonged anymore. But home was a good place to figure it out.

CHAPTER 18

Meg

There were roses, red ones, on the kitchen island when I got home. At least a dozen of them, still wrapped in cellophane from the grocery store. Not for Valentine's Day or Mother's Day, my birthday, or our anniversary. Thanks, an apology, a romantic gesture . . . The reason didn't matter. John was trying. The effort was everything.

My eyes welled.

John must have heard the back door open, because he came in from the living room. I blinked, taking in details, the cuffs turned back on his wilted cotton shirt, his blond hair sticking up in front like DJ's or Daisy's after she'd cut her bangs.

"You're home," John said. *Finally,* he did not say.

I nodded, my fingers itching to smooth that errant cowlick. To touch him.

He stuffed his hands in his pockets. Took them out again, looking as awkward, as unsure, as I felt.

I shifted DJ in my arms. "How . . . How was the tournament?"

"Good." After a pause, he offered, "We won."

"That's *great,*" I said.

"Thanks," John said dryly. Okay, maybe I did sound a little like I was praising DJ for using the potty. He strolled toward me. "How was the farmers' market?"

"Busy. Lots of people Christmas shopping." *Just* talk *to him,* Jo urged in my head. I cleared my throat. "I saw Lisa Roberts. Patrick and Jason's mom?"

"Jason's a good kid. Good wrestler. No pin, but he scored a couple takedowns. Won on points. He keeps it up, he could make Regionals."

"His mom seemed really glad you were there with him. She actually thanked me." Nobody ever came up and thanked me because my husband had arranged financing for their car.

"Sorry I couldn't watch the kids today. I hope they were okay."

"The kids were fine. Everything was fine. John, what I said about Lisa . . . I was proud of you."

Faint color stained his cheeks. He shook his head, dismissing the compliment. "Did you see your buddy Carl today?"

"He stopped by." I changed the subject. "And Sallie Moffat took the twins to the park."

"Nice of her."

"Yes." I searched for something else to say, some topic to bridge the gap between us. Something that would make our conversation less like a bad first date. "She and Ned are going to Hawaii in January."

He gave me an unreadable look. Nodded at DJ, sleeping in my arms. "Daisy in the car?"

"Yes. They fell asleep at Mom's," I said apologetically.

"I'll get her."

"Thanks." He moved around me. Not touching. Even when we weren't connecting, he was a dutiful dad. "Thank you for the flowers," I added softly.

He stopped in the doorway. "I couldn't find a vase."

He'd jammed the bouquet into the pitcher I used for iced tea. I smiled, my heart unfurling like one of those roses. "That works."

"You need to fix them to make them look better." His gaze met mine. "You're good at that."

Was that what he thought? That I had to rearrange everything? "They look beautiful to me."

He smiled a little. "Glad you like them."

"I do." Two simple words, like the echo of a promise.

He leaned his forearm on the doorway above my head. I felt a little flutter, a tingle of the old attraction. "I bought a bottle of wine, too."

"Wine is good." Wine made it easier to talk. To say yes. *Yes* to laughter and vulnerability, to love and letting go. I moistened my lips. "Sorry I wasn't home for dinner."

He leaned closer. He smelled good, warm and familiar, like fabric softener and sweat. Like John. "We can open it later."

His gaze dropped to my mouth. The tingles spread. I raised my face for his kiss.

DJ mumbled and burrowed deeper into my neck.

John straightened, his hand dropping briefly to our son's head. "Better get this little guy to bed."

I swallowed my disappointment. "Aren't you coming up?"

"As soon as I get Daisy."

Daisy! In the car. I'd totally forgotten.

"That would be good. Great," I said. "Thanks, honey."

It took time to transfer the twins to their own beds, to strip off Daisy's shoes and socks, to put DJ in a clean diaper, all without waking them up. I turned out the lights in the babies' room and eased the door shut, still thinking of those roses.

John had always been better at actions than words. Maybe we didn't have to talk, I thought. Maybe I could show him how I felt.

And maybe I was afraid of where our conversation could go.

"It's not like I'm going to quit my job," he'd said.

John was waiting in the hall. He stuck his hands in his pockets when he saw me. "You want that wine now?"

Yes. No. If we went downstairs, down to the crumbs on the counter and the bills by the door . . . Definitely no. Better to stay upstairs.

"Jo opened a bottle of wine with dinner," I said. Keeping my voice low, so I wouldn't wake the kids. "I probably shouldn't drink any more tonight." Casually, I walked toward our bedroom with its sturdy door lock and comfortable queen-size mattress. Hoping John would follow.

A load of unfolded clothes sat in the middle of our bed.

Okay. I could move the laundry basket to the floor. Or . . . We didn't have to do it in bed. When we first bought the house, we'd made love on the living room floor. Under the Christmas tree. Even on the washing machine, once. Before the bills and routines, before the scars and stretch marks.

"How is Jo?" John asked.

"Oh. Well." I blinked at him, distracted. "John, she slept with Eric."

"The chef guy? Good for her."

"I've always wanted Jo to find somebody." Automatically, I reached for the laundry basket. "But he's so much older than she is. Divorced. With two kids. Not to mention he's her boss."

"Do I need to go to New York and beat him up?" He was smiling. Half-serious. I knew Jo privately considered my husband kind of dull, but he was a good man. Protective. And he'd always been fond of Jo.

"All I want is to take care of you," he'd said. *"You and the kids."*

I folded his briefs in thirds. "She says not. She came on to him, she says." Poor Jo.

"That doesn't sound like your sister."

I reached for a nightshirt, keeping my hands busy while I told John the rest, slowly relaxing into my sister's tale. It was nice, talking about something besides our schedules and the twins. Like the old days, when we'd critique our friends' romances and congratulate ourselves on how lucky we were.

"Then last night they had a big fight about her blog, and she quit," I concluded.

John folded a T-shirt in half and then in half again, the way he did before we got married, and put it on the pile. "Bad move."

"It takes two people to make a relationship work," I said.

He grunted, his big hands painstakingly matching the twins' tiny socks, butterflies with butterflies, stripes with stripes. A wave of tenderness caught me by the throat. "Seems to me this chef guy needs to get over himself."

"Just like that," I said skeptically.

"Did she trash his restaurant on her blog?"

"No."

"Post naked pictures?"

A laugh spurted out of me. "No!"

"Then it's easy. If he loves her."

"I thought he did," Jo had said. *"But he didn't want me."*

"She's hurt," I said.

"So she ran."

"You think she should have stayed in New York."

"If she loves him, yeah. You have feelings for somebody, that's what you do. You stick around. You work things out. You don't give up."

I raised an eyebrow. "Put your head down and bull through?"

"That's what I'd do," John said.

That's what he *did*. Solid, uncomplaining, utterly reliable John. I loved him so much. "I think they should talk," I said. Testing.

"Maybe. Maybe he just needs time to cool off."

"Or Jo does." I sighed. "I'm worried she's going to end up all alone."

"She's not alone." John glanced up from the laundry, a smile in his eyes. "She has you."

"That's what I told her. But it's not enough."

"Don't underestimate yourself." He held my gaze. "It's enough for me."

My heart melted. "Oh, John."

"I told you." He reached for the flannel pants in my hands. "You can make anything better."

He tugged on the pants, drawing me close, bringing me against him. A little jolt, familiarity and lust, shivered through me as our bodies connected. We kissed softly and then not so softly. I wrapped my arms around his neck. His hands slid under my shirt, seeking skin.

"Mommy!"

The door swung open. We sprang apart. DJ toddled forward, beaming. "Beckfast," he announced.

I pulled down my hem. "It's not breakfast time, baby. It's time to sleep."

"Cookie."

"No cookie." I glanced at John. Reached for DJ's hand. "Let's get you back to bed."

"Daddy!" Evading me, he scampered toward John.

John captured him in a hug. "Come on, buddy." He hoisted DJ onto his shoulders. "Bedtime."

DJ chuckled in delight, drumming his feet against John's shoulders. This was playtime, I thought in dismay. I'd never get him back to sleep now.

"I'll do it, John. It'll be quicker," I said.

But I wasn't quick. Deprived of both a cookie and Fun Time with Daddy, DJ escalated from fretful to demanding. Mindful of Daisy sleeping in the next bed, of John waiting in the next room, I rocked him, sang to him, read him a story, rubbed his back. But every time I laid him down, he bounced up again.

"DJ, hush," I begged.

John appeared in the doorway. "I've got this. Go to bed."

I hesitated. "You've had a long day."

"You, too. You had the kids all day." He nudged me. "Go."

Reluctantly, I let go of DJ's hand.

"No, Mommy. No!"

I sank back down on the side of the mattress. "I don't want to upset him."

John's jaw set like DJ's. "I've been thinking. About what you said. About us being partners."

I stared at him. *Now* he wanted to talk?

He plowed ahead. "The thing is, my dad was never around much. Your father, he's not much better. I can be like them and not do anything. Or . . ." He met my gaze, his eyes steady, his jaw firm. "I can try to be your partner. But if we're partners, sometimes you've got to let me do things my way."

Something inside me softened and relaxed like a fist letting go. My heart. My womb.

DJ crawled out from under the covers, his arms warm and clingy around my neck.

"He'll wake Daisy," I warned.

"Then I'll deal with it." John sat beside me, lifting DJ from my lap. "Say good night to Mommy."

DJ twisted and struggled. "No! Mommy!"

"Mommy's tired." It was John's coach voice. "Daddy's putting you to bed."

DJ gave a heartbreaking sob. "Mamama . . ."

I escaped to the hall, my face flushed, my heart pounding in guilt and relief.

DJ was still sobbing in outrage as I brushed my teeth, as I pulled on yoga pants and a T-shirt and folded the rest of the laundry. I heard Daisy's voice raised in sleepy protest and John's quiet murmur as he tried to settle our babies to sleep.

Gradually, the noise across the hall subsided. I waited.

No John.

Fearing the worst, I padded across the hallway and peeked in the bedroom door. My husband slumped against the wall of DJ's bed, a child cuddled in the circle of his arm on either side, Daisy holding tight to his finger. All of them fast asleep.

Something moved in me, deeper than words.

This was love. Not holding back, not keeping score, but doing things for each other. Giving to each other. Not out of obligation, but generously, because it was a joy to offer.

Head to one side, I considered the family pile on the bed. And then—carefully, so carefully, so I didn't wake the kids—I crawled across the mattress, and laid my head on John's sprawled leg, and joined them in sleep.

CHAPTER 19

Jo

My father kissed my forehead when he came downstairs the next morning—a rare mark of affection usually reserved for birthdays, holidays, and straight As on my report card.

When I was growing up, I used to think we enjoyed a special, cerebral bond, like Lizzy and Mr. Bennet.

Maybe my coming home was an opportunity for us to develop a deeper understanding. I wasn't quite ready to discuss my love life with my father. Or the state of my finances or my sudden unemployment. I was here to be a help, not a drag. He had more important things—people—to worry about. Suicidal veterans. Mom.

But maybe now we would finally talk, really talk, about the toll of Iraq on his soldiers and himself, the difficulties of settling into life back home after losing so many friends. It would be the start of a new, closer, adult relationship between us, and years from now, he would say, *Yeah, I had some trouble adjusting. But when I realized I needed someone to talk to, my daughter Jo was there for me.*

I wiped my hands on a dish towel. "I fed the goats," I volunteered. "Made breakfast, too. Biscuits."

The tang of baking powder and buttermilk hung in the air. I'd used my mother's recipe, squishing the soft dough between my fingers the way she did, but left her round biscuit cutters in the drawer. I'd cut the dough into squares instead, the way Constanza taught me. "*Sin desperdicio,*" the garde-manger had said, her gold tooth flashing in a smile. *No waste.*

My father glanced at the clock. He was already dressed in khakis and a button-down shirt with the sleeves rolled up, like the Duke Divinity student he had been thirty-five years ago. "No breakfast for me, I'm afraid. Services start at nine."

"Oh. Right," I said.

It was Sunday. Brunch day in New York, another day of work, a chance to catch up on my blog or sleep or laundry. A week ago, I'd worked the line in the morning and spent the afternoon in bed with Eric.

My father smiled slightly. "You're an adult, of course. It's your choice whether you attend services or not. But if you would like to join me . . ."

My heart went all squishy. In his own way, my father cared about me.

"I can be dressed in five minutes," I promised.

"Take your time," my father said, with another glance at the clock.

I'd packed in a blur of tears and fury, throwing everything into the battered suitcase I'd taken to college. It took me seven minutes to strip off my barn jeans and dig out a balled-up pair of leggings. I sniffed the armpits of my sweater before dragging it on. Stuffed my feet into my city-girl boots. When I came downstairs, my father was waiting by the door. The biscuits were untouched.

"You should eat something. At least have coffee," I said.

My father eyed the freshly brewed pot. "One mug, then. Thank you. To go."

I prided myself that my life was not my mother's life. But here I was, in my mother's kitchen, pouring my father's coffee into a travel mug.

I handed it to him. "How is Mom?"

My father hesitated, as if words were coins and each one cost him.

Maybe they did. Maybe my mother's long illness had beggared him. "She has an infection of the bone—osteomyelitis—which has weakened her back. Quite curable. But she's having an operation on Friday to strengthen the affected discs and alleviate the pressure on her spine."

"I know. Meg told me." No need to mention she'd spilled the beans before I left New York. "How long will she be in the hospital?"

"At least overnight. Then she goes back into rehab for two or three more weeks."

"So long?"

"She needs to continue on IV antibiotics for six weeks. She could go to a clinic as an outpatient, but it takes several hours to administer all her medication, and travel is difficult for her now. It's easier to do it there."

"But how *is* she?"

"The doctors say the procedure will make a great difference."

I waited expectantly. But apparently that was all he had to say. All my mother wanted him to say?

My father patted my hand. "'Do not let your heart be troubled.' Your mother doesn't want a lot of fuss. We must have faith."

I appreciated his reassurance. But I wasn't one of his ex-parishioners or vets. I was his daughter. I wanted more. Also, I was supposed to be supporting him. I plunged ahead. "And how are you?"

"As you see." He sipped. Grimaced slightly. "Shall we go?"

When I was younger, my father spoke from the pulpit with the voice of God. Or how I imagined God sounded, anyway—sort of kindly and remote and just above my level of comprehension. The new pastor sounded like a camp counselor. I half expected him to hand out participation trophies to the congregation simply for showing up to church that morning.

The service over, the people flowed from the pews and out of the church, dividing between their new pastor in the vestibule and my father on the steps outside. Aunt Phee sailed through the crowd, bearing down on us like a luxury liner in a red jacket and pearls, Miss Wanda in her wake.

Crap. I'd forgotten to tell my father she'd dropped by the house last night.

"Um. Dad . . ."

"Ashton." Aunt Phee stopped directly in front of him. "I've made a reservation at the club for dinner. Five o'clock. If that's convenient." Her tone made it clear she expected him, convenient or not.

My lanky father stooped to kiss her cheek. "Thank you, Phee."

"You may pick me up at the house. You might come early so we can have a proper visit."

"We'll see," my father said. "I have open hours at the veterans' center this afternoon."

"But it's Sunday," I said.

"The Lord's work is never done," Wanda Crocker said piously.

"Even the Lord rested on Sunday," I muttered.

"You may join us," Aunt Phee said to me. A command? Or a question? Her gaze swept from my sweater to my boots. "You'll want to change first."

Bite me, I thought. "Thanks, Aunt Phee, but I thought I'd go to the rehab center today. I want to spend some time with Mom."

"Your mother is in no shape to entertain visitors," Aunt Phee said.

"Jo isn't a visitor," my father said. "She's Abby's daughter."

I threw him a grateful look.

"Suit yourself." Aunt Phee's mouth puckered. "You always have."

Now that I'd dodged her dinner invitation, guilt crept in. "Maybe another time," I offered.

She sniffed.

"Thanks for the rescue," I said to Dad when she was out of earshot.

He did not return my smile. "Phee has been very generous to us. To you," he said. "You might try to have more sympathy for her."

"I do try," I protested. "She's always criticizing me."

"Because she doesn't want to see you repeating her mistakes."

"You mean, staying in Bunyan all my life?" I asked flippantly.

"That's unworthy of you both. You and Phee have a lot in common. You both care deeply about family. You have strong minds. Strong wills." My father leveled a mild look at me. "And you both sometimes speak without considering the full impact of your words on the people you care about."

My face flushed. I'd always joked that Aunt Phee had no heart. But maybe she hid her heart because she felt things deeply. Because she refused to appear vulnerable. Had my rejection of her dinner invitation, my rudeness over the years, actually hurt her?

But she kept inviting me. She kept showing up.

Another lesson there. Or being home, going to church, was messing with my head.

M y mother's eyes were closed, her face shrunken and naked. Her faded hair straggled flat across her forehead, squashed of vitality. Only her chest moved, up and down, her breathing slow and sonorous.

"Why is she breathing like that?" I asked the aide who had accompanied me to her room.

Keisha, her badge said. She stood by my mother's bedside, taking her pulse. My mother's wrist looked thin and light in her hand, like the bones of a bird.

When Granny died, all us girls went to the visitation. I remember our mother protesting that a funeral parlor was no place for little children, but in her grief over her mother's death, she was overruled. Anyway, there was nobody to watch us. Everybody in town was there to see my grandmother laid out and pay their respects to the family.

Meg moved with twelve-year-old dignity through clusters of our neighbors, taking care to keep Amy away from the open casket at the front of the room. Not that our little sister could see over the sides of the coffin. Beth was hiding under the white-skirted table that held the guest book. But I marched right up and looked in, curious and unafraid. I loved my grandmother, who never cared if I got dirty and always smelled comfortingly like her kitchen. Besides, I'd never seen a dead person before.

She looked . . . wrong. Not like Granny at all. I recognized her Sunday dress, her gold earrings. But her face was a funny color, like an old peach crayon, and a rotten sweet smell hung over her like dying flowers.

I'd wanted to throw up.

I wasn't going to throw up now. But my stomach churned with the same sense of *wrongness*. The shock. Where was my mother?

"It's the drugs," the aide said. "That fentanyl patch is helping with the pain, but it does make her drowsy." Keisha leaned over my mother's pillow. "Abby, you have a visitor, hon. Your daughter's here to see you."

"Oh, don't wake her," I protested.

"It's all right," Keisha said. "It's time for her lunch tray."

"Not hungry," my mother mumbled. And then, "Meg?"

I swallowed hard. "It's Jo, Momma."

"I have to listen to your heart now, Abby," Keisha said. "Then you and your daughter can have a nice visit."

My mother nodded obediently, like a child. I stood back as Keisha moved the stethoscope over my mother's thin chest.

"Still beating," my mother joked when the aide was done.

Keisha smiled. "Yes, your heart is good and strong. Do you think you can sit up now?"

My mother pressed her lips together. Nodded. A grimace flickered across her face as the aide raised the head of her hospital bed. I winced in sympathy.

"Thank you." My mother shifted, trying to get comfortable. "I think . . . A pill?"

"It's not time yet, hon. After lunch, when I come in with the IV, okay?" Keisha looked at me. "You see if you can get her to eat something."

It felt rude—*wrong*—talking over my mother's head, as if she wasn't there. "I brought biscuits," I said.

"Whatever tempts her appetite. Fruit would be good," Keisha added. "Those pain meds stop her up something awful."

I sat beside my mother's bed. Took her hand. An empty IV port ran into her arm, the skin around it purple with bruising.

"Jo." Her fingers squeezed my hand with none of my mother's strength. "Love you, honey."

"Love you, too, Momma."

She used to pester me with questions. *How was your day . . . your date . . . your doctor's appointment? Are you finished with your homework . . . your college applications . . . your taxes yet?* In high school and later, coming home from college, I'd tended to brush her concerns away, saving my stories for a more appreciative audience. Saving them for my father.

I'd originally planned to fly home on Christmas Eve. Changing my ticket so close to the holidays had pretty much emptied my checking account. But she never asked me what I was doing at her bedside. Maybe she didn't have the breath or the energy. Maybe she'd lost track of time. Or maybe, in some bone-deep, heartfelt, drug-induced place, she simply accepted I was where I belonged. I didn't need a messy breakup to justify my presence at her side. She was sick. I was her daughter. Where else should I be?

My phone buzzed. A text from Eric. Where the hell are you?

Right. I was scheduled to work today. Well, screw him. Aaron was covering my shifts for the next two weeks. He didn't need me.

I was suddenly, fiercely glad I'd come home.

After lunch, another aide—not Keisha—came to take my mother to physical therapy. She couldn't get out of bed.

"Abby, you have to try," the aide said with barely veiled impatience.

She'd been trying, without success, for almost twenty minutes.

My mother closed her eyes. The small gesture—of defeat, of resignation—terrified me. My mother never gave up.

"Listen, she didn't choose to feel like this," I snapped. "She's in pain."

"I understand. But we have patients waiting who are willing to do the work."

"My mother has worked her whole damn life. She'll get out of bed after her surgery."

"Jo, it's all right," my mother said. "Don't fuss."

But after the aide left, she cried, silent tears of frustration leaking from her closed eyes. It was a relief when she slept.

It rained all week, a thin, cold rain that darkened the shortened hours and drove the goats to seek shelter under the lean-to. The days until my mother's surgery stretched gray and empty. I visited her every day, driving an hour each way past frozen fields and huddled houses, my windshield wipers beating against the gloom.

When I got home, I fed the goats and my father, but he was rarely around.

"The holidays are a difficult time," he explained. "Particularly for people who are dealing with sickness or loneliness or separation."

Tell me about it, I thought.

I'd always relished my own space. But the house felt haunted by the ghosts of Christmases Past. I missed my sisters: the smell of Meg's nail polish, the plunk of Beth's guitar, even Amy's messes scattered everywhere. Meg loved me. But she had John and the twins to care for. I couldn't expect her to babysit me all the time.

There were worse things in life than being alone, I reminded myself. Anyway, it's not like I didn't have stuff to do. Laundry. Cleaning. I could haul out more Christmas decorations. Let Trey know I was back in town.

Or . . . I grabbed my hoodie and went out to the barn.

Shoveling straw was like cooking on the line—hard, dirty, sweaty work. After twenty minutes, I paused to pull off my hoodie. It felt good to use my muscles, to occupy my hands, to find my rhythm. To feel appreciated, even if it was only by the goats.

But as I lay in bed, listening to the creaks and pings of the old house at night, a message lit my phone screen. Eric.

Are you all right?

My throat cinched tight. Chefs were egotistical, temperamental jerks. But Eric . . . Despite his unforgiving standards in the kitchen, he had a basic decency, an innate kindness I admired. He looked out for his employees.

Or ex-employees. Ray must have told him by now I wasn't coming back to work.

Fine. I chewed my lip, staring at the single, stingy word on the screen. Added, You?

He texted back instantly. I want to see you. Let me in.

He must be at my building, waiting at my door, expecting me to buzz him up. My heartbeat quickened. Was he looking for an apology? A retraction? A booty call?

No. You were right, I typed, hoping he'd contradict me. Me working for you was a mistake.

I didn't say mistake, he corrected. A problem.

Big problem. He thought I was using him. Which . . . Okay, I had. He'd served up his big heart on a plate, and I'd taken his passion to feed my own. But I put myself out there, too, in my words, on my blog. When I wrote about him, I revealed a piece of my heart. And he didn't see. Or maybe he didn't care. He'd belittled my blog. And that made me feel small.

I couldn't forgive that.

I poked at my phone. Well, I solved it for you, didn't I? I quit.

No reply.

Worry niggled inside me. To my neighbors, Eric might not look like an award-winning chef on a booty call. What if they saw him as a large black man hanging around the building entrance? Ringing Doorbells While Black. What if they called the cops?

Three dots appeared. Eric, typing. I drew my breath in relief. We need to talk, he said.

I scowled at my phone, resenting the echo of my own advice to Meg. Talk? Maybe when I was cooler. Maybe when I was calmer. Maybe when I'd figured out what to say.

I think we said enough already, I answered. Anyway, I'm not . . . My fingers hesitated. Not *home*, I thought. New York wasn't home anymore. Not there, I added.

Where are you?

The question yawned like a chasm, threatening to swallow me up. I teetered on the edge of answering. I'd left Bunyan because I didn't want to be an accessory in Trey's life. A possession. A decoration. I thought I'd found a place in Eric's world. But I didn't shine there. It was all reflected light. I was a satellite, the moon to his sun. I could lose myself in him, in his life, so easily. More easily, because I loved him.

My fingers hovered. Eric, I . . .

Oh God. Oh God, I didn't want this, this terrible *yearning.* He couldn't simply show up at my apartment and expect me to give up. To give in. The temptation to do both sucked at me like a tide. I was terrified that I could lose myself in him, that I would become less right when my family depended on me to be more. I couldn't deal with this now. I needed to focus on Mom.

But at least I could save Eric from an altercation with the police.

I mashed DELETE. Typed, Go away.

Turning my phone facedown beside my bed, I buried my head in my pillow.

But when I finally fell asleep, it wasn't my mother's face I saw.

The buzz of my phone jarred me out of sleep. *Eric,* I thought dreamily. I reached out in the thin gray light of morning, my fingers fumbling across the nightstand. "'Lo?" I croaked.

"Jo?"

Beth. She had always turned to me for confidence. For reassurance. I spoke up for her at the dinner table, stuck up for her at school. But before this week, I'd never realized how much I counted on her quiet presence at home. Even after she went away to college, she was always in the background of my visits to Bunyan, like the teddy bear on her bed, a comforting talisman of our childhood.

"Hey, sweetie." I struggled to sit, pulling up the covers against the attic chill. "How are you?"

"I talked to Meg. She said Momma's having surgery on Friday."

"Um." I fought to wake up. "Friday. Right."

"I want to be there." Beth's voice was thin and determined.

Yes.

No.

"Hang on, I have to pee, okay?" I threw back the quilt, using the pause to collect myself.

Our father was right. I needed to learn to think before I spoke. The right word—or the wrong one—would bring Beth flying home. But this once, I couldn't be selfish. Couldn't think about what I wanted. Now that Beth had finally left the nest, I couldn't be the one to clip her wings.

I splashed water in the sink. "Beth. Sweetie. You know I'd love to see you. But it's not necessary, really. Mom's going straight from the hospital right back into rehab. She has all kinds of people taking care of her. There's no reason for you to come home."

"What if something happens?"

My stomach hollowed. "Nothing's going to happen," I said firmly. "Mom's going to be fine."

"I still want to be there for her operation."

I looked around for a towel. "But what about your show?"

"I'll quit."

"You can't quit." I dried my hands on my shirt.

"You did."

I opened my mouth. Shut it. "That's different," I said. "I'm doing what Daddy told me to do." Every time he went to war. *"Take care of Momma and your sisters for me . . ."*

"Sorry," Beth said humbly. "I didn't mean . . ."

I cleared my throat. "No. No, it's okay."

Crap. I'd always presented my best self to Beth, fearless and reassuring. To protect her, I told myself. Or to protect my pride. Like a hedgehog, showing off its spines. But that wasn't what she needed from me now. If I wanted her to stay in Branson, I had to tell the truth.

"Bethie, I came home because . . . Well, because I've got nowhere else to go."

"What are you talking about? You have your cooking. Your writing. Your blog."

"Cooking was never more than a side gig to pay the bills. And I'm having trouble with the blog."

"Oh no." Her sympathy was warm and immediate, flowing over the connection. "I love your blog. I feel so much closer, reading your posts. Sometimes it's like I'm right there with you in New York."

My sisters were the best. I'd always thought of my writing as separate from my family, something I did in isolation. And all along they'd been right there with me, reading and supporting me. "Thanks, Mouse."

"And I'm not your only fan," Beth said. "Look at all the comments you got on your last post."

"Not me," I said. "Chef."

"Is that your boss?"

I nodded, forgetting she couldn't see. "Eric. Yeah."

"He has amazing arms."

"You should see the rest of him."

Beth giggled, sounding about six years old. I grinned in triumph. "So, what's the problem?" she asked.

My smile faded. "He's not such a fan."

"Of your blog? What doesn't he like about it?"

"I think he felt I . . ." *"Took something that was personal, private, and put it on your fucking blog without telling me."* "Should have talked to him about it first."

"Please. You have a gift, Jo. You need to share it."

"So do you," I said. "Seriously, Beth, this show could be your big break. When you get a chance at doing something—something you love—you have to grab and hold on with both hands. Don't let go."

"You sound like Colt," she said.

Colt Henderson, the show's star. "Is that a bad thing?"

"Not bad. Just not me."

Something in her voice triggered my protective instincts. Beth had always been our little homebody. Not ambitious like me or discontent like Amy or eager for a family of her own like Meg. Meg's worries that Beth was starstruck, that she was in over her head relationship-wise, came back to me. "Is everything all right?" I asked. "With the show and everything?"

"Everything's fine," Beth said. "I just miss you all. It doesn't feel like Christmas without you."

I swallowed the lump in my throat. "You're an angel in a Christmas show," I pointed out. "It doesn't get more Christmassy than that. This is your shot, Mouse. Don't throw it away."

"Are you quoting *Hamilton* to me now?" The smile was back in her voice.

"Whatever works," I said.

"I don't know." Beth sighed. "What if I'm not—"

"Scrappy?" I suggested. "Hungry?"

"—good enough?"

I swallowed. "Oh, Beth. You're so good. You're so *talented*. We all think so. You know Momma would want you to stay."

"No fair using Mom," Beth protested.

"It's true," I said, comfortable now that we were back in our familiar roles. "Promise me you won't quit the show."

"Only if you promise to write me a special blog post for Christmas," Beth said.

So I promised.

But when I opened my laptop, my brain and fingers stalled. A Christmas blog brought up too many memories. Of writing to Dad all those years he was away. Of New York. Of Eric.

A week ago, before our fight, I'd thought we could go together to Bryant Park to sip hot chocolate and watch the ice-skaters. Or search out the few remaining chestnut vendors on Sixth Avenue. But what did I have to write about now? Who wanted to read about my life in Bunyan?

I scrolled through past posts, hoping for a spark. The speculation from strangers had died down, but there were plenty of new comments from regular readers who felt they knew me, followers who liked me, their comments ranging from teasing to concern.

Did you really work at Gusto? Not anymore, I thought.

Is Eric Bhaer your boyfriend? In another universe, maybe.

What are you doing for Christmas? Nothing. Nada. Zip.

A sense of what I'd had, of what we'd lost, of what could have been, choked me. *When you get a chance at something, don't let go.*

I went downstairs to my sisters' old bedroom. Beth's teddy was still there among the pillows. Hugging it tight, I climbed back to my attic and crawled into bed. Then I opened another tab on my laptop and typed "osteomyelitis" into the search bar.

CHAPTER 20

Meg

You really don't have to stay home from work today," I told John early Friday morning.

He leveled a patient look at me. "Your mom's having surgery. Her family should be there."

But we wouldn't be there. Not all of us. I'd told Beth and Amy not to come in two long, agonizing telephone conversations. Amy had argued, I remembered, and Beth had cried.

I swallowed. "I'm meeting Dad and Jo at the hospital. And I already asked Sallie to watch the kids. She'll be here in"—I glanced at the big kitchen clock—"an hour."

"Good." My gaze flew to his. He smiled. "That way I can go to the hospital with you," he explained.

The tight band of pressure holding me together relaxed. "Oh, John, that would be wonderful. I know she'll be happy to see you."

"I want to see her, too. I love your mom. But I'm going for you, Meg." He held my gaze. "I want to be there for you."

I moved into his arms, resting my forehead against his chest. "Thanks."

John cleared his throat. "Anytime."

I closed my eyes as he stroked my hair. I wanted to stay like that forever.

But of course I couldn't. Daisy was missing a barrette and DJ, a sock. I needed to load their breakfast dishes into the dishwasher and write down last-minute instructions for Sallie. The twins were surprisingly okay with being left with their new playground friend.

John dropped me at the hospital entrance while he parked the car. Even so, by the time I found the surgery unit, Jo was alone in the waiting room.

The main lobby had been decked with artificial trees and plastic poinsettias, the fake cheer of the Christmas season. But the surgical waiting area was beige and bare and quiet, as cold and sterile as I imagined the operating room must be. I shivered. Our mother had already been admitted behind the painted metal doors.

"Dad's with her," Jo said.

"I want to see her."

Jo scowled. "She can only have one person, the nurse said."

John strode in, putting his hand on the small of my back. Straightening my spine, I approached the nurse's desk. "I'm Meg Brooke. Abigail March's daughter. How is she?"

"She just went back."

"I know. Could you let her know I'm here? Please?"

The woman in purple scrubs referred to her computer screen. "I'll go check."

I shivered. A flat-screen TV in one corner droned with a morning news program. The other big screen displayed strings of numbers highlighted in glowing yellow, red, and green.

"Patient numbers," Jo said. "Red for waiting, green for surgery, yellow for recovery."

"Which one is Momma?"

She shrugged.

The nurse reappeared, smiling, and beckoned. "You can come back for a minute."

We all stood.

"Just you," she said to me.

"And my sister," I said.

Her gaze went from me to Jo. "I guess . . . Just for a minute."

"Go," John said.

"You're lucky we're not that crowded today," the nurse said, leading the way back.

"Why not?" Jo asked as we followed her down a bright, narrow aisle of curtained cubicles.

"It's the holidays. Nobody wants to spend Christmas in the hospital. We don't have any elective procedures at all scheduled for tomorrow. Here we go." She grasped the edge of a striped curtain. "Abby, your daughters are here."

Our mother lay flat, attached by tubes and cords to an IV drip and an array of flashing, beeping machines. The partitioned space barely held her gurney and a chair for our father.

I edged past his knees to kiss my mother, her pale face framed by a blue paper shower cap. "Hey, Momma."

She smiled with parched lips. "Hey, baby." Her voice was thick, her words slurred.

"Jo's here, too." I squeezed back to let my sister through.

"Mom." Jo stooped, her curtain of hair falling to hide her face.

Our mother stroked her head. "Iss fine, sweethear'. I'll be fine."

The curtain rattled. "Okay, we're ready for you, Abby," a different nurse announced cheerfully. "You all can have a seat in the waiting room," she told us. "Or get yourselves some breakfast. Cafeteria's open."

We kissed our mother again before she was wheeled away. It felt horribly like good-bye.

The nurse gave our father a card with our mother's surgery number. Carrying the plastic bag full of her things, we returned to the waiting room. A family crouched forward in their chairs, looking up anxiously as we came through the door. A man worked on his laptop. A woman in a pink tracksuit turned the pages of a magazine while a teenager played with his phone.

Our father walked to the window and stared out at the rain, hands clasped behind his back.

"How's your mom?" John asked.

"Fine," I said. The alternative—that she was *not* fine, that she wasn't going to be fine—was unbearable.

Jo looked fierce, a sure sign she was trying not to cry. "What if she's not?" she asked in a low voice. "She could have nerve damage. She might need another surgery. There could be complications."

"You've been reading Dr. Google," John said.

"How did you know?" Jo demanded.

"Meg does the same thing every time the kids get sick. Sit down. You want coffee?"

While John fetched coffee, we sat. Jo had brought a book and her laptop. I had my phone, fully charged. But my eyes, my brain, could not focus on my newsfeed, my friends' adorable kid pictures and cat videos. I watched the numbers on the big screen in the corner, waiting for the color to change from red to green.

"March family?"

My father turned from the window.

"Dr. Chatworth just started the surgery," the nurse liaison said. "Everything looks good. He was able to go in with a minimally invasive technique. Abby is doing well."

"What do you mean, started surgery?" Jo said. "We've been out here an hour already."

"It takes a while to get your mother prepped," the nurse explained. "If you want to get something to eat, now's a good time, so you don't miss the surgeon when he comes out. I'll update you again in two hours."

"Thank you," our father said.

Two more hours. "I should call Sallie," I said.

"After you eat," John said.

I shook my head, watching the nurse move from family to family. Observing their reactions—relief, resignation, tears. "I'm not hungry."

"He's right," Jo said. "You should eat something."

"You go. You've been waiting longer than me. I'll stay with Dad," I added as she looked at our father.

Not that he was paying attention to us.

"Can I get you anything, Dad?" Jo asked.

"No, thank you."

Hospital time is measured in moments, weighted with worry. The count of my contractions, the catch of my breath, the day the twins were born. And then a nurse whisked DJ away, and time stopped altogether, along with my heart. We could only wait, for news, for reassurance, while the experts did something just out of our sight. I'd felt anxious. Helpless. Powerless. Just like today.

Jo came back with another foam cup of coffee and dropped gracelessly into a chair. "I wish the girls were here."

I nodded. *"Don't come,"* I'd told them. *"Momma will be fine."*

"I talked to Beth," Jo said. "Meg . . . What if something goes wrong?"

Our eyes met. Amy, I thought, would cope somehow. Tenderhearted Beth would forgive me. But I'd never forgive myself.

I reached across and squeezed Jo's hand.

At least I had John to keep me company. Poor Jo didn't have anybody but me. And our father. I glanced at him, sitting in the gray light from the window, silently reading a book with disciplined attention.

Time crawled. John kept checking his phone. He'd taken off work to spend the day—all day—with me. Of course he'd want to keep in touch with the dealership. All those end-of-year sales.

"Everything okay?" I asked.

He nodded. "Just texting Trey."

Jo jumped up to pace, unable to sit still. "How is he?"

"Haven't you seen him?" I asked.

"Not since I got back."

John started to say something and stopped. I threw him a grateful look. Now was not the time to offer my sister relationship advice.

Infected by Jo's restlessness, I called Sallie. The twins were fine. I texted Beth and Amy, typing reassurances in place of actual news.

Eventually, the nurse emerged with another update. My father closed his book to listen, one finger between the pages to keep his place. "*Not finished . . . vital signs still stable . . . another few hours . . .*"

Jo yanked on her ponytail. "Why is it taking so long?"

"I really can't say," the nurse said.

"Is everything all right?" I asked.

Her eyes were sympathetic. "The doctor will be out to talk with you as soon as he's finished."

"When?" Jo demanded.

The nurse looked regretful. "I really . . ."

"Can't say," Jo finished grimly.

"Yes. Please let us know if you leave the waiting area."

The nurse continued her rounds of waiting families. I heard a gasp. A whisper. A whimper. *Bad news.* My heart constricted in sympathy. I met Jo's gaze, my own shame-faced relief reflected in her eyes. At least our mother was all right. *Vital signs stable.* She had to be all right.

My father got up and approached the family hunched on the chairs. I couldn't hear what he said to them, only the low murmur of his voice before he sat down. After that he hardly spoke at all. He sat with his elbows on his knees, his head cocked, listening.

"What's he doing?" Jo muttered.

I swallowed. "I guess . . . being there." Being present. He was good at that, with strangers.

When the other family got up to leave, the older woman hugged my father, tears in her eyes. "God bless you, Captain," she said. "Are these your daughters?"

"Yes." He turned, courteous as always, to introduce us. "Margaret and Josephine. My son-in-law, John."

"Meg." I held out my hand. "I hope your . . ." *Mother? Father? Child?* "I hope everything turns out."

She hugged me, too. "Thank you, darling. Your father has been such a comfort. A real angel of the Lord."

"I'm glad," I said.

Wistfully, I watched as he walked with them to the elevator. There were more hugs, more murmurs, one of my father's rare smiles. Hot pressure burned behind my eyes. I didn't need him to be a saint or an angel. I just wanted him to act like a dad. What was missing in us, or in him, that made him go away? That made him available to everybody but us.

He resumed his post staring out the window at the dreary parking lot.

John put his arm around me. I rubbed my cheek against his sleeve, absorbing his solid warmth. "Let's go for a walk," he said. "I'll buy you a candy bar."

I nodded against his arm. "We'll be right back," I told Jo.

The hospital gift shop smelled like a fake, cold Christmas, like peppermint gum and pine cleaner. Small, chilled bouquets jostled for refrigerator space next to bottled drinks and waxy-looking fruit.

"What do you think?" I asked John, holding up a bud vase: four white rosebuds tied with red ribbon.

"I think you should wait until her surgery's over before you buy her flowers." He looked at my face. "Or we could get them now and they'll be waiting for her when she's admitted to a room."

I held on to them like hope. "I want her to see them when she opens her eyes."

"Sure. You want to get anything else? A book? Magazines?"

I shook my head. "Sometimes flowers are enough," I said. Trying to tell him that I loved him. Thinking of the red roses on our kitchen island, waiting for me when I got home.

His warm, brown eyes met mine. "I can do better."

My chest ached. He was trying so hard. I never wanted him to think our life together wasn't enough for me.

Maybe I was afraid to hear it wasn't enough for him.

"You don't need to do better," I assured him. "You don't need to do anything."

He frowned. "Meg . . ." His phone buzzed with another text. He fished it from his pocket and glanced at the screen. "We should get back."

"What is it?" I asked, instantly anxious. "Is it Jo? Mom . . ."

"No word yet." He paid for the flowers and a candy bar before taking my arm and steering me out of the gift shop.

"Who was the text from?" I asked.

"Trey."

I forced a smile. "He must be swamped with people buying new cars for Christmas."

We reached the waiting room. My father had returned to his book. Jo was prowling the narrow aisle between the chairs.

"He wasn't texting from work," John said.

"Then what . . . ?"

A man strode down the corridor from the opposite direction, raindrops shining in his hair and darkening the shoulders of his jacket—a young man with bright black eyes and a wide smile.

"Trey!" Jo stumbled over a chair and launched across the room.

He opened his arms, lifting her half off her feet. A moment's sunshine lightened my heart. Jo could protest all she wanted that she and Trey weren't meant to be together for always. But he was here now, when she needed him. That had to count for something.

He turned his head, catching her mouth in a kiss.

Jo broke free, her cheek fiery red. "I didn't mean . . . I was so surprised . . . What are you doing here?"

Trey grinned, looking awfully pleased with himself. "I brought some people with me." He stepped aside, revealing the girl behind him.

"Beth," I whispered.

"Beth! Oh, Bethie!" Jo flew at her, laughing and crying.

And . . .

"Amy!"

In a short black skirt and tall black boots, toting a giant carryall. "Meg!" she cried. "Daddy! Jokies!"

Thrusting my flowers at John, I ran forward, wrapping my arms around the girls. We squeezed one another tight, a sister sandwich. "But how did you get here?"

"I picked them up at the airport," Trey said.

"John bought my ticket. He told me to come." Beth hugged me, then John, then Jo again. "Thank you."

"But your show," Jo said. "Your duet."

"Colt said he could do a solo."

"For how long?" Jo asked.

Beth's thin face flushed. "I have to go back Christmas Day."

"Our Mouse is old enough be guided by her own judgment," our father said, hugging her close.

She looked at him anxiously. "You don't mind?"

He kissed her forehead. "Your mother will be happy to see you."

Beth beamed.

I looked over Amy's head at John. "You bought her plane ticket?"

He nodded, slightly smug.

I wanted to kiss him. "But how . . . But why . . ."

"I knew your father hadn't said much to the girls, and you'd never ask them to come home. So I called them."

"It was a bitch traveling so close to Christmas," Amy said. "I had to fly into JFK."

"How did you even get a seat on a plane?" Jo asked.

"Trey used his miles." John met my gaze, smiling. "Bumped her up to first class."

My heart swelled, too big for my chest. "Why didn't you tell me?"

"I didn't want you to worry."

"Good job, Trey." Jo threw her arms around Beth. "Oh, I'm so glad to see you!"

Good job, John. Somehow he'd known what I wanted, when I couldn't even admit it to myself. He'd given me my sisters. I blinked back happy tears, feeling as if the sun had come out. *Whatever happens, we have each other.*

"March family?" the nurse liaison called. "The surgeon will see you now."

An icicle trickled down my spine. John took my hand as we all turned, our father's face set like stone.

"All of you?" the nurse asked.

Trey put his arm around Beth. "We can wait here."

"No," Amy protested.

"Yes," Jo said at the same time.

The nurse looked at our silent father. Shrugged. "All right. This way."

We barely fit into the family consultation room. My father and I sat in two of the three chairs, leaving one empty for the surgeon.

"Dr. Chatworth will be right with you."

The next ten minutes dragged by, almost as long as the five hours that had gone before. Amy's face was white. Beth picked at her fingernails. The neurosurgeon came in, still wearing scrubs, and shook hands with our father. I tried to focus, but he spoke so rapidly, his words dissolving into meaningless clips and medical phrases. *"Decompression of spinal canal . . . neural function . . . stable bony fusion . . ."*

I fixed my gaze painfully on his face, as if his expression, his tone of voice, could give me a clue to my mother's condition.

". . . be significant postoperative discomfort," he said. "But your mother should wake up feeling much better." He paused. "Merry Christmas."

Like a present.

Jo was grinning, Beth pink with happiness. "Thank God," our father said.

Shaken with relief, I turned my head into John's shoulder.

An hour later, we all crowded into her hospital room as my mother was admitted upstairs. Amy tripped in her eagerness to get to Mom's side and was caught by a handsome orderly. "Careful," he said.

But I barely heard. I didn't care. I saw our mother's face as her bed was wheeled in from the hall, as her gaze traveled around the room, recognizing each face, and finally lit on the white roses in my hand. I saw her smile.

Merry Christmas.

CHAPTER 21

Jo

We couldn't all spend the night at the hospital. *"One overnight visitor per patient,"* the nurse explained with a touch of regret. Even at Christmas. So, for the second night in a row, Beth slept in the recliner in our mother's room.

"It's Christmas Eve. You're not coming home at all?" I blurted, and then bit my tongue when Beth looked stricken. "Of course not," I answered my own question. "You're flying back to Branson tomorrow. You should spend as much time with Mom as you can."

So, while Meg went home to John and the twins, I went back to the farmhouse with Dad and Amy. Somebody had to feed the goats.

The joy of being all together, the relief of our mother's successful surgery, had buoyed us through the first night. But by the second day, we were reverting to our childhood selves. Poor Amy was used to being petted and spoiled and loved. And while I loved her—she was my sister—I found her primping, her chattering, her constant need to be the center of attention, a little irritating. I tried my best, but I was guiltily aware that we weren't as close as sisters should be. Meg said I still hadn't forgiven Amy for deleting my long-ago letter to Dad.

Or maybe I hadn't forgiven myself for almost killing her.

When we got home from the hospital, Amy went to her old room to lie down, pleading jet lag. She *was* pale, I acknowledged. Or maybe she wanted to get out of helping with the farm chores.

After the darkness of the starlit yard, the barn was warm and golden, the smells of straw and livestock hanging in the air. The goats bleated when they saw me, the pregnant lady goats sticking their heads over their pens, rubbing and butting like cats. Clover, the all-white matriarch of the herd, chewed on my hair as I scooped grain pellets into her trough. I twitched my braid away, rubbing between her horns.

It struck me I was in a stable on Christmas Eve, where, according to legend, animals talked and love came down to earth. There was a message there somewhere. I should be nicer to Amy. Maybe when she got up we could put up the tree together.

"Dad, do you know where the tree is?" I asked when I came in from the barn.

He glanced up from his reading, a faint frown between his brows. "What tree?"

"Our Christmas tree. The one we used when you deployed."

"I took it to the center," my father said. "Many men and women don't have a tree of their own."

I shouldn't feel cheated. I should be proud of him, proud to be his daughter. But I felt as if he'd taken something away from us. Especially when he left the house not fifteen minutes later, responding to a call from a soldier.

"It's you and me, cat," I told Weasley.

He jumped up on the couch, purring. Maybe when I went back to New York, I should adopt a cat.

Swallowing a yawn, I opened my laptop. Tomorrow was Christmas. Now that Beth was home, I figured I was off the hook for the special Christmas story I'd promised her. But I hadn't posted in a week. For the foreseeable future, my only income was the blog. I needed to write. I needed a topic. A subject that didn't use Eric for inspiration.

I missed him so much. His dark, curling lashes. The smell of his neck. His big, scarred, competent hands. I wondered what he was doing this Christmas Eve. Visiting his boys, he'd said. Seeing his ex-wife.

Christmas cookies . . . Christmas dinner . . . Christmas gifts for cooks . . . Christmas gifts from your kitchen . . . Traditional Christmas recipes . . .

This was not our traditional Christmas. Not without Mom. Not without Dad. And when the hell was Amy getting up?

Christmas family favorites . . .

There was an idea. My mother's Christmas dinner could induce a food coma. Basically a repeat of Thanksgiving, with even more sides: roast turkey with corn bread and sausage stuffing, Coca Cola ham, macaroni and cheese, duchesse potatoes, and candied yams. Good Southern cooking, y'all. For dessert, red velvet cake and pecan pie.

A memory slid into me like a knife—Eric's stunned face as he looked down at the pie dish in my hands. *"Jo. I love that you made pie . . . Nobody ever cooks for me."*

I closed my eyes. I needed another memory.

Okay. Not dinner. One year, my mother made this breakfast casserole, layers of egg-soaked bread and cheese, a cross between French toast and a soufflé that sat in the refrigerator overnight, ready to pop in the oven when we got home from church on Christmas morning. But after the service, my mother had learned that our neighbors, the Hummels, had lost all their food when their power was cut off for nonpayment of their electric bill. So our Christmas breakfast had gone to feed the Hummels. I'd never eaten that casserole, but I could still use the idea, right? Even the story. Very Christmassy. My father would approve. I could tweak the recipe later, swap prosciutto for the sausage, maybe, use Dijon instead of yellow mustard . . .

But no matter how I labored over the story, the warmth felt forced. Fake. I wasn't feeling the Christmas mood at all.

The chime of the doorbell was a relief.

Not Dad, I thought as I uncurled my legs from the couch. My father wouldn't ring. I crossed the living room, registering movement at the top of the stairs. Amy, getting up.

I tugged on the front door. "Trey! What are you doing here?"

"I came to bring you this." He held up a leopard-print scarf.

I grinned. "Delivering presents early?"

As I reached to take it, Trey put a hand on my waist, moving in with easy confidence. I felt the scrape of his man-child stubble, the whisper of moist heat as his lips parted over mine.

I took a step back in confusion, aware of Amy trailing down the stairs. "That's mine," she said.

"You left it in my car yesterday," Trey said.

"Thanks. I thought I lost it at the airport." She looped it around her neck, her gaze cutting from Trey to me. "Where's Daddy?"

"He had to go out. He got a call from one of his clients."

Her face fell. "But it's Christmas Eve."

Her disappointment went straight to my heart, an echo of my own.

"The holidays are tough," I said gently, parroting the explanation he'd given me. Defending him, the way our mother would have. "Especially for people with mental or emotional challenges."

Amy sniffed. "You always did make excuses for him."

My mouth dropped open.

"Since he's not here, can I take you out for a drink?" Trey intervened smoothly. His hand was still on my waist.

Amy's gaze went from his hand to his face. "I owe you a beer, at least. I haven't thanked you properly yet for my flight home."

"You don't need to do that," Trey said.

"I want to," Amy said. "It meant a lot to me."

Trey hitched his shoulders, looking uncomfortable.

Amy smiled, fluffing her blond hair with her fingers. "I should go up and get changed." Even fresh out of bed, she looked fabulous, her black lace top clinging to her small breasts, her mouth a bold, rich red.

I frowned at Trey as she ran back upstairs. Had he meant his invitation for both of us? Or just for me?

Not that it mattered. We needed to talk. The sooner the better.

"Let's go," I said, grabbing the hoodie I'd worn to the barn.

A gleam appeared in his eyes. "You want to thank me properly, too?"

I flushed, remembering that impulsive kiss at the hospital. "In your dreams, Laurence. Move it."

"You want to, ah . . ." He glanced after Amy. "Wait?"

"Nope," I said.

"My place? Granddad would love to see you."

I considered the idea. I liked old Mr. Laurence, and for some reason he'd always liked me. I wasn't the sweet Southern debutante he hoped his grandson would marry one day. But in high school, when Trey and I were in and out of each other's houses all the time, he'd always ask politely after my parents and then excuse himself to go upstairs, leaving us alone in the firelit library with a full decanter of bourbon. Back then, I'd thought Trey's house was the perfect setting for long, deep talks, for my first taste of whiskey. My first kiss.

"Or we could go to Alleygators," I said.

Trey's brows rose.

I grinned evilly. "Unless you're chicken." He never could resist a dare.

"You're on." He opened the door with a sweeping gesture. "Right this way."

Amy would be pissed. It *was* pretty rotten, leaving her alone on Christmas Eve, I thought with a flash of guilt. But we hadn't actually promised to take her with us. She'd *said* she was tired.

And there were things I had to say to Trey I couldn't possibly tell him with my little sister as an audience.

G raffiti and license plates covered the walls at Alleygators. Glowing strings of chili peppers festooned the bar, glinting off dingy bottles. Judging from the cobwebs, the Christmas lights stayed up all year.

The regulars, on mismatched barstools, looked like they'd been there almost as long.

Everyone, including the bartender, gave us the once-over as we walked in and then proceeded to ignore us. Trey and I found a sticky booth in the back, away from the pool tables. By unspoken agreement, we'd stuck to random, neutral subjects on the drive over. But once we fetched our beers from the bar, there was no ignoring the elephant in the room. I felt its weight on my chest.

"Thanks for picking up Beth at the airport yesterday. I'm so glad she's here."

Trey cocked an eyebrow. "My pleasure."

"And Amy, too," I added. "It was really nice of you to help with her ticket."

"No problem." He leaned forward. "I'd do anything for you. You know that, Jo."

"Er . . . Yes." I took a deep breath and then the plunge. "The thing is . . . I kind of overreacted when I saw her. You."

His dark eyes fixed on my face. "You were happy. I was happy. It's all good."

Help. Why did this have to be so awkward? "Right. The thing is . . ." Crap. I was repeating myself. I picked at my peeling beer label. "See, I can't . . ."

A swirl of cold disturbed the close air. I looked up. My sister Amy stood framed in the dark doorway, her hair glowing like a candle in the dim light.

"Oh hell."

Trey turned. Started to get up.

"Hang on," I said. "I'll talk to her."

He sat. Reluctantly, I thought.

Amy had changed back into her skirt and boots and tossed a jacket over the black lace. She looked hot and lost and alone—a recipe for disaster in a dive like Alleygators. But my little sister seemed unaware of her danger. Or maybe she was enjoying it. She strolled forward, her boots clacking on the grimy floor. The regulars swiveled to watch. The pool players nudged one another. One of them said something, and the rest guffawed. In another minute, she'd be swarmed by burly patrons eager to offer her a drink, a joint, or a quickie in the restroom.

I hurried to reach her before they did. "Amy, what are you doing here?"

"You said you were going out for a drink. It's not like there are a lot of bars open on Christmas Eve." She looked pleased by her own resourcefulness.

I wanted to shake her. "But how did you get here?"

"Uber."

"In Bunyan?"

She fluttered her fingers. "Uber is everywhere."

I didn't have the heart to send her away. "Listen, Ames, I'm sorry we came out without you. It's just . . . Trey and I are trying to talk."

"Fine. I'll wait." She drifted toward the jukebox, a fluffy yellow baby chick surrounded by alligators.

"You'll be all right?"

She smiled just a little, her eyes unreadable. "Aren't I always?"

Amy took care of Amy. Always. And she must have developed some street smarts in Paris. "Don't talk to anybody," I warned.

"Mm." She turned her attention back to the jukebox, tiptoeing her fingers through the music selection.

I dashed back to the booth. "Okay, here's the deal," I said to Trey, speaking rapidly. "You and I need to get things straight."

"What?" He was still watching Amy. So was every other man in the place, along with a few disgruntled women.

I cleared my throat, determined to get through my speech and get my sister out of here. "We're friends. Good friends. But that's it. You can't kiss me anymore, Trey."

I had his attention now. "*You* kissed *me*."

I winced. "Yeah. My bad."

"I waited for you, Jo," he said, an edge to his voice. "I went to work for Granddad while you got this whole New York thing out of your system. When you came home this time, I figured you were finally ready to settle down. And instead—"

"I told you this summer we were through. I'm sorry."

"*Sorry?* Come on." He reached across the table, covering my damp hand on the beer bottle. "Jo, I *love* you."

My chest hurt. "I love you, too, Trey. Just not . . . like that."

"But you could. I know you could," he insisted. "Maybe you don't feel the way I do—yet. I can live with that."

"But I can't."

"Things change. People change."

"Not in Bunyan," I said.

His eyes blazed. "That's why I need you. I can't stay old Mr. Laurence's grandson for the rest of my life."

"And I won't be young Mr. Laurence's wife."

"So you said." His tone was bitter.

I swallowed and looked away. My sister had joined the pool players, good ol' boys in flannel shirts, feed caps, and various stages of drunk, playing a drinking game: miss a shot, take a shot. The tables around them were littered with empty beer bottles and dirty glasses. A tall, bearded dude at the bar said something to the bartender, who shook his head.

Trey followed my gaze and then turned back to me, his face tight. "It's him, isn't it?"

"Who?"

"The guy from the blog. You're dumping me for the guy with the tattoos. That old cook, Wolfgang Fuck, whoever the hell he is. Wherever he came from."

"His name is Eric Bhaer." Distracted, I watched Amy toss back a shot while her new pals hollered encouragement. "And he's not an old cook, he's a talented, passionate, incredibly accomplished chef with his own restaurant. Anyway, that's over."

Trey's fingers gripped mine against the cold glass. "Then there's still a chance for us."

I regarded him across the table, my oldest pal, my closest coconspirator. Who would I be without Trey? For years, we'd laughed and studied and played together, gotten each other in and out of trouble. But this was one stupid thing I wasn't going to let myself get talked into.

I had loved three men in my life. My father, who made me feel smart and special. Trey, who made me feel upbeat and happy. And Eric, who had made me feel . . . whole. Maybe I didn't have the stuff to make a real relationship work. To make it last. But I knew now how it should feel. And I didn't feel that way with Trey.

Gently, I slid my hand away. "No."

Something flickered in his face. He drew his breath. "Jo . . ."

A raucous cheer rose from the pool table.

Trey glanced over his shoulder. "Christ. What is she doing?"

Amy downed another shot and tossed her head, almost as if she were aware of his gaze. Stroking her cue, she sauntered to the table. At the bar, the bearded guy sighed and shook his head.

"Yeah, baby," somebody yelled.

There were leers and whistles as she bent over to take her shot. Planted her feet. Wiggled her hips in that short, tight skirt. The guy behind her grabbed her ass, and she straightened, whirled, and cracked her cue over his head.

Oh shit.

Trey shouted. I lurched from the booth at the same moment Bearded Guy launched from the bar, muscling in between Amy and the guy she'd just clobbered.

Chairs scraped—customers pushing to their feet, jostling to get closer or away. Beer spilled. A woman screamed. Her boyfriend threw a punch at one of the pool players, who swung back. *Damn it, damn it, damn it.* Breathless, I shoved through a blur of bodies, beer, and sweat, desperate to get to Amy. I threw my arm around her. Bearded Guy had grabbed her elbow on the other side and was hauling her toward the door. I hung on, looking back for Trey. He was at the bar, his wallet out.

"She with you?" I heard the bartender ask.

"Yes."

"Get her out of here."

We were already out, pushing through the door, spilling into the sputtering neon light of the bar sign. Amy wobbled as the cold air hit her. Among the pickups in the parking lot, Trey's low-slung Italian sports car was easy to spot. We crunched toward it over the gravel, our breath fogging in the dark.

"Thank you," I said to Bearded Guy. Was he the bouncer? He looked vaguely familiar.

He frowned down at me. "Does your ma know you girls are here?"

Thanksgiving, I thought. He'd come to our house for Thanksgiving dinner.

Amy hiccupped. "Momma's in the hospital."

He went still. "She gonna be okay?"

"She had back surgery," I said. "She's doing much better now."

"Glad to hear it. Nice lady, your mother."

Trey appeared, striding onto the scene like a Disney prince, lean build, dark hair, great teeth. "Are you all right?"

Amy turned her face into my shoulder, refusing to look at him. She was probably mortified. "Fine," I said. "Thanks to, uh . . ." Well, shoot. I couldn't remember his name.

Trey extended his hand to our bearded rescuer. "Appreciate it, man."

The man ignored his gesture. "What the hell were you thinking, bringing these girls to a place like this?"

Trey scowled.

"It was my idea," I said hastily. "My fault."

My fault. Amy's fault. We brought out the worst in each other. We always had. Me running away, her following . . . Disaster.

"People change," Trey had insisted.

But where my sisters were concerned, I hadn't changed at all.

T he next morning Amy staggered downstairs looking wan. "Coffee," she croaked.

I glanced up from my laptop, fighting my own fatigue. "You should eat something first."

She turned paler, if that were possible. "I can't."

"Hangover?" I asked sympathetically.

She sank gracefully into our mother's chair, closing her eyes. "Jet lag."

I snorted as I got up to pour her coffee. "Still?" I set the full mug on the table in front of her, bending to kiss her brow. "Merry Christmas."

She smiled without opening her eyes.

I got back to work on my blog. The recipe was fine. I'd tested it last night. The problem was the tone, which was preachy and treacly and heavy-handed. Ugh.

My phone chimed with a text from Meg. Merry Christmas, darling sisters!

It didn't feel like Christmas without any stockings or presents. Without a tree. Without our mother home. It was even worse for Amy, I imagined. She must miss all the holiday trappings and fuss. She used to wander through December in a little cloud of glitter, trailing ribbons and glue.

Another ping. Beth, from the hospital. Mom feeling better!!! Best Christmas present ever!!!

I smiled at the news and the string of joyful emojis. Can't wait to see you all, I typed.

When can you leave???

As soon as Dad gets back from church. I'd stayed home this morning, out of guilt, so Amy wouldn't wake up alone.

"Who are you texting?" she asked.

"Meg and Beth. They messaged you, too," I offered.

She sipped her coffee. "I thought maybe it was your boyfriend. The arm-porn guy? From your blog."

I could have explained that Eric was never my boyfriend. I could have pointed out that Amy had never expressed any interest in my blog before. "We broke up," I said.

Amy nodded sagely. "Guys always break up with you before the holidays. That way they don't have to buy you presents."

I smiled, amused in spite of myself. "So young and yet so cynical."

"Not cynical. Realistic. Most couples break up over money. Or sex." She rested her head on the back of her chair, closing her eyes again. "Either they don't have enough or they're not comfortable talking about it. Look at Meg and John."

Meg had always protected Amy. It wasn't my place to confide her worries about John. Even sisters were entitled to some secrets. Anyway, Meg and John had seemed happy enough at the hospital. "Meg and John are fine. They're like Jane Bennet and Bingley."

Amy raised her hand. *Stop.* "Please. Not *Pride and Prejudice* again."

"*Pride and Prejudice* is a timeless novel. I love *Pride and Prejudice.*"

"Of course you do. Because you get Darcy. You're always Lizzy, and Meg gets to be Jane, and who's left? It's like Beth and I don't count."

"I guess . . . Beth could be Mary." The quiet one who played the piano. "Although obviously Beth is much nicer," I added. "And a better singer."

"You know what your problem is?" Amy demanded.

"I'm sure you're going to tell me."

"You pigeonhole everybody. Like we have to fit into the same little boxes we had when we were kids. The responsible one. The smart one. The talented one. The pretty one. But real people aren't all one thing. We're all mixed up."

Her criticism stung. Maybe because it was true. "I never said you were."

"Uh-huh. Which sister am I?" Amy asked.

I flushed. "What?"

"Which Bennet sister?" Amy narrowed her blue eyes. "Lydia, right? The slutty one."

I set my laptop on the coffee table. "This conversation is ridiculous. I'm going to get you some breakfast."

"I'm not hungry," Amy said.

"You'll feel better after you eat," I said.

The cheesy casserole I'd put together the night before was keeping warm in the oven. I put a big slice on a plate and dug out the red napkins, arranging everything as nicely as I could on Momma's special "sick" tray.

Carrying the tray to the living room, I set it proudly on the coffee table in front of Amy. "Merry Christmas," I said, satisfied I'd done my best to save Christmas.

Until she vomited all over my open laptop.

CHAPTER 22

Meg

The tree lights twinkled. The Christmas stockings were emptied and flung on the floor. DJ, ignoring his new toys, climbed into the carton John's mother used to mail their presents. Daisy was burying him under discarded wrapping paper.

"Snow!" she cried, tossing sparkly tissue paper high.

I smiled ruefully at John. "That's it. No more presents. Next year, I'm giving them a box."

But they looked so adorable, giggling in their matching Christmas pajamas. I took a picture to send to Momma and my sisters.

John smiled back at me, his eyes warm. "Maybe one or two more." He laid a flat rectangle in my lap. "For you."

"Oh my goodness." I flushed with pleasure and surprise. He'd even wrapped it himself, with a stick-on bow and corners secured with tape.

We'd already exchanged the usual, practical gifts, the way you do when you're on a budget, shopping from each other's preselected wish lists, a socket wrench set and a jacket for him, an electric toothbrush and a sweater for me. Underwear. Socks.

Only John had given me a present that wasn't on my list. The best gift ever—my sisters for Christmas. And now . . . This. It was too much.

"Wait." I scrambled up. "Let me give you your present first."

I fetched an envelope tied with ribbons from under the tree, my heart beating in anticipation.

John shot me a bemused look as I handed him the envelope. I held my breath as he unstuck the flap and slid out the pages inside. A computer printout of the North Carolina High School Wrestling Association schedule. A Greensboro map. Hotel reservations.

John stared at the pages in his lap, his face unreadable.

I hurried into explanations. "I called Ben Hardy. At the high school? He said you wouldn't be reporting scores until next month, but that Jason and some of the other boys had a good chance of making Regionals. Maybe even States." I took a deep breath, willing John to smile. Praying I'd got this right. "Tickets for the championship aren't on sale yet. But I made hotel reservations. For both weekends." I smiled tremulously. "In case your team goes all the way."

"That's Valentine's Day weekend," John said.

"I know. Not so romantic, to spend it with a bunch of sweaty high school wrestlers. But I thought it was important." *To you. To us.*

"This is . . . wonderful. Thank you, honey." He got up to kiss me. "You've thought of everything."

Not everything. My stomach sank even as his lips warmed mine. I'd been so eager to get this right, to get him right, the way he "got" me. He deserved that. "Is something wrong?"

He nodded toward the gift I'd set aside. "You haven't opened your present yet."

My fingers traced the lines of the package. "What is it?"

"Open it."

I fumbled with tape. Ripped the paper. It was a photo, framed. A selfie of the two of us together, standing on the Carolina Beach boardwalk, taken on that first night. I'd been laughing too hard to pose, my hair blowing in my face, but that was all right because we both looked so happy, John slightly stunned, me, almost smug. His arm—the one that wasn't holding the phone—was around me. Behind us, the Ferris wheel lit up the sky like stars.

Tears pricked my eyes. "It's beautiful." I half laughed, moved and embarrassed. "I was so skinny."

"You look great." His gaze met mine. "You always look great to me."

My heart melted. "Oh, John. Thank you."

His smile seemed forced. "There's more. Turn it over."

He'd taped an e-mail on the back. A rental confirmation for an ocean-front suite on Carolina Beach. "Oh, John."

"It's not Hawaii, but . . ."

"It's perfect," I said. "I love you."

"Love you, too." He cleared his throat. "I already talked to Hannah. She said she can stay with the kids that weekend."

I scanned the e-mail, searching for the date. "Valentine's Day weekend?"

John shrugged.

I laughed. "Can we change it?"

His gaze held mine. After a moment, the corners of his eyes crinkled. "I already paid the deposit. But I guess . . . If you want to. If the team makes the championships."

A warm feeling settled in my chest. "They'll make it," I predicted.

And so, I thought, would we.

We kissed. I drew back, flushed with happiness. "You said you had something else for me?"

"Yeah." He smiled again, more easily this time. "For you and the kids."

He went to the kitchen. The door to the garage opened and closed. Another new car for Christmas, I thought, another dealership car I could drive for a year and give back. I arranged a properly delighted smile on my face.

I heard a wild scrabble across the kitchen floor.

"Iss a puppy!" Daisy shrieked.

It was not a puppy. It was a large, hairy dog of indeterminate breed with a red bow tied to its collar, lurching forward, straining against John's hold on its collar. Oh God. The very last thing I needed. Something else to take care of.

DJ crawled out of his box.

Daisy danced forward. "What it name, Daddy?"

No. Don't name it. A lifetime with Bethie's strays had taught me once we named it, it was ours.

"Lady." John pressed his hand to the dog's haunches. "Lady, sit."

The dog obeyed, tongue lolling, eyes swiveling anxiously between John and the kids. Even sitting, it was almost as tall as Daisy.

"It's very . . ." *Big.* "Pretty." Black and white and tan, with funny patches like eyebrows.

"She's part golden," John said proudly. "Maybe collie."

Or German shepherd, I thought, regarding those sharp teeth.

John squatted, uncurling Daisy's fingers from the dog's thick fur. "Not like that. Like this, see?" He guided her hand.

Daisy patted the dog's shoulder, her face pink. DJ hung back, clutching his blanket.

"Where did you get her?" I asked.

"She showed up at the dealership about a week ago. Must have been dumped on the highway."

My heart gave an unwilling tug. *Abandoned.* "Poor thing. Beth says it's because people don't like to turn their pets in to shelters. They think they're better off on their own in the country."

John's jaw set. "Yeah, well, a week ago she was half-starved and covered in fleas." He looked at my face. "I took her to a vet. She's had all her shots. And she's housebroken."

Daisy was hugging the dog, her arms as far around its furry neck as she could reach. DJ took a cautious step forward. Before I could react, the dog's head lunged forward. Her tongue swiped his face.

DJ stumbled back a step, his face clouding. "Ick." Or maybe he said *lick*.

John laughed.

"It's a doggy kiss," I said. "Lady kissed you."

DJ's expression cleared.

"I want a doggy kiss," Daisy said jealously. "Lick me, Lady. Lady, lick me."

I looked from our children's flushed, excited faces to John's open one.

He'd never had a dog growing up, he'd told me once. Never had any pet at all. His mother struggled hard enough to provide for John and his brother. A dog—that would need food and visits to the vet and attention—was out of the question.

He wanted this, I thought. In all our discussions about getting a pet, he'd never said so. I couldn't remember the last time John had told me he wanted something for himself.

Maybe I should have asked. Because he wanted this dog. For our children, yes, but also . . .

I leaned forward and kissed him. "What a great present."

His answering smile made my heart swell. Three sizes, like the Grinch.

Tubes and wires anchored my mother to the bank of machines by her bed. We all barely fit inside her hospital room. But her breathing was steady, her eyes soft with warmth and love. The twins had been warned not to bounce.

"Here, give him to me." Amy took DJ from my arms. "Can I have a kiss?"

DJ licked her nose. Jo snickered.

"Doggy kiss!" Daisy said.

Amy turned bewildered blue eyes to me.

"John gave us a dog for Christmas," I explained. "Lady."

"Puppy," DJ said.

I smiled. "Not exactly a puppy. She's a golden-collie mix."

"She sounds beautiful," Amy said.

"And smart," Jo said from her perch on the windowsill. "Which is more important."

"The vet thinks she's about four years old. I figured an adult dog would be less trouble for Meg," John said.

Jo snorted. "Yeah, because it's so much easier to scoop the poops of an animal the size of a small pony."

I coughed to cover my laugh. "I'll have lots of help."

"Where did you find her?" Beth asked, beaming approval as John told the story.

Our mother smiled. "Rescuing the homeless."

"Not exactly," our father said dryly from the recliner.

Presents heaped the hospital tray and the foot of the bed. I'd bought our joint gift to Momma, a silk scarf she'd admire and tuck away as too good for everyday wear. Jo had picked out Dad's present, a gloomy-looking book called *Aftermath* about the war in Iraq. We exchanged our gifts to one another in order of age: scented soaps from me, notebooks with funny sayings from Jo, fuzzy socks from Beth.

Amy's gifts were different. She'd made them herself, with unerring taste and her almost desperate desire to please, stitched from leather and canvas with bright colors and bold graphics. A folder for Beth's music with a cubist guitar. A scribbling rat on a padded laptop case for Jo. A square-patterned tote that didn't look anything like a diaper bag for me.

"These are beautiful, Amy," our mother said, stroking the stitching on my bag. "You've learned so much in Paris."

"It's good to see you use your talent for others," our father said. Even compliments were teaching moments for Dad.

Jo regarded her present, a funny expression on her face.

"I'm sorry I puked on your laptop," Amy said.

Oh no.

Beth's eyes widened in sympathy. "She threw up on your laptop?"

"It's fine," Jo said.

"It was an accident," Amy said.

Jo wrapped her ponytail around her hand, securing it in a bun with one vicious stab. "There are no accidents, according to Freud."

"Picasso," Amy said in a small voice.

"What?"

"Freud didn't say that. It was Picasso."

I hid a smile. Jo sometimes forgot our baby sister was an artist, as ambitious, as talented in her own way as Jo. Amy disguised her determination beneath a bright, shallow surface, but the two were more alike than either wanted to admit.

"Ash, will you read to us now?" our mother suggested. Smoothing things over, the way she did. The way I did. "Before Beth has to leave for the airport."

Every year that he was home, as far back as I could remember, our father read the Christmas gospel to us in his deep, beautiful preacher's voice. The memories washed over me as he told the old, familiar story. The hospital noises faded away, squeaking shoes, beeping monitors, the jabber of the TV in the next room. Jo and Beth stood by the window, their arms around each other. I looked from our mother's serene face to John cradling Daisy to the fluorescent light gleaming on our son's head, resting on Amy's shoulder. I was surrounded by love, a lovely pull at my heart, a tug in my womb.

My father stopped reading.

In the silence, Beth's voice rose, singing "I'll Be Home for Christmas," the melody achingly clear as angel song.

I blinked back tears as my sisters joined in. Jo was flat, as usual. John caught my eye and smiled.

Christmas *wasn't* perfect this year. It was messy and flawed and human. It was real. It was wonderful.

I sang, my voice blending with my sisters'.

CHAPTER 23

Jo

D ad took Beth to the airport. I swallowed tears as we said good-bye in the hospital parking lot.

"I wish I was staying," she said, clinging to me. "We barely had any time together at all."

"Oh, honey." I squeezed her tight, like a teddy bear. Tried to smile. "You have to go. Your fans are waiting."

She blushed. "That's what Colt says."

"Anyway, you'll be back before you know it. New Year's is only a week away. We'll have a long visit then."

She looked away, across the parking lot.

"Bethie?"

She took a deep breath. "Colt . . . He asked me to come with him to Nashville after the show closes. He wants to record my song in his studio. But—"

"But that's wonderful," I said heartily.

She met my gaze. "It's a long time to be gone."

My heart wrenched. "Mom would want you to go. Did you tell her?"

She nodded. "Last night. Will you be okay?"

She was worried about us. About me? I pulled myself together, channeling Momma, determined not to make her leaving harder. "We'll be fine. I'm so proud of you." I hugged her again. "Nashville! You have to tell me all about it when you get back. Promise?"

Her thin face broke into a smile. "Promise."

I waved wildly as Dad's car pulled away, satisfied that Beth, at least, was on her way to where she belonged. Following her passion.

And Meg was going home with John. She told me, smiling, that she had given him a weekend away at some wrestling competition for Christmas and that he gave her a weekend at the beach. The same weekend, apparently, but she seemed confident they could work it out.

"It's like 'The Gift of the Magi,'" I said.

Meg looked blank.

"The short story. By O. Henry?"

"English major." Meg pointed at me, then tapped her own chest. "Accountant."

"Right. I just meant . . . Well, I'm glad you guys are happy."

"Thanks, sweetie." She kissed me as she took Daisy from me to load her into her car seat. "You want to come over for dinner? You can meet the dog."

Without my niece, my arms felt empty. I thought of the cheerful chaos of my sister's house, full of twins and food and noise, and wanted desperately to say yes. But Meg and John had already spent half their Christmas at the hospital. They deserved some family time together, without me hanging around.

"Maybe later," I said. "I'll see what Dad wants to do."

"Okay. I'll call you."

More hugs, more waves, and she was gone. Leaving me standing in the parking lot with nowhere to go, except home.

No word from Eric since I'd told him to go away. Not a call, not a text, nothing. Nada. Squat. Not that I expected him to . . . Okay, fine. Maybe I hoped he would wish me Merry Christmas or something.

I could call him. We lived in the modern world, after all. I didn't have to wait for him to message me. But what good would that do? He wanted me to take down my blog. And I wouldn't. Anyway, I wasn't intruding on his Christmas with his sons. His ex-wife.

"I am with you now." An image of Eric smiling at me across my alcove desk crashed over me like a wave. Eric, naked in my shower. Eric, bounding up the stairs with a bag of Chinese takeout in his hands. For a second it was hard to breathe.

I dug in my pocket for my keys, feeling tired. The drive to the farmhouse seemed suddenly long and lonely.

"Shades of middle school," Amy said as we got in the pickup.

Right. Not lonely. Amy was with me. *Yay.*

I flicked on the wipers. It was raining again. "What are you talking about?"

"You driving me home in Mom's truck."

"Gotcha." I glanced across at the passenger seat. In the spangled light through the windshield, her face was pale. Her eyes looked bruised, as if she hadn't slept. Concern pricked me. I wasn't Mom or Meg. Amy and I had never been close. But I was still her big sister. "Listen, I'm the last person to tell you how to live your life," I began.

"Then don't," Amy said.

"But maybe you shouldn't drink so much."

Amy sighed. "I don't, usually. Last night, I was just dealing with some stuff, all right?"

I nodded understandingly. "Mom."

"Mom and Dad, and you and Trey, and . . . stuff," she said.

I flushed with guilt. "We should have taken you with us."

"No. No, I should have let you two go. I don't know what I was thinking."

"Gee, maybe that you didn't want to be alone on Christmas Eve?"

"Something like that." She smiled crookedly. "At least I didn't drown this time."

A joke.

Amy had changed, I thought. Or maybe I was finally learning to see her, the grown-up Amy, not the image of her I carried in my head. I'd always seen her bids for attention, her focus on appearances, as an irritating character flaw. Spoiled, shallow Amy. But now I saw how hard she really tried to please. Those Christmas gifts, for example. She wasn't showing off her talent. She'd put real thought and work into our presents, taking the time to create the perfect, practical, individual gift, something each of us could actually use. She was more perceptive than I was. The thought was humbling.

"You really did learn a lot in Paris," I said.

Amy looked away. "You have no idea."

We drove past bare trees and brown fields and ditches that never drained. "I was wrong," I announced.

"Well, duh," Amy said. A pause. "About what?"

"About you. You're not Lydia Bennet. You're Marianne Dashwood."

"Who?"

"The younger sister in *Sense and Sensibility*. The emotional one. She makes some dumb decisions, but she always acts with her whole heart."

"Bet she doesn't marry Darcy, though."

"Well, no, since he's in another book. She marries Colonel Brandon." Amy still looked blank. "Alan Rickman, in the movie," I said.

"The old guy?"

"He's not that old," I said, oddly defensive.

"Well, not anymore. He's dead."

A snort escaped me.

Amy heaved an exaggerated sigh, her eyes sparkling with humor. "It's not fair. You—your character—gets Colin Firth in a wet white shirt and I get stuck with Professor Snape."

I grinned. "Yeah, but he's crazy in love with you. And rich."

"Richer than Darcy?"

I hesitated.

"Never mind," Amy said. "I don't need some selfish, entitled asshole in my life. I'm going to start my own design label and become fabulously wealthy on my own."

"Now you sound like me," I said.

"Shoot me now," Amy said. But she was smiling.

Eric wasn't an asshole, I thought as I turned up the drive to the farm. He was a proud, private man. A good man. A good boss. Until he fired me. Or I quit. I wasn't sure anymore. Either way, my working for him was a problem. I didn't belong on the fringes of his life in New York any more than I belonged on the fringes of Trey's life in Bunyan.

Where did I belong?

I yanked my hair into a ponytail and went to feed the goats. When I came in from the barn, Amy met me at the door.

"Somebody left this," she said, handing me a brightly wrapped package. "For you."

My first thought was that Trey had brought my Christmas present. But the handwriting on the note wasn't Trey's. Or the signature.

Sorry I missed you. Eric.

My heart stopped. "He was here?"

"Who?"

"Eric. The guy who brought this."

"I don't know. It was at the front door when I came in."

I clutched the note, my insides swooping and tumbling like a flock of swallows. "He was here, and I missed him."

"At least he brought you a present," Amy said. "Aren't you going to open it?"

I pulled at the wrapping paper, my fingers trembling with some emotion I couldn't name. Fear? Happiness? Hope?

"It's just an old cookbook," Amy said, disappointed.

"It's Eric's copy of *The French Laundry*. Signed by Thomas Keller." I turned reverently to the title page to show her. There, under the author's signature, Eric had written another note.

"'To Jo. Write your story. Eric,'" Amy read aloud. "What does that mean?"

I stroked the message without answering, replaying our conversation in my head. *"He kicked me out."* Eric's voice had been easy, amused, as he spoke of his old boss. *"Time to fly on my own, yeah? Cook my own food. Find my own voice."*

Write my own story.

I didn't know my story. At least, I couldn't see the ending. But I thought I knew where it began. In a room of my own.

⌢

Singers put out Christmas albums. Chefs cook Christmas menus. Writers tell Christmas stories. This one is mine.

HOME FOR CHRISTMAS
by Jo March

"Christmas won't be Christmas without any presents," I grumbled, lying on the rug.

White Christmas was playing on the TV, but this year the scenes of soldiers far from home made my throat ache. It felt weird to be watching the movie without Dad. Everything felt wrong this year.

I raised my head, glancing from the laptop screen—my mother's, and thank God she kept her passwords in a desk drawer with her checks—out the funny peaked window at the view of fields and trees. Good. Yes.

I loved having my own space.

Ten-year-old Amy looked up from the coffee table, where she was making something out of the scraps she'd begged from Miss Hannah's quilting bag. Christmas ornaments, I thought. A mess.

Amy called up the stairs. "I'm going to Meg's. You want to come?"

"In a minute."

Or ten. Or twenty. I typed in fits and spurts, by feel, from memory.

"I'm leaving," Amy shouted.

Christmas dinner, I thought. I should see if Dad was ready to join them. But the story drew me back, drew me in.

> "We're having turkey, too," I said, clutching the phone, hungering for his attention. His approval.
>
> Momma held up a finger. "One minute left."
>
> "I love you," Dad said. "Take care of Momma and your sisters for me."
>
> I swallowed hard. "I will."

I hunched over my requisitioned laptop as the light faded. Remembering, fixing, fiddling, deleting.

> "We're getting cut off," Dad said. "Love you, too, honey. Merry Christmas. God bless you."
>
> "Merry Christmas!" we all chorused.
>
> The connection cut off. Silence fell, as cold as snow. Beth's eyes swam with unshed tears. Amy's face was blotchy.
>
> God bless us, every one, I thought, echoing Tiny Tim.

I stretched my neck. Shook my cramped fingers. Not done. Not done yet.

I put in our presents to Momma, put it all down in bursts of feeling and snatches of recollection, like setting words to music, like hearing my sisters singing in my head. When I was finished, my heart pounded as if I'd completed a four-mile run. A naked run. This was something different, all right. This was me. This was my own story, under my own name. Would anybody like it?

I read the blog over, breathless and exposed.

Before I could chicken out, I took a deep breath. Hit POST.

So quiet.

Against the drumming of my heart, I could hear the patter of rain on the roof and the sound of my father, moving around downstairs. It was dark outside. He must be hungry. Stiffly, I made my way down the attic steps.

Light shone from my parents' room. There was an open suitcase on their bed.

My brain stuttered. "Dad? What are you doing?"

My father turned from his dresser, T-shirts in hand. I wondered who had folded them for him. "Packing."

My skin prickled. He didn't need a suitcase to spend the night in the hospital. "For what?"

"The caregivers' conference."

"You're not still going." As if my saying so could make it true. "Mom's in the hospital."

"She'll be released to rehab tomorrow."

Paralyzed, I watched him walk back to the suitcase, trying to reconcile the man methodically stacking underwear with the father of my childhood, the one I'd written letters to, the dad in my story. "Have you told her?"

"She knows."

"What did she say?"

His mouth compressed. "I don't believe I have to share the details of our conversation with you."

Heat stung my cheeks like a slap. But this was my *father*. The man who had taught me to speak up for myself, to hold true to what I believed. "I don't need details, Dad," I said in an even voice. "But an explanation would be nice."

My father sighed. "Your mother isn't the only one who requires support, Jo. There are people—veterans who have sacrificed every-thing for their country, many of them homeless or wounded—who don't have anyone else to advocate for them. No one to share in their grief and their joy, no one to care for them or their families. I have a duty to be where the suffering is greatest. If you had any kind of calling yourself, you would understand."

"This isn't about your high-and-noble calling. And I'm not going to let you make it about me. About my writing. This is about Mom. And she needs you."

"I can't be here now. Not the way she . . ." His gaze met mine, briefly. "Not the way you seem to want."

"You can't just leave," I blurted. "We're your family."

His brow creased, as if in pain. For one giddy moment I let myself hope that I had won. But I'd forgotten I was fighting my father.

His forehead smoothed. His eyebrows rose. "For someone who has pushed away any intimacy in her own life, it's rather disingenuous of you to question my choices."

I sucked in my breath. It was like the end of *To Kill a Mockingbird*, when Atticus Finch doesn't heroically save his client, when he loses at trial and Tom is shot escaping from prison. Except my father wasn't even trying to do the right thing.

I folded my arms, burying my shaking hands in my armpits. "At least I'm trying. I'm not running away."

But my father was no longer listening. He frowned. "Do you know where my navy sweater is?"

I stared at him in disbelief. "I'm not going to help you pack. Find your own damn sweater." I spun on my heel.

His clear voice followed me to the door. "Who's running away now?"

His words tripped me at the edge of the carpet. But I didn't stop. I pressed my lips together, the way I'd seen my mother do a thousand times, and went out, closing the door.

My father, my hero, would rather minister to wounded warriors than deal with his own family.

He'd always seemed so wise and impartial, presiding with loving fairness above the girl drama the rest of us lived in, Beth crying in her room, Amy shouting down the stairs, Meg fretting over her hair or her shoes. I'd wanted to be like him. I was too impulsive. Too hotheaded.

"*Passionate,*" Eric said.

My throat was tight. My father wasn't impartial. He just didn't *feel* anymore.

I went into the bathroom to cool my hot cheeks. The mirror above the sink gave back the same reflection it had in high school: the same thin face, the same familiar scowl, even the same hair. My father's hair.

"*For someone who has pushed away any intimacy in her own life . . .*"

No more.

I was in the bathroom a long time. When I came out, my parents' door was still shut. I climbed the stairs to the attic.

The browser was open to my blog. My cursor hovered over the link. Clicked.

To: chef@gusto.com

Sorry I missed you. I miss you. Thank you.

I gnawed my lip over the closing. Sincerely? Always? Love?

Merry Christmas, I typed at last and hit SEND.

CHAPTER 24

Meg

G o potty," I said to Lady, the way I did to the twins a dozen times a day.

The dog stopped rambling around the yard long enough to give me a patient look.

"Is that some kind of special dog command?" Amy asked.

"No idea," I confessed. "This is all new to me. I've never had a dog before."

"I always wanted a puppy. A little one I could carry around in my bag. Like Kylie Jenner."

"Or Aunt Phee."

Amy laughed. "I can't believe she brought her dog to Christmas dinner."

Yesterday, after Jo and Dad turned down my invitation, I'd steeled myself to call Aunt Phee. Our great-aunt had arrived on our doorstep at precisely five o'clock, bringing her dog, a box of pralines for me, and board books for the children. Despite her Yorkie's determination to show the much bigger Lady who was boss, the evening had been surprisingly pleasant.

"It wasn't so bad," I said. "At least she was polite to John."

"She also said nice things about the turkey."

I bit back a grin. Lady sniffed at the muddy ground. "Potty," I repeated.

Miraculously, the dog squatted.

"She peed, Mommy!" Daisy said, clapping her hands.

"Good dog."

"I pee, too," DJ said, and, yep, there was a dark, spreading stain on the front of his overalls.

"Okay," I said. "That's okay. Let's go inside and get everybody cleaned up."

Daisy scowled. "No."

The twins were tired of rain, bored with playing inside.

"You go," Amy said. "I can watch Daisy."

"Lady, too!"

At the sound of her name, the dog waved her plumy tail uncertainly back and forth.

"And Lady." Amy smiled. "Don't worry."

It was so nice to have her here, I thought as I took DJ inside. My own sister in my own house for Christmas dinner.

Last night, after Phee had left, John took the twins upstairs so Amy and I could talk. In my heart, I knew John and I needed to talk, too. But my sister was here for only a short visit. And the sound of my husband putting our babies to bed, wild bursts of giggles, slippered feet running down the hall, lulled me into thinking any heavy discussions of our future could wait. In the end, Amy and I had stayed up to watch *White Christmas* until Amy fell asleep on the couch.

As I changed DJ, I caught myself humming the "Sisters" song.

When I returned to the yard, Amy and Daisy were stacking pinecones into Christmas trees. Well. Amy was stacking, and Daisy was scattering pinecones and laughing.

"Look at you getting all dirty," I said affectionately.

Amy flashed me a quick smile. "It was this or mud pies."

"I'm sorry the kids woke you so early."

"It's fine. I don't get to spend enough time with them." There were faint purple shadows under her eyes, smudges of jet lag or unhappiness.

"Is everything all right?" I asked. She bent to the pinecones, not meeting my eyes. "Amy?"

"Did you ever want something so much that you convinced yourself to see it when it wasn't really there?"

"I'm not sure," I said. "Do you want to talk about it?"

She shook her head. "It's not my secret to tell. I don't want to make things worse." She balanced another pinecone on the stack. "There are other people involved."

The tiny hairs on my arms prickled. "Do we need to have the talk about good and bad secrets?"

Amy looked up and saw my face. "No. Whatever you're imagining, please stop."

"All right. But if there's ever anything you want to tell me . . ."

She grinned, wrinkling her nose at me. "Are we having a Momma Hen and Little Chick moment, like in the movie?"

I laughed. "I just want you to know I care."

"You're so sweet. I love you, too."

A pickup truck edged to the curb in front of our house. Mom's truck, with Jo at the wheel. The vehicle door slammed and Jo strode up the driveway.

"Oh my God," Amy said. "What happened to your hair?"

Jo flushed. She met my gaze, her eyes filled with pride and embarrassment, satisfaction and regret. "I cut it."

We could see that. Her thick, long, beautiful hair—our father's hair—had been chopped to jaw level. Even shorter in the back.

"With what? Hoof trimmers?" Amy said.

"Sweetie, why?" I asked.

Jo shrugged. "It was always in my way. In the kitchen. In the barn. I got tired of messing with it."

"But to cut it! Your beautiful hair. It's . . ."

"Awful," Amy said.

"It's not awful," I said loyally. "It's . . ." Words failed me.

Jo gave a choked laugh. "It is pretty bad."

"If you wanted a haircut, why didn't you tell me? I could have made an appointment for you with my stylist."

"Nope. I've had the same hair since high school." She stuck out her chin. "I'm ready for a change now."

I would never, ever cut my hair like that. But it was such a Jo thing to do—fearless, impulsive, defiant. I hugged her. "Good for you."

"Dad's gone to D.C.," she said against my shoulder.

"What are you talking about?" Amy asked.

"Some conference," I said. "Remember? He mentioned it at Thanksgiving."

"But he didn't say good-bye."

"I need to talk to Mom," Jo said. "Do you want to come?"

I drew back, my Momma Hen sense tingling again. "I'd love to. Oh, but the twins . . ."

"I can stay with them." Amy looked at me. "Please tell me they nap."

"No nap," Daisy said. "Play. Play wiv us, Auntie."

"Play," DJ said, grabbing her hand.

"Right after lunch," I promised Amy. "They'll be down for an hour at least."

We were in my mother's room, waiting for her transfer to rehab. She held the plastic bag of her possessions on her lap, the T-shirts and sweatpants she needed for PT. The winter sun, slanting through the hospital windows, outlined the strong, clean lines of her face, bleaching the tips of her hair and eyelashes. She'd always been low maintenance. *Beauty is as beauty does,* she liked to say.

But even she couldn't fail to notice Jo's drastic haircut. "Bit sudden, wasn't it?" she asked.

Jo ruffled her hair, shoving the longer strands behind her ears. "Clover kept eating my braid. I got tired of fussing with it."

"I see." Our mother's gaze was sharper than it had been in weeks. "The shorter style suits you."

I didn't see that at all. Jo's head looked like the goat had kept on grazing. Her hair was shorter than Momma's now.

Our mother folded her hands. "Girls, I have something important to tell you," she said. Which was how she had announced every one of Dad's deployments, the death of our grandmother, the move to the farm. I felt that warning tickle again.

"You know," Jo said with obvious relief.

Momma raised her eyebrows. "Know?"

"About the conference."

Of course she knew. Honestly, it was too bad Dad was leaving now. But not unexpected. It wasn't like our mother needed him at home. As far as I could see, his trip wouldn't make any difference to her care or schedule at all.

"At least this time we're sure he's coming back," I said.

Our mother cleared her throat. "Actually, that's what I want to talk to you about. He's not coming back. Not for a while."

"You mean, while you're in rehab."

"And after I get home," our mother said. "Your father's not coming back to the farm."

My brain stumbled. "I don't understand."

"He left you," Jo burst out. "I will never forgive him."

"No, honey. No. Ash didn't leave me. And he hasn't left you girls. I asked him to move out."

"What?"

My world lurched. "Why? Don't you love him anymore?"

"Your father is an amazing man," our mother said carefully. "He does wonderful work, important work, that he loves. I admire his commitment very much. But that's not enough to sustain a marriage. I told him if he went this time, not to come back."

Jo's face was stormy, her eyes betrayed. "But where will he go?"

"Aunt Phee has invited him to stay with her at Oak Hill. It's his heritage, after all. Just as the farm is mine. And yours," she added. "Your heritage from my side of the family."

Our *heritage*? Like she was dying. How could she do this to our father? To our family?

"You just had surgery," I said. "I don't think you should be making any sudden decisions right now. Wait until you feel better."

"No, no." Our mother half laughed. Wiped her eyes. "I'm fine. I've been thinking about this a long time. Now that you're both here to manage things, it seems like a good time to make a change. I don't expect you to stay forever, of course. You both are moving on with your lives. It's time for me to move on with mine."

I grasped for words. "But yesterday . . . Christmas . . ."

Our mother patted my hand. "I wanted to get through the holiday before I said anything to you girls."

"What about Beth?" Jo asked.

"I'll tell Beth when she comes home in January. I didn't want to say anything before she left for Nashville."

"And Amy?" I said.

Our mother sighed. "I'll talk to her. I want to tell them myself. I'm sure they'll have questions, too."

That struck a memory. A lot of memories, actually. Whenever my father was deployed, my parents never sat us down and broke the news together. It was always Momma, explaining and reassuring. If we had fears, we took them to her. If we had questions, she answered them. *"We need to be strong for your father,"* she always said. *"Let's not worry your father."*

She'd spent our whole lives sparing his feelings. Protecting him from ours.

I sat up straight. "Where is Dad, anyway?"

"Gone."

"Already?"

"A soldier from his old unit is at Walter Reed hospital. Your father left early to visit him." Our mother's smile twisted. "He's been a great comfort to the young man's family."

"Comfort, my ass," Jo muttered.

Momma looked at her sharply, but for once she had no gentle rebuke, no wise saying, no guidance for us.

Jo was silent in the car going home. My heart wrenched in sympathy. She had always idealized our father. I wanted to do something to make her feel better. To make myself feel better. To fix things, like my mother. But I didn't know where to begin.

Y ou're back," Amy said with relief.

Lady woofed in welcome.

"Mommy, Mommy! Auntie Jo!"

I removed the dog's nose from my crotch and doled out kisses, one on top of each smooth blond head, Amy, Daisy, DJ. A rush of protective love surged over me. I understood Momma's desire to tell Amy personally about the separation. But the secret squirmed inside me, seeking to get out.

"Hello, my little monsters." Jo snatched up DJ, making gobbling noises into his neck as he squirmed with delight.

"You look terrible," Amy said to her.

"Gee, thanks."

"It's the shock," Amy said sympathetically. "You'll get over it."

"What?"

"You've had the same hairstyle since high school," our little sister said. "Losing your hair is like losing your identity. It's like you're in mourning for your childhood."

"Sometimes you're so perceptive, it's terrifying."

"I'm just saying, you'd feel better with a good haircut," Amy said.

"I want haircut," Daisy said.

"No haircuts," I said automatically. What was that smell?

"But I *want*—"

"No haircuts now," Amy said. "We're doing pretty fingernails now."

Ah. Nail polish, that was it. Daisy waggled her fingers in the air. "Pretty."

"So pretty, sweeties," I said. DJ pulled his thumb from his mouth. Both my babies had rainbow manicures. I eyed the bottles—eggplant, scarlet, navy in some brand I'd never heard of—spilling from Amy's bag. "Is that . . ."

"Nontoxic," Jo said, looking up from her phone. "And vegan. I Googled it."

"Good job," I said.

"Which one of us?" Amy asked.

So competitive. "All of you," I said. Making peace. I started cleaning, tissues, cotton balls, purple smears on the kitchen table.

Jo made a strangled noise. I looked up. She was staring at her phone, her face red and stunned.

"What? What is it?" Amy crowded closer to peer over her shoulder. "Oh, him. The arm-porn guy."

"Who?" I asked. "Where?"

"Eric." Jo's voice shook. "He commented on my blog."

"I recognized his avatar," Amy said. "That's the same photo, right? With the tats."

"Well, that's good," I said cautiously. Anything that took her attention off our father had to be positive. "Is that good?"

Jo's eyes welled with tears. "He posted his mother's recipe for *pfeffernüsse*."

"Bastard," Amy said. "What's *pfeffernüsse*?"

"Bat turd," DJ said.

Amy shot me a guilty grin. "Oops."

Jo snorted.

I smothered a laugh. "Nothing wrong with his hearing. Come on, my babies."

I settled the twins with a video in the family room and returned to my sisters in the kitchen.

"She wrote about us in her blog," Amy said, looking up from Jo's phone. "Like, a story from when we were younger. It's so weird."

Jo sniffed. "But do you like it?"

"Yeah, it's cool. It's good." She scrolled, still reading. "Was I really such a spoiled brat?"

"You're not a brat," I said.

Jo grinned. "Just spoiled."

Amy stuck out her tongue. "You always did have to play the hero."

"Hey, it's my story," Jo said. "When you write the story, you can be the hero."

"You just wait," Amy said.

"So." I opened the fridge and pulled out a package of chicken thighs. "Eric's reading your blog now."

"I sent him a link. I never expected . . ." Jo got up from the table and started assembling ingredients for a salad. "I guess I thought . . . I hoped he would text me."

"You're disappointed."

"No. I mean, this is better, right?" My sister's eyes were shining. "He commented on my blog."

Amy filched a carrot from the cutting board. "Lots of people comment on your blog. I don't see why that's so special."

"That's why they broke up," I explained. "Because of something she wrote."

"Oh. So, it's like a peace offering."

"His mother's recipe," Jo repeated, like she couldn't get over it.

Amy shrugged. "I still think he should have called. Or texted. This is sort of stalker creepy."

"He is not a stalker," Jo declared.

"He left you a package on the porch. That says *stalker* to me. You should be more careful about setting boundaries."

Jo's eyes narrowed dangerously. And then she laughed. "Look who's talking. Instagram queen."

Amy smiled like a cat in the cream.

"All right, children," I said. To my sisters? The twins? "Time to wash up for supper."

Peace restored, we cleared away the nail polish and set the table.

It wasn't until much later, after my sisters had left for the farm, that I had a chance to open my computer and read Jo's blog for myself.

A wave of longing rolled over me as I read. The story was so Jo. It was so *us*, the way we used to be. The wave receded, leaving an ache behind.

I was reading the comments—almost a hundred of them—when John came into the kitchen. "Down for the count," he reported.

I managed a wobbly smile. "Thanks, honey." Bedtime with Daddy was becoming a routine. A good one, for all of us.

He put his hand on my shoulder. "You okay, babe?"

My throat felt tight. "Jo wrote a story on her blog. About the first Christmas Daddy was deployed."

"And that upset you."

I swallowed. Nodded. "It's just . . . It made me remember a lot of things. How special it felt. How close we all were."

"You were. You are. Your family intimidated the hell out of me when we started dating. Still does, sometimes. Especially Aunt Phee."

I grasped his hand. Squeezed gratefully. "You were wonderful with her last night."

"So what's the problem?"

I told him about the visit to the hospital, about my father's trip to D.C., about my mother asking him to move out. John listened in his quiet way, not interrupting, his warm, brown eyes on my face. "I thought their marriage was perfect," I said. "That my mother was perfect. But now . . ."

"Your mom is great."

"My family is a mess."

"You're still a family."

"John, my *parents* are *separating*."

"My dad walked out on my mom. That makes him a lousy dad. But it didn't make us—Mom and my brother and me—less of a family."

I flushed. "It's just . . . Reading Jo's story, it took me back. It's all true, but it's not true. Like everything I remember, everything I felt, wasn't real."

"People change," John said. "Bad things happen. That doesn't mean the good things didn't happen. You can remember the good things."

"My mother did everything for my father."

"Well, that's their problem right there. He took her for granted."

"She never complained."

"Because that's not who she is. Abby's not going to tear your father down. Not to you."

"I just don't understand why she would ask him to leave now."

"She's been thinking about it a long time, you said."

"I don't understand that, either."

John rubbed his jaw. "Okay. Say I've got this team. One great returning senior and a bunch of other guys. And my star, the senior, he's all in. He comes to every practice, he busts his ass, he breaks his heart, he wins all his matches. But he's only one player. He can't carry the team by himself. At some point—maybe he gets injured, maybe not—the other wrestlers have to pull their weight. They have to put up points for the team to win. When Abby went into the hospital, you stepped up. Your sister stepped up. And your dad walked away."

"He didn't simply walk away," I said. Remembering what Mom had said. "He had a commitment."

"He made a commitment to your mom first. She should have been his first priority."

"John." I looked at him, this man I had married. "Are you sorry you decided to leave coaching? Teaching, I mean."

"We decided together. So you could stay home with the kids."

"But you love coaching."

"I love you more."

A little flare of warmth as I digested this. "Do you think my father loves my mother?"

"As much as he can."

"He was always bringing her flowers. Every time I went to visit, she had a different bouquet."

John didn't say anything. I watched the blush creep up his neck and realized. "It was you," I said. "The poinsettias, the flowers . . . They were all from you."

"Big deal," John said gruffly. "Anybody can buy flowers."

"But you did. Oh, John." I threw myself into his arms. He held me tight. This, *this* was real. My parents' marriage was a fantasy, a happily-ever-after that was ending now. And, oh, it hurt to let it go. "I always wanted a marriage like my parents had," I said, the words muffled against his shoulder.

"Then you married the wrong guy."

"John!"

He smiled a little. "I'm nothing like your dad."

"No," I said, relaxing against him. "No, you're not." I laid my head against his chest, lightness creeping in to fill the hollow inside me. "I guess I don't have to be like my mother, either." Doing everything by myself. Fixing everything by myself.

"I've always admired Abby," John said. "But she's more than somebody's mother. She's more than somebody's wife. She's a strong woman. You take after her that way."

"Thank you." I sighed. "You're wrong about one thing, though."

"What's that?"

I raised my head, smiling. "I married exactly the right guy."

CHAPTER 25

Jo

Eric commented on my blog again. It felt wonderful, intimate, and the teensiest bit intrusive, like having him in my apartment. Correction—like having him in my apartment while everybody I knew hung around the fire escape, peering through the window and trying to figure out what we were doing.

I didn't know what we were doing.

But when those tattooed arms popped up in my comment feed, my heart gave a happy little bounce. He started by replying to comments on his mother's cookie recipe. A top chef, commenting on my blog. My readers loved that.

There were comments that weren't all about me or about Eric, too. Remarks about the two of us together, curious questions from total strangers, excited encouragement from friends, funny stories from readers about couples who cooked together or worked together or wanted to one day. Traffic on the entire site was up 500 percent, and my affiliate account was going to reward me with a nice deposit at the end of the month.

My pal Rachel called from Portland. "Oh my God, Jo, why didn't you tell me you were seeing Eric Bhaer?"

"I'm not." Technically, it was true. I hadn't seen him for almost two weeks. Thirteen days and ten hours, if I was counting. Which I wasn't. "I work for him. Worked."

"Really? Because according to your blog, you two are a thing."

I squirmed with pleasure and discomfort. "It's complicated."

"That's a Facebook status. Not something you say to one of your closest girlfriends."

I laughed. "When—*if*—I ever have something to tell, you'll be among the first to know."

She told me about spending Hanukkah with her boyfriend's family in Lake Oswego. She hadn't found a position with a design firm yet, but she was working as a barista not two blocks from her new apartment, serving coffee to freelancers, hipsters, and stay-at-home moms. I didn't know if I could relocate for love, the way Rachel had. But she sounded so happy. I was happy for her. We ended the call with promises to catch up again soon.

The farm was quiet. Too quiet, with my father gone, even though Amy was staying in her old room down the stairs and Meg came over with the twins almost every day. I wrote another post about the short dark days of the dying year, the fallow pastures, the resting goats. How, under the sleeping surface, the land slowly renewed itself for spring. My old advisor would have sniffed at such an obvious metaphor for the creative process. But Eric wrote back to me. That is, he wrote a long comment about the kitchen in early morning. How he used the quiet hours, the review of old ingredients, the delivery of fresh ones, to create each day's menu.

And my readers ate it up. Other chefs commented. I recognized the names. So many hits. So many clicks. More links. More shares.

Ashmeeta called. "So, you're in North Carolina," she said without preamble. "What happened?"

I explained. Not about Eric, but about my mother and the farm.

"But you're going back, right? To New York? To Gusto? I mean, obviously your boss wants you back."

Yearning caught my heart and squeezed. "You really think so?"

"Nah, I bet he stalks all his kitchen staff online," Ashmeeta scoffed. "Of course he wants you."

I reached for my hair to tug it into a ponytail and encountered . . . curls. I was done with running away. And I wasn't going back. "Actually, I was thinking of letting the apartment go. I mean, I can write anywhere."

"So come to Boston. It's cold, and I'm lonely."

I felt the pull of old friendship. "Tempting, thanks." But I wasn't making another move without a clear direction.

"Come on. Clam chowder. Baked beans. Me, on the nights the boss from hell doesn't make me work late. What more do you need?"

"I'm not sure." I looked around at the bare bones of my attic room, the exposed beams of the roof, the hand-stitched quilt on the bed, the shining glimpse of water from the window. "But I'm in a good space for now. And my mother needs me." Or the goats did.

I promised to visit soon.

The goats didn't need much, just fresh water, clean bedding, and alfalfa hay. The pregnant does ambled around their enclosure, their bulging sides making them look like boats or balloons or basketballs, round and hard.

"God, I remember that stage," Meg said when she dropped in that afternoon. She pressed a hand against her stomach. "I thought I'd never see my toes again."

"I've seen your toes. You're not missing much." The curl of her fingers, the curve of her mouth . . . "You're not, um . . . ?" I glanced at Daisy and DJ, playing peekaboo in the hay.

"Oh no." Meg laughed. "We just got a puppy. I don't need another baby."

Clover came up and rubbed against the fence. I scratched her forehead. "Speaking of babies, kidding season starts in a couple of weeks. I'm going to need some help."

"Beth will come home from school on the weekends. And Mom

usually gets some kids from 4-H to help with the bottle-feeding and cuddling."

"What about a vet? Does she still use Dr. Dunn?"

Meg's brow creased. "I think so. I have to look at the bill."

"I can just call his office."

"Wait until I see how much we owe him, okay?"

"Why?" Her lips pressed together. I felt a tickle of apprehension. "Meg, how much *do* we owe him?"

She sighed. "You might as well know. Mom took out a loan on the farm. I made the payment for December from the farmers' market deposit, but I want to see how the numbers look going into January before we take on any more debt."

"And you're just now telling me this?"

"We were sort of preoccupied with Mom."

"Have you talked to her about this?" She nodded. "Dad?"

Meg looked away.

I felt sick. "And he left anyway?"

She wouldn't meet my eyes. Because I was Dad's favorite. Because she wouldn't criticize him to me, would never make me choose between my loyalty to our father and the rest of the family. "Don't worry. I'll take care of it," she said. "I'm meeting with the buyer for All Seasons next month. Or if that doesn't work, I'll find a food broker. Getting into stores would make all the difference in the world. If we can make it through the kidding season, we'll be fine."

A rush of affection filled me, along with a familiar sense of inadequacy. Responsible Meg.

Except real people weren't all one thing, Amy said. Maybe Meg was as mixed up—as full of different strengths and fears, impulses and dreams—as Amy. Maybe she was the responsible one because we didn't give her a choice. Mini Mom by default.

I started to apologize. Squeezed her hand instead. "We'll take care of it together."

Amy took the news of our parents' separation better than I expected. "It's weird thinking of them apart," she said when she got back from the hospital.

"They've been apart before," Meg reminded her. She held out her hands to the twins, playing in the kids' pasture. "Every time Dad was deployed."

Daisy and DJ straggled out of the enclosure, muddy and rosy and tired.

"Yeah, but he always came back," Amy said.

"He'll come back this time, too," I said with more certainty than I felt. "He'll apologize or something."

"You're just saying that because you're his favorite," Amy said.

"I'm saying it because nobody could actually live with Aunt Phee."

"I could." Amy tossed her head when I stared. "What? It's a big house."

"She came for Christmas dinner. It was nice," Meg said.

"But she's so judgmental."

"She wasn't judging us." Meg's mouth curved. "She was silently correcting our mistakes."

Amy snickered, which set us all off.

Sobering, Meg said, "I don't think Mom will take Dad back."

"I wonder what he did to piss her off," Amy said.

I latched the gate carefully behind us. "Besides leaving town while the farm is in debt and she's recovering from surgery?"

"I think he stopped seeing her," Meg said quietly.

"He visits her every day."

"Visited." *Past tense.* I winced.

"He visits lots of patients. He prays with them and cries with them and comforts their families. He shows up for perfect strangers. But not for Mom," Meg said. "Not for us."

Amy feathered her fingers through her hair. "Then she should have said something to get his attention."

"She did," I said.

We all were silent.

"Men suck," Amy said.

"Not all men," Meg said.

"All men but John. And Arm-Porn Guy," Amy added generously. "Unless you're still mad at him."

I shrugged as we walked toward the house, trying to shake off my discomfort. "I'm not mad. I'm grateful. I figured when I changed the content—when I posted that Christmas story—it would turn off a lot of readers. And instead, they're more engaged. And I've got a lot more of them. Which is good, right? Only my blog's not all about me anymore. It's about us. Me and Eric. It's . . . weird."

"Oh my God, you poor baby. People are reading your blog. What a disaster," Amy said.

I smiled reluctantly.

Meg hugged me. "So Eric's been a help. I know you don't like relying on other people. But it's okay to accept a little help sometimes."

Amy sniffed. "Says the control queen."

"I'm reformed," Meg said.

Which made me laugh.

A red Ferrari muscled up the drive, tires spitting gravel. "Car," Meg said, reaching for the twins.

"It's Trey," said Amy.

"Magnum, P.I.," I said.

"Hello, March girls." His smile was the same, quick and charming. "I came to see . . ." His gaze narrowed. "What did you do to your hair?"

I raised my hand self-consciously to my head.

"She cut it, genius," Amy said.

"Hey, Trey," I said. "How was your Christmas?"

"Dull. Grandfather and I had dinner at the club. I came to see if you'd go out with me tonight. I owe you after Alleygators."

"You paid the tab. And the damages," I said.

"Yeah, but I usually show a girl a better time."

"They probably fake it. To protect your ego," Amy said.

That dark gaze sliced to her. "I thought you'd be back in Paris by now." I frowned. It wasn't like Trey to be rude.

"I'm going to New York first."

Which was news to me. "When?"

"For New Year's. A friend of mine is playing in a band. I leave tomorrow."

I watched as he visibly pulled himself together. "Need a ride to the airport?"

"I'd rather walk."

His smile stiffened to a rictus grin. "Come on, Amy. Don't be like that."

She tossed her head. "I'm the same as I ever was. You're the one with consistency issues."

"What is up with you guys?" I asked.

"Ask him," Amy said at the same time Trey said, "Nothing."

Nothing? The air almost crackled between them. Meg and I exchanged glances.

"I had a layover in Paris this summer," Trey said after a charged silence. "Amy offered to show me the sights."

"I didn't know you went to Paris," I said.

"You weren't returning my calls at the time."

Meg lifted DJ into her arms. "I can take you to the airport tomorrow," she said to Amy. Making peace.

Amy shook her head. "It's okay. I'll call an Uber."

"I'll take you," I said.

"Great." She flashed a smile at Trey. "So I guess you're not needed here."

"I see that. So . . ." He glanced at me. "Tonight? Seven?"

I looked into his handsome, smiling face, his dark, anxious eyes searching for the response he wanted. All our history was naked in his face. "I can't," I whispered. "I'm sorry." So, so sorry.

He drew a sharp breath. "Really, Jo? Can't you?"

"Trey, I wish I could!"

"Right." His expression shuttered. "I'm outta here."

"Trey!"

The car door slammed.

"Well, that was fun," Amy said into the silence a few moments later.

I wiped my eyes. "So much fun."

"Vroom," DJ said. Meg hugged me, and he kicked me in the stomach. Which felt about right.

"Come on." Amy gave me a quick hug. "Let's go inside, and I'll fix your hair."

H ow long are you going to be in New York?" I asked when I was seated on a kitchen chair, a towel over my shoulders. Amy danced around me, waving a pair of scissors.

She shrugged. "A week?"

"So long?" Meg asked.

"I'm only in the way here."

"No, you're not," Meg said.

Amy snipped. "Momma doesn't need me. And I need to get away for a while. I'll come back when she's out of rehab."

"Can they spare you at work that long?"

"Nobody is there over the holidays. And since I basically work for free . . . Anyway, I told Monsieur I'd visit the Garment District. I want to see the Fashion Institute. And Mood!"

I resisted the urge to point out that she could have seen all those things if she'd come to visit me at any time over the past few years. "Where are you staying?"

Amy busied herself with the scissors. "With the band."

Meg and I exchanged glances.

"At their hotel?" Meg asked.

"It's not what you're thinking," Amy said. "Vaughn and I are friends."

If anyone could get her friends to spring for a week in New York at the height of the holidays, it would be Amy. But still . . .

Meg bit her lip. "Maybe . . ."

"You could use my place," I offered. "It's not much, but it's empty. And the location is great."

"Really?" Amy hugged me, nearly jabbing me with the scissors. "Oh, that would be so awesome!" She hugged Meg. "You are the best sister."

"Hey, it's my apartment," I said.

Amy beamed. "You're the best sister, too."

And I was, I thought on Friday as I knuckled my mother's truck through traffic. I really was.

The departure lane at the airport was clogged with people leaving town for New Year's Eve. Or maybe going home after the holidays—back to work, back to school, back to bases across the country. The curb in front of the terminal teemed with soldiers with duffel bags, students with backpacks, gray-haired seniors in wheelchairs.

I found a spot behind a black SUV and parked. Amy pulled her suitcase from the backseat.

"Got the key?" I asked.

"Of course."

"Text me when you get there."

"I will."

"I'll see you in a week."

"I might stay a little longer."

I sighed. "Just don't be stupid, okay?"

She smiled crookedly. "I love you, too."

She kissed me on both cheeks—very French—and strode away through the sliding doors, her boots tap-tapping on the sidewalk. The walkway teemed with suitcases and families saying good-bye. A woman in camouflage hugged a toddler tight, her cheek to the child's hair. A mother reached up to hold her son. In the space ahead of me, the SUV's doors swung open, and Eric got out.

My heart lurched.

He saw me, and the pleasure on his face slashed me like a razor. "Jo! You are on my flight? To New York?"

"Uh . . . No." Disappointment made me dumb. "I'm here to drop off my sister." I waved vaguely toward the terminal. "Amy."

"Ah." He turned to the two lanky teenagers standing by the curb. "My sons. This is Miss March."

I flushed. "Jo, please."

"Hey. Bryan." The tall one in the red jersey, with the straggling chin patch, shook my hand.

"Nice to meet you." He had his father's watchful eyes.

He nudged his brother, who started forward. "Alec."

Dinosaur sandwiches, I remembered. The boy shot a startled look at Eric. Oh crap. I'd said it out loud. "Sorry," I mumbled. "Your dad mentioned when you were little, he used to cut your sandwiches into, um, dinosaur shapes."

The confused look melted into a grin. "Cool. Yeah, that's right."

Such lovely boys. They went to open the back of the SUV, leaving me standing with their father on the curb. So awkward.

"Thanks for the book," I said. "And . . . and everything."

"Thank you for the link," Eric replied politely.

"You've been here? All this time?" Without seeing me.

"There is a soccer tournament. In Florida." He gestured toward his older son. "We are back yesterday. And you? You return soon?"

I risked a look at his expression. Did he want me to return? "No. No, I'm staying. To take care of my mother."

"How is she?"

"She's good. Better," I amended. "Her surgery went well. She'll be in rehab for a couple more weeks. I'm helping out until then."

Bryan dumped his father's bag on the sidewalk, and they all did that one-armed hug thing men do, with lots of back patting. Their obvious affection for one another, their ease, brought a lump to my throat. I sidled toward my car, feeling like an intruder, trying to get out of the way.

"Jo." Eric's voice tripped me up. I turned as the SUV pulled away, Bryan at the wheel. "Jo." Eric took a step closer, his beautiful hazel eyes focused on me. Seeing me. "You look . . ."

I ducked my head self-consciously. "Scalped?"

"Ah, your hair." He raised his hand. Just the touch of his hand on the ends of my hair electrified me. His smile started at the corner of his mouth and settled in his eyes. "No. You look . . . content. Your writing, your blog, it is going well?"

I swallowed. "Thanks to you." *Content.* Content? Was that a compliment? "Half the comments are about you."

He waved the acknowledgment away. "*Nichts zu danken.* You are a good writer. I saw Michael commented yesterday."

A car honked behind me. "Who?" I asked.

"Michael Burdette. From Squeal."

My breath rushed out. Burdette owned three renowned restaurants in North Carolina, including the pork-themed Squeal in Wilmington. "Wow. McSqueal is Michael Burdette? I didn't know."

"You should call him."

"I'm not looking for a job."

"About your cheese. He's on the lookout for local suppliers."

"Oh. Right. I will. Thank you."

"Vivian, too."

A security guard in an orange traffic vest approached. "Ma'am, I've got to ask you to move your truck."

I ignored him. "Vivian *Howard*?"

"The Chef and the Farmer."

"I know who she is. You want me to call *Vivian Howard*?"

Eric raised an eyebrow. "Connections. They are important, yeah?"

"Absolutely." My eyes drank him in hungrily.

He hesitated for a second and then said, "You have time for a coffee?"

Yes. Anything. "I can't leave the truck."

"Of course," he said politely. "You must go."

"And you have a plane to catch," I said.

"Yes."

The guard was back. "Ma'am . . . Your truck."

I clutched the keys in my hand. Eric was leaving. And I hadn't said half of what I needed to say. "I'm sorry," I blurted.

"I am sorry, too. I lost my temper with you."

"I overreacted. I shouldn't have run away."

His eyes crinkled in that appealing half smile, his gaze clear and a little sad. "Maybe you run to something, not away, yeah?"

"I think so. I hope so."

He inclined his head. "Then I am happy you have found it."

I could feel him leaving, withdrawing from me, and there were no words, I couldn't find the words in time to make him stay. "I'll be back," I babbled. "Sometime. I mean, I have to clear out my apartment, right?"

"Ah. Yes. Maybe you will call me when you . . ." Another tiny hesitation. "Visit New York."

Like a booty call. My heart sank. "Yes. Of course."

He half turned away. Turned back. His arms wrapped around me, half lifting me off my feet. He hugged me hard, muttering something into my hair.

"Ma'am." The security guard sounded pained.

Before I could react, before I could say anything, Eric released me and walked away without looking back.

"Ma'am, you can't stay here. You have to move on."

Stupid phrase. *Move on. Moving on.* I watched Eric's broad back all the way into the terminal.

Are you sure you're all right staying home with the twins?" Meg asked. She and John were leaving for a New Year's Eve party at Belle Gardiner's. My sister looked fantastic.

"Absolutely." I waved them away. "You kids have fun."

John smiled, one hand at the small of her back. "Thanks."

"You, too," Meg said.

And I did. Daisy and DJ were at their most adorable, popping in and out of a giant carton that doubled as a fort/cave/spaceship, snuggling with me on the couch to read *Where the Wild Things Are* before bed. We paraded like monsters up the stairs, all of us in our pajamas.

"Yum, yum, yum," I growled as I tucked them in, nuzzling their sweet necks. "Must. Eat. Children." And they squealed and hugged me with their chubby arms. DJ gave me his slow, wide smile and a kiss.

"I love you, Auntie Jo," Daisy said.

My heart filled. "Love you, little monsters. So much."

One day, I thought, turning out the lights.

But, God, I was exhausted. Lately I seemed to be tired all the time. There was a bottle of champagne chilling in the fridge, a pint of Ben & Jerry's Salted Caramel Core in the freezer. I got the ice cream and a spoon and sat down with the dog to watch *When Harry Met Sally* almost to the bitter end, when Billy Crystal ran through the streets of New York to find Meg Ryan. Their eyes met, caught, and held across the crowded room as the party counted down around them. Not because he was lonely. Not because it was New Year's Eve. But because he saw her. Because he loved her.

Crap. I checked my phone for messages. Zilch. Zip. No voice mail. No e-mail. No new comments on the blog.

He was working, I told myself. Everyone in the restaurant world worked on New Year's Eve. There would be two seatings and a special menu. The kitchen would be hot and crowded and intense, crackling with energy. At midnight, there would be a special champagne toast, and Eric would circulate through the dining room, making every guest feel welcome.

"Maybe you will call me when you visit New York." His long-distance booty call. But, oh, that look in his eyes when I told him I wasn't coming back . . .

I grabbed my phone. Not calling. Come see me, I texted.

Not that I was counting on an answer. I'd broken up with him. Or he'd broken up with me. Besides, he was in the middle of service. The kitchen would stay open as long as people were there and ordering. He probably wouldn't even check his messages until morning.

I switched to the ball drop in Times Square. Nothing like watching puking hordes of tourists in the Hellmouth to make me feel better about missing New Year's Eve in New York. I wondered how Amy was faring with her friends. I hoped she was happy. Or at least warm.

The dog put her head on my knee, fixing me with Disney dog eyes.

"Happy New Year," I said, and let her lick the spoon.

My phone pinged. I lurched for it, rousing a bark from Lady.

A single word. When?

A grin started on my insides and spread to my face. He was coming! He was coming? He'd just been down here to visit his boys. He rarely left the restaurant. I couldn't hope . . . I didn't expect . . .

NC is beautiful in the spring, I typed, and held my breath.

I'll be there. Happy New Year, beautiful Jo.

My whole body suffused with smiles. Happy New Year.

I fell asleep on the couch, covered with a blanket, breathing in the good Christmas-tree smell. Sometime during the night, the dog crawled up on the couch with me, a heavy, comforting presence.

In the morning, the dog slunk down, and Daisy and DJ took her place. "Auntie Jo!"

"Oof," I said as DJ's knee found my stomach.

"Sorry." Meg, flushed and pretty, appeared at the bottom of the stairs. "I told them to let you sleep."

I cuddled them close, ignoring my queasiness at the faint whiff of diaper. "It's okay."

Meg frowned. "Are you all right?"

I reached for my phone under the blanket. Smiled. "Too much ice cream last night."

Meg nodded. "I'll make coffee."

"Coffee would be *great*," I said fervently. "Thanks."

She laughed and corralled her herd, driving them toward the kitchen.

I sat a minute, taking slow, deep breaths. Checked my phone. No text from Eric.

That's okay, I told myself. At least I wasn't running away anymore. I was moving forward. Even if I couldn't quite see my destination yet.

I staggered into the kitchen. The smell of coffee, rich as chocolate, earthy as soil, hit me like a slap.

"Here you go," Meg said. "Half-and-half?"

I gripped the carton, the sides wet with condensation. Added a dollop to my mug. The cream swirled and sank, dark and light in an acid brew.

Nausea rolled in my gut. I forced it down. Took one sip, and bolted for the bathroom.

Humiliating minutes later, Meg stood in the bathroom door, pity in her eyes. "Oh, Jo."

I spat into the toilet. "I'm fine," I said weakly. "It's just something I ate."

"Or didn't eat." She disappeared. Came back a minute later with a juice glass full of—ginger ale?—and some saltines. "Here."

I shook my head. "I'm not hungry."

She set the glass by the sink and handed me the crackers. "Try it."

Clearly, she wasn't going to budge. To please her, I took a sip of ginger ale. Took a bite of saltine and let it dissolve in my mouth.

"Better. Thanks." I smiled, but my sister's worried expression didn't go away. "Really, I feel better. It's probably just a stomach bug or something. I hope the kids don't catch it."

"Are you sure it's a bug?"

"What do you mean?"

Meg bit her lip. "Jo . . . When was your last period?"

Oh. "I don't know. Right after Thanksgiving?"

"You don't keep track?"

No. "It's not like I have sex all the time," I said. Until recently. Until Eric.

My sister was diplomatically silent.

Oh. My stomach lurched again. Not the ice cream. Not a stomach bug. Oh *no*.

CHAPTER 26

Meg

The cashier at the drugstore glanced at the pregnancy test before putting it in the bag. "Good luck, dear," she said, her tone nicely balanced between congratulations (in case I wanted to be pregnant) and sympathy (in case I didn't).

"Thank you. Happy New Year," I said, and hurried to the car.

I'd wanted to spare my sister the awkwardness of running into anybody we knew. Jo was waiting for me at home. Getting started on dinner, she had explained to John when he invited her to go with him and the twins to the park. I'd bought a spiral-cut ham, figuring it would be no work. But Jo was determined to prepare the traditional New Year's Day dinner. For luck. *"Rice for riches, peas for pennies, collards for dollars, corn bread for gold,"* our mother would say. Jo had promised to bring a plate to her tomorrow.

Along with the news that she was going to be a grandmother again?

I went in the kitchen door. Jo was stirring a big pot of greens on the stove. "Just like Momma's," I said.

"I made collards and corn bread for staff dinner once," Jo said. "For Eric."

I nodded. I didn't know what to say.

Jo's chin raised. "Right." She wiped her hands on a dish towel. "Let's do this thing."

I pulled the pregnancy test from the bag. "It's supposed to be most accurate first thing in the morning."

She ripped the box open. "I have to know now."

"Do you want me to come with you?"

Jo smiled crookedly. "I can pee by myself," she said in a fair imitation of Daisy. She grabbed a wrapped stick and marched with it into the downstairs powder room.

I remembered taking my pregnancy test, getting up extra early so John would be home to share the results. The anticipation. Our joy when those two little lines appeared.

My poor sister. She'd been in the bathroom a long time. I glanced at the clock. Longer than three minutes.

The back door opened and John walked in, bringing the twins and the cold air with him. And the dog. And . . .

"Trey!" I said, dismayed.

"Hey, Meg. Happy New Year." He bent to kiss my cheek, smelling of the outdoors and deodorant and rather pleasantly of sweat.

I looked over his shoulder at John, who had the grace to look a little shame-faced. "He was running in the park. I asked him back for a beer. Not for dinner," he added.

"Unless you want to invite me," Trey said.

"Of course, you . . . That is, I . . ." I kneeled, hiding my confusion by helping DJ out of his coat.

"Do I smell corn bread?" Trey asked.

"Corn bread, yes. In the oven." I busied myself with Daisy's zipper. "Jo made it."

"Meg." John was staring at the kitchen island, the open drugstore bag, the distinctive pink box with the top ripped off. "What's this?"

It was obvious. Even if he didn't remember the box, the lettering was clearly visible on the side: First Response Early Result Pregnancy Test.

"What?" Trey looked. "Are you . . . Oh, hey. Congratulations."

No. Oh no.

I smiled weakly at John. "Everything's fine. I'm fine. I'm not pregnant."

"Two lines." Jo burst out of the bathroom, clutching a pee stick. "Look! Should I do the other one now or . . ." She stopped abruptly. "Shit."

Trey's face went white. "Jo?"

Jo's face went red. "Trey!"

"What's going on?" John asked.

"That's what I'd like to know," Trey said.

I stood. "Trey, we love you, but Jo and I really need to talk. Why don't you, uh . . ."

"Let's get that beer now," John said, taking his arm.

Trey shook him off. "Jo?" he repeated.

Her throat moved as she swallowed. "I don't . . . I can't . . . Not now," she said in a constricted voice. "I'm sorry."

Something flashed across Trey's face and was gone. He looked at John. "Got anything stronger?"

John nodded. "Right this way. Come on, kids."

He herded them all out of the kitchen, and Jo lurched forward into my arms.

"Ssh. It's all right. Everything's going to be all right," I murmured, as if she were no older than the twins. As if this was nothing more serious than a scraped knee or bruised feelings, something I could kiss and make better. Her breath shuddered, in and out. "Whatever happens, we have each other." I petted her hair the way Momma used to do, her new, short curls springing back against my touch. "What are you going to do?" I asked after a while.

"I don't know." She gulped. "I have to think."

John returned and stood awkwardly inside the doorway, hands in his pockets. "Everything okay in here?"

Jo made a muffled noise against my shoulder. A laugh? A sob?

"We're fine," I said, and prayed that it was true.

"Good." He grabbed the bottle of bourbon and two juice boxes. "We're watching *Frozen*. You let me know if you want me to beat anybody up," he said to Jo.

She raised her head at that. "No." Her eyes were wet, her face pale and surprisingly composed. Somehow she managed a smile. "Thank you, though."

He nodded, shifting the bottle under one arm to pat her shoulder. "Anytime. Whatever you need."

He was such a good guy. I loved him so much.

"Jo," I said after I'd set her down at the kitchen table and made us both a cup of tea. Decaffeinated, because . . . Pregnant. "Do you want me to make an appointment for you with my doctor?"

She grimaced into her tea. "Isn't it a little early for that?"

"You need to start prenatal vitamins." I bit my lip. "Unless you want to . . . Jo, do you want this baby?"

She swallowed and set down her mug. "I don't . . . I don't know." She pressed her hand to her middle, her fingers curving protectively around her still-flat stomach. "I don't think I could . . ."

Have the baby? I wondered. *Terminate the pregnancy?*

"I just found out myself," my sister said. "Can we just not tell anybody for a little while?"

I thought of Trey in the next room, drinking bourbon and watching *Frozen*. "It's a little late for that."

"You're right." She reached for her ponytail. Tugged on curls instead. "Oh God. How am I going to tell Mom?"

"Forget Momma. What are you going to say to Eric?"

She stared at me, her mouth slightly open. "I have to tell him."

"Er, yes."

She slumped in her chair. "Crap. Oh crap!" She jumped up. "The corn bread!" She pulled the skillet from the oven and set it on the stove top, tapping, testing the surface with her fingertips. "Only a little burnt."

"It looks wonderful. Do you want to dish up now?"

"I'm not very hungry," my sister confessed.

"You should try to eat something."

Jo lifted an eyebrow at me. "For the baby?"

"For luck," I said, and got up to set the table.

I don't like to think of her all on her own," I said to John as we got ready for bed that night.

Jo had turned down my offer to spend another night on our couch, declaring she would be more comfortable in her own bed. Anyway, she had to go back to the farm to feed the animals.

"She's not alone," John said. "She has us."

My heart turned to mush.

"Relax," my husband advised. "Things will look better in the morning."

"I'm pretty sure she'll still be pregnant when she wakes up," I said. "Although I did tell her to take the second pregnancy test. Just to be sure."

John grunted.

I sat on the closed lid of the toilet, watching him brush his teeth, my quiet, solid, reliable husband. "Sorry about the scare earlier. When you saw the box? I wanted to tell you it wasn't for me. But I couldn't. Not with Trey standing there."

"It would be okay if it was. Yours, I mean." John met my eyes briefly in the mirror. "If you were pregnant again."

My heart wobbled. "John . . . Do you want more children?"

It made sense. He was so good with the twins, such a conscientious provider, such a caring coach.

"I want what you want. You always said you wanted a big family. Four kids. Like your parents."

"I do. Well. I did." I cleared my throat. "I actually kind of like our family now. I like our life."

"Good." He leaned over and spat in the sink. I waited for him to say something more. He didn't.

"What about you?" I asked.

"I like our life, too."

"I thought maybe you wanted to make a change. Start coaching again."

He filled a glass at the tap. "I am coaching."

I sighed. "You know what I mean. Go back to teaching."

He rinsed the sink carefully. "I make more money doing what I do now. Maybe when the time is right . . ."

"Maybe the time is now," I suggested.

He didn't say anything.

"When I went back to work, you said it wasn't about the money," I reminded him.

"It's not. As long as you're happy, that's what matters to me."

"Exactly." I watched his reflection. "John, are you happy at the dealership?"

A muscle bunched in his jaw. We could say so much without words. Neither one of us found it easy to talk about our feelings. I'd been proud of our unspoken understanding, pleased that we didn't fight. But sometimes words were necessary. I tried again. "If it weren't for the money, would you go back to teaching?"

His shrug belied the tension in his shoulders. "I guess I'd consider it."

My own muscles relaxed. I felt like he'd given me another present— his trust, his dreams. "I could run the numbers," I offered. "Look at the budget with both our incomes."

He smiled slightly. "Taking this partners thing seriously, aren't you?"

A little glow started in my chest. "Yes."

He nodded. "I'll think about it."

Of course he needed time to mull it over. He did everything carefully, deliberately, my John. Except for falling in love with me.

"I love you," I announced suddenly.

He held my gaze in the mirror. "I love you, too."

I closed the distance between us, sliding my arms around his waist, resting my cheek against his broad, smooth back. "I mean, I really love you."

"Good to know. Because you're everything to me." His voice was husky. His hands covered mine, clasped together over his stomach. "I get that we're not trying for another baby right now. But you want to fool around?"

The glow spread. I smiled against his back. "I'd love to."

CHAPTER 27

Jo

I was still pregnant in the morning. First I threw up, and then (since I was in the bathroom anyway) I peed on the second stick. Two lines. So after I downed tea and toast and fed the goats, I drove to the rehab center. I had never in my entire life sought my mother's advice or approval. I had always been Daddy's girl. But I needed her now.

When I got there, my mother was down the hall in physical therapy. I sat in the room's one chair to wait for her.

"Honey?"

I jerked awake. My mother was standing—standing!—in front of me, the aide at her side. The hated port was still in Mom's arm, but she was no longer trailing an IV bag and a pole. I blinked. "You're up!"

My mother nodded. "Up and walking."

"Thirty minutes today," the aide, Keisha, said.

I watched as she helped my mother maneuver to the bed, raising the head so she could sit upright.

"I saw the caseworker yesterday," my mother said. "I'm being discharged in a week."

I looked at Keisha. "So soon?"

Keisha tucked the bed control where Mom could reach it. "She's doing great."

"I can't stick around here forever," my mother said. "There's too much to do at home."

So much. I had memories of Momma rubbing VapoRub on my feet for a cough, holding my hair when I puked. But I didn't know anything about nursing. How was I supposed to take care of her at home?

Some of my panic must have shown in my face, because my mother said, "Don't fuss. I'll be fine on my own."

Keisha adjusted her tray table. "As long as you don't—"

"Bend, twist, or lift anything heavier than a gallon of milk," my mother finished for her. They smiled at each other with obvious affection before Mom turned her attention back to me. "Anyway, I've got it all figured out. Beth can come home on the weekends, and Meg and Hannah are close by if I need them."

"But the farm . . ." I objected. She couldn't afford to hire help for the farm, Meg said.

"Your father knows a veteran who's willing to help out for food and a place to stay. So you don't need to worry about me."

"When did you talk to Dad?"

"I called him after I spoke with the case manager. He's decided to stay another night in D.C."

And hadn't bothered to notify any of us.

"That's enough about me." My mother settled back against her pillow. "What are you doing here?"

I could hardly tell her in front of the aide. "I brought you lunch," I said, gesturing to the knotted shopping bag. "Black-eyed peas and corn bread."

My mother smiled. "For luck in the New Year."

"I can put that in the fridge for you, if you want," Keisha said.

"That would be wonderful," my mother said.

I waited until Keisha left the room before I said, "Momma. I was thinking I should move back home for a while."

"Not on my account. You should go back to New York. Get on with your own life." She studied me. "Unless . . . Is there a reason you want to stay?"

I opened my mouth, but my voice had dried up.

My mother sighed. "You never wanted my advice. You'd ask your father sometimes about school stuff. But not me. Even when you got your period, you took care of it yourself." She smiled a little wistfully. "I didn't hear about it until Meg complained you'd used up all her supplies."

"I was embarrassed," I muttered. But that wasn't the whole truth. Before puberty hit, I was happy with my body and my life. I didn't want to change.

"You didn't want to grow up," my mother said. "I worried maybe I'd failed you somehow, that you wouldn't come to me. I thought maybe when you got older . . . Anyway, I'm here now. If you want to talk."

"I'm pregnant," I announced baldly.

She took my hand. "How far along?" Pragmatic as always.

"Five weeks, I think. I didn't plan it." *Obviously*.

"Well." She patted my hand. "Life is what happens while we're making other plans."

"What should I do?"

Her gaze sharpened. "Do you want my opinion? Or my sympathy?"

"I want . . ." All my feelings rushed in. Burst out. "I want my mommy."

My mother's expression melted. Transformed. "Oh, Jo." She tightened her grip, and I tumbled from my chair, doing my best to hug her despite the brace and the hospital bed. Even with all the hard edges in the way, it was a good hug. When I finally drew back, my eyes were wet. So were hers.

"My little girl." She kissed my forehead. Wiped my tears with her thumbs. "You'll figure it out."

I sat back, keeping tight hold of her hand. "That's it? After twenty-eight years, that's your big maternal advice?"

My mother sniffed. "You've never in your whole life listened to what other people had to say. Even your father. I trust you to make the right choice for you. Besides . . . It seems a little late for us to have the birth control talk."

"We used birth control. Every time."

"Nothing's one hundred percent effective." Her smile took a wry twist. "Your sister Meg proved that."

I nodded. "When she got pregnant with the twins."

"When I got pregnant with her."

I goggled. "You didn't . . . I never . . . I didn't know."

My mother folded her hands. "No one knew, except my mother. Well, Phee guessed when we moved the wedding date up. But she wouldn't say a word that would reflect poorly on your father."

I couldn't wrap my brain around it. "You and Dad had to get married?"

"We didn't *have* to get married. We wanted to. I would have liked to finish college first, but I loved Ash so much. And we'd talked about starting a family together." Another wry smile. "Just not so soon."

"I'm not ready for marriage."

"Mm." My mother made a sound that might have been agreement. "Where is your baby's father in all this?"

"In New York. It's Eric. Eric Bhaer."

She nodded. "From your blog."

"I thought you didn't read my blog."

My mother sent me another of those new, sharp looks. "You've always been so independent. I didn't want you to think I was stalking you online. But of course I read it. I'm your mother. So, have you told him yet?"

Him. Eric. I shook my head, humbled by her perception.

"Do you love him?"

Not a question my father would have asked.

"I didn't mean to. I never expected . . . Ma, he's such a good man. I wish you could meet him. I think you'd approve. He gets me. He accepts me." At least, I thought he did. "But I don't know how he fits into my life. Or if I could fit into his. He has two sons already. Teenagers."

"Tell him," my mother said. "If he's as good a man as you say, he'll support you whatever you decide. Just don't let this stop you from doing what you want. Or rush you into something you're not ready for."

"Thanks, Momma."

"Just remember, I'm here for you. You can stay at the farm as long as you want."

"You could always come home," my mother had said when I graduated from college. And again, when I lost my job. Her offers of support used to make me feel like she was waiting for me to fail. But now I heard them differently—not as an invitation to fall, but as a soft place to land.

"Just until I'm back on my feet," I said.

My mother patted my hand again. "Guess we'll be learning to walk together, you and me."

Her words carried me through the week. For the first time, I could see where I came from leading clearly to the place I wanted to go. I wasn't on my parents' path, or my sisters'. I wasn't following the map I'd made for myself in college.

But I was finally moving forward.

I was writing. Stories of the farm for the blog, usually with a food tie-in. Stories from our childhood that sometimes made it into the blog (#sistersfarm) and sometimes into a folder labeled simply "Chapters."

I wrote on my mother's laptop or in notebooks the way I used to do, sitting up in my attic room at night, filling the silence of the empty house with words. Not clever words. Words as plain as my mother's blue glass bottle on the windowsill or useful as the pump in the yard. The ambient noise of the city was very far away. The sounds of the countryside were different, distinct and staccato—the creak of the stairs, the crack of a branch, a dog barking at an owl or a fox or at nothing at all. I was learning to be still and listen.

When the page got dark, I pulled on my hoodie and went out for a last barn check. The security lights flickered on, throwing deep shadows in the corners, turning dust motes into fireflies.

The goats jostled against their enclosure, crying for attention. I rubbed heads and shaggy coats, refilled their water trough, pulled down hay.

My mother had called this farm our heritage. I did not have her connection to the land. I'd been so eager to get away to make something of myself, to forge a new, grown-up identity far from home. But being back stirred so many memories. I felt my roots digging deep, drawing stories from the earth. The farm was not my heritage, but the stories were. I wanted to pass them on.

Lately a female tabby had taken to hanging around the barn, seeking shelter from the rain. There would be kittens in the spring, I thought. I'd posted a story about farm cats and bodega cats, including a shot of the tabby rolling flirtatiously in the straw, another of Weasley posed like a miniature lion. Eric had responded in the comments with a photo of the black cat eating from a plate in the alley behind Gusto. My cat. He was feeding my cat. Your friend misses you, he wrote.

My heart stumbled.

And my readers loved it. Not just cat owners and cat lovers, posting pictures of their felines, but an organic pet food company offering to buy ad space. A homesteader in Washington State and another in Virginia. A bodega owner in Flatbush. Farm-to-fork restaurants in Wilmington, in Raleigh and Asheville.

Comments on the blog had fallen from the peak of speculation over Eric's identity, but overall traffic was up. City dwellers responding to some fantasy of getting away from it all, maybe. Or voyeuristic interest in Eric's and my relationship, hinted at in pictures and replies.

I had a growing audience, it seemed. Or he did.

I was thankful for the interest. And the income. But even the success of *Hungry* left me unsatisfied. I felt a longing, a root-deep yearning for . . . something else. Something of my very own.

Tell your story.

I touched my stomach lightly. *Is it you? Are you part of my story?*

A slow, blind rising welled. Like a flood filling me up, like love or faith or certainty. I was having a baby. With or without a job, with or without Eric. *There you are. Hello, baby. Hello.*

Meg came over to drop off the twins, dressed for her meeting with the All Seasons rep in what I thought of as her bank clothes, the bag from Amy doubling as a briefcase.

"You look good," I told her. "Happy." Glowing, which is what they said about pregnant women. Not that I was glowing much after throwing up.

"I am happy," Meg said, loading the samples into the back of her big white Explorer. "You sure you're okay out here all alone?"

The girls, Amy and Beth, were both still gone. For once, I was the one left at home. There was no place I would rather be. I'd always been happy with my own company.

But I missed Eric.

I swallowed the ache in my throat. "I'm not alone." The twins scampered around the kids' paddock like a pair of baby goats, Daisy stamping through puddles in her glittery pink galoshes. "I have these guys. And Mom gets out of rehab next week."

Meg closed the hatch and turned. "We should all have dinner before Amy flies back to Paris. The way we used to for Dad when he got home. A dinner for Mom."

"Beth's classes start the Tuesday after Martin Luther King Day. Maybe that weekend? Before she goes back to school."

"I wish she hadn't gone to Nashville."

I watched DJ try to climb up the bottom of the toddler slide. "Colt Henderson invited her to record her song in his studio. She can't turn down an opportunity like that."

"Or she can't turn down Colt Henderson. I don't trust him," Meg said.

"You've never met him."

"I don't have to meet him to form an opinion about him."

"You've never met Eric," I pointed out.

She raised her eyebrows without speaking, a trick she got from Mom. *And look where that got you.*

I flushed. "I should probably make that doctor's appointment soon."

The look dissolved into concern. "You want me to come with you? I can hold your hand."

She was the world's best sister.

"I've decided to keep it. The baby," I said.

"Oh, honey." Meg hugged me tight. "You'll be a wonderful mom."

"You think?" I asked, almost shyly.

"I know. Look at you with these two. Auntie Jo." She pulled back, smiling. "Maybe you're more like Mom than you thought."

"Right. Both of us knocked up."

Her mouth fell open. I snickered. She giggled. And then we were snorting and gasping with laughter, clutching each other for balance, collapsing against the car. The twins stopped their play to watch us.

"I should go," Meg said, straightening up.

I nodded. "Good luck with your meeting today."

She flashed another smile. "Thanks."

"There are a couple restaurants who are interested in our cheese," I told her. "You think you could meet with them?"

"You should do it. You know what they're looking for."

I didn't see Michael Burdette from Squeal seeking my input, but I nodded anyway. It wasn't fair to make Meg do all the work.

"Or . . ." Meg hesitated.

"Or?"

"We could do it together," Meg said.

"Sisters' Farm," I said.

"Sisters' Farm." Meg smiled. "Sounds good to me."

"Me, too." *Together* sounded even better.

⁓

J ohn says you're keeping the baby," Trey said when I answered the door that night.

"Hello to you, too," I joked.

His expression didn't change in the porch light. "Can I come in?"

"Sure. Want some soup?" The flood of sympathy casseroles had dried up once my father moved out, but I'd left a big pot of minestrone simmering on the stove. The smell of Tuscan beans, thyme, and tomatoes filled the downstairs.

"I'm not here for dinner."

I stepped back. "Come in anyway." I led the way to the kitchen.

"Have you told the father?" Trey asked.

I lifted the lid off the soup. "Not yet."

"You need someone to take care of you," Trey said. "You and the baby."

I stirred. "Not your job."

"It could be." His tone was uncharacteristically grim. Resolute.

I turned. His face was pale, his eyes very dark.

He was serious, I realized with a curious twist of heart. He was . . . Trey. My buddy. But at some point, when I wasn't paying attention, he had become something more, this quiet, determined man set on doing the right thing. *"I can't stay old Mr. Laurence's grandson for the rest of my life."*

He was right, and I was wrong. He had changed.

And I had, too.

Marrying Trey would be the perfect romance novel solution, where the pregnant heroine enters a marriage of convenience and finds true love with her best friend. I could be Elizabeth Bennet, living happily ever after at Pemberley. Trey was kind. He was rich. He would always take care of me.

Only . . . Lizzy loved Darcy, right?

"Trey." I put down the spoon and sat, taking his hands across the kitchen table. His hands were long and elegant. No scars, except for a white puncture at the fleshy base of his thumb where he'd jabbed a fish hook once. No tattoos.

I swallowed. "I appreciate the offer. I do. Really. But I don't want to marry you." I squeezed his hands. "And you don't want to marry me."

Something flashed in his eyes. Relief? "It's complicated."

"Well, yeah," I said dryly. "I'm pregnant."

He didn't smile. "I still want to help."

"You can. You will. You'll be an amazing uncle."

He sighed and released me. "I'm better at playtime than diapers anyway."

"You're good at a lot of things." I got up to serve us soup. Somehow I knew that now he would stay. "You want to start a college fund, I won't say no. My job prospects don't look so good right now."

"What about that guy? The father."

"Eric."

"Yeah. He ought to pay."

"You mean, like child support."

"That, too."

"Ha. I'm glad you can joke about it."

"Who says I'm joking?" Startled, I turned, soup dripping from my ladle. Trey was smiling crookedly, the old Trey smile, but his eyes were deadly serious. "You have to tell him," he said quietly.

"I know. I will. I want to. It's just . . ."

"Complicated," he finished for me.

"Yeah."

"If you're worried about how he'll react—"

"No," I said quickly. Not in any way I could discuss with Trey. "I trust him to do the right thing." Whatever the right thing was. "It's just . . . It's not the sort of news you break over the phone."

"So you're going to see him."

Come see me, I had written on New Year's Eve. NC is beautiful in the spring.

I'll be there, Eric had texted back. Before he knew—before *I* knew—I was pregnant. Could my news wait until March?

"I thought I'd ask him here," I said.

Trey grinned, a sharp, feral grin. "Good."

"You have to be nice," I warned.

"No, I don't. Not if he's taking you away from us."

"Don't be ridiculous. We're having a welcome-home dinner for Mom," I said, changing the subject. "Next Sunday. You're invited."

"Great."

"And your grandfather, too."

"If you're feeding him, he'll come. Thanks, Jo," Trey said quietly. His dark eyes met mine. "Still friends, then?"

"Always." I leaned my head against his shoulder. "You will always be in my life," I promised.

I only wished I could say the same about Eric. We were expecting a baby together. Well, I was expecting. Eric didn't have a clue what was about to hit him. I could take care of myself. And our child, too. But I had to tell him.

Soon.

CHAPTER 28

Endings and Beginnings

Like birds returning to the nest, my sisters had come home.

First Amy, her suitcase bursting with fabric samples and knock-off scarves from New York. Then Beth from Nashville, toting her guitar. And finally Meg, bustling in the back door, bringing the twins and two pies.

"Lot of fuss," our mother said, taking them from her. "Not that I don't appreciate it."

"No fuss," Meg said. "They're from Connie's."

I looked at the perfectly finished crusts. "Store-bought? Good for you."

Meg smiled. Shrugged. There was an ease, a confidence, in her that wasn't there before. As if she'd found her balance with work, with John, with everything.

"I was working last night. No reason to be a hero, John says."

I grinned back at her. "Or a martyr."

The kitchen filled with women's voices. I sat at the table with DJ on my lap, breathing in his little-boy smell and the golden scent of onions sautéing in butter.

"It's so wonderful to all be together!" Beth said.

Not quite all. Daddy wasn't here.

The words lingered unspoken on the air.

"Actually." Our mother cleared her throat. "I'm expecting a few more for dinner."

"John will be here as soon as he gets off work," Meg said. "After he takes the dog out. Four o'clock, he said."

My phone chirped from my pocket. "That's what I told Trey," I said.

"Your father will be here at five," Mom said. "He's coming with Aunt Phee."

Amy looked up from the centerpiece she was constructing of milkweed pods and magnolia leaves. "You invited Dad?"

"This is a family dinner," our mother said evenly. "He is still part of this family, girls."

Beth slipped her arm around our mother's waist. "Do you miss him very much?"

"I've been missing your father most of my life," she said dryly. "Could be he's missing me, too. At least now when I call him, he shows up."

Another chirp from my phone.

"Should you get that?" Meg asked.

"It's just a blog comment." I shifted my weight to one hip, holding on to DJ, reaching for my pocket.

"I liked that post you did about the cats," Beth said.

"Everybody liked that one," Amy said. "But your branding is wrong. You need a new logo."

"If you want to redesign something, look at the farm website," our mother said.

I stared at my phone screen. My heart ricocheted to my throat. Not a comment. Not a text. A phone call.

"Who is it?" Beth asked.

Amy craned to see. "Eric. Oh my God, is that him?"

"Answer it," Meg said.

"Hello?" I croaked.

"I talk, Auntie Jo!" Daisy demanded.

Meg hushed her.

"Jo." His voice; oh, his deep, remembered voice.

"Hi."

Daisy, denied the phone, broke into wails. Meg picked her up, murmuring soothing sounds.

"You are well?" Eric asked politely.

I'm pregnant.

"I'm fine. That's Daisy. My niece." It seemed absurd to be making small talk after our online flirtation, the intimacy of his late-night comments. "How . . . How are you?"

"I am here. In North Carolina. Bryan has a tournament this weekend. I did not call before because I did not know his schedule. If his team would advance. But I would like to see you before I go." His deliberate sentences, his Old World courtesy, made him sound very formal. Or possibly . . . nervous?

Warmth filled my chest. He wanted to see me!

"He has a playoff game this afternoon," Eric continued in that deep, delicious voice. "But when we are finished, perhaps we could visit you. If that would be okay."

My brain scrambled. "Here? Today?"

"This is a problem?"

Meg grabbed my arm. "He's coming here?"

"Who? Eric?" Amy asked.

I flapped my hands at them to be quiet. "It's just . . . There are people coming over."

"You have a party."

"It's only family. A dinner for my mother."

"I'd like to meet her," Eric said.

"But your boys . . ." I objected weakly.

"They have been asking about you since the airport. I want them to know you. I want to see you."

"Invite him," my mother said.

"Jo." Eric's voice was quiet. Serious. "*'Come,'* you said. If this is the wrong time . . . If you have changed your mind . . ."

No running away. No pushing away. "No," I said. "I want you."

"Then I will be there."

My heart swelled. "Stay for dinner," I said recklessly. "You and the boys."

"Everybody's dying to meet them," Amy said, loudly enough to be overheard.

Our mother gave her The Look.

"Thank you," Eric said. "We may be a little late, but we will come. After two days of fast food, we all are hungry for a good meal."

"Great. That's . . . Great."

We said good-bye. I sat there, stunned.

Meg smiled. "I should have brought another pie."

Three hours until dinner. Then two. Then one. Beth cleaned. Amy set the table. I helped our mother in the kitchen while Meg got Daisy and DJ up from their nap.

Beth gave a contented sigh. "This is nice. All of us working together."

Amy handed a spoon to DJ, who promptly stuck it in his mouth. "Like old times."

We were still us, I thought, looking around at my sisters. There was no one else who shared our history, who spoke our secret language, who could summon the past or drive me crazy with a single word. And yet . . . "It's the same," I said. "But not the same."

Meg cuddled Daisy, all rosy with sleep. "It's more."

"Because you girls are more," our mother said. "I'm proud of you. Each one of you. Not just as my daughters, but because you're all becoming wonderful women."

"It's a new beginning," Beth said, her eyes shining.

Amy gave a little nod. "I'm launching my new brand this year."

"I have a new business," Meg said.

"And Jo has a new blog," Beth said.

"A new book," I said. Saying it out loud like that made it all the more real.

"Not to mention the new baby," Meg said.

"What? Jo!"

"You're pregnant?" Amy exclaimed, delighted. "You slut!"

Oops.

Meg gave me an apologetic look. "I thought you told them."

My sisters descended on me for hugs and explanations.

"Nobody tells me anything," Amy complained.

"I'm not telling anyone yet," I said. Only our mother. I bit my lip. And Meg and John. And Trey, who was sworn to secrecy. "Not until I see the doctor this week."

Beth squeezed my hand. "Does Eric know?"

"I have to talk to him," I said. "We'll take it from there."

"Who cares about Eric?" Amy said. "You've got us."

"You've always got us," Meg said.

"Whatever happens," Beth said.

I hugged my sisters tight, choked with emotion. I'd always prided myself on living my own life, on making my own way alone. With or without Eric, I was finding my path forward. But I wasn't alone. I had my sisters. And my mother. And my father, detached as he was. I had prickly Aunt Phee and loyal Trey and friends on both sides of the country. I had a story inside me struggling to get out. And seven months from now, I would have a baby. Imagine.

A smile worked its way from deep inside. "I'm so lucky."

My mother met my eyes and smiled with perfect understanding. "We're so lucky," she said.

"Oh, hey," Amy said. "I almost forgot." She dug in her pocket. "This is for you."

I looked at the wad of cash without touching it. "It's a little early for baby presents."

She lifted her chin. "It's not for the baby. It's for you." She put the bills on the table. "For a new laptop. Because I puked on your old one."

Stunned, I started to count. "Amy. Honey. What did you do? Sell a kidney?"

"Of course not, silly. I left some of my bags with that friend of Meg's. Sallie Moffat? She works at that boutique? She sold them for me."

"Your bags. You mean, bags you made? You sold them?"

She nodded, her blue eyes meeting mine, seeking my . . . approval?

"That is so sweet," Beth said.

"Generous," Meg said.

"You didn't have to do that," I protested. "I don't know what to say."

"Say, *thank you*," our mother prompted.

"Thank you," I repeated. "Oh, Ames, thanks!"

She beamed. "You're welcome."

And then we were hugging again, and I was crying,

"Hormones," Meg said.

The family started arriving, first John—he brought the dog with him—then Trey and old Mr. Laurence. Hannah came, with pictures of her grandbabies. Finally, Aunt Phee's white Mercedes pulled into the drive, our father in the passenger seat, her little Yorkie perched on his lap.

Phee greeted me with a kiss and a demand to know what I'd done to my hair.

Polly yapped and shook in our father's arms, desperate to establish dominance over Lady. Dad held the dog awkwardly, a guest in his own home. I felt a hot surge of resentment and then a tug of pity. All this togetherness couldn't be easy for him. He'd always held himself a little apart in family gatherings. Maybe I only noticed it now that he didn't have his study to retreat to.

I took the dog from him, taking care it didn't bite. "Hi, Dad. How was your conference?"

I stayed with him, listening, while my ears strained for the sound of the doorbell. While Trey juggled DJ and a conversation with Aunt

Phee, and old Mr. Laurence got on the floor with Daisy, and John cornered Meg for a kiss in the hallway. Amy flitted around with a platter of crudités.

"Let me get that," Beth said, taking a bowl from Mom and setting it on the table.

And still Eric didn't come.

"I spoke with your mother," my father said, recalling my attention. "You're . . . all right?"

Our entire relationship was in the question and in the silence between. My father cared about me. He just couldn't get involved in the messy emotional details.

But my first stories were letters I had written for him. He was the one who had encouraged me to read, who took me to the bookstore to buy *Harry Potter and the Deathly Hallows* at midnight. Who urged me to apply to grad school. Who taught me to stick up for what I believed in.

"I'm fine, Daddy."

He looked relieved. "Good." He cleared his throat as if he might say something more. Patted my shoulder instead. "Good."

I blinked back tears. It was all he could offer. It was enough.

I found my sisters in the kitchen and took my turn at the sink, looking out on the empty pasture. The sun was sinking into the trees, taking the temperature down with it. The sky was stained pink. Slowly, the days were getting longer.

Eric was late.

Maybe his son's game had been delayed. Or he'd changed his mind. Or there was traffic, an accident on the highway, maybe. My heart jerked. Oh God, what if Eric had been in an accident? What if . . .

I took a deep breath, scrubbing a pan with renewed vigor.

"I will be there," he had promised.

"Did you know Beth's song got, like, a million hits on YouTube?" Amy asked.

I smiled over my shoulder at Beth. "Because she's amazing."

Beth blushed. "Not because of me. Because of Colt."

"But it's your song," I said. "You wrote it."

"You'll be a celebrity when you go back to school," Amy said.

Beth focused on drying a pot. "I'm not going back to school this semester."

"What?" Meg asked.

"Of course you're going back," I said.

"Why?" asked Amy.

Beth raised her chin, anxious and defiant. "Colt asked me to go on tour with him, and I said yes."

"I thought you threw up every time you went on stage," Meg said.

I looked at her sharply. Beth hadn't told *me* that.

"Colt says I'll get over it. I want to be stronger. To be more . . . To be *more*, like Momma said." Beth's gaze sought mine. "Be happy for me. Please?"

Amy was right. As much as I wanted to protect Beth, we couldn't stay in our little pigeonholes forever. Let Beth follow her heart.

And I would follow mine.

"Of course we're happy for you," I said staunchly.

The doorbell chimed.

"I'll get that," Amy said.

I dropped the pan into the soapy water, my hands suddenly shaking. "I've got it."

I dashed across the living room. Flung the door open. "You're here!"

"I told you I would come." Eric cupped my face in his large, warm, rough hands. I caught my breath. He smelled of grass and sweat and cold. He kissed my forehead, then my nose, then my lips, kissing me as if his sons weren't standing right there on the porch, as if my family weren't watching from inside.

I curled my hands around his thick wrists and held on, kissing him back with my heart on my lips.

"Who is this?" my father asked.

I broke away, feeling my face flush. Taking Eric's hand, I led him into the living room, nearly bursting with pride and love and worry. "This is Eric. Eric Bhaer. And his sons. Bryan." I tugged him forward. "And this is Alec."

They murmured greetings and shook hands with the awkward grace of the young.

Phee craned her neck to look at them. "You're very . . ."

I stiffened. *Please, please, don't say something horrible.*

"Tall," Phee said.

"They're growing boys, Aunt Phee." I grinned at them. "Hungry?"

Bryan nodded, smiling faintly.

Alec flashed a grin like his father's. "Starved."

John stepped forward. "Right this way. I hear you play soccer," he said, leading them back to the kitchen.

I loved my sister's husband.

Phee switched her attention to Eric, taking in his dark skin and heavy stubble beard, the tattoos under his pushed-up sleeves. "What is it you do, Mr., ah . . ."

"Eric," he said pleasantly. "I cook."

"He's a cook," she remarked to no one in particular.

"He's a chef, Aunt Phee," Meg said.

"I worked at Eric's restaurant in New York," I said. "Gusto."

She ignored us. "And what brings you to North Carolina?" she asked Eric.

"Soccer tournament," I said at the same moment he said, "Jo."

My heart jolted.

"I'm with Jo," he repeated, holding my gaze. His eyes crinkled in that way he had of smiling without smiling, and something moved in my chest.

I grabbed his hand again. "Let me show you around."

Phee raised her eyebrows. "I would think the tour of the farm can wait."

"It actually can't," I said. *I can't.*

"Well, really, I . . ."

"Let the girl go, Phee," my mother said.

Whatever Aunt Phee replied was lost as I pulled Eric back outside, dragging him off the porch and out to the barn. Not that he took much dragging.

The barn was cold and smelled of hay. My heart hammered as I turned to face Eric. "I need to talk to you. Alone."

The creases by his eyes deepened in amusement. "Alone is good," he agreed.

My knees turned to custard. I straightened my spine. "I'm pregnant."

His face stilled. Before I could decipher his expression, he hauled me into his arms and against him. His body was as hard as oak. His arms were so strong and he felt so good against me, solid and strong and right. I sagged against him, giddy with relief. For a long moment, we just stood there, holding on to each other, his warmth surrounding me. With me. *I'm with Jo.*

He pulled back, his big hands gripping my shoulders. "But . . . How?"

"The usual way. The first night, probably." My smile twisted. "Apparently I should have checked the date on the condom box."

His gaze was dark and intense on my face. "How do you feel?"

"I feel fine. I'm seeing the doctor on Thursday." His expression did not change. I realized suddenly what he was asking. "I want this baby. And I want you to be part of his life. Our lives. If that's what you want," I added.

His hands tightened almost painfully. "That's what I am here for. To ask you. If you will be with me."

My heart stuttered. "Where?"

He smoothed my hair back from my face, his touch lingering in my short curls. "Does it matter?"

I shook my head. "No. Not if we're together."

"You can do better."

"I am doing better," I protested. "Telling my story, like you said. I'm writing a book."

"I cannot wait to read it. But, Jo . . . I do not care what you do. No."

He frowned. "I mean, whatever you do, I respect *you*. I admire you. To me, you are perfect. You can do better than me."

"There isn't anybody better," I said, my voice husky. "Not for me."

"Then . . . Jo, will you marry me?"

My mouth dropped open. My courage had taken me only as far as telling him. My imagination hadn't taken me much beyond that. "I . . . It's a little early to be making plans."

He gave me a patient look. "You are having a baby, yeah?"

"Not for seven more months. Our baby won't care. Besides, your boys need time to get used to me. My mother still needs me. And I . . . I'm not ready to leave my family."

"*Einverstanden*. You are here. My boys are here. I will stay."

"But the restaurant . . . Your job is in New York. *Oh*." I yanked my hair. "I have to *think*."

Eric smiled. "You think. I will wait. And then we will get married."

I crossed my arms. "You're not marrying me because I'm pregnant."

"No," he agreed. "I am marrying you because I love you." His face softened. "Beautiful Jo."

My eyes were wet, which made it hard to see, but I thought his were, too. I kissed him. We kissed a long time, until Amy called us in to dinner.

"Sorry to interrupt," my sister said cheerfully. "But in another minute John is going to come out and demand to know your intentions, and the rest of us are hungry."

We went inside, where we were met with a considering look from Trey and a quick smile and thumbs-up from Meg. DJ had stripped off his diaper and ran giggling around the living room, pursued by John. Alec galloped by with Daisy on his back. Lady pressed against the sofa, whining adoringly up at Weasley, who stared disdainfully back. Aunt Phee was directing the placement of the dining room chairs while Beth and Hannah tried to get food on the table.

"Welcome to March Family Madness," I murmured to Bryan, and was rewarded by a flickering smile.

We all trooped into the dining room. John helped our mother to a chair at the head of the table. After a pause, my father took a seat beside Aunt Phee. So that was different.

"Ashton, will you say grace?" my mother asked.

That, too, was new, my father needing an invitation to speak.

We joined hands around the table. Eric's knee, warm and firm, pressed mine.

My father bowed his head. "Lord, bless this food for our use and our bodies to your service. May we lay up for ourselves treasures in heaven, riches that endure. For where our treasure is, there will our hearts be also."

"Amen," our mother said, and we all echoed, "Amen."

"Not that there's anything wrong with a little treasure here on earth," Aunt Phee added. She leveled a look at John. "What's this I hear about your quitting your job to go back to teaching?"

I smothered a grin.

Dishes were passed. Plates were filled. Everybody was shoveling food and talking. Trey dealt manfully with Phee while John discussed working summers at the dealership with old Mr. Laurence. My father said something (I heard the words *noble calling*) that won a surprised look from John and a nod from the old man. Amy broke off a conversation with Hannah to show Bryan something on her phone. Beth had overcome her shyness to draw out Alec about an upcoming school play.

Here was my treasure, I thought, gathered around the table. Here was my heart. I was surrounded by family. By love.

At the head of the table, Mom held herself stiffly—she had to wear the brace for another week—but her face was warm and relaxed. I'd never realized how much of her mealtime was spent jumping up to serve others, how much of her energy went into taking care of my father. Now she listened as Meg described the recent buyer's meeting. Eric nodded, adding something about establishing standing orders to restaurants.

He fit in, I thought. He belonged.

"So, when is there going to be another wedding?" Aunt Phee demanded.

Conversation stopped.

Eric took my hand. "That's up to Jo." He looked at me, that little crinkle at the corners of his eyes, and for a second I forgot to breathe. "Slow and steady, yeah?"

My heart, already full, flooded. I loved him so much. "Not too slow," I said.

Eric laughed. And there, in the sight of both our families, he leaned forward and kissed me.

Meg
&
Jo

VIRGINIA KANTRA

QUESTIONS FOR DISCUSSION

1. *Meg & Jo* is inspired by Louisa May Alcott's classic story. What versions (book or movie) of *Little Women* are you familiar with? In what ways did *Meg & Jo* confirm your impressions of the characters? How did they surprise you?

2. The March sisters often repeat their mother, Abby's, sayings ("If you can't say something nice . . ."; "Whatever happens, we have each other.") What sayings did you hear as a child? Do you ever find yourself repeating them? How did they direct your life?

3. Which of the sisters could you most identify with, and why?

4. Meg and John both show love by actions, not words. How does this work for and against them? Does it change? What would you say your style of showing love is?

5. Jo feels especially close to her father. Do you think her desire for his approval affected her other relationships? How did her perception of him change throughout the book? What did you think of Ashton as a man, husband, and father? Did you agree or disagree with Abby's decision at the end of the book?

6. When the original *Little Women* was published, many readers were disappointed that Jo chose older Professor Eric Bhaer over her childhood friend, Laurie. How do you feel about her choice between Eric and Trey? Which sister do you think is a good match for Trey, and why?

7. Meg tells Jo that she's unfair to Amy. Can you remember examples from the book that make you think this is true or not true? How would you describe Jo and Amy's relationship? Does it remind you of sisters you know?

8. Major scenes in *Meg & Jo* involve food. What does cooking in the book mean to different characters? What does it mean to you? Do you have family or holiday traditions involving food?

9. The March girls find themselves reverting to their childhood roles when they are together. How does that compare with your own experience? What is your family role? Has it changed over time?

Keep reading for an excerpt
from Virginia Kantra's next novel

Beth
&
Amy

Coming soon from Berkley!

Amy

I t's always a mistake to sleep with a man who's in love with your sister. Even in Paris. Even if they'd broken up again—for good this time, he said. Even though I'd been in love with him since I was eleven years old.

But I was young and dumb and homesick. So. Whatever. I had a one-night hookup in a foreign city with Trey Laurence, the rich boy next door, after my sister broke his heart.

Three years later, I was older and a whole lot wiser. But returning home for my sister's wedding was still going to be all kinds of awkward.

Not that I hadn't been back to North Carolina before. For holidays, and that awful time when Momma got sick, and when my nephew Robbie was born. But even though my sister was about to be married to another man, I still couldn't face her without a squirm of guilt. I'd had sex with Jo's ex—a clear violation of the Sisters' Code. As for the other guilty party, Trey . . . Well. Just because he'd found a way to forgive himself didn't mean I had to forgive him. Or myself. Mostly I avoided him.

Which was going to be a lot harder to do now that we were members of the same wedding party. (And no, my heart wasn't holding on to some pathetic hope that now that Jo was finally marrying somebody else, Trey would pull his head out of his ass and realize it was me he loved, after all.)

But maybe being a bridesmaid in Jo's wedding would bring me and my sister closer. Maybe this was my chance to prove to Trey—or at least to myself—that I was over him. I had better things to do with my life than obsess over a stupid childhood crush. My handbag business, Baggage (*"Own It"*) had taken off. Meghan Markle herself had recently been photographed carrying one of my totes, and demands for the re-christened "Duchess" bag were pouring in, threatening to flood my Bedford Park apartment.

"It's like a goddamn rainbow puked up in here," my assistant, Flo, had said before I left New York. She zipped tape across the top of a carton, adding to the boxes of custom orders packed and stacked for pickup by the door.

I glanced from her Frida Kahlo T-shirt (ASK ME ABOUT MY FEMI-NIST AGENDA, read the cartoon bubble from the artist's mouth) to her natural hair, tipped this month in fiery red. "Yeah, I know how much you hate color," I said, making her laugh.

I skirted a rack of bins to get to my worktable, piled high with wallets waiting for snaps and trim. Purses, totes, and cross-body bags in bright colors and various stages of assembly overflowed every surface. I was already renting storage from the dry cleaner's downstairs. My bedroom was so filled with bolts of vinyl and leather, I couldn't find my mattress. Not that I had much time to sleep anyway.

The truth was, we needed a bigger workroom. A second sewing machine. More shelving. More light. Maybe even a little retail space, although a storefront in Manhattan was totally out of my price range, at least for now.

I reached for a punch tool. "You sure you're all right filling these orders while I'm gone?"

"Mamey." Easy. Flo Callazzo was a real New Yorker, a proud Afro-Dominican Puerto Rican daughter of the Bronx.

Me? Not so much. In Paris, my schoolgirl French had marked me as irredeemably "other." I'd reckoned being back on American soil would feel like home. But my first week in the city, I'd realized my down-home accent made me stick out among the fast-talking Yankees all around me. Waitresses asked me to repeat myself. Buyers assumed I was uneducated. Guys figured I was easy. Or naïve. A dumb hick blonde.

Which worked to my advantage, sometimes.

"You're not getting out of your sister's wedding on account of me," Flo said.

"I'm not trying to get out of anything." I busied myself inserting a snap. "I'm flying down early to do some store checks."

Three days after Easter. I didn't actually need to visit clients on my way to my sister's wedding. But I loved walking into a store and seeing my bags, my brand, displayed on the gleaming shelves (#bagsinthewild #ownit). I loved the expensive smell of the boutiques: citrus, sandalwood, jasmine, bergamot. The accounts were always happy to see me, flattered I'd gone out of my way to visit.

Not like going home at all.

Not that my family didn't love me, I told myself as I left the last client store and hit the highway for my mother's farm. They did. All of them, even Jo. But my sisters were too busy with their own lives to care much about mine.

Our mother, who never took a day's vacation in her life, had encouraged all of us girls to work hard and follow our dreams. Meg was the perfect mother to two perfect children. Jo was a bestselling author. Beth was a budding country star. And I . . . I made accessories. It didn't matter how many Instagram followers or employees I had. In my family's eyes, I was still little Amy, playing with scraps from Miss Hannah's quilting bag.

And yet . . . There was comfort in the familiar landscape rushing by, the tall pines stretching to the wide blue sky, the sunlit ditches full of cattails and turtles, the poppies blooming by the side of the road. I turned up the gravel drive marked SISTERS' FARM, the stones spitting beneath my tires. The square-frame house, the old mule barn, the child's playset in the baby goats' paddock.

Home.

Too bad nobody was there. No car. No truck. Nobody.

I got out of the car and took a deep breath of country air scented with hay and the river. Also . . . goats. Brown goats, black goats, striped and spotted goats, all sizes, smelling like cheese left out on the counter too long. They crowded to the fence, bleating and bumping for attention, the babies skipping around the paddock like they were auditioning for YouTube. Cute, if you liked that sort of thing.

Our mother loved them. Not more than she loved us girls, of course.

Our mother, Abigail March, could birth a goat and kill a copperhead. She could find anything—toys, shoes, missing homework. Fix anything, except a broken heart. She made sure we got our shots and permission slips on time, taught Meg to cook and me to sew, and came to all our school performances. But her time and attention were always rationed between us and the farm.

Meg said things were different before Daddy quit his job as a minister and went to Iraq as an army chaplain. I remember I cried when we left the parsonage and all my friends in town. But I was only ten when our mother moved us girls out to the farm. Most of my memories were of her working.

It wasn't like her to be gone in the middle of the day.

I didn't expect to see our dad. Mom had asked him to move out almost three years ago. But I felt his absence like poking at a missing tooth with your tongue.

Stupid. All my sisters were grown and gone while I was still in high school. I should be used to coming home to an empty house by now.

I leaned against the front fender as I called Momma's cell. She didn't pick up. Typical. *"Why would I ignore somebody standing right in front of me to answer the phone?"* she liked to say. But I could call Meg, my oldest sister. Meg was busy, too—her twins were about to turn five, and she kept the books for several farms and businesses in town. But she always found time for me.

A guy walked around the corner of the barn. A tall, older guy, his face creased with hard living behind a don't-mess-with-me beard.

I kept a hand on my phone just in case he turned out to be, oh, a serial killer or something. Living in New York had taught me caution. And out here in the country, nobody was around to hear me scream. "Hi."

He nodded in greeting. The strong, silent type, obviously. Beneath the beard, he looked vaguely familiar. Well. Everybody looked familiar in Bunyan. Because of inbreeding, Jo said. But it was more that everybody had a cousin who used to go to your daddy's church or went to school with your sister, strands of connection twined and knotted like macramé.

I tried again. "Do I know you?"

He looked at me, no expression at all. "Sam Harkins."

I smiled encouragingly, waiting.

"I work for your ma."

So he knew who I was. Or at least that Momma was expecting me. I relaxed my grip on the phone.

Our mother came from tough Scottish stock, too proud—or too cheap—to pay somebody else to do her work. But after she was hospitalized a couple years ago, she'd hired one of Dad's vets to do the heavy lifting. (Literally. Those full-grown milking goats weighed a ton.) Mom was better now, but as her herd and business grew, she'd kept on some of her new hires to help around the farm.

"Where is my mother?" I asked.

"Over at Oak Hill." A pause. "Helping your sister."

Jo, being Jo, had taken a casual approach to her wedding. She and her love, Eric Bhaer, were already living together. They had three kids—baby Rob and two teenage sons from Eric's previous marriage. It was only now that Eric's ex-wife was deployed and his younger son,

Alec, was coming to live with them that Jo decided it was finally time to get married. "I don't need a poofy dress and a big, fancy wedding," Jo said when she called me. "I just want to marry him."

So. No bachelorette parties, no bridal showers, no save-the-date cards or hair and makeup trials. *"No fuss,"* our mother would say. It wasn't quite an elopement—our great-aunt Josephine had offered her big old house at Oak Hill for the wedding, and all the family would be there—but it was pretty close.

Still, there must be a million things to do before the ceremony on Sunday. Food. Eric was a chef. And maybe I could help with the flowers or something.

"I guess I'll go give them a hand," I said.

Because nothing says *I'm so sorry I slept with your old boyfriend* like a flower arrangement. Anyway, spending time with my sister couldn't be more awkward than hanging out here with Silent Sam.

With a little wave, I got back in the car, flipping down the visor to check my lipstick (Parisian Red). The little flick of eyeliner I'd applied so carefully this morning was only slightly smudged. Good enough, I decided. It wasn't like I was going to see Trey. And Jo didn't care.

But Aunt Phee would, I thought as I turned in the long sandy lane toward Oak Hill. Nothing mattered more to our great-aunt than appearances.

Our father grew up in the big white house on the hill. Not that we girls ever lived there. When Daddy deployed to Iraq, Momma refused to move in with our father's aunt Phee, moving us instead to her parents' small farm. Over the years, the land had been sold off, but Oak Hill manor and some of the original outbuildings remained. Too much space, Aunt Phee said, for one old lady. Our father had moved into the carriage house after Momma kicked him out.

I could see signs of recent activity as I approached. The dark magnolias had been trimmed back from the house, the columned porch freshly painted, and the grass mowed all the way down the long slope to the duck pond. Azaleas and early roses bloomed everywhere, clouds of pink, red, and white, transforming the scrubby gardens into the perfect wedding venue.

I pulled into the long circular drive behind our mother's battered blue pickup. A white van with the Taproom logo—Eric's new restaurant in town—was parked by the side of the house.

And there was my sister Jo, laughing and chasing Robbie over the grass. He was grinning at her over his shoulder as he pushed a toy lawn mower, his fat little legs moving as fast as they could go, a wake of bubbles rising in the air behind him.

Gladness and guilt surged inside me. And maybe . . . a pang of envy? She looked so happy.

"Jokies!" I cried, getting out of the car.

Which is what I always called her. We had always been rivals, for Dad's attention and, later, for Trey's. She didn't confide in me, the way she did in Meg. She didn't baby me, the way she did Beth. But we were sisters. The funny pet name was my way of establishing a special bond just between us.

Robbie looked in the direction of my voice, stumbled over the mower, and fell.

"Oh, shit. I'm sorry."

"It's okay. You're okay," Jo said. To which one of us? She scooped up her baby, smooching his cheeks and propping him on her hip. She smiled at me over his head. "Hey, Ames."

I hugged her awkwardly, the baby between us. He peeped at me from her neck, his shy smile revealing a string of little pearl teeth. He had his daddy's dark skin and curly hair. Eyelashes to die for. "Hello, handsome." I kissed his forehead gently. "You're getting so big," I marveled.

"Nineteen months." Jo shifted his weight. "Good to see you. Mom wasn't sure when you were getting in."

"I wanted to come early to help. Not that you need help," I added. "Everything looks wonderful."

"Thanks. Wait till you see the inside," Jo said.

I trailed her up the wide, shallow steps to the high, shaded porch. Planters of ferns flanked the leaded glass door.

Oak Hill manor was built in 1852 in the Greek Revival style. Aunt Phee's style of furnishing was almost as old. But the faded velvet drapes and most of the oriental carpets were gone, the pine floors refinished, the walls painted a creamy neutral. The whole effect was light, bright, and inviting.

"Wow." I surveyed the changes. Tables had been set up in the living and dining rooms. Dining chairs were stacked in the hall. "I thought you wanted a simple wedding."

"Oh, it's not for the wedding." Jo's face lit with excitement. "Tell her."

Only one man brought that light to my sister's face. I turned to see her honey, Chef Eric Bhaer, striding from the direction of the kitchen. Arm-Porn Guy, I'd dubbed him when they first got together. He kissed Jo and hefted their baby in the air, making him squeal with delight, before wrapping me in a big bear hug.

"Amy! *Spatz!*" *Sparrow*, in German. I felt a little glow at the special pet name. "It's so good to have you here."

Here was the welcome I'd hoped for. Eric was such a great guy. There was a time I couldn't imagine how Jo could possibly reject Theodore Laurence III in favor of, well, any other man. But obviously my sister had made the right choice. Which only proved—didn't it?—that I was over Trey. "Tell me what?" I asked.

"Eric's opening a restaurant," Jo said.

"Another one?" I asked.

Jo nodded, beaming. "Here at Oak Hill."

"Thursday through Sunday only," Eric said. "During the season, yeah? I want to spend more time with my family. So we hire a sous chef for the Taproom, and I work from home this summer."

"Eric has hired a whole new staff," Jo said with a glowing look at him. "Local kids who can't afford culinary school. Working at Oak Hill will give them a chance to learn the high-end food business without going into a bunch of debt."

"That's . . . Wow. That's amazing. But here?" I couldn't wrap my brain around it. "How did you get Aunt Phee to agree?"

"It was her idea. She wants Oak Hill to stay in the family, and she wants me to stay in North Carolina. So she offered us Oak Hill."

"But where will she live?" I asked.

"She's moving into the carriage house. At least for now."

"Aunt Phee is going to live with Dad?"

Jo hesitated. "I think they're still working that part out."

"She is in the library with your mother now," Eric said. "They will be glad to see you."

"They were arguing about the seating chart for the reception when I left," Jo said.

"Oh." Well. I'd come to be helpful, after all. "I'll go . . . referee."

Jo grinned. "Better you than me."

". . . have a responsibility," Phee was insisting as I came down the hall.

"Not anymore." My mother's voice was flat.

I blinked. Abby March was all about taking responsibility.

"He's still your husband," Phee said, and my stomach sank.

They weren't talking about the wedding. They were arguing about Dad. I pasted a smile on my face and pushed open the door. "Hey, Momma," I said brightly. "Hi, Aunt Phee. Am I interrupting?"

Phee glowered. She and my mother faced off across the library desk. My mother's hands and lips were pressed together, a sure sign she was angry. But she smiled when she saw me.

"Hey, sweetie. What are you doing here?"

Like I needed another reason to feel de trop. I felt my smile slipping and dragged it back. "I thought I'd come in early. To help." I gave Momma a quick hug before going around the desk to kiss Phee's cheek. The little dog in her lap growled.

"What about your work?" my mother asked.

"Flo's handling orders while I'm gone. That's the advantage of owning your own business," I said. "I can take time off."

If my mother was impressed by my entrepreneurship, she didn't show it. "Jo doesn't want a lot of fuss."

"I thought I could help with the flowers."

"Meg ordered the bouquets already."

"What about table arrangements?"

"I'm picking up flowers when I go to the farmers' market on Saturday." Something must have shown in my face, because our mother added, "You could arrange those. You did such a nice job for Meg's wedding."

Phee sniffed. "You want to make yourself useful, you can take Polly for a walk."

"Nice to see you, too, Aunt Phee."

I eyed the bad-tempered Yorkie on her lap. The dog didn't seem any more excited at the prospect of a walk than I was. But I was obviously in the way here. Anyway, our family owed Aunt Phee. She had paid for my postgraduation trip to Europe. She had opened her home to Dad. And she was doing such a generous thing for Jo and Eric, letting them have the wedding here. Letting them have Oak Hill.

Hm, I thought as I clipped the lead to Polly's collar. I wasn't jealous. Exactly. But if Phee was going to invest in her great-nieces, why not me?

We meandered toward the duck pond, the little dog stopping frequently to sniff. The sun sparkled on the flat water. A faint breeze rippled the surface, stirring the reeds at the water's edge, loosening a shower of petals from the nearby apple trees. In spite of the smell of decay from the pond, all the scene needed to be perfect was Colin Firth in a wet white shirt.

Polly growled and quivered. A family of Canada geese was browsing on the bank, the adults standing at attention over five little goslings.

"Don't even think about it," I told her sternly. "They'll eat you for lunch."

Polly snorted and busied herself with a stick. Let her. I didn't care if she made herself sick.

While Polly rootled at the ground, I contemplated the azaleas, wondering how long the blooms would last if I cut some branches to use in wedding arrangements. A burst of yapping grabbed my attention. Polly tugged against my hold on her leash. There was a squawk. A honk.

A splash.

I looked. Polly had seized one of the goslings by the neck and stood with her struggling prize on the bank, triumphant and seeming slightly bewildered by her success.

Shit. I started forward. But not before Momma and Poppa Goose lunged, necks outstretched, black beaks open and hissing.

"No!" I shouted. "Polly, stop! Drop it!"

Wild-eyed, the dog obeyed. Or maybe the gosling freed itself. Peeping in distress, the bird ran for its mother. But it was too late. As Momma Goose shepherded her baby to safety, Poppa attacked.

Polly yelped and stumbled under the rush of the bird's wings, tumbling into the water.

"No!" I yelled again. "Shoo!"

The goose paid no attention, fixing its beady eyes menacingly on the dog.

Crap, crap, crap. I ran into the pond, my sandals sinking in the muck, and scooped up Polly. The Yorkie bit me, drawing blood. The indignity of it—after I'd rescued her, the little monster!—slapped my senses. The goose advanced on us, hissing, head moving side to side like a snake's. I clutched Polly to my chest.

And then, apparently deciding I wasn't worth it, the big bird folded its wings and launched past me, rejoining its family in the center of the pond.

The ripples faded in its wake. I stood there, dripping and shaking with shock. In my arms, Polly shook, too.

"I thought I heard a commotion," said Trey's voice.

I swayed. I was hallucinating. Unless . . . I turned. Nope. There he was, in the flesh, on the bank, golden-skinned and lean and perfect, the only boy I'd ever loved.

Of course he would show up now, I thought despairingly. When I was wet, muddy, and bloody. At a total disadvantage.

Our gazes locked. "Little Amy." He smiled crookedly. "I should have known it would be you."

My vision grayed. And I realized two things.

One, I was quite possibly going to faint.

And two, I wasn't over him after all.

Photo by Michael Ritchey

New York Times bestselling author Virginia Kantra is the author of thirty novels. Her stories have earned numerous awards, including two Romance Writers of America RITA® Awards, ten RITA® nominations, and two National Readers' Choice Awards.

Carolina Dreaming, the fifth book in her Dare Island series, won the 2017 RITA® Award for Best Contemporary Romance: Mid-length, and was named one of BookPage's Top Ten Romance Novels of 2016.

Virginia is married to her college sweetheart, a coffee shop owner who keeps her well supplied with caffeine and material. They make their home in North Carolina, where they raised three (mostly adult) children. She is a firm believer in the strength of family, the importance of storytelling, and the power of love.

Her favorite thing to make for dinner? Reservations.

Ready to find
your next great read?

Let us help.

Visit prh.com/nextread

Penguin
Random
House